REWERA RISING

Devil Within

Book One

Daria M Paus

Cover Designer: Daria M Paus

Internal Designer: Daria M Paus

Editor: T. L. Hanigan

ISBN:

978-91-986433-3-6 (paperback)

978-91-986-433-4-3 (eBook)

For my man, whose many devilish ideas made it into this book.

Who survived endless lonely hours while I wrote this. (And many more to come.)

fight DARKNESS with LIGHT

Before war and corruption controlled humanity, the Devil once spoke to an Angel.
He spoke of a way out of Hell and into the midst of innocence.
Of infiltrating the human race and growing like a sinister seed of sin and darkness in the human brain.
"I'll take over the world—one generation at the time."

The angel replied.
She spoke of love—of fighting Darkness with Light.
"You can take their bodies and their minds, but you can never take their hearts.
They will fall in love with me, again and again, and Good will conquer Evil."

his flesh. Black dots danced before his eyes as warm blood trickled down his body. He bit back any sound of pain, knowing it would only make it worse.

Be strong, be brave…

"Son," his mother's faint voice breathed light into his dark, and without a second glance at his father, he pushed through the nauseating pain, bent down to scoop her up from the floor, and ran toward the door.

His father's voice thundered in his head as he fled. "You can't save her."

Darek didn't listen, and when he stepped outside in the pouring rain, his father's words echoed in his mind.

Tick tock. Tick tock.

Across the street, the windows of Dr. Pedersen's house shone yellow, and on the front porch, a hammock swung with the wind.

Darek took the stairs in a flying step, and while he cried out for help, he kicked the door over and over until it flew open from the force.

Dr. Pedersen appeared in the dimly lit hall, his long unshaved face startled. He wore sweatpants and a white tank top, looking like he was interrupted in a workout session.

"Help her, please! You've gotta help her."

The look on the doctor's face hardened when he recognized Darek. His eyes flickered from the boy's drenched form to the mother in his arms. He held out a hand to prevent Darek from coming any closer. "I can't. Get out of my house."

"She'll die. I beg you."

Dr. Pedersen grabbed the small silver cross hanging from his neck. "Child of Satan," he stepped away with a disgusted look on his face. "Leave. Now!"

"She's never done anything bad to you. Doctor—" Darek's voice broke, and he only managed a trembling, "Please."

"Leave this house."

A thin woman came up behind the doctor, glaring at Darek through slits of green eyes. "You heard him," she snapped. "Go to hell where you belong."

5

She grabbed a vase off a pedestal and hurled it at Darek. Swirling to the side in an effort to protect the woman in his arms, the object caught him across the side of his face, slicing through his skin before falling to his feet.

When the doctor's wife reached for an umbrella and hoisted in the air, ready to strike, Darek turned and ran.

The rain beat down on him. A thousand needles prickling his skin. His bare feet hurt from the rough street as he ran aimlessly, desperate to find someone willing to take mercy on them. Cars swirled out of his way, angrily honking their horns.

He'd never asked for anything, from anyone. He'd stayed out of the way, suffered the whispers and the looks from the narrow-minded people of the one-street town.

Never before had he been desperate enough to demand the attention from the people who'd shunned his family for as long as he could remember, but he was now.

Darek's screams for help washed away in the thunder above. Pedestrians huddling under umbrellas scurried from his path, and as the minutes ticked on, Darek's desperation grew.

Shifting the body to one arm, he used his free arm to grab at people but was repeatedly shoved away.

"She needs help," he cried out. "Anyone?"

His hand closed around the arm of a man. "Sir, please!"

One look at his face was enough for the man to recoil and shake him off. "Get away from me."

Darek reached for him. "I need an ambulance, it's my mom, don't go!"

"Sorry, I can't help you."

Tears blurred his vision. No one ever could. In a small place where rumors spread like wildfire and everyone's beliefs mirrored the bible, fear grew like weeds until it covered rationality and common sense. His fathers' reputation had darkened everyone's mind long before Darek was born. Rumors of a man possessed by evil, a devil on earth, spread fear so dark and cold over the sleepy little town, no one dared to see what went on behind closed doors. People crossed the streets to avoid encountering the unholy family, turned their heads to the abuse they all saw on the broken skin of the little boy every time he walked alone to school.

Darek never truly understood. He grew up knowing something was different about his father, but he never considered the truth behind the name-calling and accusations.

Laughter reached his ears, and as his frantic eyes landed on a group of teenagers smoking outside of the pub, images of the abandoned birthday cards flashed through his mind.

"Get the fuck off the streets!" one of the guys called out. "You're scaring people."

"You and your family should be locked up at some zoo!" another voice added.

A hard shoulder bumping into Darek made him tumble to the ground. Clutching his mother's body in his arms, he looked up, pleading with the man who stopped and stood looking down at him. "Help her."

The church tower struck six, drowning the reply with bells echoing across the street. Darek felt his mother's body become limp in his arms. His breath stopped along with hers. His body, frozen in the moment as his blood boiled in his veins. He lowered her onto the ground, stroking her wet hair as a slow burning built up deep in his core.

Traffic swirled by him as if he was nothing but an obstacle in the road. In the distance, laughter from partying teens and the drum of a base thundered in rhythm with Darek's heartbeats.

With every thud, his blood grew warmer until his body was on fire. Shaking with held back tension, Darek breathed through parted lips as the world spun in circles around him. Tilting his head back, he allowed the rain to wash the blood from his face and the tears from his eyes while the suffocating feeling spread in his chest.

"Get out of here and take the witch with you!" a voice snaked its way into his mind. His fists clenched. A sharp pain as something hit his arm snapped his head in the direction of the voice. The group of teenagers screamed in a choir, chanting the word "*Devil*," over and over as they hurled beer bottles at Darek.

Darek narrowed his eyes, glaring at the bottle flying toward him. He sat motionless, taking the assault while the growing anger rose inside of him. When one bottle landed on his mother's chest, the pressure exploded inside of him. Like a dam bursting, he allowed all the feelings he'd held back to flood free, and as he shot to his feet, a wave of power blasted from him. He screamed into the night as flames licked their way up the teenagers' legs.

The brief flicker of surprise vanished the moment his eyes fell on his mother's body at his feet. The sudden anger stilled to a low simmer, and as he carried her away, silent tears fell from his eyes.

— * —

Darek dug her grave in their backyard while his father's words resounded in his head.

"Stupid child, do you think the church will bury her? We don't go there."

Heavy rain fell from the sky and thunderclaps shook the earth. Darek worked in silence, guided by the flickering porch light and the crisscross of lightning in the sky. One thrust of the shovel after the other until the hole was deep enough to fill up with water. He slipped on the muddy ground and fell but got back up and pushed on.

"Let her rot in the street. Rat food. That's what she is."

The tears ran dry, and as he pushed himself to the limit of collapse, he promised himself he'd never cry again. What good would it do in a world that hated him?

The lash of the belt burned across his chest, but it wasn't the first time he'd taken the punishment of being a wuss. His father's theory seemed to take *'what doesn't kill you makes you stronger,'* to a whole new level, and maybe he was right?

But Darek didn't feel strong now. His muscles ached with exhaustion and his heart hammered in his chest. But he couldn't stop. He couldn't allow his father to take this away from him. He'd taken everything already.

This was one thing he needed to do. What she deserved. If Darek was the only one who cared, he'd rather die than let her down. This was the last thing he could ever do for her. He wasn't going to stop until she was safely covered in the ground. Away from the monster she'd been trapped with for over twenty years. Away from pointy stares and whispered insults as she walked the streets. She'd be safer here, tucked away from the world. No one could hurt her again.

When he lowered her body into the ground, the first rays of morning light broke through the clouds.

"Goodbye, Mom," he whispered. For a moment he closed his eyes, allowing the pressure behind them to build up, but snapped them open before the feeling had a chance to manifest. He refused to cry.

His arms shook as he shoved the dirt back into the hole and once it was done, Darek sunk to his knees in the mud.

This night would haunt him. But somehow, he didn't dread it. Remembering meant more than sleepless nights and images of dead bodies with worms crawling across pale skin. It meant lessons learned. It meant mistakes to never be repeated. And it wouldn't. At that moment Darek swore on his mother's grave to never let anyone step on him again. To never allow himself to be vulnerable, and most of all, to never let anyone live long enough to laugh at his expense.

— * —

When Darek kicked the door to the doctor's house open, only one thought was on his mind.

The man appeared. "Didn't I tell you to leave us alone?"

A calm authority settled over Darek, and the panic that drove him the previous visit was just a memory.

"You did." His voice dipped into a low growl as he went on, "Pity I didn't listen." His eyes glowed a deep red as he glared at the doctor. "She died. Because of you."

Dr. Pedersen took a few startled steps back.

"It's time to return the favor."

Before the doctor could turn and run, Darek grabbed him by the throat and lifted him into the air. Dr. Pedersen's strangled cries awoke a strange feeling of satisfaction within Darek, and he tightened his grip. Holding the struggling man at arm-length, the sudden strength registered in his mind. The man must've been twice his weight, still, he could lift him as if he wasn't heavier than a cat. The sudden fire flashed before his eyes, and the whispers of the people slithered through his mind.

Demon. Devil. Freak.

A sharp cry snapped Darek back to the moment. A young woman, dressed in nothing but a towel, stood frozen in the doorway.

"What are you doing? Let him down!"

"Hmph," Darek scoffed, turning his eyes back on the doctor who was beginning to turn blue.

"You're killing him!"

Darek chuckled softly.

"Close your eyes, darling, or leave." With a flick of his hand, he snapped the doctor's neck before tossing him aside.

The girl backed away in shock, held-back sobs shaking her body.

"I warned you."

When Darek walked back to the cottage, his mind was in chaos. Flickers of remorse and shock shook his hands and weakened his knees. Images of the dead man and his twisted neck haunted his vision, but at the same time, he never felt more at peace. He *deserved* it. Revenge never felt sweeter, and the thought empowered Darek.

Everyone who'd ever let him down was going to pay. Humanity was going to suffer. It was what they deserved. He'd bring hell to earth and watch it all burn with the same intensity as the venom within him. How could people be so cruel? How could they watch an innocent mother die and laugh at the son's despair?

Darek would never forget. The feeling that night was forever etched into his soul. He would never be helpless again. He'd take the power back, one soul at a time, he'd make them all crawl at his feet. Make them beg and show them no mercy. Show them what evil was all about. When he'd been the one crumbling to pieces, all they did was laugh and curse his existence.

Now the tables were turned. A power he didn't understand coursed through his veins, but at the moment he didn't care what it was or where it came from. He welcomed it, and the strength and determination it brought with it. He'd be the evil everyone said he was.

"You will face darkness, but don't ever let that darkness take you."

His mother's words resounded in his mind.

"You are stronger than you know. Use it for the right cause."

Darek fell to his knees on the doorstep of their home. Tears sprung to his eyes, and he angrily wiped at them.

She knew. She saw it coming. The warnings now made sense. And how he wanted to listen to her, to grow into the man she wanted him to become.

"Mom," he whispered. "I killed a man."

Dr. Pedersen's blue face tortured his memory. Disgust and regret eating away at him until he wanted to cry. He killed a man …

Then just as fast, the doctor's actions snaked into his mind, bringing the darkness back in full force.

"He deserved to die."

The sudden voice speaking inside his head froze Darek mid-breath. Glancing around, he almost expected the owner of that deep velvety voice to be standing behind him. He was alone. But he was not. The presence which he denied, brushed off as loneliness or imagination over the years, never felt stronger. *He* was there. Right inside his head. Whispering to him. Tempting him. The voice, dark as sin but smooth as velvet, seducing him with promises of power he'd never known.

"They all do."

Darek closed his eyes, breathing through parted lips as he was pulled in two different directions.

"Let go," the voice urged. *"Take the power back."*

Darek's eyes flashed red. He buried his mom and the world laughed. He suffered the abuse of his father for over eighteen years, he'd been desperate to belong with the people who made him bleed, who beat him black and blue. All he wanted was to be accepted by a world that did nothing but reject him.

"You don't have to feel that pain," the voice promised.

"Who are you?" Darek whispered out loud.

The low chuckle inside his head sent a shiver down his spine. *"You know who I am."*

Darek gulped. Did he? The whispers of the people. The rumors were on everyone's lips. The strength, the cruelty, the way the sky went from blue to thunder and lightning the moment his father lost his temper. It had been there as long as he could remember, right in front of his eyes.

Possessed by evil. Ungodly. Demonic. Darek shuddered at the words as he was forced to face the truth. Was that what he'd become? A copy of his father? A vessel for... what?

"You're disappointing me," the voice taunted.

Child of Satan. Devil. Demon. Abnormality. Freak. Darek backtracked his thoughts, stopping on the word that felt... right. The word, amongst many, had been flung at him endlessly. He could not hide from it. It was true. He'd never been surer. He felt it. The untapped power simmering below the surface. The heat was vibrating under his skin. Something within him had shifted. He was no longer the same.

Devil.

The low chuckle vibrated within him, confirming his thoughts, pushing him on the right path.

"That's right, son. You can have it all. You can rule the world."

Darek let out a shuddering breath, slowly rising to his feet. That didn't sound all too bad.

"Let go."

Turning his face toward the starlit sky, he whispered a broken, "I'm sorry, Mom." Then he clenched his fists, allowing the anger to take over his senses. Once let free, it flowed like a river, filling every cell of his body until the blood in his veins and the breath he breathed filled with a smokey darkness that burned below his skin.

The front door swung open, and there his father stood, filling up space with his massive frame and a sinister scowl on his face.

"You little rat," he hissed. "Give it back."

Darek took a step forward, not understanding the meaning of the words, but no longer afraid. "Oh, I'll give back, how do you want to die?" he snarled, surprising himself with the venom in his voice.

But his father didn't flinch, and as his hand shot out and grabbed Darek by the throat, the voice in his head hissed, *"Now."*

Acting on pure instinct, Darek let go of everything he knew to be true, allowing a blinding pain to take over his body as it transformed into something new. Filled with burning hatred toward the man in front of him, he didn't pause to think, to feel afraid of what he turned into. He felt it. Waiting. Lurking. Ready to spring forward the moment he let go. He knew he would never be the same, and in the moment fighting for his breath in the mercy of a lifelong torturer, he welcomed it.

The massive leathery wings poised on his back, and claws worthy of a lion filled Darek with a strange sense of home. He had nothing to fear. This was who he was meant to be.

Reaching out, he grabbed the hand still clutching his throat, burying claws into his flesh before tearing the hand off him. Darek let go with a shove powerful enough to send the man flying back, crashing to the floor and sliding across it into the house.

Darek lowered his gaze, settled it on the cottage that contained a life of fear and pain, disappointment and broken dreams—memories of a time he could never get back.

The person he once was died along with her. He'd been reborn into something better and stronger, risen with the fire that consumed him. He was suddenly someone they could never break with turned backs, held-back affection, or neglect.

"What are you waiting for?"

"Your birthday surprise, what else?"

Darek clenched his jaw as the realization finally hit. He knew. They both knew.

Flames shot up the walls of the cottage, and as Darek watched it burn, he locked away his heart and threw the key into the fire.

DAREK

CHAPTER 1

Present time

Rounding a bend in a blur of speed, Darek pushed the motorcycle to its limit, taking the slick mountain road with fearless abandon. The danger and the icy wind in his hair made him feel alive. Naked trees swished by in shapeless colors of brown and gray, blending with the snow-coated mountains siding the roads. Darek played with death because he didn't think he could die. He had turned into a killing machine. The power burning inside him not only made him immune to the cold winter air, it also filled him with a deeply rooted frustration. *He was fire. He was destruction. He was fear.* And he loved it—but he wanted more. Whatever *more* was...

The car came out of nowhere. In the blink of an eye, it was speeding toward him, giving him no chance to brake or steer clear of the inevitable crash.

Darek's eyes locked on the face on the other side of the windshield, and the world around him slowed down. Two dark eyes stared back at him. The panic and the fear were his own, even though he wasn't afraid.

Wings sprouted from his back, ripping his shirt right off his body and lifting him into the air microseconds before the bike slammed into the car. The ear-piercing screech of bent metal and screaming tires all drifted away as he flew unharmed through the thin winter air.

He never cared about a human life. Not since *that* day. They all deserved to burn in hell. And he would gladly offer them a ride right down to the flaming gate. He never stopped to think, never felt the regret, and never had a second thought about who he left to die. The need to go back and check on the car both stunned and angered him. Why should he care? What was another soul to him?

Still, those eyes haunted him. The way they looked straight at him. The way they touched something deep within him that had laid untouched for years.

Darek cried out from the feeling, then did a one-eighty and flew back. Nearing the site, the smell of gasoline tickled his nose, and a faint pillar of steam rose into the air. The hissing and crackling as the vehicle trembled in the aftermath sent a wave of satisfaction through him. There was nothing better than the sound of destruction. The sound of revenge... The sound of screams was music to his ears.

He landed, changing back into human form before inching closer to the wrecked car. Peeking inside, his eyes landed on a female body, slumped over against the wheel. Black hair covered her face.

Something in Darek clenched. A sliver of regret. A bolt of fear. He reached for the door. It didn't open. One fist to the glass shattered the already broken window. He grabbed the frame, and with one sharp tug, yanked the whole door off. Throwing it aside, he leaned in, grabbed the woman's shoulder, and pulled her back against the seat. Her body was limp but still warm. Her head rolled to the side, hair falling away with the motion, and the moment Darek's eyes fell on her face, something shifted within him. The sudden feeling made him jerk back in startled shock. He hit his head in a hurry to get away and cursed out loud from the sudden pain.

The woman stirred, and his eyes snapped back to her just in time for hers to open. Her gaze as it landed on him, hooded by sleep and clouded from unconsciousness, drew Darek in like a moth to a flame.

Darek's lips parted in a soft gasp as the fire within him calmed. Her gaze brought along a cool breeze through his soul. Soothing and calming, allowing him to breathe a deep breath for the first time in years.

She blinked at him, her mouth opening as if she wanted to speak. Several tries later, she found her voice. Her eyes narrowed as they bored into Darek's. "You."

The hidden accusation in the word sent a chill down Darek's spine. During her short moment of terror, before he slammed into her car, she'd seen him. She recognized him. She blamed him.

"Hmph." He pulled back. "Wanna die in here?"

She turned her face away, revealing a slow but steady trail of blood trickling down the side of her face. The stark contrast of dark red against her white skin stirred something within him, and when he spoke his voice was just a growl. "You're injured."

"Yeah." She snapped her head back to glare at him. "That's what happens when some asshole runs their bike into my car."

Ignoring her, he muttered, "You have to get out." It was only a matter of time before the car caught fire. He'd burned down towns and reveled in the screams of hundreds of souls caught in the flames. But the thought of this stranger's soft body consumed in the inferno made him sick to his stomach. She was the perfect picture of beauty. She was exquisite. She was innocent, and fierce, she was everything he *shouldn't* bother with. Darek had never cared for anyone, never felt the need to be close to anyone. One look at this hauntingly beautiful creature, all of it changed, and he didn't have the will to fight it.

He didn't even know her name, but he wanted her, needed her. She was the calm in his storm. The lighthouse in the dark. The blood on her soft skin made his chest tighten with a sudden wave of guilt.

Darek ripped off her seatbelt, then slid an arm around her waist with no regard to her protests. He wasn't going to let her die just because she was too stubborn to accept his help.

Once she was free, he scooped her up in his arms, carrying her away from the car. He didn't even flinch as the blast shook the mountain, and the heatwave pushed against his back. He held her tighter, breathing in her jasmine-scented hair with a desire burning just as hot as the car.

"Let me go!" She pushed against his chest. A growl slipped past Darek's lips. He wasn't ready to let her go.

"Put me down!"

Darek abruptly stopped, dropped her to the ground, and stood glaring at her as she scrambled to her feet and away from him. When she turned her eyes up to glare right back, a twisted grin spread across his lips.

MILA

CHAPTER 2

Mila wasn't sure if her through-the-roof heart rate was because of the blood running down the side of her face, or if it was from staring up at the ridiculously handsome man who supposedly just saved her life. She could count the beat of her pulse, each tap as it pounded against her skull.

"Don't give me that look." She shot him an annoyed glare.

Darek arched an eyebrow. "Which one should I give you then?" His husky voice dripped with sarcasm as he went on, "No need to thank me."

The undertones of danger that laced each letter sent shivers up Mila's spine, but she refused to be intimidated.

"If you hadn't hit me, I'd be halfway to—" she cut herself off, scowling at the man. "I don't have time for this."

Arrogant son of a bitch. Mila added under her breath, turning on her heels to get away. She wobbled on her feet as dizziness swept over her, and immediately a tight grip around her upper arm steadied her. The heat from his skin burned into hers. She stiffened, biting back another snappy retort just because she needed his support not to collapse as her head spun.

One look at this man and she knew who he was. Everyone in the area did. His reputation didn't do him justice, though. While everyone spoke of the young man with unexplainable strength, the man who burned down cities and left people dying in his wake, the man with the raven black hair and the steel-gray eyes and the scars on his face—they'd forgotten one thing. How irresistibly mouthwatering gorgeous he was. One look at him had her blood pumping through her body like he lit it on fire. She hated him for making her ache to touch that ripped chest and peel those leather trousers off of his strong legs. She hated him for making her feel *anything*.

The rumors pinned him as some sort of a monster. Something not human, someone with no heart and no remorse. An outlaw who took what, and *who* he needed. The stories of women claiming to have encountered him and fallen for his charm, only to wake up in a strange house in an empty bed the next morning, made Mila sick to her stomach. She had no problem believing in the playboy stories, but the non-human part, she shunned as some sort of gossip to make up for the fact no one had caught him in action, no matter how many he murdered and left behind. It was based on fear, of the shame of being outsmarted by one man who roamed the states and left destruction in his wake.

"Tell me your name," he demanded, snapping Mila back to the winter road.

"Why? So you can track me down and finish what you've started? I'm not one of your toys. You've already done enough." She gestured to the damaged car with her free hand, trying to tug her arm from his grasp. "Let go!"

His low chuckle made her skin crawl.

"If I wanted to kill you, you'd be dead long ago."

Mila steered her gaze straight at him, challenging him with her eyes. "What do you want from me?"

His eyes locked on hers, and she refused to cower under his burning gaze. She wasn't going to let him scare her.

His voice dipped into a seductive growl, "I want *you*."

Something in Mila clenched, and before she could stop

it, a soft gasp slipped past her lips. His grip on her arm tightened as he pulled her closer. The way he looked at her made her feel naked, even though she was covered in her red winter coat and a black-and-white checkered scarf.

Mila's eyes flickered to his hand, then back up. Pausing at his bare chest, she couldn't help wondering about the series of rough scars against his otherwise perfectly tanned skin. Abandoning the thought, she trailed her eyes along a tattoo that followed every curve from his chest, down his abs and a perfectly toned stomach, to disappear into his trousers.

"You like what you see?" he asked, snapping her out of her head and back to the cold reality. Tearing her gaze away, Mila tried not to blush. There was no denying it, the man was god-made. It should be illegal to have that body and display it in public...

"I've seen better." She turned her face away from him. "Where's your clothes?"

"I lost them."

"It's minus degrees," she muttered.

"I don't feel cold."

The way he said it made her feel like he meant it as a permanent fact, not just about this moment. But that was impossible.

Mila shook her head. Why did she even bother? This man was insane, she needed no more proof. The rumors were more than enough. When she should be running for her life, she stood there arguing with him. She wasn't surprised. It wasn't the first time she reacted to the fight or flight instinct with the former, even though she knew damned well she should have chosen the latter. Fear made her brave when she shouldn't be. But if it was one thing she hated, it was to be one of those women who trembled under the hands of a man. She'd dated enough assholes to never let herself be the victim again. And the man staring her down was no exception. She refused to admit being frightened, even if it meant masking her feelings with snappy comments and fake courage.

"I have to go," she tugged at her arm, but his grip never loosened. "Let go of me!"

Darek's fingers twitched, as if he was debating with himself. Then instead of removing his hand, he pulled her closer. One hand landed on her head, fingers curling into her hair before yanking her head back, tilting her face upward. Mila held her breath, keeping still to minimize the painful tug of her hair. The way he studied her, his hot gaze roaming over her face made it impossible for her to look away. The hand on her arm shifted to her face, and with a notable gentleness, he ran his knuckles across her cheek. Mila shuddered under his touch, keeping her eyes fixated on his face. There was no denying it, he could snap her neck with a flick of those strong hands, yet, he traced the outline of her jaw with featherlike delicacy until she forgot about everything but the trail of fire left on her skin and heat spreading through her body.

"You need to get that stitched. Come." His arm snaked around her waist, snapping Mila out of the trance.

"No!" She jumped away from his reach. "Don't touch me. I'm not going anywhere with you!"

"You're bleeding."

Mila stared, for a moment torn between the strange pull toward the man, and the need to get away. "Leave me alone." She began to walk. She'd flag the first car that came this way. Anything was better than staying with *him*.

A hand shot out, grabbing her shoulder, yanking her back. Mila spun on her heels, slapping a palm across his cheek. The few seconds of stunned silence filled the air. Then faster than she could react, his fingers were around her throat in a death-grip. "Do that again..."

"Or what?" she wheezed. "You'll kill me?"

Darek let go of her with a shove, sending Mila stumbling backward.

"I know who you are. *Rewera*." She backed away as he came closer. "The devil? Did you pick that name yourself? I'm not scared of you."

"Then why are you moving away from me?" His eyes glowed a deep red as he stared at her. "You *are* scared. You *should* be."

Mila stopped, locked her eyes on his, gathered up the last

remains of courage, and hissed, "Try me."

His low chuckle made her blood run cold, but she stood her ground. No way she was going to give him the satisfaction of seeing her afraid.

"You shouldn't have said that, darling." Darek's lips twisted into a sinister grin as he drew near her.

Mila held her breath, standing still while every cell of her body screamed at her to run. To get as far away from the man as she could. She refused to believe in the stories. It was just a name he'd taken. He was no devil. He was just some sick bastard who—

A scream tore from her throat.

"Scared now?" he asked.

Her jaw dropped. She couldn't move. All she could do was stare as his nails grew into claws, and horns, just as sharp, emerged from his skull. When he closed in on her, Mila staggered back, stopping as she felt something touch her back. It was sharp. Warm. Alive. She froze, forcing her head to turn slowly, not wanting to see but not able to resist either. The moment her eyes fell on a snakelike tentacle, she regretted the decision. Tracing it back to the man, she refused to accept the fact that he had a tail. A fucking tail! Mila squeezed her eyes shut in denial.

She felt the touch, the gentleness as those claws scraped across her cheek, tipping her chin up so she had no choice but to look at him.

"You won't hurt me," her voice trembled.

"I could."

Mila swallowed. "You won't."

He flicked the tail, cracking the air like a whip, and chuckled as she jumped. "Just do as I fucking say."

Mila scowled. The attraction she'd felt toward this man was long gone, leaving only a burning hate in her core. He was everything she despised. Dominant, manipulative, and arrogant. The way he seemed to find some sick satisfaction in taunting her, scaring her, made her want to scream.

"No, thanks," she said. "You have to kill me before I let you touch me. You sick fuck!"

He huffed. "I'm taking you to the hospital, not raping

you."

Wings burst from his back, and before Mila could scream, he snatched her up.

She saw the mountains grow small, felt his warm body pressed against hers as the icy winds tugged at her hair. Then her vision turned black…

DAREK

CHAPTER 3

Darek dropped her at the helipad at the hospital's roof. She staggered away from him, stumbled, and fell. His arm was around her waist before she hit the ground.

"I got you." The moment he said it, he was perplexed. What was wrong with him? Why did he care if the stubborn woman cracked her skull? She was nothing but an annoyance, resisting and arguing as if she had no fear in her body. He should've left her in the car to burn. It should've been the most normal thing for him to do, but just thinking about it made Darek's stomach churn.

Mila got to her feet, pushing away from him with an angry scowl. "So it's true? What people say?" The tremble to her voice gave her away. She could pretend all she wanted, he smelled the fear on her skin. She was scared of him—she *should* be.

Darek flexed his wings, making her jump further away. He chuckled at her expression.

"How?" she asked, suspiciously eyeing his devil-features. "How can you—" she gestured with a flick of her hand, leaving the sentence hanging. "You are—"

"I am."

"How—"

Darek shrugged. There was no manual. The thing he turned into didn't come with instructions. He had no idea of how and why, but he felt it. Just as clear as he knew he was human, he was also something so much more sinister. Demon. Devil. People called him all the names they could think of, long before he grew into what he was now. What crushed his spirit and broke his heart now empowered him. If they wanted to call him the devil, he'd show them just what kind of a devil he could be. Was it a self-fulfilling prophecy? Did he turn into the beast he was now, just because everyone claimed he was as evil as his father? Or had the constant torture he suffered at the hand of the same man, shaped him into what he needed to be to take the power back? Darek didn't know. He never cared enough to find out. He just rolled with it. Used it to his advantage. He learned to control the power inside of him, he let it turn him into someone no one could step on again.

Mila's voice snapped him back to the moment. "Your name... are you..."

"The devil?" Darek filled in, raising a dark eyebrow at her expression. "Yes." He said it with such certainty he stunned himself. It came naturally. He didn't even think about it. He realized at that moment—he always knew. He simply never stopped long enough to think or feel.

Mila gulped, inching backward as she managed to whisper the next words. "Why me?"

"*Why you,* what?"

"Why did you save me? I know what you do. The rumors—"

"Don't believe everything you hear."

She looked around as if searching for a way to escape, then blurted, "Why don't you kill me?"

Her straightforward question caught Darek off guard. Why didn't he? Why had he bothered to fly her all the way from the damned mountain to the hospital when he could've left her to burn in that car? Why did he even bother at all?

He stared at her, trying to assemble any sense of thought or sanity. She was hauntingly beautiful, but so were many women. It never affected him before. She wasn't the first pretty girl he came across, but she was the first one to ever make him ache with the desire to be near her. He never cared for anything more than sex and taking what he needed, but she was the first to arouse him in ways he never knew possible. Hell, he was hard from just imagining her soft skin hidden under the coat. Darek let out a shuddering breath. He *couldn't* kill her. He couldn't even imagine her dead. He imagined her in more exciting ways than lifeless in a coffin.

"Hmph." Darek shook his head free of disturbing thoughts, gesturing to the wound on her forehead. "Get that fixed up, then we'll talk." He grabbed Mila's arm, dragging her to the edge of the roof, and stood looking down while she struggled to break free.

"Can you stop!" he snapped. Mila stilled, but stood, trembling under his grip.

"I'm *not* jumping off the roof!"

"You don't have much of a choice, darling."

Darek held out his hand, producing a ball of fire in his palm, then sent it flying through the air, smirking as a car far below on the street exploded into flames.

Mila gasped. "What did you do that for!"

"Diversion."

Ignoring her screams and pathetic attempts to get away, he grabbed her and jumped into the air. Landing safely on the ground, he folded his wings and the rest of his devil-features vanished with them. "No one saw a fucking thing."

She gaped, eyeing the people scurrying around the fire. "You could've hurt someone."

"So?"

"SO?"

Darek shrugged. "*Devil*, remember?" He gave her a push

toward the entrance. "Go. I'll wait for you."

Mila scoffed. "Thanks for the *ride*, but you're not seeing me again."

Darek glared at her. Smoothing back his hair, he battled the feelings inside. Something about her words stirred up a panic in him which he hadn't felt since holding his dying mother in his arms. He was desperate to save her even when all hope was lost, refusing to let her go.

"Bye, creep." Mila turned on her heels and stalked toward the entrance. Darek's eyes narrowed. He couldn't lose her. He only just found her. Catching up, he slung an arm across her shoulder. "Not so fast, darling."

"Go away," she hissed, shrugging his arm off her. Darek followed close by as she stopped in the reception. Standing behind her, he had to resist the urge to wrap his arms around her waist and feel her body against his.

"Step through the doors here, miss, a nurse will see you soon."

Mila moved, stopping to shoot Darek a cold look. "You're not coming with me."

"Sir?" The receptionist blinked at him, her cheeks red as she tried to look anywhere but at his bare chest. "Are you family?"

Darek looked straight at Mila and said, "I'm her husband."

Mila's jaw dropped. "Wh—"

He slung one arm around her waist, guiding her through the doors before anyone could ask. Leaning in, he growled in her ear, "Don't fight it."

She tensed, her breath hitching in her throat as a shudder rippled through her.

"I know you want me."

"In your dreams," she hissed. "Now shut up."

MILA

CHAPTER 4

His gaze burned into her back as the nurse cleaned her wound. The small talk she attempted drowned in the thunder of her heartbeat and the whirlwind of unspoken words boiling inside of her.

How dared he! Who did he think he was? She didn't even know him, and there he was, pretending to be her husband. If she'd been alone, she would have slapped him. Devil or not, he was a monster, who now had eyes on her. Even though she knew she should be scared, she wasn't anymore. She was annoyed, she was frustrated, and she'd do anything to get rid of him. But it wasn't out of fear. Somehow, she believed him. If he wanted her dead, she would be dead. There was no doubt about it.

"There you go." The nurse smiled, patting Mila's arm before getting to her feet. "It will heal up in no time."

Mila's eyes paused on the young woman's face, taking the time to fully see her since walking into the room. She looked kind, like the type of person Mila would have loved to befriend. Her curly blonde hair was pulled into a ponytail, and her face free of makeup. She hadn't even tried to hide the mole on her cheek.

"Thank you." Mila threw a look over her shoulder. Darek stood by the door, his arms were crossed over his chest as he casually leaned back against the doorframe. Mila gulped, trying to stay calm. He looked every bit the predator he was as he stood, motionless and staring at her. He didn't even blink.

She shuddered, letting the anger drive away the fear. She was no one's snack, she'd show him. That self-absorbed son of a bitch!

"I need to use the restroom. Do you mind showing me the way?" she asked the nurse.

"Of course, hun." She waited for Mila to stand, gather her coat, and then held the door open.

Mila shot Darek a look, forced a smile, and said in an overly sweet voice, "I'll be right back, my love, you can wait for me in the waiting room."

"Hmph," Darek pushed off the wall. "I'm going with you."

"I can pee by myself," Mila hissed. "I said I'll meet you in the waiting room!"

His features hardened, the smirk flattening into a threatening glare that couldn't quite hide the fire burning behind the gray. His muscles flexed as his hands curled into fists. Mila scowled. Nice move, asshole.

"Is there a problem, miss?"

"No," Mila shot Darek a look, then followed the nurse as she guided her down a corridor. His eyes followed her every move, a palpable heat encircling her as she increased the distance, darkness swirling in the air until she found it hard to breathe. Mila picked up the pace.

"Call the cops or the freaking fire department," she hissed to the nurse as they walked. Rounding a corner, she threw one look over her shoulder and breathed a sigh of relief. "*That* is Darek Rewera, you must've heard of him?"

The nurse faltered, then picked up her pace to catch up. "You're married to *him*?"

Mila stopped, grabbed the nurse's arm. "He's not my husband, he's a freaking stalker. Help me out of here before he finds me!"

The nurse paled, looked around as if she expected Darek to be standing there, there she nodded.

"Here," she guided Mila toward a door. It opened to a new corridor that ended in a flight of stairs. Reaching the bottom, the nurse gestured to one more corridor, and Mila saw the green light above a door. *Emergency exit.*

"Miss," the nurse held on to Mila's arm. "If you believe you are in danger, I'll have someone—"

Mila cut her off. "No, it's ok. I have to go. I'm already late."

The nurse hesitated but let go. "I don't like this."

Mila flashed her a smile. "Is there a phone I can use? I lost mine."

"Believe it or not, there's an old phone booth right across the street."

"That will do."

Mila hesitated. "Be careful. He's dangerous. All those stories online, they're true."

"I believe you, I can see auras. His is dark. Go, get away from him, be safe."

Mila gave the nurse a quick hug, then turned and jogged toward the exit.

She pushed the door open, blinked against the bright winter sun, and stepped outside. The door swung shut behind her.

Mila started walking, heading across the street just as the nurse said. She imagined Darek pacing the waiting room, a bunch of female eyes glued to his chest. It suited him right. She hoped they'd be all over him. It would teach him a lesson. Mila's eyes landed on the phone booth and steered straight toward it. She needed to contact the rental company, she needed a new car. She also needed to report the accident to the police. She groaned, picking up the phone. Already knowing it would be a long process, she dreaded the phone call. She didn't have time for this.

Answering question after question, Mila started to lose her patience. How hard could it be to write the accident into their system and let her rent a new car? Insurance this, insurance that. Mila wanted to cry. And it was all HIS fault. If he'd been driving like a normal person, he would have had time to stop.

"I don't have a car!" Mila snapped. "I can't get to the station. I'm at the hospital." She tried to restrain from yelling at the man and plucked old paint off of the red walls while she listened. "A day? I don't have time!" Mila slammed the phone, turned—and ran straight into a person. She didn't need to look to know who he was. The unnatural heat radiating off him spoke for itself. She froze, cold fear rushing down her spine. He found her. Her heart skipped a beat, then sped up, pumping her blood through her body in hot waves, driving out the cold and spiking her temper.

"Get out of my way!" She shoved an elbow to his side hoping to push her way past him. He didn't even stagger.

"Not so fast, darling."

Mila cursed the authorities who kept her on the phone long enough for Darek to find her. She cursed herself for being naive enough to think she outsmarted him. She cursed *him*, for not taking the fucking hint. She didn't want him! She didn't even want to look at him.

Darek stepped into the booth, forcing Mila back with his body against hers. Two palms up against the glass, he trapped her within his arms, leaning down to growl into her ear. "You can't escape."

Mila gulped, pressing up against the wall to avoid touching his skin. His scent filled the tiny space, a mix of freshly extinguished candles and burnt wood. Mila wrinkled her nose. No wonder he smelled like fire. Just one more thing to remind her how abnormal he was.

"Where do you want to go?" he asked in a low seductive tone that made her belly clench with unexplainable desire, and her hatred skyrocket as a result. What was it about this man that evoked such reactions in her? She wasn't attracted to him, she despised him. So why did his proximity make her tremble and his intoxicating scent making her yearn to breathe him in?

"Nowhere," she breathed. "Now let me go." She hesitated, her hands hovering in the air before she dared to touch him. Her hands flat against his chest, she faltered. The intention to push him away was overshadowed by the strange sensation rushing through her. He was hard as a rock, his body sculpted out of marble. And he was on fire. No human was supposed to be that warm. A traitorous gasp slipped past her lips, blending with a low hiss from him.

Mila's eyes darted to his lips, her breath hitching as she saw his, parted in a silent moan.

Snatching her hands back, she ducked under his arms and slipped away. She didn't know what was wrong with her, but she refused to stay and find out.

She scanned the street for any sign of a taxi as she hurried away. Footsteps behind her made her pick up her pace until she was jogging.

One hand on her shoulder yanked her to an abrupt halt. "I'll take you."

Mila's eyes widened.

"Wherever you want to go," he clarified with a huff. Gesturing toward a black mustang parked down the road, he added. "I'll behave."

Mila snorted. Tempted to take him up on the offer, she shook her head. As much as she needed to get to that shelter, she wasn't desperate enough to hitch a ride with the devil.

DAREK

CHAPTER 5

"Why are you following me?" She shouted over her shoulder as she strode away from Darek. "What do you want from me?"

"You."

Mila stopped, swirling around to face him. "Why? Why me?"

Her question caught Darek off guard. He didn't have an answer. He couldn't explain the intense feeling, the desire to be near her. She allowed him to breathe, to rest. He didn't know how badly he needed that stillness until he'd seen her. Once he got a taste of it, he couldn't live without it. She was the missing piece. He needed more, and staring into her dark eyes, he knew it was her. She was the *more* he'd been craving.

Mila shook her head, sneering, "You don't even have

an answer." She continued down the street, making Darek cry out in frustration. She was slipping away. Balling his hands into fists, he looked down at the fire leaking through his skin, making his veins glow orange with the pressure inside. Breathing through clenched teeth, he tried to still the suffocating heat, tried to keep himself together. Lifting his eyes, he watched her walk away, taking everything he needed with her. Something in Darek snapped. He couldn't lose her. Couldn't let her get away. He didn't even know her name.

Dashing back down the street to the awaiting car, he slid into the driver's seat and hit the gas. Catching up with her, he rolled down the passenger window. "Get in the car!"

She didn't even look at him. "Piss off!"

Darek hit the brake, put it in park, and left the engine running as he rounded the car and grabbed her by the neck. Mila screamed as he yanked her toward him. Spinning her around, he gripped her upper arm tight enough to leave bruises. "I. Said. Get. In."

Her eyes locked on his, making him flinch from the sudden wave of calm rolling over him.

"No!" She spat in his face, using the few seconds of stunned stillness to rip her arm free.

Darek's eyes flashed red. In a blur of speed, he slung her over his shoulder, carrying her kicking and screaming to the car, and dumped her in the back seat before slamming the door. Before she could assemble any sense of direction, he was back behind the wheel, and the car shot forward.

"You won't get away with this!" Her voice trembled, and when he threw a look in the rearview mirror, Darek caught a glimpse of real fear in her eyes. A stab of regret shot through him. He didn't mean to be that rough. He didn't mean to... what? Abduct her? What was he going to do with her?

As if she read his mind, she asked, "Why are you doing this? What do you want?"

Darek remained silent, clenching his jaw until his head throbbed with the tension. What had he done?

"Kidnapping me, huh?" Mila snapped. "Nice. What a gentleman you are."

Darek glared at her through the mirror. "I'm the devil for fucks sake," he snarled. "What did you expect?"

She scoffed but fell silent. Darek let out a shuddering breath, stomped a little harder on the gas. He couldn't outrun this, but it didn't stop him from trying. He hated her with a sudden intensity that made his blood boil and his body vibrate with the heat. He hated her for what she made him feel. He hated everything she brought back. No one liked him. He accepted that long ago, he stopped caring. Humanity was nothing but a sea of faceless insects. He didn't need them. He didn't need *her*.

"Did you steal this car?"

"Do you really wanna know?"

Mila opened her mouth to reply but closed it. When he thought she'd given up, she blurted, "Yes, I wanna know."

"Yes." Darek saw no reason to lie. "Killed the scumbag who drove it too."

When Mila's eyes bulged, and her skin visibly paled, he couldn't help but smirk.

"Was that too much for you?"

She swallowed, letting out a low, whimpering sound before shaking her head and averting her gaze.

Darek drove in silence, contemplating the next step. Taking her was an impulse acted upon, where he was going, and why he even bothered to stuff that stubborn hot-tempered, brave, human into the car, he didn't know.

"At least turn down the heat."

A look in the mirror made his breath hitch and his pulse skyrocketing. Mila had removed her scarf, and soon her coat followed. She wiped her forehead, tucking her hair behind her ears while muttering, "Some people are dressed."

Darek scoffed at the hint, her words cranking up his anger levels further. She didn't know, it was *his* heat filling the car. His fucking fire burning him like the strongest fever known to man. He couldn't stop it. He could barely breathe.

They rode in charged silence until Darek caught a glimpse of her, removing her sweater. She struggled in the narrow seat, dragging the fabric over her head. Once she was free, she tossed it to the side, brushing her hair out of her face, and leaned back. Sitting in only a white skin-tight tank top, her eyes shot to the mirror. "What?" she hissed.

Darek tore his gaze away, letting it rest on the slick road ahead as he tried to fight through the sudden feeling within him.

"Where are you taking me?"

It took a while for Darek to find his voice, and when he spoke, it came out as nothing but a hoarse growl, "You tell me."

She straightened, her interest piqued. "You're serious? You're driving me to the Moon-bridge? Why?"

"Moon-bridge?"

Mila shifted, leaning forward with a suspicious look on her face. "You're not kidnapping me?"

Darek let out a sharp laugh. "I'm the devil, not a fucking rapist. When will you get that?"

"You won't touch me?"

"Not until you beg me to."

Mila jerked back, crossed her arms over her chest. "Not gonna happen."

Darek let out a slow breath. Promising her was the hardest thing he'd done, and honoring that promise would be even harder. Every time he looked at her, he wanted to rip her clothes to shreds and feel her body wrapped in his. He wanted to taste her, to devour every inch of her skin and make her scream.

"It's a dog shelter, up in the mountains. Moonpike Ridge, by the hiker resort." Her shaky voice abruptly ripped him from his thoughts. One glance in the rearview mirror was all it took. Her eyes were on him, those dark depths mirroring the desire that had his body in an iron hold.

"I know where." Darek swallowed, awkwardly shifting in the seat as his trousers suddenly clung to him, painfully tight. A low groan escaped his lips as the fabric rubbed against him.

Mila leaned forward, letting her hair brush against his shoulder, and asked with fake innocence. "Something wrong?"

Darek gripped the wheel tighter.

"If you as much as lay one finger on me..." she brushed a finger across his bicep as to demonstrate, "I'll be gone before you even know what hit you."

"Don't taunt me," Darek growled.

She leaned in, letting her breath tickle his neck before hissing in his ear. "Or what?"

Darek knuckles whitened with tension, the wheel caving under his grip. Her hot breath on his neck was more than he could stand. Claws grew from his fingernails, curling around the wheel seconds before his horns tore from his skull with the same burning ache as the fire in his loins.

Mila jerked back, a small gasp slipping from her throat. Darek let out a breath of relief, but before he had the chance to return his heart rate to normal, she was back, a hand reaching for a horn. Darek held his breath as she slid the tip of her finger over the bone.

"They're..." she let the words drop, and her trembling fingers caressed the length, from top to bottom before she withdrew her hand, "Hard."

Darek hit the brake, twisting in the seat before the car came to a full stop. He caught her hand, yanking her toward him.

"The fuck are you doing?" His voice was just a breathless hiss. Her face was inches from his, so close he could feel her breath on his lips. Her body trembled from the sudden shock and her lips opened in shuddering breaths as his hovered over hers.

"Don't you dare," she breathed.

"Then don't fucking taunt me if you don't like the consequences."

MILA

CHAPTER 6

Darek let go of her with a shove, sending her flying back against the seat. Regaining her composure, she raised her gaze to glare at him. Pleased with herself, she adjusted her top, deliberately pulling it a little lower to reveal a cleavage of smooth white skin. She got the answer she needed. He kept his promise, even though it was clear he was struggling.

Mila didn't understand why she pushed him. She was stuck in a car with a sexually frustrated devil who had his eyes on her. Did she *want* him to jump her? Mila was appalled by her own behavior. She wasn't a tease, and she was certainly not into casual sex with random strangers, no matter how hot they were. It wasn't about that. She wanted him to suffer like the pathetic loser he was. She wanted to watch him squirm, to make him throw her out of the car in frustration. She wanted him gone.

Mila wet her lips, keeping her eyes locked on his. She wanted to watch him suffer and burn in those tight leather pants. And by the looks of him, she was doing something right. Mila cocked her head, sending her hair dancing across her shoulders. Two people could play the game. His drop-dead features had no effect on her. She wasn't shallow enough to fall for his looks when it was obvious that it was all there was to him. His soul was black, and his mind just as twisted.

"Gonna drive, or stare at me?"

Her voice made him huff, but his eyes never left her body.

Her voice dipped into a throaty purr. "Wanna touch?"

His jaw tightened, veins bulging from his throat as he tensed. When his eyes glowed red, Mila faltered. Taunting the devil surely wasn't the smartest thing she'd done, but she couldn't help but enjoy his struggle more than she should. What had he expected? He toss her into his car as if she was a bag of potatoes, and she just lie there? Willing and waiting for him to satisfy his sick needs? She wasn't that kind of woman, and he found out the hard way. Mila hoped he regretted his decision to snatch her. She hoped he was as uncomfortable as he looked. She hoped he was *hurting*.

"Stop," he hissed.

Mila let out a sharp laugh. "Me, stop? You're the one who dragged me into your car and keeps eye-fucking me," she snapped. "*You* stop, pervert!"

Darek's claws dug into the seat. The sound of tearing leather made Mila's skin crawl. Then just as fast as he turned on her, he shifted back with an inhuman snarl erupting from his throat.

Without another word, he started the car, hit the gas, and steered toward the mountains.

He took the curvy roads at flying speed, and every time Mila was sure the car was going to slide off the road and tumble to certain death, he steered clear of the danger.

Her protests did nothing to slow him down. He didn't listen to her, didn't even look, but his face reflecting from the mirror made her shiver. She'd seen tension, but he looked like he'd snap from it. Those red eyes caught hers, but she couldn't bring herself to look away. She could've sworn his grip of the wheel was nothing but a distraction to keep him from gripping her, instead.

The tension in the car was palpable. The air, thick and warm. It didn't take long for the windows to steam up.

Little drops of moisture trailed down the glass in slow, teasing patterns that painted images in Mila's mind. Images she didn't want.

When the car came to a sliding halt, Mila wiped the steam off the window to look out and gasped. The sign hanging from two chains planted a seed of guilt on her gut. He had taken her right up to the gate. He meant every word. She hesitated, hand on the door, as the uneasy feeling grew stronger.

"Listen—"

"Get out," Darek growled. "Get out before I do something I'll regret."

Throwing on her sweater, Mila grabbed her coat and flung the door open. The cold air hit her like a wall. The sudden temperature shift made her cough as the icy winds filled her overheated lungs. Shrugging on the coat, she buttoned it up to her chin and wrapped the scarf around her neck.

Throwing one look at the car, she turned her back to it and strode toward her destination.

Stopping outside of a wooden building, she read the logo printed on the door with nervousness spreading within her.

Moon-bridge Dog Shelter.

The mountain shelter was the last on her list. She traveled across the state in hopes of finding the missing dog, and even though every effort, every tip, every call, had led to nothing but disappointment and crushed hope, she kept going. Bosco was out there somewhere, and Mila wasn't going to give up until she found out where.

Stepping through the door, the first thing she heard was the heated argument of a voice she never expected to hear this far from Seattle. Her eyes darted to a man, and even with his back to her, the mere sight of him made her want to vomit. Scott Trenton. The man who did everything to screw up her life. If he wasn't the biggest asshole to ever walk the earth, she didn't know who was. He'd done everything in his power to get back at her as if she was the one needing punishment. The minute she put her foot down, she was the bitch. Maddie, the dog, paid the price. She died, locked up in Scott's basement before Mila could locate her.

Mila's eyes narrowed as she eyed his jeans west above a red flannel shirt. Dressed like the freakin' farmer he was far from being, he stood there with the audacity to pretend to be worried about the missing dog. *Her* missing dog. She wouldn't be surprised if he was the one who'd taken Bosco, too.

"Hey!" she called out. "Asshole!"

Scott spun around, eyes landing on her and a grin spread across his face. "I'd be damned. Princess Shikawa."

Mila scowled at his ridiculous nickname. "As if you didn't know I'd be here," she snapped, stalking up to the man, she jabbed a finger to his chest. "Bosco is mine. You have no right."

Scott laughed, showing a set of crooked teeth. "Yours? This paper says differently." He waved a paper in the air, and when Mila tried to snatch it, he held it above his head.

"You need to grow some legs, shorty."

She glared up at his tall frame and hated him more than ever. "I'm not short, you're the one who's abnormally tall."

He laughed. "Either way, you're not getting the paper or the dog."

Mila restrained from shouting. It wouldn't solve anything, especially not when there was another human being in the room. Mila's eyes traveled to the woman at the desk, the poor soul who Scott fought with.

"Ma'am," Mila smiled. "Is there a problem?"

"As I've tried to tell your…" she made a sweeping gesture toward Scott as if waiting for someone to fill in the missing word. Mila glared at Scott, who just grinned back at her.

The woman behind the desk cleared her throat, giving a polite cough before going on, "As I said. The shelter is closed for the day, you have to come back tomorrow if you want to meet the dogs."

"But—"

The woman held up her hand. "It's the rules. My hands are tied."

Scott opened his mouth to argue, but Mila beat him to it. "At least tell me if you've recently taken care of a gray

Pitbull. I've traveled all the way from Seattle on nothing but words that my dog was seen here. Please?"

The woman's face softened. "Ah, you are the woman who called earlier? Mira? I was expecting you earlier."

"Car problem," Mila muttered, not bothering to correct the name. "I'm sorry I'm late."

"Give me a moment." The old lady pulled out a drawer, starting to browse through an endless row of files.

"Pitbull, you said?"

"Yes."

Mila tapped her nails against the counter as she waited. When the woman finally produced a file, her heart leaped in anticipation.

"There's a Pitbull." The woman flicked through the file. "Gray, you said?"

"Yes!"

The lady produced a picture, and Mila's heart sank. The dog in the picture, though similar, was darker in color. She shook her head. "Bosco is more silver. It's not him." The disappointment welled up in her eyes, spilling down her cheeks before she could stop herself.

"I'm sorry, miss." The woman's voice was apologetic. "I have your number, I'll call if there's any news about your dog. If he was seen in this area, there's a chance he might show up."

Mila wiped her eyes, whispering, "Thank you."

She turned to leave, but Scott's voice stopped her. "Too bad about the doggo," he said, looking Mila up and down. "Staying in Westwood?"

Mila shot him a cold look, and instead of answering, she continued toward the door. When she stepped out into the fading evening light, the first thing she saw was Darek, leaning back against his car. Arms crossed over his chest and his eyes locked on her as she stopped dead. She forgot about him. Somehow, she assumed he would have left. But no such luck.

"Hey," Scott brushed his hand across her back, "Shame he wasn't here."

"Why are *you* here?" Mila asked. "What makes you so

interested in my dog?"

"Thought I'd help you find him."

"Bullshit. You're still angry about Chrissie."

Scott laughed. "I don't care about the kid, Mila."

"Yeah, you kinda made that clear when you hit her!" Mila turned to face Scott, tilting her head up, and went on, "If you don't want her back, then what is it? Why are you harassing *me*? She's better off with Peter and we both know it. I did what anyone would have done."

Scott slung his arm across Mila's shoulder, and her eyes darted back to Darek. His eyes were bright red, following Scott's every move. Mila gulped, already having a feeling this wouldn't end well.

DAREK

CHAPTER 7

Darek's blood burned in his veins. The icy winds did nothing to cool him down, and the more he thought of her, the more he craved her. She'd been gone for no more than fifteen minutes, and the ghost of a touch still lingered on his skin, the trace of her fingertips tingling in memory of the feeling. Images of her porcelain skin were etched into his mind. The soft curves of her chest, her slender arms, and those delicate fingers which he couldn't help but imagine in better places than his goddamn horns.

His eyes snapped up to the sound of a door slamming shut. Mila stepped out, her usual graceful strides slow and her face shadowed with sorrow. Something in Darek stirred. A different need. A different ache. Before he could make sense of the sudden feeling, a man stepped through the door. Darek held Mila's gaze, and when the man brushed his hand across her back, grinning down at her, Darek's eyes flashed red. How dare he touch her? How could *she* let him, when she made it perfectly clear she didn't want Darek anywhere near her. He huffed at the thought. She'd change her mind. He refused to accept anything else. Giving up on her wasn't an option.

Pushing himself off the car, he sauntered over to them, keeping his eyes locked on Mila. "What's wrong?"

Mila shook her head, but Darek knew better. Her eyes were shiny with tears, and even though he'd seen her bleeding and scared, seeing those tears in her big black eyes did something to him. He never cared for tears, never bothered to feel anything but hatred toward people. They begged, they cried, they screamed, and he reveled in their misery. Revenge had never felt sweeter, and knowing he'd once been the one begging and crying only fueled his anger, adding to the pleasure. But he found no pleasure in Mila's tears. Instead, they touched him somewhere deep inside, pulled at his heartstrings until he had to shove his hands into his pockets to avoid reaching for her.

"Why are you crying?"

"Forget it!" Mila snapped. "Why are *you* still here?"

Her harsh words stung, he had no way of denying it. It ripped apart something inside of him, stirred up feelings he'd sworn to never feel again. Didn't she know he'd never leave her in this remote place with no way of getting back to the city? Didn't she know the fifteen minutes without her felt like hours? Didn't she understand what she did to him?

Scott chuckled, eyeing Darek's lack of a shirt with an amused sneer. "Isn't it too cold for that?"

Darek didn't take his eyes off Mila. He didn't have time, or even the opportunity to find a new shirt, and he didn't care.

"Hey," Scott raised his voice. "Stop staring at her, you freak!"

Darek's eyes darted to him, his voice just a growl as he shifted closer, "What did you say?"

Scott stepped closer, accepting the unspoken challenge. "Fucking. Freak."

46

In a flash, Darek had his throat in a death-grip, lifting him off the ground with zero effort. His eyes burned with the intensity of the sudden rage inside as he glared up at the man who gripped Darek's arm in a useless attempt to free himself. Darek tightened his hold, squeezing until Scott's eyes bulged and a gargled sound escaped his lips. No one spoke to him like that and lived to regret it. He had enough of name-calling. Enough of the bullying. Darek's fingers twitched with the desire to snap his neck. The only thing holding him back was Mila's horrified eyes as she stared back at him in stunned shock.

"Stop!" She found her voice. "Let him go!"

Darek squeezed tighter, feeling the itch in his fingertips. The prelude of claws. He'd slit the bastard's throat and watch him drown in his own blood. He'd—

"Darek!"

Hearing his name roll off Mila's lips made him falter. He never heard her say it and wanted to hear it again. The way her tongue caressed it made him shiver.

Mila's hand landed on his arm. The tremble of her fingers vibrated within him, spreading a calm through his system until the rage dimmed and the fingers around Scott's neck loosened. He let go with a shove, sending Scott's body sliding through the snow. Darek let his hand drop and stood staring at the unconscious body as the last waves of hatred washed through his system.

Mila snatched her hand away, taking a few steps back with a disgusted look on her face. "You're a monster."

Darek stood frozen, still reeling from the sudden shift within him. Her touch was magic. Her hands were like a calming balm to a burning wound. Not until he experienced the calm control did he realize what he'd been missing.

Ever since his eighteenth birthday, he lived on the edge. Driven by the hatred for everything and everyone, controlled by the fire raging within him. He barely slept a day in three years, not finding the peace to close his eyes. He enjoyed the power and he used it well. But he let *it* use him, too. The evil that took residence within him was running the show, and he did nothing to stop it. Why would he?

When the world deserved to burn and humanity deserved to suffer. He made sure they did, but he suffered too. Darek couldn't remember being able to breathe, to sit down and eat a normal meal without the unslakable itch in his bones and the pressure in his veins.

Looking at Mila made him realize there was a third option. He didn't have to be consumed by the flames to watch everyone else burn. He could bend them to his will. He could take control. He could control the devil. The realization made a smirk creep onto his lips.

A groan from Scott snapped him back to the moment, and as his eyes fell on the man, anger flared up within him anew. He never wanted to kill someone as bad. He never fought so hard to keep from acting out on those impulses. Never been as torn in two.

"Touch me."

Mila's eyes widened in surprise. Then she scowled. "You wish."

"No!" Darek grabbed her hand, placing it on his chest. "Do as I say or I'll burn that pathetic excuse of a man to a crisp."

Mila hesitated but kept her hand plastered to his skin. Darek closed his eyes, searching for the feeling, but it wasn't there. Instead of quenching the fire, she redirected it until he gasped from the sudden sensation rippling through him. He jumped back, watching her arm drop and a perplexed look settling on her face.

"I can't do this anymore," she said. "I'm going home. Don't follow me."

She started walking down the road. Darek's eyes darted to her, then back to Scott. He clenched his fists, more than tempted to release a ball of fire to ease the pressure inside. Darek let out a cry of frustration and swirled to watch Mila's back as she increased the distance between them.

"I'll drive you!" He called out. She held up her hand, flipping him off with a middle finger.

MILA

CHAPTER 8

The humming of the engine and the crunching of the wheels against the hard-packed snow reached her before the car appeared next to her. When it stopped, she didn't have any other choice but to get in. Walking back to the city would take hours, and she'd be dead long before that. At night the temperature dropped drastically in the mountains. The cold seeped through her coat. Her thighs had grown numb long ago and her fingers were frozen stiff.

The door opened, and the heat rolled over her like a blanket. Mila threw him a look just as frosty as the air outside the car, then slid into the passenger seat without saying a word. Her frozen fingers didn't have the strength to pull the door closed, but it didn't stop her from trying.

Darek leaned over her, grabbed the door, and yanked it close. "What were you thinking?" he growled. "You could have died out there."

Mila glanced up, flinching from the sudden intensity in his gaze. Looking down at her numb hands, she remained silent. Why would he care? He was the freaking devil. He nearly killed Scott. Not that she cared what happened to that scumbag, but the fact remained, the man next to her was a monster. He was a bomb ready to explode at any given time. He was as unstable as she was stupid. Mila couldn't believe she willingly got into a car with him. This time she had no one to blame but herself.

"Give me your hands," he demanded.

When Mila didn't react, he let out a frustrated growl, abruptly collecting her hands and wrapped both of them between his. The heat spreading from him drew a low moan from her lips. It felt good. For a moment, Mila couldn't remember why she was supposed to be angry with him, why she was supposed to be scared of him. All she could think of was those strong hands covering hers, and the extreme heat seeping from his skin into hers. Her fingers began to tingle, her bones aching painfully as the heat spread within her.

When she dared to look at him again, the expression on his face made something inside of her clench. His usual hard features softened. His lips slightly parted and his eyes hooded as he gazed at her.

Mils swallowed down the sudden lump in her throat, removing her hands. "It's enough."

He shifted, gripping the wheel and for a moment he just sat, motionless and still, staring blankly at the road ahead.

Mila couldn't help but watch him as the silence filled the car. The slight tremble of his hands as he squeezed the wheel piqued her curiosity, and also made her narrow her eyes. Did those hands itch to strangle her, as he did with Scott? Was his tension just another attempt to keep from ripping her to pieces?

"Are you warm?" His voice made her jump. "I can—"

"I'm fine." She averted her gaze. "Just take me back to the city."

He let out a slow breath but didn't make any move to drive. What was he waiting for? Her eyes drifted back, catching him looking straight at her. Fighting the urge to look away, she held his gaze.

"How did you get those scars?" she asked, eyeing the rough white lines across his chest and stomach. She'd seen them on his back, too, but never gotten the chance to ask. When Darek didn't reply, she reached out to trace a ragged line sliced across his upper arm.

"What happened to you?"

A shudder rippled through him, his muscles tightening, and before he turned his gaze away from her, she could have sworn she saw a shadow of pain in his eyes.

His voice was nothing but a hiss. "Nothing."

"That's not *nothing*," Mila pushed. "Someone did this to you."

When he didn't deny it, she eyed the scars with a newfound horror and an unexplainable need to touch him. She was right, she was sure of it. And against her better judgment, she found herself sympathizing with him. Did it matter what he was? That he wasn't human... Before she could think about it, she let her hand land on his shoulder, brushing it over his damaged skin as she whispered, "Whatever happened, I'm sorry."

His whole body tensed up, muscles flexing under her fingers.

"Don't."

Something in his voice made her frown. The threat was there, the warning, but there was something else, something she never expected to hear from someone as confident and fearless as him.

"You walk around shirtless but you don't like it when people look?" she asked, no longer able to keep it to herself. It made no sense. "You've made it perfectly clear that you'd like to fuck me in the backseat of this car, but you don't want me to touch you?"

Darek's hand landed on hers, closing around it and removing it from his skin. He held on to her hand for a moment, then placed it back into her lap.

"Why?" Mila reached out, testing her theory. Before her hand fell on his arm, he snatched it, holding her wrist until she winced from the pressure. He released her with a huff.

"Don't provoke me."

Mila gathered her hands in her lap, muttering under her breath. "Fine. Just drive. I don't want to be here anymore than you do."

For once, he did as she said without argument or anger.

As the minutes dragged along and silence settled over them, Mila let her thoughts wander to Bosco. Where was he, was he still alive? The thought of the beautiful creature somewhere far away from her broke her heart. Was he with another family? Was he happy? Or did he miss her, did he wonder why she'd abandoned him, and did he wait for her to come and pick him up? Mila swallowed down the emotion rising in her throat. If he was safe, she could live with it, but not knowing was worse. Being left wondering what happened to him hurt more than anything. Was he out there in the snow? Was he freezing?

"What's wrong?" Darek's low voice brought her back to the car. Mila blinked tears from her eyes, shooting him a brief look before averting her gaze.

"Tell me."

Mila no longer had the energy to get angry at his dominant behavior. She just wanted to sleep and forget the whole day, but instead, she found herself opening up to him.

"My dog." She glanced at him. "He's missing. Presumably stolen. I followed a lead here, but it was a dead end. I don't—" her voice broke into a sob. "I don't know where he is."

When he didn't say anything, Mila dared another glance. His brows were furrowed in a frown.

"A dog?" he said at last. "You're crying over a dog?"

Mila's face hardened. "You wouldn't understand," she muttered. "I should have realized." She turned her head so she didn't have to see him. Of course he didn't understand. Had he ever loved anything in his life? Mila doubted it. He was the last person to feel her pain, and still, she'd been dumb enough to try to get his sympathy. Angry for letting herself fall into his trap, she swore to never be that stupid again.

"I never had a dog," he said.

Mila wanted to ignore him, but couldn't stop herself from snapping, "That shouldn't matter! It's basic human emotion, but I suppose you're not capable of that, either!"

"Hmph."

"Hmph?" Mila echoed. "You're not human, what am I

supposed to think? You know what, Scott was right. You're a freak! A coldhearted son of a—"

The car swirled to the side, dangerously near the edge, cutting Mila off mid-sentence. A scream tore from her throat, her arms flying out to grasp hold of something as images of the car flying off the cliffs passed before her eyes.

"I can fly if we crash," Darek growled. "You can't."

DAREK

CHAPTER 9

Darek parked the car outside of the hotel Mila had directed him to. As soon as the car came to a halt, she threw the door open and tumbled out.

"Thanks for the hell-ride!" she snapped. "Have a good life." She slammed the door and stormed toward the entrance. Darek watched her disappear through the doors and out of sight.

He let out a long breath. That woman was something special. She was fucking amazing. The way she dared to speak back to him, how she wasn't even afraid of his devil side was more than he could understand. Everyone reacted in the exact way he predicted, and desired, but not her... *her*... He didn't even know her name. She'd refused to tell him.

Stepping out of the car, he closed the distance in a flash, throwing the door open, and stalked up to the reception. "The girl with black hair," Darek gestured toward the empty lobby. "I need to see her."

The man behind the desk cleared his throat, speaking in a polite tone. "There's no one here, sir."

Darek leaned forward, hands on the counter. The man, despite his tall frame and tattooed arms, took one step away.

"Don't lie to me."

"I'm not. No one's passed here in hours, man."

Darek straightened, looking around the hall with a growing sense of dread.

"Is there a backdoor?"

"Only the basement, stairs are right beside the—"

Before he could finish his sentence, Darek pivoted and rushed back the way he came. Stopping right inside the main doors, he located a second door a few steps down. Holding his breath, he yanked it open, revealing a flight of stairs leading down. Cursing under his breath, he took the steps in a flying stride. The corridor was dark, fenced storage rooms on both sides. Darek dragged his hands along the net as he walked, his eyes locked on a window at the end of the corridor. Running the last steps, he screamed out loud as the truth slammed down on him. She was gone.

The slit of an opening was big enough for a child to squeeze through, but with her petite size, she could manage. Slamming a fist into the wall hard enough to crack it, he leaned his forehead against the cold bricks and focused on the pain, and tried to breathe through the desperation.

She was *gone*. The blood boiled in Darek's veins. He didn't even know her name. Digging his nails into the brick wall, he felt them grow into claws as a cry erupted from his throat. The overwhelming sense of loss shook his body as the pain turned into anger. The control he swore to master while he'd been with her vanished, too. And why should he care? Let the inferno loose, let it all burn with the same intensity as the raging fire inside. The devil took over, ripping through his bones as horns and wings exploded from his body. His shriek shook the building, and as he flew his arms out, a heatwave spread from him, rippling in rings of fire around him.

Darek flexed his wings, unleashing the true power in a blind rage. The hotel crumbled around him as he rose upward, clearing the collapsing masses with powerful wing strokes.

Darek flew until he had no energy left and the city was a dot on the map. Gliding through the air, he let his wings relax, allowing the image of her to fill his mind. For a brief moment, the same cool tranquility came over him as he soared.

Then he opened his eyes, and the reality slammed back like a punch to the stomach. He lost her, let her slip through his grasp.

Darek swooped down, beating the air with angry strokes. He'd find her. If it was the last thing he'd do. He'd find her and once he had her, he would never let her go.

— * —

When the first rays of morning light broke through the night, Darek sank to the ground, folded his wings, and let his devil features withdraw.

Stepping through the door to the house he stayed in, he slammed it shut and started to pace the floor. His whole body was exhausted, but he couldn't rest. Not until he found her.

Looking at the unfamiliar place, a sting of longing zapped through him. Everything was at the tip of his fingers. He could eat and drink everything he wanted, he had a bed to sleep in, even though he barely slept. He had a wardrobe full of clothes, a whole house packed with things he could use in whatever way he pleased. But it wasn't *his*. None of it was. He lived the life of the perfect outlaw for years and enjoyed every minute of it. Only recently he started to grow bored.

He wanted something to call his own. He wanted his own home, his own bedsheets, and his own couch, not some dead guys. He wanted his own car, not one he'd stolen. Swiping a hand across a table, he flung a dozen papers and books into the wall. He'd grown tired of this place anyway. The four walls that pleased him not long ago now made him claustrophobic. It was too small, too closed up, too fake.

Collapsing onto the couch, he flicked on the TV, zapping through the channels until he found what he looked for. But the naked bodies of strangers did nothing to him. Once he got a taste of *her*, he'd never settle with anything less. She was the definition of beauty. She was intoxicating, she was delicious. Everything about her set his body on fire, and just thinking of her did more than the porn ever could. Darek hurled the remote onto the screen, watching it light up in flames as his frustration leaked through every fiber of his body.

Darek ignored the fire, he was immune to the smoke and flames. Instead, he closed his eyes, keeping her image alive in his head as he reached down to tug his belt open. Imagining her hand in the place of his, he let his head fall back as the pleasure rolled over him. He'd been on the verge of bursting with tension all day, and the delay only increased the feeling as he finally allowed himself the release. Her face flashed before his eyes, her imaginary hands on his skin. The memory of her hot breath against his neck...

Darek's free hand dug into the cushions as the feeling exploded within him. His back arched off the couch, his head tilting back as he cried out into the raging inferno.

MILA

CHAPTER 10

Mila couldn't shake the nagging feeling of disappointment as she got into her new rental and steered toward the highway. Westwood was her last hope of finding Bosco. The last lead she had. She didn't want to give up, but she also didn't know where else to look. But the uneasy feeling in her belly had nothing to do with Bosco, and no matter how badly she tried to convince herself, she couldn't lie.

Lingering images of *him* occupied her brain. She saw something of him in every stranger she passed on the street, heard his voice every time someone shouted in the nearby park. She could have sworn his scent still clung to her coat, and no matter how much she tried to not sniff it, she found her nose going there anyway.

Cursing under her breath, Mila stopped the car, shrugged out of her coat, and flung it into the backseat. There! No more scent to distract her. She didn't even like it for God's sake! It was disgusting. He smelled like something burnt. Like the candles she liked to light in her apartment on rainy fall nights...

Mila shook the thought with an irritated snort. He was nothing like those candles. They represented calm and cozy. He was the polar opposite.

Five minutes down the road, she was shivering. Cranking up the heat, she tried to not imagine *his* heat and focused on the snowy road. This was going to be a long night, and all she wanted was to be back home, lie in her own bed, and forget this last day ever existed.

A strange tingle spread through her body seconds before the abstract image flashed through her mind. Flashes of fire flickered before her eyes, dancing flames encircling her, and heat just as intense settling between her legs. Mila clutched the wheel, briefly allowing her eyes to drift shut as the unexplainable feeling rushed through her. It was over just as fast, leaving her breathless and quivering as she tried to understand what happened.

Only one thought was stuck in her head as she drove, and it annoyed her like nothing else. How one man could have such a hold on her after barely a day in his company was more than she could grasp. She didn't fall easily for anyone. Growing up in a home of big brothers and no sister, she learned how to deal with boys. How to make them lose their minds and how to keep them away. But Darek had slipped past her defense even though she did everything she could to avoid him.

She didn't even like him. In fact, she hated his guts. He was the worst example of a sex-obsessed control-freak she could think of, and yet, she couldn't get him off her mind.

Turning on the radio, Mila sang along to the music and enjoyed the distraction as she turned onto the highway leading her back to Seattle.

When the music turned to the news, she reached to tune in to a new channel. A man spoke of a sudden fire that destroyed a hotel and a suburban area, all in one night, and her hand froze on the button.

A chill ran down her spine. She didn't need more information to understand. He followed her inside like the goddamn stalker he was, realized she tricked him, and threw a fire tantrum. He burned down the hotel to find her.

Mila shivered despite the heat, and suddenly she was glad she was on her way far away from that man. She called him many things, and she was right. It didn't matter he was sexy as sin, he was a cold-blooded killing machine who wouldn't hesitate to bring hell to earth. How many lives were lost in the fire?

Mila tried not to think of it, tried not to feel guilty. If she didn't choose that hotel as her escape route, the families staying there would still be alive. Blaming herself was stupid. All she did was get away from a stalker, the rest was on him. She couldn't take responsibility for a madman's actions. Still, the nagging feeling of guilt refused to leave her alone.

Pushing down on the gas harder, Mila exceeded the speed limit in a hurry to leave as much distance between the car and Westwood as possible.

— * —

The next morning, Mila stepped through the red door to Lucky Paws Pitbull rescue center with a smile on her lips. A night in her own bed left her feeling refreshed and everything that happened in Westwood was a little dimmer. Memories of Darek were fuzzy as if maybe she imagined him. In her world, there were no such things as devils and demons. Only the human ones. The ones who abandoned and abused innocent animals. Those people were the real devils, and Mila was hellbent on making those bastards suffer as much as the dogs that were rescued out of their cruel hands.

"You're back!" A honey-blonde head popped up from behind the front desk. "Just in time!"

"For what?"

"Riley rescued a mother and her pups, they're ok. The asshat who had them, not so much."

A warmth spread within Mila. These were her people. People who cared and loved as deeply as she did. She thought of Riley and chuckled. It wasn't hard imagining Riley dragging some thug, kicking, and screaming into the police station. Despite his *boy-next-door* look, he was tough when he needed to be. He would never take justice into his own hands, none of them would, even though they were all more than tempted every time a bad situation arose.

Mila was on her way through the back doors to see the dogs, when a thought struck her. "Hey, Jenny? Have you seen Scott around?"

"No, why?"

Mila shrugged. "Never mind."

She found Riley and his girlfriend, her best friend, Kate sitting on the floor, cooing and squealing to the little creatures crawling around their hands.

"Oh, my God!" Mila exclaimed. "Aren't those the sweetest!" She sat too, gently picked up a puppy, holding it up for inspection. "Little bully baby." She stroked the pup's dark fur. "Where's the mom?"

"With the vet, she'll be back soon." Kate sat back, eyeing Mila while adjusting her chocolate-brown hair gathered in a messy bun at the back of her head. "You didn't find him?"

Mila stroked the puppy's back and shook her head. "He wasn't there, but guess who was? The son of a bitch Scott. Can you believe he's also searching for Bosco? I mean, for what reason? To annoy me?"

Kate grimaced. "After what he did to Maddie, he has no right to even go near a dog."

"Right!" Mila put the puppy down, drew her knees up, and wrapped her arms around them. "Men are assholes, every single one of them!"

Riley pretended to clear his throat. "I heard that."

Kate slapped his arm playfully and Mila groaned. "You're the only exception."

He chuckled, getting to his feet and held out both hands, one for Kate and one for Mila. They got to their feet.

"Why the sudden man-loathing?" Kate asked, brushing dog hair off her jeans.

Folding blankets to keep her mind busy, Mila muttered. "They're just—self-absorbed, dominant, sex-obsessed—"

Kate's laugh cut her off, and Mila spun on her heels to glare at her best friend who was busy untangling her hair

61

from the hair-tie.

"It's not funny!"

"You need to get laid, missy!"

Mila tried not to blush as images of Darek flashed through her mind. "Certainly do not!"

Kate wiggled her eyebrows. "Wait!" She pointed a finger at Mila. "You *did*, didn't you?"

"No!"

"Then why are you blushing?"

Mila groaned. There was no hiding things from Kate. Her nose was like a dog's, she could sniff out the truth from under every stone and corner.

"I met someone in Westwood." Before Kate had a chance to get too excited, Mila rushed to add, "I didn't sleep with him, what do you think of me? I don't do one-nighters. I learned that lesson long ago."

"But you wanted to?"

Mila snorted. "I'd rather have killed myself." She tried to shake the images of Darek's perfectly sculpted body from her head. The harder she tried, the clearer the image became. He was so warm, so smooth despite the rough scars littering his skin. Touching him was like touching a marble statue. A steamy hot one...

Kate's brown eyes demanded the truth, making Mila squirm under her stare. "Okay, okay, he's sexy as sin, but he's a dick. An ass. Self-centered—"

Kate finished the sentence, "Dominant, sex-obsessed?"

Mila rolled her eyes. "He gave me a ride to the Moon-bridge."

"That's such an asshole move."

Kate's sarcastic tone made Mila groan. There was no way she could tell Kate the full truth. "It is if they force you into the car after you turn it down. It is if they drive like a maniac and keep undressing you with their eyes, it is if they're sporting a boner the whole ride and not even trying to hide it."

The way Kate gaped at her made her feel somewhat satisfied. It wasn't just her. If she managed to shock her best friends with only half of the story, then it was bad.

"Holy cow!" Kate breathed. "That's intense."

"That's not even half of it. The guy is a freaking stalker. I wouldn't be surprised if he shows up here."

"How would we recognize him?" Riley had been surprisingly quiet but suddenly spoke up.

"He looks like a freaking Greek God, couldn't be that difficult," Mila muttered.

Riley pretended to gag, and Mila couldn't help but giggle.

Then she sighed and added, "He has scars on his face, three parallel lines, looks like a cat scratched him. Impossible to miss." Mila tried to ignore the sudden sadness tearing at her heart. Why would she care about his pain? He wasn't even human. Was he even capable of feeling emotion? Of sympathizing? Judging by his behavior when he chased her down and threw her into the car, she doubted it. He didn't care about her fear, about hurting her. All he wanted was to fuck her.

"Wait." Kate held up a finger, her eyes wide. "Are you saying you met *that* guy?"

Mila pretended to not understand. "Who?"

"The scars, the sexy psycho? You know who I mean."

Mila gulped. She did know, but for some reason she didn't understand, she didn't want her friend to know.

"No," Mila muttered. "Forget about him. It was just some random asshole."

DAREK

CHAPTER 11

Darek snatched a black shirt off a rack as he walked down the shopping strip. Not even bothering to look to see if he was caught stealing it, he shrugged it on and buttoned it halfway up.

The smell of smoke still clung to his trousers, and as he pushed his way through the crowded street, people whispered.

Darek tried to ignore them, but their low voices and pointed looks made his skin crawl.

Whispers from a distant time and place crept into his head, cracking his walls and making his confidence waver.

Go back to hell where you belong.

Freak.

Loser.

Child of Satan.

Darek picked up his pace. He didn't need the reminders, the scars were just as clear on the inside. Years after years of being treated like a ghost, of listening to cruel whispers and suffering physical abuse, never went away just because Darek pretended it was no longer there. The pain and the scars left behind didn't go away just because he grew into something better and stronger. No matter what he did, how good the revenge made him feel, it still hurt—every time those whispers reached his ears.

Darek curled his fists into tight balls. He'd give them something to whisper about. He was no longer an innocent little boy they could step on. They'd all regret even looking at him in the wrong way. Feeling the power course through his body, burning its way through his veins like hot lava just waiting to be released, he channeled it into his hands until they shook from the energy and flames leaked through his fingers.

In the blink of an eye, he switched into devil form, flung his arms out, and the street around him turned into a sea of fire. In the midst of the chaos, no one noticed his wings as he shot into the sky and away.

Darek watched the chaos from a rooftop, still fuming with the lingering memories of their whispers. They were all the same. It didn't matter where he went, which town he came to. They were all the same backstabbing, gossiping, whispering little insects he couldn't stand to even look at.

Humanity was a disease, and he was more than willing to help wipe it out. They were nothing but vessels of pain and misery, ready to inflict their torture on anyone who came in their way. He'd been in their way and unable to break free. No more!

Darek no longer knew if his inner world was his or the devils. When they merged into one, he could use the power whenever he needed it, with zero effort. It was just there, waiting for him to sink his teeth into the next victim. And he did, gladly.

Except with *her*...she was the only exception. The only human he couldn't imagine hurting. Only around her did he feel separate from the devil. Only with her, did he feel the need to be gentle, to be human...

Darek shuddered at the thought. He had to fight the devil when he was around her, but it wasn't the power-struggle that bothered him. It was the fact he'd gotten so lost he didn't feel the devil's dominance anymore.

Powerless his whole life, left to the mercy of his father's cruel hands and the never-ending torture. He suffered under the glares of the people, dancing on their threads like a puppet. Scared to go out, scared to be bullied, and even more scared to be ignored when all he ever wanted was the opposite.

He was still a puppet, only this time he was controlled by the devil.

The realization washed through Darek like a bolt of electricity and suddenly he knew. She opened his eyes. Shone a light into his dark. The stillness she allowed him to feel had been enough to make him see himself in a new light. And Darek didn't like what he saw.

He swore to avenge his past, and he had, he was still doing it, and he would never stop. But he was doing it wrong. The short-lived pleasure of burning down cities left him with a hollow ache inside.

He needed a purpose. Something to focus his energy on. Aimlessly drifting across the country and burning things in his wake became more of an annoyance than something fun. All he was left with was the rage and the hollow darkness inside that could never be filled, no matter what he did. It was a part of him for so long, he got used to living with the pain. Until *her*. In her absence, he felt it stronger than ever. She showed him paradise, then ripped it away just as fast. She left him falling, burning in his own hell, and he didn't know how to escape it.

Darek looked out across the burning city. He would show them all, give them something to whisper about, and he would do it with style.

But first, he had to find *her*. He needed her like he needed air. Darek stopped trying to rationalize or understand. He didn't care why or how, he didn't even care if his desire for her went against everything he was. He needed her, and he was going to make her his.

— * —

Darek paced the sidewalk outside of the burnt hotel. The sun hung low in the sky. One more day gone by. One more day wasted in absolute despair. Darek wanted to punch something or scream, but bottled the anger up and headed over to the first taxi that rolled to a halt.

Leaning into the rolled-down window, he asked, "Were you here last night, right before the fire?"

The driver shook his head. "That's the night cars, their shift begins at midnight."

Darek huffed but nodded.

Leaning back against the ruins of the hotel, he waited as the hours dragged by too slow. When he thought he'd snap, the distant church bell struck twelve. Darek ran a hand through his dark hair, adjusted his shirt, and eyed the two cars creeping onto the street. The first driver was a man who looked to be in his early thirties. Darek glared at him and went to look into the second car. An older man smiled up at him.

Darek chose him, imagining *she* would have, too. Sliding into the car, Darek remained silent.

"Where to, sir?"

Darek shook his head, asking the same question as he asked earlier.

The man nodded. "I was right here," he shuddered visibly, holding his head as if to avoid fainting. "The sound, oh, it was terrible. And the heat. I thought it would take the car too, and the poor girl was so scared, not that I can blame her."

"Girl?"

"A pretty young lass, oh, I still remember her, she reminded me of my daughter."

Darek could barely keep his voice from trembling. "Red coat, black hair?"

"Oh, yes, do you know her?"

"My wife."

"Oh, dear, you must be worried sick."

Darek's voice dripped into a growl. "Where did she go?"

"The Five Oaks, I waited until she was safely inside."

Darek's claws dug into his palms as he tried to remain patient. She was just a few blocks away, and he was stuck in a car with an old, babbling—Darek tried not to scream.

"Take me there."

— * —

Darek stormed up to the front desk of the hotel, impatiently hitting the bell until a woman emerged from a back room.

"My wife's staying here, I need to see her."

The receptionist nodded and smiled as she produced a ledger. "What's your wife's name, sir?"

Darek opened his mouth but closed it as he realized his mistake.

"Sir?"

"I don't know."

The woman let out a chuckle as she eyed him with suspicion. "You don't know your wife's name?"

Something in Darek snapped. The control he tried to hold on to bursting like a volcano. He reached out, grabbed the woman by the collar of her shirt, and dragged her across the desk in one swift motion. Her screams turned into gargled gasps for air as he pressed her up against the counter, one hand to her throat. "Black hair, red coat. Where the fuck is she?"

The woman tried to speak, and when Darek let go of her throat enough for her to breathe, she started to cough.

"SPEAK!" he shouted, and the woman started to cry, squirming under his grip.

"Please," she sobbed. "Don't hurt me."

"Tell me where she is," Darek hissed. "Or I'll do more than that."

"I don't know," the woman sobbed. "I haven't seen her, please."

"Last night," Darek growled. "After midnight."

"I wasn't here," she whimpered. "Aaron works the night shift."

Darek let go with a shove, watching her collapse and curl up on the floor.

"Call him," he snapped. "NOW!"

The woman scrambled to her feet, fell back down, and crawled on her knees to safety behind the desk. When she pulled herself to her feet, Darek stood leaning over the counter, red eyes focused on her as he snarled. "Now."

Her hands trembled so bad she could barely pick up the phone, and once the voice drifted through the line, Darek snatched the device from her sweaty grip.

"Aaron?" he barked.

"Yes. W-who's this?"

"Your worst nightmare," Darek hissed. "The whimpering excuse of a woman here dies if you don't speak." He held out the phone to record the crying, and when he brought it back to his ear, Aaron seemed to have gotten the point.

"Okay, okay, calm down. What do you want?"

"The girl with the black hair, and the fucking red coat," Darek snapped. "Is. She. Here?"

"What?"

"Don't play games with me." Darek entertained a flame in his palm. "Do you like fire?" he asked. "Do you want this place to burn with the rest of the city?"

"No, no, please. I saw her. She sat in the lobby for about five minutes. I thought she waited for someone, then she got up and left. She didn't come back."

Darek curled his hand around the receiver until the plastic bent under his grip. With an ear-piercing shriek, he hurled the piece into the wall.

MILA

CHAPTER 12

When Mila closed the door to the shelter and stepped outside, small flakes of silent snow danced in the light of the streetlights. The ground was still dark, but Mila suspected by the end of the night, it would be white.

Giving an annoyed huff, she began to walk the ten minutes to her apartment. She didn't mind the overtime especially when it was for a good cause, but no matter how much she loved her job, she could barely keep her eyes open.

Taking a shortcut through the park, Mila didn't notice the shadow ducking behind a tree. Nor did she feel the eyes on her back as she hurried through the cold.

When she closed the front door to the apartment complex, a shadow stood in the darkness across the street, out of reach from the glare of the lights.

Mila unlocked the door to her apartment and stepped inside the warmth. She hung her coat on a hanger and threw her scarf on the shelf above, then flicked on a lamp in the kitchen to make herself a cup of warm tea.

Looking out the window while the kettle boiled, she watched the snow slowly turn the pavement white. As she was about to turn back, she caught a glimpse of movement.

Her eyes flickered across the street, first seeing nothing. Then, out of the shadows of the old oaks lining the road, stepped a tall figure. Mila sharpened her eyes, trying to see beyond the dark. The person stood, immobile, looking straight at her. She jerked back, and when she looked again, the shadow was gone. Mila's hands trembled as she pulled the blinds. She hadn't imagined it. Someone was watching her. Someone tall, dark, and...devil? Her stomach clenched as the image of his leather trousers flashed through her mind.

Mila's eyes darted to the now blocked window. Could it be? Did he have some kind of tracking ability? Maybe he could smell her, like a dog? She didn't know anything about his kind. Hell, he wasn't even supposed to exist. Mila wasn't one to shun the spiritual world, she believed in ghosts and the things a normal person believed in. She was born into a Christian family, but she's only been to church on Christmas and Easter. She never even considered the possibility heaven and hell could exist.

Meeting Darek had forced her to rethink. He was the living proof of the existence most people only dreamed of seeing. Or feared. She didn't know which category he belonged to. The line was fuzzy, and even though the sight of his wings and horns freaked her out, she wasn't scared. She was curious. And if she thought about it, the lack of fear frightened her as much as the undeniable pull toward him.

Mila threw one more look toward the window, reached out to separate the blinds so she could peek through. She wasn't scared before, but the way the tiny hairs stood up in her neck and the chills running down her spine, it was fair to say, she was now.

If he found her here, there was nowhere she could hide. His intentions with her were clear, and what scared her more than his seductive voice and rough hands, was the small spark of excitement in her belly.

Turning off the stove, Mila pulled the kettle off and steered straight for the front door. Pushing it open, she stepped out on the top platform of the stairs. Trying to keep her voice from trembling, she called out, "I know you're there!"

Only silence greeted her. Mila shivered in the cold wind, whispering his name as if to taste it. She left Westwood hoping to never have to see him again. But standing there now, the silence creeped her out more than his presence would.

"Darek?"

Mila turned her eyes to the sky, almost as if she expected him to drop down in front of her. Snow fell on her face, and for a moment Mila stood there, letting the cold flakes melt on her skin. Then she turned and shut the door, trying to ignore the uneasy feeling in her gut. Had she been wrong? She wasn't the only one living in this building, whoever was out there could have looked for someone else. Was she being paranoid? Was the knowledge the freaking devil *did* exist making her imagine things? She was sure it was justified to be skittish after what she'd seen. But it wasn't like her to be nervous.

Forgetting about the tea, Mila went straight to bed.

Instead of getting a peaceful sleep she craved, she tossed and turned as images of faceless men and dark figures haunted her dreams. She felt as if she was trapped in a horror movie, her consciousness flickering between scenes like a TV with a bad antenna.

Mila woke up gasping for air, her heart pounding in her ears. Reaching for the nightstand lamp, she drew a breath of relief as the room flooded in light. Her bedroom was still the same. Her teal walls and the dark blue curtains, just as calming. The paintings of her dogs still hung on the wall above the bed, and the mirror held no shadow image as she gazed into it from across the room,

Relaxing, she laid back down, pulled the blanket up to her chin, and soon drifted off to a dream that felt as real as if he was right there.

His blood-red eyes as sharp as she remembered, his hands just as rough as he snatched the blanket right off of her. Mila hoisted herself up on her elbows, watching him tug

72

at his belt, finally revealing what he'd hidden under black leather. Mila wasn't disappointed. His warm skin burned against hers as he pressed her down with the weight of his body, and as she wrapped herself around him, the same fire burned within her.

Mila woke with her heart in her throat and fire in her loins. Dragged from the dream by the sounds from the city, she blinked into the sudden brightness. Not fully awake, she clung to the dream, squeezed her eyes shut to try to return to the sensation. Absentmindedly, she traced a hand down her body, over her belly, and further down as the images of his hands replaced hers. Mila's head rolled to the side, her lips opening in a soft moan as her fingers actualized the dream. Drifting in and out of reality, she lost herself to the moment, feeling the burning warmth of his body against hers as if he was there, moaning his name as the heat consumed her.

DAREK

CHAPTER 13

Darek drifted through the night like a restless ghost. His hope of ever finding her crushed and the anger consumed. For the first time in forever, all he wanted was to lay down and sleep. To find some kind of rest in a world that refused to let him.

With nowhere else to go, Darek collapsed onto a park bench. Leaning back, he let his head fall back to watch the flurry of snow across a dark canvas. The snow swirled into the shape of a face, and before Darek could stop the visions, he saw her before him. Her hair tousled from sleep and her eyes hooded and dreamy.

Darek jerked upright, blinking into the dark and the image was gone.

Growling into the cold air, he swore he was losing his mind. The obsession with this unknown woman was becoming a burden, but yet, he couldn't stop the thoughts of her any more than he could control his rising temperature. Her mental presence was enough to set him on fire.

Darek had no energy left to fight it. Falling back against the hard bench, he allowed her lingering memory to overpower his mind. Fragments of images flashed through his mind. *Delicate fingers on soft skin. Colors swirling into a kaleidoscope of teal and blue.* His pulse sped up until his body quivered with intensity.

He felt her body against his, the soft curves of her breasts pressing against his chest, the warmth as she wrapped around him and the hum of blood coursing through his veins.

Darek groaned into the night, hands gripping the bench to keep from touching himself as her energies rolled over him in powerful waves.

Just as fast as it started, her presence dispersed, leaving him aching and trembling in the aftermath. Darek shifted, once again cursing the tightness of the trousers. Why did he insist on wearing them, when all they did was cause him discomfort?

Scowling at the fabric digging into his over-sensitive skin, he pushed off the bench and stood, glaring down at the ground. The snow melted around him, leaving an unexplainable circle around the bench. Darek unleashed his wings and launched himself into the air. He'd rather fly anyway. It was less frustrating than walking. It was faster. It gave him a safe distance from people and their pointy stares. It gave him an outlet for the fire raging in his body.

Days turned into weeks, blurring together into endless darkness that refused to release its grip. It surrounded him, closed in on him as if he was stuck on a sea and couldn't swim. When he wanted to sink, to give up and let it all go, he couldn't do that either. Was this what hell was like? Had he been transported there without knowing it? It sure felt like it. He was stuck in a nightmare with only the raging fire inside him as company. Without her, he was lost.

Darek didn't bother to take a new home. He couldn't sleep anyway. He could barely eat. All he could think of was her and the calming feeling she stole as she left. He needed it back.

Weeks turned into months. She was still gone. Her disappearing without a trace made Darek doubt. Had she been there at all? Had he imagined her? Was she nothing but an illusion planted in his life to torture him further? Show him heaven, then plunge him into hell. A little extra salt in his wounds. Darek wanted to cry but refused to accept the pain. He hadn't cried since the night he buried his mom, and he swore to never shed a tear again. He was a man, not a little boy. Crying was for the weak, and he was everything but.

Accepting the truth also meant accepting the feeling it brought with it, and Darek wasn't ready. She had to exist. She had to be real, he felt her. That night on the frozen park bench wasn't the last time. He had feelings that weren't his own, felt his body ache with pains he didn't have. He saw images dance before his eyes, forming shapes and colors of places he'd never seen. She had to exist, or he was losing his mind.

Darek refused to give up, even though he was too tired to go on, either. He ran out of places to look for her. There was only so far he could fly, so many towns to roam until he had to face the fact. He'd never see her again… He needed to stop, to forget.

The months crawled by, winter turning into summer, and summer into fall. Darek still flew, still ran. But no matter how far or how high, he could never escape her memory.

It was imprinted in him, from the moment he met her, to the moment he'd die. He couldn't explain it. She was like a disease, slowly eating away at him until he'd go insane. She infiltrated his mind with her haunting beauty and pale skin. She was inside of him no matter where he went.

The sun peeked over the horizon as Darek zoomed in on the building sticking up from a canvas of city lights. Like a needle on a map, it pulled him toward it. Once he landed on the top, he studied the endless city below in awe.

Growing up in a one-street town and spending the years after breaking free from the hell aimlessly drifting through small towns, the big cities were nothing but distant dreams. Something he'd seen on TV but been afraid of. The millions of people and the crowded streets were enough to make him shudder in horror.

But perched on top of the round disc that overlooked the city mapped out far below, Darek started to realize his mistake. If he wanted to blend in, the bigger the better. Who was he in a city of millions?

The buzz of the morning traffic and the activity below awoke something in him which he hadn't felt before. Excitement, ambition, hope. He could be more than the demon spawn that everyone spat at on the streets. No one knew who he was here. He could start over, take his power back.

At that moment, Darek looked out across the endless cityscape and made a promise to himself. This city was going to be his. He'd make it a home, a life, and he'd make it good. He'd find a better way to get back at the insects that crawled up and down the streets. Darek imagined a place just like this. A place above the city, a position of power and authority. The dream no longer seemed as distant. His promise to himself, no longer impossible. Darek flexed his wings, stirring up a whirlwind of foggy air that swirled around him as he overlooked the city. A golden hue spread over the rooftops, making the trees sparkle in yellow and orange far below.

He landed here by a coincidence, but he didn't want to leave. The city spoke to him, whispered of possibilities he never imagined, of promises of a life so different from how he lived. A smirk crept onto Darek's lips. He was home.

MILA
CHAPTER 14

"You've gotta come here!" Kate's voice was on the verge of hysterics. Mila blinked into the sharp morning light seeping through her kitchen window trying to clear her head from the dream she'd been abruptly pulled from. Judging from the long shadows falling across the street outside, the sun had just risen. No one ever called her *that* early.

"What's going on?"

"Someone has burnt down Lucky Paws!"

Mila dropped the phone. She heard Kate shout her name, but could only manage to stare at the wall and fight off nausea. Lucky Paws, burnt? She couldn't wrap her mind around it.

"MILA!"

Mila's mind spun.

Burnt…

The dream she just had flashed through her head like a bad omen, filling her with a deep sense of dread. She'd seen this. Fire. Destruction. The devil, engulfed in hot flames that didn't burn him, but everything in his way. She dreamt of him more times than she wanted to admit, and not until now did she realize the dreams might have been more than that. Mila swallowed the nausea.

Was this Darek's revenge for leaving him and disappearing for months? Did he find her? Was this his way of letting her know? Could he really be that cruel? She knew the answer even though she didn't want to accept it. He was the devil, what did she expect? Roses and love letters? She pissed off the devil and this was the consequence. Mila clasped a hand to her mouth and just made it to the toilet before her belly revolted.

When she stumbled back to the kitchen, Kate had hung up. She dialed the number to the shelter, but the line was dead. Darting back to the bedroom, Mila slid out of her nightdress, tossing it aside on the bed. Grabbing the first clothes available, not stopping to see how she looked.

Mila ran through the park, startling the few early birds who were jogging as she darted past them. When she stopped outside of the shelter, a sheen of cold sweat coated her skin and she panted for the air she forgot to breathe. Her eyes fell on the blackened walls and the bile rose a second time.

"Mila!" Kate threw herself in Mila's arms, and when she finally stepped away, her eyes were red from crying.

"The dogs?" Mila only managed a whisper. "Are they..."

"They're safe," Kate sniffled, making Mila sag in relief. She expected the worst, imagined the animals burned to crisps, imagined their terror and their pain.

"Oh, thank God," she breathed. "Where are they? Who got them out?"

"The police station. Riley worked late. If he hadn't…" Kate's words trailed off into a sob, and the unspoken words made the hair on Mila's arms stand up.

"We have to find them a new location fast," she added.

Mila's head spun. Relief, fear, despair.

"Who would do such a thing?" Kate cried. "Who'd want to hurt innocent animals?"

Before Mila could form a reply, Riley came walking up to them. His face, a mask of anger. "Nothing on the CCTVs, the son of a bitch knew what they were doing. The cops don't think it's an accident. We have many enemies." He hit a fist against his palm, then shook it and cried out from the pain. "The place's gone, it will take months to rebuild it. We'll lose all the dogs."

"They'll get placed in new shelters, they'll be fine," Kate tried to comfort him even though she was crying herself.

"If no one takes them they'll be put down," Riley muttered, turning from the girls as he fought to keep his eyes free of emotion. Mila watched Kate hug him while her brain went right back to the dream of Darek she'd been ripped from. She didn't know how to kill a devil, but she would damn well try.

Mila looked around, almost as if she expected to see him lurking in the shadows, reveling in their pain as the freaking sadist that he was.

She tried to forget him, to push him far out of her mind. How could one person, a person she despised, linger in every fiber of her body no matter how badly she tried to rid herself of the memory?

She spent one day—*ONE*—and suffered over six months as a result. The never-ending dreams, the way he refused to leave her mind, whether she was asleep or awake made her want to scream. The more time passed, the more she hated him.

"Are you happy now?" she shouted to the busy streets. People stopped to stare, but she didn't care. "Are you satisfied, you sick bastard!"

"Mila!" Kate's hand on her shoulder made Mila spin to face her. Her stunned expression made Mila grimace.

"I know who did this."

Kate and Riley stared at her, exchanged puzzled looks before returning their attention to Mila. Kate's face paled as she seemed to catch Mila's thoughts. "The sexy stalker? I thought he was long gone?"

"Don't call him that!"

Kate frowned. "What, stalker?"

"Sexy!" Mila snapped. She didn't need to be reminded of his looks. She didn't need to be reminded of how incredibly dumb she'd been. The sick dreams, the image of his bare chest ingrained in the back of her head, his strong hands on her body...

She'd felt him. She still remembered the night in detail, but it hadn't been the last. Her hands had been his, and she enjoyed it. Mila shook her head, cursing her own stupidity. She'd been fantasizing about the devil while he burned down her life. How fitting.

"Son of a bitch!" Mila growled.

"Wait," Kate began. "Has he even been around? You haven't mentioned him since the day you came back from Westwood."

Mila sighed. "I've...dreamt about him. About fire. This is his way of letting me know he—" She cut herself off as Kate's confusion reached her overheated mind. Of course, Kate didn't understand. No one would if they hadn't seen what Mila saw. And the fact she kept her mouth shut and denied the devil's existence did nothing to help her. Everything she tried to close her eyes to now caught up with her. What happened to Lucky Paws was her fault...

"When I get my hands on that man..." Riley left the sentence unfinished, but Mila felt a little better knowing she had backup. Darek Rewera was going to pay. She just didn't know how. All she knew was she'd make him suffer. She'd make him feel the pain, crush him and everything that mattered to him, just like he crushed her.

"Just..." she thought of how to warn Riley. If she began to speak about the devil, they'd think she'd lost it. *That* was a thing you had to see to believe. "He's dangerous, be careful."

Riley let out a bark of a laugh. "He'll see about danger."

Mila winced. If only he knew. No longer wanting to think of Darek, she changed the topic. "We have to find a location for the dogs. Anyone have an idea of who could take them?"

"They're all full, already contacted every shelter in the city," Riley said, and Mila nodded. It made sense. The biggest and most known dog rescue centers were never empty. The pressure they had, was nothing compared to the Lucky Paws. But Mila had never wanted something that huge. She wasn't in it for the business, she was in it for the dogs. And even though she'd gladly house thousands of rescues, she was happy with her small family of twenty. She wanted all the dogs to get the attention and the time they deserved. She wanted them to feel at home until they found their real home with the right person.

Even though Riley and Kate were the owners, they never treated Mila like an employee. They shared everything, even though they mostly waded in expenses. But Mila never cared about the money either, as long as she had enough to have a good life, she was happy doing the thing she loved.

"I'll just take them home if I have to," Kate said. "We'll share equally until we find a place for them."

Mila couldn't help but smile as she imagined a dozen of dogs hogging her bed. Her apartment was too silent in Bosco's absence anyway. Besides, with a devil out to get her, she could use a team of four-legged guards until she thought of a more permanent solution to get rid of that sick bastard.

"Deal."

"No need," Riley held up his phone. "It's solved. Lisa's Kennel takes them."

Mila sagged with relief. "Oh, thank God."

DAREK

CHAPTER 15

A bolt of fear zapped through Darek. He scrambled to sit, slipped on the slick surface, and slid down on the fresh layer of rain before regaining his composure. Cursing under his breath, he held on to the antenna sticking up in the middle of the sky-disc he apparently fell asleep on. Squinting through the foggy morning air, he tried to still his pulse.

Deep despair filled him and it wasn't his own. It was *her*... it wasn't the first time he felt her. He couldn't explain it, but he'd never been surer. She was somewhere far away, but she never felt closer. *Her* pain coursed through *his* body. *Her* anger made him scream into the cold rain falling on him.

Smoothing back wet hair, Darek looked out across the city as he had done every day since landing in this new place. He made the top of the Space Needle his home, in the lack of a better one. The view was breathtaking, a reminder to stay focused. To stay on top. He'd sworn to have a view just like this one day, and he still held on to that dream. He just didn't know where to start. The life he wanted to escape followed him like a tail. He dreamed of power and authority, still, he slept under the stars and roamed the streets like a homeless man. Darek hated every second of it but didn't know how to break the circle.

Wings spurted from his back, launching him into the air. He needed to find her, needed to know why the feeling inside of him made him want to cry.

Hours of walking, of asking strangers if they'd seen a girl in a red coat made Darek ache to burn it all to the ground. If he saw one more set of eyes roaming over his body, he'd break someone's neck. He had to find a fucking shirt, and he had to learn to think before unleashing his wings that tore his clothes right off his body.

Dressed in a new and stolen black V-neck, his confidence level rose with the decreased number of eyes glued to his chest.

After two more hours of aimlessly wandering the streets, he considered giving up. His stomach ached painfully from lack of nutrition, and the disappointment weighed heavy on his shoulders.

Stepping into a restaurant, he ordered a pizza and slipped into a booth at the far corner where he could sit undisturbed. Where he could disappear without drawing attention to himself after finishing the meal.

A female waitress caught his arm as he tried to leave, stopping him right before he could step out onto the street.

"I believe you haven't paid for that."

Her accusing tone triggered Darek's anger. But instead of killing her right on the spot, he tried to smile. "Seemed to have forgotten my wallet."

"Nice try," the waitress sneered. "Now pay up, or I'll call the cops."

Darek shifted closer, leaning in to whisper in her ear. "I

can pay you in other ways."

His seductive attempt was regarded by a slap to his cheek. Darek exploded in a whirlwind of rage, flinging her up against a wall before he could stop to think. Ready to rip her throat, he reigned in the devil microseconds before it was too late. Letting go of the waitress with a shove against the wall and a frustrated scream, he spun on his heels and ran back to the street. Fuming, he picked up his pace, not caring whether he knocked people down in his hurry to get away.

Dropping down onto a park bench, Darek considered his options. He'd gotten by on thievery and destruction, taken what he wanted and left no one alive to complain. He no longer wanted that. He wanted to matter. To be something more than a thug. Darek didn't know where to start. He had nothing, he never did.

All he had was anger and a broken life. When it came down to it, he was still that boy who cowered under his father's whip. He'd taken the beating knowing he deserved it. Knowing he was the pathetic wuss everyone said he was.

Be a man.

His father's words echoed in Darek's head, the memories of the pain as the whip bit into his flesh making him shudder.

Sitting alone in the midst of a crowd made Darek feel just as small as he'd been back then. All the power of the devil meant nothing. It was a temporary pleasure. An explosion that filled him with the sweet taste of revenge, but then it blew over just as fast. The satisfaction never stayed, the power never giving him anything more than a brief rush. When he came down from the high, he was just as powerless, just as pathetic. Darek lifted his gaze, looked around him, letting his eyes scan the sea of faceless people. No matter how many he killed in a blind rage, they would never end. They'd always be there to look down on him, always be the backstabbing bloodthirsty insects they were.

There was no escape.

"You look like you need something." A young woman sat down next to him, snapping Darek out of his head and back to the buzzing city. "What is it?" She eyed him up and down, lingering for too long at the scar on his face.

Darek stared back. She was dressed in a ridiculously short skirt and a top that showed her stomach. Her lips were painted black and made her teeth shine bright as she flashed him a crooked smile. His eyes were stuck on two pink stripes in her auburn hair as she asked, "What do you want, huh? Money, sex, drugs?"

Darek looked around, too confused to reply. Was she offering?

"I have what you need." She stood, winked at him, then began walking. Darek stared at her as his mind spun. Then he jumped up and followed. He had nothing to lose.

Darek's eyes narrowed as she led him through dark alleys and finally stopped far out of sight from the rest of the city. He looked around. They stood in some sort of a small backyard. An open square in the corner where two buildings came together. The air smelled of garbage and piss, and the cobblestones under his feet were sticky and slick from the rain. Darek considered leaving when a door opened and three shadows emerged.

"What do we have here?" one of them asked.

"He's perfect," the girl said.

Darek huffed. "For what?"

The shadows turned into three young men, maybe around his own age. Some sort of gang members by the looks of them. Their buff bodies and tattooed arms didn't scare Darek. Neither did the knife in the leader's hand.

"Why should we trust him?" one of the guys demanded. His shaved head was tattooed and the torn jeans he wore looked like they had never seen the face of a washing machine.

"The fuck is this about?" Darek snapped.

"A job," one of them said. "Carla thinks you've got what it takes."

Darek cocked an eyebrow. "What's in it for me?"

The knife was up against his throat. "Cash."

"What do I have to do?"

"Deliver a package to a friend."

"Hmph." Darek wasn't dumb. That package was most

likely drugs and that friend was most certainly someone as disgusting as the trio breathing down his neck. Tempted to let the devil loose on them, he saw the opportunity. Quick cash. It wouldn't be the first time he'd been the courier for someone's shady business.

"How much?"

They chuckled. "If you get back here alive, I'll give you ten percent."

"Deal." Darek flew an arm out, knocking the knife from the guy's hand, and growled. "Don't threaten me."

They faltered, shooting each other startled looks, but then laughed. The guy snatched the knife off of the ground, and in the same flowing movement pushed Darek up against the wall. He felt the blade against his throat, the pressure as it cut through his skin.

"Nice try, motherfucker," the guy snarled. "Cross us, and you're dead!"

Darek clenched his teeth, balling up his fists to avoid burning them to the ground. He needed the money, and he wasn't going to let his anger issues get in the way this time. What was a little pain anyway? He'd been through worse.

Darek's body shook from the effort of holding back. He let the knife cut him, closed his eyes, and focused on the stench from the street to keep the pain from triggering the devil.

MILA

CHAPTER 16

Mila's hand flew to her throat, a cry tearing through her lips.

Kate spun in her seat next to Riley in the car, shooting her a startled look. "What's wrong?"

Clutching her throat, Mila met her best friend's eyes, trying to breathe through the sudden sharp pain that came out of nowhere.

"You're scaring me!" Kate cried.

"It hurts," Mila whimpered, trying to rub the pain off her flawless skin.

"What does?" Kate shot Riley a desperate look. "Take her to the ER!"

"NO!" Mila gasped. "It's okay." She squeezed her eyes shut, sucking in a deep breath, then let it out. She repeated the pattern until the pain faded, leaving only a lingering feeling of fear in her gut.

When she removed her hand and held it out for inspection, she almost expected it to be red. The sight of her white skin, spotless and free of blood made her frown, suddenly confused as to why she even expected to bleed in the first place. She was safe in Riley's Ford pickup. No one was hurting her, yet she felt as if she'd been stabbed.

"What the fuck was that?" Kate exclaimed. "Are you ok?"

Mila only managed a shaky whisper. "Yeah, I'm fine. I don't know what happened." She swallowed, testing the function of her throat. It still worked. The pain was gone, just as fast as it started. Falling back against the seat, she let out a quivering breath, trying to understand.

The Ford pulled up outside of Mila's apartment complex. She left in such a hurry in the morning, she'd forgotten her wallet. She planned to fetch it and be back in the car in seconds. Nearing the front door, which to her surprise was ajar, Mila paused mid-step. The moment her eyes landed on the broken lock, something cold settled over her. She swallowed, slowly reaching out to push the door open.

Stepping inside, the first thing she saw was her clothes, thrown on the floor, the full-length mirror tipped over and cracked. Mila's blood ran cold. She knew before daring to move, the rest of her home would be in pieces, too.

Looking into the kitchen, she couldn't stop the whimpers. Drawers were pulled out, their contents in a mess on the floor. The kitchen table had been her workplace, now, every paper and folder were on the floor amongst scattered pasta, rice, and a crisscross of silverware. Mila backed away, unable to take her eyes off the destruction that was supposed to be her calm space.

When she looked into the living room she was prepared for the worst, same with the bedroom, and she was right. She could barely find an empty spot on the floor to walk on, and the moment her eyes fell on the empty jewelry box, she knew what this was all about. She didn't have much of value, *except* the jewelry, but it wasn't the money that made tears form in her eyes. The money she'd get back. Those pieces of gold meant more to her than their value, they were memories. Gifts.

Mila sank onto her bed as the feeling started to creep up on her. She shivered despite the warm coat. The thought someone had been in her home, touched her private belongings, made the little hairs in the back of her neck stand. Images started to spin in her head, bringing tears to her eyes at last. The shadow she'd seen on and off the last months. The burnt shelter, the psychopath stalker. Ever since she got back from that disappointment of a trip, her life had not been the same.

Footsteps echoed on the stairs. Mila held her breath. Then Kate's horrified shout reached her and she relaxed. Her friend's face peeked into the bedroom. "Shit!"

Mila looked up. "You can say that again."

Riley cursed somewhere in the apartment, and Kate stared at the mess around her. "You think..."

"I don't know," Mila muttered. She knew what Kate was thinking, she'd been thinking the same thought. As much as she wanted to blame that devil, it didn't seem like him to rob her place and leave. He made it perfectly clear he wanted *her*, not her things.

Was he playing games with her? Scaring her so she'd have no option but to fall into his arms? Mila's face hardened at the thought.

"Seems like the son of a bitch was looking for something," Riley appeared in the doorway. "Anything missing?"

"Just the jewelry."

He frowned. "It can't be it. Someone turned the whole place upside down. They were hoping to find something."

"Riley!" Kate snapped. "Stop being a detective. Can't you see she's upset!"

"Sorry, I'm just—" he threw a look around. "I'm fucking pissed."

"Me too." Mila got to her feet. "You're right. It doesn't make sense." She started to walk, careful not to step on items as she scanned the sea of strewn about things. "What was he looking for? I have nothing worth stealing!"

"He?" Riley asked.

Mila stopped, picked up a broken frame, and took the picture out. Running a finger along the image, the break-in was no longer a mystery. It was as clear as day and she was surprised she didn't think about it sooner. It wasn't the first time the son of a bitch had taken what was hers. He'd taken Maddie, he'd once taken her wallet and used her

Mastercard to score drugs, and she knew damn well who'd taken her jewelry now.

"I know who did this."

"The stalker guy," Kate clarified to a dumbfounded Riley.

"No," Mila held up the picture.

"Maddie?" Kate eyed the Pitbull dog with a confused wrinkle in her forehead. "I don't—" she cut herself off as the realization hit. "Scott?"

"Who else?" Mila carefully placed the picture into her coat pocket.

"What makes you so sure it's not that other douchebag?" Riley asked.

"If he'd take something, he'd take *me*."

"As sick as that sounds, you're right. But Scott? I thought he was clean?"

"He's a liar. This—" Mila made a sweeping gesture, "Proves it. He needed money. The sick son of a bitch!"

"You have to go to the police," Kate said. "You need protection. He can be dangerous, especially if he's back on drugs."

DAREK

CHAPTER 17

Darek held two thick piles of cash in his hands, turning them over as if not trusting their authenticity. He'd never seen this much money at once, hell, he'd probably never seen it in his life. If those dumb excuses of men thought he'd return and settle with ten percent, they must lack a brain. Who'd be that dumb to come running back when they could take it all?

Darek shrugged. People were cowards. After being nearly decapitated by that knife, no one would have the balls to ignore such a threat. No one but the devil. Darek grinned at the money. Fuck those idiots. They'd never see the trace of this. It was his and it had been the easiest thing he'd ever done.

He'd simply waited until dark, unleashed his wings, and flown right up to the spot. Darek didn't understand what the big deal was. What was the supposed danger, the *if* he'd get back alive? Huffing, he attempted to shove the money into his pants pockets but realized quickly it would never fit.

His first stop would have to be a clothes store. Again. He needed a jacket. He needed pockets, and if he ever hoped of blending in, he probably shouldn't walk the streets half-naked.

Scouting the street for any sign of a store, he caught a whiff of burned plastic and wood. Darek's eyes landed on a building, or the remains of one squeezed in between two taller ones and sneered. Humans didn't need him, they burned themselves down just fine. Idiots, all of them.

The squeaking of a metal sign dangling by a chain made him shiver. How he hated that sound. Darek threw an annoyed look at the source of the sound and faltered as the dog paw printed on the board catapulted him back to that car ride six months ago. To *her*.

"You're crying for a dog?"

Darek groaned. He regretted it the moment it left his mouth. But then it had been too late. He didn't understand the fascination people had for the canines, he'd never gotten close enough to one to even touch. They hated him since he was a child, and Darek never thought too much about it. He simply didn't care. It had been normal, even the humans hated him, so why wouldn't the animals, too?

But the hurt in her voice and the tears in her eyes still haunted him. She masked it with anger, throwing insults at him until he snapped. He would never have hurt her, but he scared her. And now she was gone...

— * —

Darek found the store he searched for, and dressed in new clothes, he studied his reflection in a window and liked what he saw. The black leather jacket was a perfect fit, and he traded the old trousers with new ones in a similar style. He smoothed his hair back, felt his pockets to make sure the cash was still there, then continued down the street. Cars swished by, occasionally spraying water on him as they took the lingering puddles too fast. Darek bit back the impulse to throw fire at them. The last thing he needed was to snap and destroy his new jacket, but God did he want to. A little chaos, a few crushed bodies, and blood-soaked streets… it called to him, a thirst he'd never been able to slake. Shaking his head clear of intrusive thoughts, Darek picked up his pace. The devil wasn't going to ruin his clothes. He fucking bought them. For money. He couldn't even remember when he last did, but one thing he was sure of. He never wanted to go back to being broke. He had enough of roaming the streets like the lowlifes he'd worked for. He had enough of being homeless. Because when it all came down to it, that's what he was. What he'd been since he burned down his childhood cottage and all the nightmares along with it. Darek lost count of how many beds he slept in, how many homes he took just to have a roof over his head and something to still his hunger.

Not watching his step, he bumped into a person, their shoulders crashing together sending both bodies twisting to the side.

"Get out of my way! Idiot!"

"Sorry," a female voice mumbled, and when Darek turned his head to shoot her an annoyed glare, her red coat made his heart skip a beat. He blinked at her quickly retreating figure, then turned on his heels and ran to catch up. Grabbing her shoulder, he pulled her to an abrupt halt and spun her around to face her.

Two pale blue eyes stared up at him, wide in terror. Darek staggered back. The disappointment rushing through him in cold waves. It hurt, physically. It pulled him down until all he wanted was to crumble to the ground along with the short-lived hope of seeing *her* again. The woman said something, but Darek couldn't hear. His head spun. The despair cut through his heart like knives as he continued to back away from her. This had to stop. He had to stop. His obsession with her wasn't healthy. He had to let her go, let the thought of ever seeing her again go, or she'd ruin him.

A wailing car-horn blasted his thoughts, and before he could react, the car slammed into his back, sending him flying into the air before tumbling to the ground. Everything spun, a sharp pain in his hip and back, a pressure in his spine. Darek tried to move, to switch into devil-form to save himself, but his body didn't respond. Blinking at the faces hovering over him, he tried to understand, but his mind didn't function either. All he could focus on was searing pain in his back and the panicked voices all around. Soon even that faded, and the world turned black.

— * —

Darek's eyes fluttered open, blinking at the white light shining down at him. A strange smell assaulted his nose, and a constant beeping made his blood pressure rise along with the anger. Struggling to lift his head, he took in the surroundings with a growing sense of panic. He'd never seen the insides of a hospital, even though he'd been in desperate need of it more times than he could count. His father hadn't cared, he left him on the floor to bleed. He'd been unable to move for days after the worst lashes. He'd cried. He'd begged until he'd learned to be silent and take it like a man. Darek tried to push the memory away and focused on the present moment. What had they given him? Why did he feel so fuzzy? So unfocused, so weak. What were those tubes and wires for? Darek pushed himself up into a half-sitting position, ready to rip it all off. He didn't need human medicine, it would only make it worse. He was the devil, he'd heal on his own, much faster than any doctor could even imagine. But he couldn't do it here, not with those ridiculous liquids forced into his bloodstream. Not in his human form.

"Hey."

A hesitant voice made his eyes snap to the source of it, and widen. Darek blinked, not trusting his eyes. She was a hallucination, a result of the medicine the doctors had injected into his blood. Six months of aching for her, and there she was—as if no time had passed. She looked the same, the perfect heart-shaped face framed with the darkest of hair. She was the most beautiful creature he's ever seen. Darek's jaw slacked in awe. How many times had he dreamt of her?

Her presence stirred something within him, and for a moment he forgot where he was, forgot about the pain, about anything that didn't involve his body wrapped around hers. A deep growl escaped his throat as the heat within him magnified. The familiar ache intensified as blood rushed through his body, gathering in his loins.

Mila inched closer to the bed he was stuck in. "You stepped out right in front of my car."

Darek gaped, looked away, blinking a few times then looked back, almost expecting her to be gone. She stood before him, like the fucking angel she was. Dressed in the red coat he'd never gotten out of his head.

"You're here?"

"Yeah," she muttered. "I see you're alive, so bye." She turned to leave.

"Wait!" Darek called out, struggling to sit. His hand fumbled with the pipes attached to his nose and ripped them off along with the needles stuck in his arms.

She grimaced at the blood trickling down his skin but remained silent. Her eyes flickered between Darek and the door, then she sighed, turned, and walked to sit in a chair next to the bed. "Tell me one thing. Did you follow me?"

"No."

She narrowed her eyes, repeating the word. "No?" She snorted, attempting to get up but changed her mind, and instead of leaving, snapped, "You've been spying on me. You followed me, don't lie to me!"

Darek huffed. "You're the one who ran me over with your fucking car."

"It was an accident. What were you doing in the middle of the road anyway?"

She was right. He'd been careless. He'd been crushed by the disappointment of never seeing *her*. He'd not watched where he was going.

She locked her eyes on him and added. "Serves you right. A few broken bones should teach you a lesson."

Darek's hand shot out, grabbed her hair, and yanked her onto the bed, onto him. He'd almost forgotten how stubborn she was, how her attitude made his blood boil. How he couldn't decide whether he wanted to hurt her or fuck her.

Holding her in place, her face inches from his, he hissed. "You broke my fucking back."

She struggled against his grip, and as he loosened it she scrambled to her feet, showing him a disgusted look while rubbing her head.

"It was an accident, I'm—I'm sorry."

Darek chuckled at the unmistakable look of shame on her face. "Appreciate that, but no need to be. I'm the devil, remember. I heal."

She scowled, this time pulling the chair out of reach, making sure he knew exactly what she was thinking. "I hoped to never see you again."

"Hmph." Dared shifted, wincing as the tiny movement sent stabs of pain through his spine. "That's why you've been touching yourself thinking about me?"

A stunned gasp slipped past her lips. She opened her mouth to speak, then closed it again. Finally, she ignored her flustered cheeks and snapped. "So it was *you*!" Her eyes shot daggers as they locked on Darek. "You've been spying on me, you perv!"

"Hmph."

"Don't pretend to look offended!" Mila barked. "Just leave me alone. I don't want you. Do you get that? I don't want you!"

"I didn't spy on you!" Darek snarled. "The fuck would I do that for?"

The question caught her off guard. A frown formed on her forehead as she thought of a comeback. Darek took the opportunity to go on. "If I'd found you before today, I'd been in your bed *with* you, not outside your goddamn window."

Mila made a face but didn't argue. She knew he was right. Darek's lips twitched into a smirk.

Mila looked down at her lap, fidgeting with her nails. When she finally looked up, her frown had deepened.

"Then how would you know…"

Darek raised an eyebrow at her indirect confession.

"Don't look at me like that," she muttered, crossing her arms over her chest. "Just tell me."

"I felt you."

"You've… *felt*… me?"

"Yeah."

"What does that mean?"

"Exactly what I said."

"How is that possible?"

Darek shrugged, having no good answer. "I didn't understand either. It was intense, sudden, and then gone again. A ghost sensation. Real but not. Mine, but not."

She nodded numbly. "Are you doing this?" Her face paled visible and when she spoke again, her voice was just a whisper. "Someone cut your throat?"

Darek's eyes widened. "How did you—"

"Holy shit!" She shot to her feet and started to pace the room. "This isn't real!" She stopped next to the bed, glaring down at him. "I wish I'd never met you!"

"Likewise," Darek snarled.

It caught Mila off guard, and the look she gave him was filled with suspicion. "Why are you here, in Seattle?"

The sound of approaching voices reached his ears, cutting his intended reply short. Darek's eyes darted toward the door, then back to Mila. "I have to get out of here." Before she could protest, he swung his legs over the edge and stood, nearly collapsing from the sudden pain slicing through his back.

"Get my clothes," he hissed. "Now."

She stunned him by obeying, rummaging through the lockers and cabinets until she found the garments. Tossing them at Darek, she remained at a safe distance from him while throwing glances toward the door.

"What are you running from?"

"People."

"But you're still hurt."

Darek bit back the pain and struggled to get into his pants.

"Whose fault is that?"

The fact he could move at all surprised him. The damage to his spine had been enough to paralyze a human being for life. The doctors would call his sudden mobility a miracle, but they'd never seen a devil. But even though his genes allowed him to heal faster, the fact he was stuck in his human form slowed down the process remarkably, threatening to leave permanent damages if he didn't get out of there.

"Dar—"

"Not now," he hissed. He had no time for explanations. No time for her pity. The damage was done.

Footsteps approached on the other side of the door, and as his eyes darted in the direction of the sound and narrowed, Mila sprung forward, caught his arm, and pulled him toward the window.

"Don't you dare hurt anyone, get out!" She pointed toward the sky on the other side of the glass, and Darek raised an eyebrow.

"Wanna fly?"

A horrified look came over her face. Darek didn't wait for her protest. His wings ripped through his back, sending a shockwave of pain through his damaged spine, and for a few seconds of terror, he thought he'd pass out from the intensity. Gasping for air, he held on to Mila, leaping through the window.

DAREK

CHAPTER 18

Hot knives tore through his spine with every wingstroke. His body shuddered as he forced it to stay in motion, willed it with everything he had to go on instead of crumble to the ground and curl up. He didn't have that option. He'd never had. Darek knew pain, and he'd be damned if he'd let it stop him from getting away.

He felt Mila's fear, her heart hammering against her ribcage, her arms clinging to him in pure terror. The tremors shook her body as she tried to scream. Her fear, her life depending on him pushed him to fight through the agony. He got her back. He refused to let her go, especially from above the rooftops.

His wings began to grow heavy, and with every passing second, the effort it took to lift them made him bite back sounds he never wanted Mila to hear. If she knew he was falling apart in the air like a broken airplane, ready to crash-land at any given moment, she'd never forgive him. Sweat coated his skin, and as he struggled to go on, his body vibrated with the effort.

One more flap of the wings sent a stab of pain through him, spreading into every nerve of his body until it grew numb. Darek bit back the cry at the last minute, but despite his best effort, he felt himself falling. His wings no longer possessed the power to keep him in the air. They refused to move, slacking to his sides as he spiraled dangerously fast toward the ground.

Mila finally screamed, and in thoughtless panic, tried to get away, to push herself from his grasp. Darek struggled to hold on, clutching her tighter. Holding her nearer. The dark alley beneath came closer, the hard surface whispering promises of broken bones and crushed skulls, of *her* blood coloring the night red. Darek screamed as the image became unbearable. She could *not* die. Losing her was impossible.

Darek twisted in the air, crash-landing on his back. His scream ripped through the air as a blinding pain exploded throughout his spine. His arms tightened around Mila, clinging to her as if she alone could make it all better.

Too stunned to act, she lay still, unharmed and safe, tucked into a cocoon of arms and wings. Her breaths warm and soothing against his sweaty skin, her heartbeat pounding in rhythm with his.

As she regained the ability to move, she pushed herself free from his grasp, scrambled to her feet, and staggered away from his wings as they twitched, only to fall limp to the ground. When his head rolled back and his body twisted in pain, Mila only stared.

Darek's eyes sought her, trying to focus on her shape as it drifted in and out of consciousness. She looked around as if searching for an escape route. Lost in his own personal hell, Darek couldn't keep himself from wishing she'd stick around to hold his hand.

Her eyes drifted to Darek, cringing at the pain he couldn't keep off his face. He didn't try to move, even though he wanted to get up and act like nothing happened. Small spasms made his wings twitch, but they lacked the power to move off the ground. The way they lay, spread out to their full width on either side of him made him an easy target. Darek never felt weaker, more exposed. He was broken, useless. Even Mila could kill him now.

The way she looked at him as if she suddenly realized he could get injured, as if surprised he could feel, made the anger boil up inside of him.

"You're not human, what am I supposed to think?"

But he was. Around her, especially. But she couldn't see beyond the wings and the horns. She made up her mind, pinning him as some sort of a monster. In one way, she was right.

Mila stared down at him, and he struggled against the overwhelming need to feel her next to him. For those soft fingers to wipe the rain off his face, for his head in her lap instead of on the hard ground.

Mila took a step toward him, and Darek's breath hitched. Had she somehow heard his thoughts? Keeping the pain off of his face, he tried to look stronger than he felt, tried to act as if he didn't need her, as if he didn't care.

"Hey," his voice betrayed him, coming out as nothing but a strained rasp.

She hesitated, inching closer. Then the sympathy on her face died and was quickly replaced by a stern expression. She scoffed.

"Can't believe I almost fell for those puppy eyes," she snapped. "I have no time for your twisted games."

Darek rolled his head to the side to stare at her, opened his mouth to ask, but an overwhelming wave of pain stopped him. He winced, clamping his mouth shut to avoid screaming.

"Don't follow me!" she snapped, then turned and ran. Disappearing around a corner, she took away the little hope he worked up. Darek closed his eyes, breathing through the internal torture, and prayed no one would stumble upon him.

Her moans and cries reached his ears, snapping his eyes wide open again. He was hurting her. She felt him, felt what he went through. He hated it. Hated she knew, that she pitied him. Suddenly wishing for her to go away, he closed his eyes and willed the pain away. If she didn't feel him, there was no reason for her to stay. No reason to feel guilty for running him over with her fucking car. No reason to pity him. She'd be gone. Out of his life but always in his mind. Blinded by pain and shame, it was all he wanted.

Mila dropped to her knees next to Darek, this time taking his hand.

Darek's eyes shot open, gazing up at her through heavy eyelids. Her skin was soft against his, her fingers brushing against his in a way that made small shivers slither up his arm, momentarily distracting him from the pain. A calm settled over him, dulling the anger as well as the stress. Darek relaxed, dropping his guard along with the tension that had his body in an iron grip. "I never stopped thinking about you," he rasped. "What are you doing to me?"

As if stung by his words, she snatched her hand away and sneered. "Did you think of me too, when you burned down the shelter?"

"Shelter?"

Mila faltered, taken aback by the confusion on his face. It was too genuine to fake, and she must have realized it, but he still added, "I haven't done anything."

"I find that hard to believe."

"Hmph."

She was one stubborn woman, and it was one of the traits that intrigued him. Darek locked his eyes on her, demanding her to believe, to realize he was more than some bulldozer that destroyed everything he came near.

Mila pursed her lips. "What? What am I supposed to believe?"

"I didn't burn your goddamn shelter."

Mila sighed, and Darek's eyes narrowed in suspicion. Was that a look of resignation? Did she believe him? He made the mistake of shifting his body, and new, sharp stabs struck his back, sending hot flashes of pain throughout the rest of his body.

Darek groaned, tightening his jaw until his bones were ready to snap, and hissed through clenched teeth, "Fuck."

Mila scrambled to take his hand back, this time squeezing it tight. "I'm sorry I did this to you. Will you be okay?"

He managed a short nod, focusing on breathing.

"You landed on your back to keep me safe."

It wasn't a question, so she couldn't possibly expect him to reply, but what came out of his mouth stunned both of them into silence.

"I'd die for you."

Mila gaped at him. Darek, too, was shocked by the words, but he didn't take them back. He simply closed his eyes, letting out slow breaths through parted lips as he tried to pretend he hadn't said something as embarrassing as what he just let slip.

He couldn't stand to see the look in her eyes. It was too raw, too emotional. As if she'd finally realized he would never hurt her, that he was capable of feeling more than she'd ever imagined. He was human, too. Darek scoffed inwardly. *Human*. As much as he hated that fact, it was true. And as much as it stunned him, everything he'd said was true. He'd do anything to keep her safe. Hell, he already had. He'd known it would hurt, he'd known he'd re-break his back by landing on it as his wings had failed to keep them in the air. He'd done it anyway. He'd done it for her.

— * —

Hours later, Darek was back on his feet. Mila still held his hand as he stood, letting out shaky breaths, trying to brace himself before folding his wings. They disappeared along with his devil features, as effortless as normal, but the pain was there, making him grind his teeth and squeeze his eyes shut in an effort of hiding it from her.

"Does that hurt?" Mila asked and Darek mentally cursed his stupid body for showing emotion. So much for hiding it. He could keep from making any sound, but he couldn't keep the tension from his jaw as little as he could stop the way his chest heaved from deep breaths. Nor could he hide the sheen of sweat glistening on tight muscles.

"Like snapping your spine in two," Darek muttered,

feeling no need to deny it.

She ran a thumb along the soft skin of his hand, and Darek couldn't keep the shudder from rippling through him. Removing her hand, she handed him the jacket she'd held on to.

"Where do they go?"

He never thought of that, but it made sense that she'd wonder. Shrugging, he took the jacket in silence, eyed the hospital shirt hanging in threads on his body, and scowled.

"This is why I don't like clothes." He ripped it straight off his body, seeing Mila gulp as she eyed his toned chest. Her eyes roamed over him until his muscles tightened under her gaze. When she looked back at his face, his eyes were locked on her, gaze burning with the same heat that radiated off of his body.

"Don't look at me like that!" she snapped.

Darek raised an eyebrow, suddenly amused by her hypocrisy. "Which way should I look at you then?"

"Just—" She forced her eyes off him, her cheeks turning hot. "Put on the freaking jacket already!"

Darek stepped closer, one hand reaching out to brush his knuckles over her cheek. Mila's eyes drifted close, her breath trembling.

"Don't run away from me again."

Mila stepped away. "Why shouldn't I?"

Darek's voice was just a growl, and as the words slipped past his lips he stunned himself with the honesty. "I need you."

She gulped, forcing herself to ask, "Why me?" She lifted her gaze, looking up at him for answers. "Why are you so obsessed with me?"

"You awaken something in me."

"What?"

Darek hesitated, then whispered, "Light."

Her forehead furrowed as she stared at him.

Darek couldn't hold back. Those eyes did something to him, stole his reason, and messed with his head. In one swift motion, he had her in his grasp, her back pinned to the brick wall, his hands holding her arms on either side of her head as he struggled to maintain a gap between his body and hers.

"The hell!" she cried out. "Let me go!"

"I can't." He leaned in, lips hovering above hers. "You're a part of me. I can't lose you."

Mila's lips parted in a soft gasp, her body moving toward his.

"You make me feel like a moth. I'm drawn to you, yet I know I'll get burned."

Her nostrils flared, her nose twitching as if taking in his scent. "You smell like fire." She spoke the words onto his lips, caressing him with the soft puffs of her breath.

"I *am* fire."

She shivered under his heat, knowing all too well he was right.

"Don't go." He touched his forehead to hers, letting her soft skin still the internal inferno. "It drives me mad not to know where you are. If you are safe. I *need* you to be safe."

Mila gulped but kept still. "You're the devil." She shifted, lifting her face to his. "You're lethal."

"I am." He stepped closer. "Don't pretend that it doesn't turn you on."

Mila rolled her head to the side, ignoring his comment. "Let me go."

Darek did the opposite. She wanted him, her whole body showed it. The way her eyes roamed over him, the way her hands struggled in his grip. She wanted to touch him, and one part of Darek ached for those delicate hands on his skin. But he couldn't allow it. Not yet, maybe never. Darek stepped closer, pressing his body against hers. Her coat tickled his skin, the cold buttons pressing into his chest as she squirmed against him. Did she try to get away, or get closer?

"Don't."

Her voice lacked the previous determination. A smirk tugged at Darek's lips as he leaned closer, hovering them over hers. She trembled under his hot breath, showing no sign of wanting him *gone* now.

Darek's head spun. He wanted nothing more than to

undress her right there and feel her skin pressed against his. His whole body ached for her, but it wasn't just lust. It wasn't just about sex, even though he throbbed with desire. He wanted her in a way he'd never wanted a woman. He wanted more than her body. He wanted *her*.

"I've never wanted to be gentle as much as I want it with you." His body vibrated against hers, his breath heavy and warm on her lips. Mila's eyes found his and he held her gaze, eyes deep red as the fire inside burned bright.

He whispered the next words onto her lips. "Teach me how to love you."

Mila gasped. The hot puff of air like a caress to his lips.

"Prove it," she whispered. "Be gentle."

A low growl erupted from Darek's throat. He was so close to kissing her, to crush his lips against hers and kiss her breathless. With her words in mind, he leaned in, brushing his lips against hers in a ghost of a kiss leaving him burning for more. Using the last of his willpower, he pushed himself off her, reigning back the claws, and hoped she hadn't noticed. Shrugging on the jacket, he tried to keep his voice steady as he spoke.

"At least tell me your name."

"Mila."

He tasted it, played with it on his tongue. *Mila.* He lifted his gaze and looked straight at her. "Stay." He frowned, adding in a dry tone, "Please."

DAREK

CHAPTER 19

"I can't believe I'm doing this," Mila muttered and Darek chuckled.

"You know you want to."

"How is it possible you have no place to live?" She held open the door to her apartment, allowing him to step inside.

"The fuck happened here?" Darek's eyes landed on the tipped-over furniture and scattered clothes and widened. "Somehow I didn't take you as the messy type."

Mila sighed, leaned against the doorframe. "Someone was here, stole my jewelry, and turned the whole place upside down. I—" she looked away. "I can't look at this right now, I have to meet my friends, it's about the dogs."

Darek tried to follow, but all he heard was '*Someone was here.*' His fists curled into balls to contain the anger. *Someone was here?* Some asshole had broken into her home, taken her stuff. Darek's eyes darted to her, and the anger leaked through his words as he growled, "Did he hurt you?"

"I wasn't even at home."

"I'll find him," he snarled. And he would. If it was the last thing he'd do. He'd make the bastard pay. A smirk came over Darek's lips as he imagined the thief begging for mercy, as he imagined his claws tearing through his flesh.

"Control yourself," Mila muttered. "I don't need you to burn the place down as well." She turned to leave.

Darek reigned in his powers, cursing himself for letting his control slip. He couldn't scare her away again. He couldn't stand the thought of losing her, *again*.

"Wait! I'm not letting you go alone."

"Darek!" she snapped. "We've been through this. Stop trying to control me! And stay here."

"Hmph."

She rolled her eyes, shot him a glare that spoke volumes, then left him standing there staring after her.

Darek scratched his head, weighing his options. The thought of her out there, when someone was threatening her bothered him to no end. She'd be with friends, he tried to remind himself. She'd be safe.

Darek shook his head at his own insanity. Since when did he care about one human's safety? He didn't recognize himself. Slamming the door, he turned to face the mess. Mila's stuff, spread out across the floor filled him with deep frustration, and a need to clean it up. His mom had always been the tidy one, picking things off the floor in a never-ending pattern. Darek had helped her as well as he could, but things always flew when his dad was around, and no matter how much bleach his mom had used, the bloodstains never washed from the walls.

Darek shuddered as the sight made him nauseous. He couldn't stand the mess, it brought up too painful memories. If he was going to survive one night in this place, he needed to do something about the goddamn chaos. Picking up the clothes from the floor, he struggled to stay in the present, to not let the images take over his mind. Blurry scenes played out before his eyes no matter how he tried to fight it. His father's screams echoing through his head. Darek couldn't stop it. Standing with Mila's soft clothes hugged to his chest, the memories washed over him.

The sound of the whip cracking the air made the tears he'd desperately held back roll down his cheeks. Closing his eyes in anticipation of the pain, Darek pressed himself against the wall and tried to remain on his feet as the material dug into his flesh. If he fell, he'd be dead. His father hated him for being weak, he had to keep standing. He had to be strong. Darek clenched his teeth and breathed through the torture, counting the lashes silently in his head. When he reached fifteen, he lost count and black spots started to take over his vision and nausea rose in his throat. In the distance, the sound of soft weeping reached his ears. His mom. In the midst of the pain, he felt bad for her. She wanted to help him, but she stopped trying. She didn't dare, and Darek couldn't blame her.

Darek felt the blood run down his back, slowly soaking his trousers and trailing down his legs until the floor turned slippery under his feet. Biting back the noises he had no power over, he slipped in the blood, feeling his body sink to the floor as his legs gave out. Collapsing face down in the pool of blood, he heard his father's snarl.

"Get up!" his voice thundered in Darek's head. "You've got to toughen up. Be a man."

The sound of his own scream snapped him back to the present. His hands shook as he untangled claws from Mila's sweater and brought it to his face. Letting the soft material muffle his gasps, he tried to calm his thumping heart. He wasn't there. He wasn't that boy anymore. He didn't have to feel that pain again. Darek bit back the emotion rising in his chest. It wasn't true. It never stopped hurting. He could never escape the memories. They were there, visible on his skin and they'd never go away. He'd changed, but at the same time, he hadn't and he hated it. Hated the human part of him that refused to let him forget, the way it clung to the pain as if it was the only thing he deserved.

After what felt like forever, Darek could breathe again. Inhaling her jasmine scent made him shiver for a whole new reason. Everything about her touched him in places he'd never been touched. He felt her in his heart, in his soul.

Folding the garment, he placed it back on the shelf and let out a ragged breath.

Shrugging out of his jacket, he hung it next to hers and studied the black leather next to a soft teal sweater. It belonged there, just like he belonged with her.

Kicking off his shoes, he ran a hand through his hair, then bent down to return the mirror to its upright position. Staring back at his reflection through the cracked glass, he saw himself for what he was. *Fragmented. Shattered. Broken.* Darek's eyes settled on the thickest line sliced across his chest and shuddered. It was the last one, and even though he'd long ago grown used to the stinging pain as his body suffered the wrath of the man he hated more than anything, his heart hadn't been prepared. A part of him died with his mother that day, but even if he wanted to be as heartless as Mila thought he was, he couldn't hide from the truth. He couldn't hide from himself and what he carried inside. Tearing his gaze away, Darek turned into a kitchen. It was a disaster. It was enough to make him shudder in horror. Darek ran a hand through his hair, smoothing back the loose strands trying to escape onto his forehead, then he began picking things from the floor. Keeping busy was the best way to distract his mind from going places he never wanted to go and feeling things he never wanted to feel— from going back there...

When one room was organized, he went on to the next. When he reached her bedroom, Darek hesitated.

Stepping over the threshold, eyes landing on the teal walls and blue curtains, he couldn't help but gasp. He'd seen this. Not in detail, but the colors were imprinted in his mind. He'd seen it, *felt* it. Felt *her.* Darek swallowed, letting out a shuddering breath as the feelings rushed through him. She'd been right here, in this bed...

Darek tried not to think of her soft skin as he slid a hand over the sheets. Picking up a pillow, he pressed it to his face, inhaling her.

Snapping out of it, Darek tossed the pillow back on the bed and began to pick items off the floor. When everything looked organized, it suddenly occurred to him she probably wouldn't find anything. He had no way of knowing where she kept each item, he'd just put things in a way that seemed logical to him. Darek shrugged. She could always rearrange. At least the place was livable.

Darek located the vacuum cleaner and the mop, and went over the floors, ridding the surface of dust and shattered glass.

When he was done, he slumped against the kitchen counter, filling a glass of water while panting for air. How many hours had he worked? He didn't even know, but judging by his rapid heartbeat and how his pants clung to sweaty skin, he realized it had probably taken longer than he'd anticipated. Where was Mila? Shouldn't she be back by now?

Darek gulped down the water, threw one look out the window, then went straight to the shower.

Clean and with a ridiculously small towel wrapped around his hips, he threw the door open and steered toward the kitchen for one more glass of water. Halfway down the corridor, the front door opened and Mila stepped inside.

She stopped dead, eyes widening at the sight of him. Darek stood motionless, following her gaze down his body, and willed himself not to react to her burning eyes on his naked skin.

"See something you like?"

She tore her eyes off him, blushing. "What are—" Her mouth fell open as she finally took in the shape of the apartment. "You—" Her eyes grew wide in disbelief. "You cleaned up?"

"I don't like clutter."

She let out a sharp laugh and Darek raised an eyebrow. "What? Thought I wasn't capable of feeling *that*, either?"

"No, I—" She dropped her gaze in what could only be described as shame, placed her shoes next to his and her coat next to his jacket, then walked past him, inspecting the work.

Darek turned to watch her but didn't go near. Two people could play the game. He'd control himself. He'd control more than the devil. He'd wait until she begged him to touch her, and once she did, he'd make sure she never stopped begging.

He'd be the good guy, the perfect gentleman.

"This is amazing." She came back, stopping close enough for him to reach her. Darek crossed his arms over his chest to keep himself from doing it.

She smiled a genuine smile. "Thank you. Really."

Darek nodded politely. "No problem."

Mila narrowed her eyes. "What's going on? Where's the devil I know?"

Darek chuckled, adding in a seductive tone. "Oh, he's here, waiting."

DAREK

CHAPTER 20

Mila's eyes kept drifting back to his body even though it was clear she tried not to look. Her gaze flickered between him and the room, until settling on him again. Darek stood motionless, not sure how to act. One part of him wanted to run back to the room to throw his clothes back on, but he couldn't bring himself to move. He was frozen under her burning gaze. She liked what she saw, and Darek took some kind of strange pleasure in that.

He was in good shape, he couldn't deny that. It came effortlessly, the kind of body any given man would spend years toning came naturally to him. He didn't need to lift weights to look ripped. He'd never thought of why, but he simply assumed that being the fucking devil provided him with just the perfect temptation for the opposite sex. That, and the fire burning within him. With his high body temperature, gathering fat was simply no option. He had been shaped into a predator, something strong and lethal, it only made sense he looked like one, too.

Mila's eyes landed on the tattoo, following the black lines over his chest and stomach, and down that carved V until they disappeared into the towel draped over his hips. He didn't move, didn't even shift as he mentally cursed the lack of clothing. When she looked at him like that, he had no way of hiding under the small towel.

She averted her eyes, a flushed look on her face. It took a moment before she dared to look back, and Darek took the opportunity to breathe. To suck in big gulps of air to calm his pulse from skyrocketing and his blood pressure to calm. Before he had any chance to regain his composure, her eyes were back, roaming over his body until he cringed mentally under her gaze.

If she had stopped at that, Darek would've been happy. But when the look in her eyes shifted from arousal to sympathy, he tensed. He didn't want her to see. He'd been shirtless around her before, but this was different. Standing under the sharp hallway light, fully exposed to her, he'd never felt more vulnerable. Every line on his body laid out for her to see, every moment of humiliation, every sign of weakness.

He had the chance to be something worth looking at, but he'd been damaged. Scratched and burned until the smooth skin he'd once had was littered with rough lines that made him avoid looking at himself in the mirror.

Darek looked away in shame.

Mila inched closer, tilting her face upward to see his. She reached out, and the moment her fingers touched the scars on his cheek, a shiver rippled through him. She swallowed visibly but didn't move away. Tracing the three lines slicing across the left side of his face over his cheek, nose, and forehead, only just barely skipping his eye, the sympathy shone in her eyes, but she didn't say a word, and Darek was glad. He couldn't talk about it even if she asked. He didn't even want to think about it, to remember, even though the damaged skin made it impossible to forget either. Every time someone stared at him, he was forced back there, forced to relive the pain.

"Darek," her voice was soft, but before she could say anything, he cut her to it.

"Don't."

"I was just—"

"Don't fucking mention it." She didn't need to know the details. The fact he was covered in scars gave her all the facts she needed; he'd been through hell, but the last thing he wanted was her pity.

"Okay," she whispered. She let her hand slide down to his shoulder then she stepped closer, circling her arms around him, and pulled him close to her. His body tensed from the sudden shock of her proximity, his muscles flexing against her, his breath hitching. She tightened her hold as he tried to pull away, murmuring into his neck. "It's okay."

Darek wasn't sure *okay* even covered it, but he couldn't find the willpower to put up a fight. It felt good. Too good.

For a brief moment, he allowed himself the comfort.

He knew pain. His body was evidence. He'd been through hell, but he'd never known real love. He'd never let anyone close enough to even try to care for him, and he'd never felt the need. But with Mila, he wanted to try. He wanted so much that he'd never wanted before.

Teach me how to love you...

His previous words echoed in his head. She'd accused him of all sorts of things. She'd said he didn't have a heart, and while he should've been glad for such words, something about it bothered him. He didn't want to be a heartless monster around her, he wanted to be so much more than that. What she did to him by simply being near him was unexplainable. Darek didn't understand why he insisted on staying around someone who made him want to be anything less than the devil he was meant to be. He should run. He should crush her like the pathetic human she was. He should take the control back, but he couldn't do any of that. He knew from the moment he saw her, she was different. The way she made him feel was like a drug. He couldn't breathe without her.

A deep growl vibrated in his chest. One of his hands

landed on her back, the other in her hair as he pulled her closer to him. Embarrassed by the way his body trembled against her, how his heart pounded too fast, he tried to hide it by pressing her closer and soon realized his mistake. Mila's soft gasp let him know she'd felt it, and how could she not? Just thinking of her made him hard, and with her body pressed up against his overheated skin, he had no way of controlling his desire for her.

Mila gulped, and Darek couldn't help but smirk. There was nothing stopping him now. They were alone together, no one could save her. There was no escape. She invited the devil to her home, what did she expect? For him to eat cookies and drink milk? He had more interesting things on his mind, and it was damn hard not to act upon those impulses when she was so close. When only a thin sheet of fabric lay between them.

Despite the sinister thoughts, Darek didn't move. He wanted nothing more than to grab her and throw her down onto her bed, but he'd sworn not to touch her, and he was going to keep that promise.

One of her hands slid over his back, hesitating as his muscles rippled under her touch. A low growl against her neck made her tense. A warning. *Don't play with fire.* His claws scraped against her skull as his hand closed around her hair and his other hand slid under her shirt. A sudden jerk of his hand tipped her head back, and when her eyes flickered to his blood-red ones, a bolt of excited fear zapped through hers.

"I can't resist you," he hissed.

He was so close he could feel her breath on her lips. His hands holding her in a fierce grip against his body.

His lips hovered over hers, and Mila's parted in anticipation of the touch. But instead of kissing her, he cried out in frustration, stepping away.

Mila gaped, shocked at the sudden change.

He stood, back to her, shoulders tense and fists clenched to his sides. "Tell me to touch you," he growled. "Tell me." It was the only way. He refused to be something he was not, even though with her it took everything he had to stay away from her.

"Darek..." she began. "I—" She closed the gap between them, laying a hand on his back. Before he could stop himself, he spun on his heels, grabbing her and backing her up against the wall.

Her back slammed against the wall from the force of his body pressed against hers, holding her in place. She tugged at her hands, but he held them in a firm grip above her head with one of his. No more touching. No more hands on his skin, he couldn't stand what it did to him. He didn't know what would happen if he let her hands free. If he let her touch him the way she wanted to, let her run her hands along his stiff muscles. Would she rip the towel off and touch him how he craved to be touched. Would he lose the last fraction of control he was clinging to, would he take her, right here against the wall, or would he bring her to the bed? Or would he run?

Pushing the uneasy feelings aside, he focused on the women in his grasp.

His free hand hovered in the air above her face, his eyes burning bright red. When the tips of his claws touched her skin, she couldn't stop a gasp. He touched her with a gentleness he'd never expected from himself, from something so lethal. The featherlike touch as he dragged those claws over her cheek made her shiver under his touch. He traced the contours of her lips, making them part for him, her tongue slipping out to wet her lips and circle his finger until his body tightened against hers and a low growl escaped his throat.

Mila squirmed under his grip, grinding her body against him until he thought he'd explode from the feeling. How could he hold on when she made him feel so damn good, how could he keep his promise when she taunted him with her body, tempting him to lose control.

"Mila," he hissed.

Her voice was just as breathless. "What?"

"Stop."

"Why?" she breathed. "You're hard as a rock, you want me."

"Of course I fucking want you," he growled. "I promised you."

She gasped, staring up at him with a look that seemed to say, *'fuck that promise.'* But before he could do anything, the doorbell chimed.

DAREK

CHAPTER 21

"Don't open." Darek tightened his grip, holding Mila in place with his body. If she wasn't touching him she was too far away. Every little movement from her, every rub against him drove him wild. He wanted her, the need was physical, a deep ache in his loins, and the longer he held back, the harder it became to stand the feeling.

"I have to." She tugged at her arms. "Let me go!"

Darek released her with a snarl. Throwing his hands against the wall, he leaned forward, digging his claws into the wallpaper.

"You're worse than a horny dog," Mila giggled. "Control yourself."

Darek pressed his forehead against the wall, trying to still his speeding pulse. He was throbbing with desire. Even the touch of the towel was torture he couldn't stand.

The click of the lock echoed in his head, then the slight squeak as the door slid opened, and then Mila's scream. Darek swirled around, watching her stagger back. He caught her before she collapsed, lowering her to the floor before darting to the door. The sound of fleeing feet disappeared down the corridor. Darek exploded into devil form in an instant, his wings tearing like knives through the walls as he took after the retreating figure. He didn't care what he destroyed, he didn't care about anyone seeing him, all he could think of was catching that son of a bitch and tearing him apart. When he reached the bend in the corridor, the only thing hinting of someone having been there was the draft seeping through the slowly closing main door. Darek's scream bounced across the walls. He'd find that cockroach, if he'd have to burn down the city, he'd get him. His hands shook with contained flames just waiting to be set free.

Mila...

The thought of her allowed him to reign back the power seconds before he snapped. He rushed back to her apartment, only to find it empty.

"Mila?" Darek's eyes darted across the empty hallway, to the spot where she'd collapsed. His voice rose into a shout, calling out her name as flames burned bright in his palms.

— * —

Dressed in his usual black, Darek rushed through the front door, nearly knocking a couple down in the process. Clearing the steps in a flying stride, he stopped, looking up and down the street, and tried to keep from panicking. The night traffic wasn't as intense as in the day, but a steady row of cars passed by, each one of them pushing his stress level up a notch. He didn't feel her how he'd felt her before. Their unexplainable connection let him know she still existed. That she was alive and well. He'd felt her anger, her fear. He'd felt her as if she'd been a part of him. Now, he felt nothing, and the emptiness inside of him scared him more than anything. Had she disappeared in one of those cars?

Taken against her will and carried away into the never-ending buzz of activity the big city provided. Was she even alive? Darek called out her name in desperation, shouting to the sky.

A hand landed on his shoulder. Darek swirled around, standing face to face with a young couple who eyed him with a mix of suspicion and confusion.

"Looking for Mila, huh?" the guy asked. "Why don't you just piss off and leave her alone?" He stepped closer, letting go of the girl's hand. She wobbled back, and when she giggled at nothing in particular, Darek caught a whiff of alcohol on her breath.

Realization flashed across the girl's face as she shamelessly stared at Darek's scars.

Darek huffed. "She's missing," he snapped. "I need to find her."

A fist to his face sent Darek staggering back. When he regained his composure, the sight of the guy rubbing his bleeding knuckles made his lips twitch into a twisted grin.

"Do you have a death wish," he hissed.

"Stay away from Mila."

Darek scoffed at his pathetic attempt to be brave. He had no idea what he was dealing with, and Darek itched to show him. The only thing stopping him from turning devil on the asshole was the fact that they knew Mila. He needed these people to stay alive long enough to help him find her.

Reigning in the power he wanted nothing more than to unleash on the bastard who'd dared to hit him, he forced himself to remain calm. "Hit me again..." he left the threat hanging, allowing his eyes to flash red for effect.

"Your eyes! How did you do that?" the girl gasped, pointing a wavering finger at Darek. "What are you?"

Darek locked his eyes on her, hissing. "The devil. Now, will you help me find her or not?"

"You're a fucking—"

"Riley!" the girl hissed, grabbing his arm. "Don't provoke him."

"I'm not scared, fucking parlor tricks!"

"You're *the friends*," Darek stated the obvious.

"And you're the stalker guy," the girl shot back. "Mila was right about the Greek God."

"Geez, Kate."

Kate gave her boyfriend a sheepish smile, then turned to Darek and her face hardened. "She told us about you. Believe it or not, she wants nothing to do with you. Go back home, find some other girl to stalk."

Darek huffed. His hands itched with the desire to burn this profoundly annoying couple to the ground. One more word from their lips and he wasn't sure he could stop himself.

"That has changed," he snarled. "She was taken from her home. Someone knocked her out. I chased after the son of a bitch, when I came back, she was gone."

The couple exchanged looks. Kate speaking up, "Wait, you were *with* her?"

Darek gave a short nod, not wanting to be reminded of how close to her he'd been. Not now, he had to focus, he wouldn't be able to do that with an aching hard-on.

"I see." Kate giggled, suddenly looking curious. "She finally let you into her pants, huh?" she snickered. "Can't say I blame her."

Darek gulped. This was going wrong fast.

"Kate!" Riley snapped. "Focus, didn't you hear him? Mila's missing."

That seemed to sober her up. "We'll find her. It's Scott, it's gotta be Scott."

Riley's face was grim.

"Well, let's go then. Where's this cockroach located?" Darek snapped, running out of patience real fast.

"God if we know, he's an addict, broke into her apartment. She believed he was the one to burn down the shelter as well, after ruling you out."

Darek groaned. Why would everyone think it was him every time there was a goddamn fire?

"What's this shelter all about?"

"Rescue dogs, that's what we do."

The pieces fell in place. Everything she'd said suddenly made sense. And there he'd been, indirectly telling her how dumb it was to cry over a dog. The strong need to apologize burned within Darek. But he'd have to find her first. And once he did, he swore he'd never let her out of his sight ever again.

Fear slammed into him, so sudden and so intense he gasped out loud. A hand flew to his forehead, rubbing the skin to ward off a sudden sharp headache he already knew wasn't his own.

"Are you all right?" Riley asked.

"She's hurt."

Before either of them had a chance to ask, the sound of a window shattering made the trio spin on their heels. Darek was first to react, taking the steps in a flying stride, Kate and Riley not far behind. Flinging the door to Mila's apartment wide open, he prepared to kill whoever was in there. It no longer mattered Mila's friends would see him in action, he'd rip the bastard to pieces and feed them down his throat. Something crunched under his shoe as he took a step further into the foyer. Dropping his gaze to his feet, the shattered glass spread out over the floor made him curse out loud.

Kate bent down to pick up a piece of paper, sticking out from a broken bottle.

"*You have what's ours. Return it by midnight or she dies. You know where.*"

Kate started to cry. "It has blood on it," she whimpered.

Darek snatched the note from her trembling hands, and as he saw the red smeared across the paper, he couldn't contain the rage. Tilting his head back, he screamed as he exploded into full devil before their eyes.

Ignoring Kate's hysterical shrieks, and Riley's *oh my Gods,* he darted back the way he came, clearing the steps in one flying stride. The moment he was outside, he spread his wings and shot toward the sky. Fuck people. Fuck the idiots who'd seen him explode. Mila was in trouble. That was top priority. Everything else he'd deal with later.

DAREK

CHAPTER 22

Darek landed with a thud, flinging a hand out to catch the man perched outside of the door by his throat before he had time to warn anyone about the intrusion.

The gargled sounds he managed were drowned in the howling wind. Darek snapped his neck, holding on to the body as he slid the door ajar to peek inside.

The deeply ingrained stench of piss reached his nose, making him grimace. He'd flown not more than five minutes, and even though the bird way across the city was faster than by car, the area was worse than he remembered it. Gutters littered with garbage and tipped over dumpsters hinted at the mentality of the inhabitants, and the house towering over him looked like it was ready to collapse.

Pushing the door open, Darek caught the sound of voices. He sharpened his ears, trying to hear the words.

"I don't like this," a man's voice hissed. *"It's too*

dangerous."

"Stop being such a pussy," another snarled.

"Something's not right man. Boss pays us for snatching some chick?"

"Does it fucking matter?"

A third voice cut in. *"He'll kill us all,"* he paused, then hissed. *"Carla's not even here to see it. What'cha think that's for, huh? She's fucking scared!"*

Darek's mind reeled. What were they talking about? Weren't they expecting him to return the money? A simple trade? Not that Darek had any intention of playing by their rules, he hadn't even brought the cash. But they didn't know that. And who was this Boss they talked about? And why would he kill—Darek cut himself off mid-thought. It wasn't their *Boss* they were scared of—it was Darek. A twisted grin spread across his lips. They were damn right about that. They should be. They should be fucking terrified.

Darek's breath stopped the moment he heard Mila's voice.

"What do you want?" she called out.

The fear in her voice cranked up Darek's anger level to extreme, drawing claws from his fingers and a deep red fire in his eyes. His whole body tensed as it prepared for the attack.

"What do you think we want, missy?"

Darek grabbed the doorframe to keep himself from bursting right in. Digging his claws into the wood, he held back—until he couldn't. The need to know who these people were was overshadowed by the need to get Mila out of there. He couldn't wait, but God, did he want a fucking name, a goddamned reason why she was down there in a cold cellar and not in his bed.

Darek inched closer, dragging the dead body with him as he ducked under a low door frame. He moved silently down the first steps and stopped, craning his neck around a corner, and froze. Mila sat, tied to a wooden chair in the middle of the room. Thick rope wired around her chest, and by the odd angle her arms were twisted, he guessed they were pulled tight behind her back and tied to the chair. She wore nothing but the clothes which he'd last seen her in. The tight light-blue top and the black leggings did nothing to block out the icy winds which drifted into the room from the glassless window high under the low ceiling. Occasional bursts of snow sprinkled through the gaps, and even though Darek was immune to the cold, Mila was not.

A man crouched down in front of her, forcing her legs apart with two hands on her thighs, and Darek saw red. His wings shot out, filling the narrow space with their mass as fire burst from his hands. One rough shove sent the dead man tumbling down the stairs. He landed at the bottom, his clothes consumed by hot flames. The hands were off Mila in a flash, as the guy ran to see what the commotion was about. His mates joined in, coming to an abrupt halt at the foot of the stairs, gaping at the burning man at their feet.

"Motherfucker's here!"

"Remember, Boss wants him alive."

"You're all idiots!" the third guy shouted. *"Look at Mac, look at his fucking neck!"*

Mila's head jerked up as she saw Darek, her mouth falling open at the sight of the fire swirling around his arms. The brief moment as their eyes met, everything around them seemed to stop. Struck by the strong urge to hold her, to shield her from the horrors, Darek almost forgot the three idiots who'd dropped into fight stances at the bottom of the stairs.

When they reached for their weapons, Darek didn't bother to move. He didn't need guns or knives —he *was* the weapon, and they'd soon find out how sharp he was.

Darek tore off the shredded shirt, setting his eyes on the thugs as he moved down the stairs, deliberately slow. His wings were pulled back to fit the narrow space, making him look taller than he already was, adding to the intimidating posture that made the men shrink back as he neared.

One look at Mila and his patience dropped like a stone. He had no time to play, she needed him and she needed him *now*. As soon as he had enough space to stretch his wings, he used them to cross the room, swooping down as he neared the men.

127

Screams and cries of pain echoed in the frosty night, blood staining the walls from swift slashes of sharp claws against their skin. Darek moved with ease, dodging the knives and punches with effortless graze. It was over as soon as it had begun, leaving Darek in the midst of fallen bodies. He lifted his gaze, and the moment his eyes locked on Mila, the red faded into his steel gray.

"Get me out of here," Mila whispered.

Darek was at her side in a flash, his claws tearing through the ropes with one swift cut. Once she was free, he scooped her up into his arms, holding her close as if he'd never let her go. Wrapping her arms around his neck, she clung to him, nuzzling her face into the crock of his neck. Darek took the moment to breathe in her jasmine scent, letting her soft body soothe the burning rage inside.

"I got you," he whispered. "You're safe." While his arms held her pressed against him, he folded his wings around her, creating a shield from the cold, cutting them both off from the world around for a brief moment of stillness. It was over. She was safe.

When Mila had stopped shivering, he unfolded the wings and carried her up the stairs and into the night without saying a word. Her arms tightened around him, her body shifting closer to his, rubbing against his tight muscles. Darek let out slow breaths that didn't quite hide the tremor of each exhale.

"Hold on."

Mila stiffened, her breath coming with short gasps as she braced herself for the flight. Darek spread his wings, lifting them into the sky before shooting forward, cutting the air, and letting the icy winds bite into his skin.

He didn't let her go until they were safely inside Mila's apartment. When he lowered her down onto her bed and tried to move away, Mila clung to him. His hands removed her arms, firm but gentle, and as he sat watching her, Darek's heart clenched from the sudden intensity of emotion. He almost lost her. The thought was enough to make him want to lock her up and shield her from every potential danger he could think of. She was too precious for this world. She was a rare flower, a pearl in the midst of pigs.

He reached out, touching the bruised skin on her forehead and Mila winced. A growl erupted from his throat, his features hardening. She was hurt. He couldn't stand the thought of what has caused it. Those cockroaches deserved something worse than death. They deserved to suffer slowly. Darek imagined all the things he'd do to them, how satisfying their screams would be as his claws cut them like the fucking pieces of meat that they were.

"Hold me," Mila whispered, bringing him back to the room. His eyes followed her gaze down to his free hand, digging into the mattress. Releasing the grip, he studied her for a long time, taken aback by her sudden request.

His lips twitched into a smile. "I thought you'd never ask." Darek pushed off the bed, stepping out of the dirty trousers, and slid down next to her in the bed while pulling the covers up. Mila settled into his embrace naturally, letting him pull her as tight to his body as he possibly could, tangling her legs with his for a perfect fit.

"You were gone," he whispered into her hair. "I didn't *feel* you. It was only—emptiness. A vacuum."

Mila shifted, finding his hand and tucking it closer to her. "I must have passed out."

Darek's chest tightened at the memory. The hollowness of her absence had terrified him. Not until that moment did he realize what she meant to him. The short moment of having lost her made him more determined than ever to never go through it again.

Darek closed his eyes, feeling how his heat crept into her, relaxing her stiff muscles and stopping her shivers. He relaxed, too, for a brief moment letting everything go. For a brief moment, he allowed himself to be human, to feel the full spectrum of feelings. When it threatened to overwhelm him, he pulled her closer, burying his face into her hair, and let her presence soothe the storm inside.

— * —

Darek stood under the bleak rays of morning sun shining

through the window. He'd fallen asleep. It surprised him. And the shock of waking up with Mila wrapped in his arms had forced him out of the bed when all he'd wanted was the opposite. He wasn't ready for the romance, he'd never thought he needed it, that he even wanted it. But with Mila, he wanted everything.

"Hey," she murmured, "Why aren't you sleeping?"

Darek turned away from the window, took the few steps back to the bed, and sat at the edge, his back toward her. "It was my fault."

The rustle of sheets as she moved made him cringe. He felt her move behind him, felt the air on his back as she sat, and forced himself to say the next words.

"They took you because of me."

Her soft intake of breath made him tense. She had every right to blame him, but he dreaded it. After a silence that seemed to stretch into eternity, she finally snapped.

"I trusted you! I felt safe with you!"

Darek turned, reached for her, but this time Mila was faster. She slapped his hand away and scrambled out of bed. Holding the bedroom door open, she snapped, "Get out!"

When Darek didn't move, she stalked over to him, grabbed his arm, and tugged. "Get out of my bed, you manipulative son of a bitch!"

With a snarl, Darek trapped her under his body, her hands pinned above her head as he straddled her, holding her in place with the weight of his body. "Listen to me," he hissed. The frustration drove him crazy. She'd gotten it all wrong, acting as if he'd been the one to take her. Didn't she know by now he'd never hurt her? Didn't him killing those bastards prove which side he was on? Darek wanted to scream. What did he have to do to prove himself to her? To make her see he was not all those things she accused him of being?

Mila shot him a frosty look. "It's all a game to you, isn't it? Have some sick douchebags rough me up, scare me enough to fall straight into your arms? Well congratulations, it worked."

Darek could only stare. Was *that* what she thought of

him? He couldn't hold back a huff, and for a confused moment, he wasn't sure whether he should feel offended, or flattered. At least she wasn't underestimating his brains or his powers.

"Let me go, I can't stand to even look at you now."

Darek's eyes narrowed in annoyance. He had enough of her stupidity. Pressing down on her harder, he drew a wince from her lips, and couldn't help but enjoy the flicker of fear in her eyes as he growled, "Not until you listen."

"You have one minute."

Darek chuckled at her threat, then he sighed. "You're awful quick to jump to the wrong conclusions," he huffed. "I didn't *get* you taken, I'd never do that."

Mila stopped struggling but stayed tense, ready to bolt the moment he released his grip.

"I did a job for some jerks, I was supposed to get ten percent. I took it all. Mila, I'm... I'm sorry?"

She stared at him, then finally let out a long breath, her body softening along with her gaze as the anger faded.

"Who's *Boss*?"

The edge to her voice made Darek wince inwardly. He hung his head, dipping his forehead to her chin. "You don't believe me?" he muttered against her skin.

"No, I..." her voice trailed off. "I do."

Darek lifted his head, staring down at her. "Then why are you still angry?"

The range of emotion on her face left him in a daze.

"How could you be that dumb?" she snapped. "They're criminals. They are dangerous."

Darek huffed. "Not to me."

Mila groaned, and Darek realized his mistake as the fear she couldn't hide flashed across her face. Just because nothing was a danger to him, didn't mean *she* was safe. They'd never stop to try to get to him, using her as bait. Darek shuddered at the thought.

"They are to *me*."

She spoke his thoughts out loud, angering him with the truth he didn't want to face.

"They're dead," he hissed. "No one will touch you."

"Just give it back."

"I can't. I have nothing, Mila. I need that money."

If that wasn't the goddamn truth. He owned the clothes he wore, and that was it. The cash made him feel a little less pathetic, and he refused to give it up.

"What happened to you?" she whispered. "Why are you on your own?"

Darek pushed off her, turning to face the window. Her eyes burned into his back, making him cringe mentally as he imagined her studying the crisscross of scars covering his skin. The mattress dipped as she moved, coming nearer. Darek threw a glance over his shoulder, fighting the urge to get up and away. The wetness in her eyes was too much. He didn't know how to deal with emotions. And the way she looked at him triggered his own, making his chest tighten and his throat close off. He couldn't do this. He needed space, he needed—

She scooted closer, snaking an arm around his stomach before he could act upon his impulses. Resting her cheek against his back, she whispered, "Talk to me."

DAREK

CHAPTER 23

"Talk to me."

Her words echoed in his head. Darek let out a ragged breath. Her proximity, both comforting and arousing, suddenly felt too real. Too close. She didn't only touch his body, she somehow slipped past the barrier of skin, and into his soul... he'd never been as vulnerable as he was now. And yet, he knew he had to let her in further.

She nudged him, touching the spot between his shoulder blades where the wings were hidden out of sight but ready to burst free at any given signal. "Have you always been... like this?"

Darek hesitated, torn between the urge to explain himself to her, and the need to shut her out. For her own good, and his.

"No."

"What happened?" her soft voice urged him on.

A pain he never managed to slake burned deep in his core. Memories he tried to banish from his head, flashing through his eyes. "I was eighteen. I don't know, maybe it was always there, but... I changed that day. I was never the same again."

"You just—turned into a—" she cut herself off, but what she didn't say was as clear as if she did say it. *Monster*.

"How is it possible?" she whispered against his back. "How can a human being just grow wings and horns and—" she again fell silent, taking a moment before asking, "Can you die? I mean—" her hot breath burned his skin as she paused to rephrase. "I mean, are you—immortal?"

"I don't know." It was the truth.

"Fire doesn't burn you," Mila stated the obvious. "You can heal injuries that would kill a normal human. It's—remarkable."

"Hmph."

"What?"

"Why the sudden curiosity about my mortality? Plotting to kill me?"

Mila chuckled softly. "I just want to know you better. Don't shut me out."

Darek's chest tightened from the sudden rush of emotion. His natural reaction was to suppress it, to turn it into anger, to survive. Mila's presence made it hard for him to keep that up.

"What happened to you?"

Her voice was just a murmur, a comfort, her words like a siren he couldn't resist. Before he understood what he was doing, he heard himself say, "I lost my mom on my eighteenth birthday, she was—" his voice broke and as Darek fought against the fresh pain of remembering, Mila tightened her arms in support.

"She was the only one who cared."

Mila's silent comfort filled him with the courage to speak about the things he never allowed himself to think of since that day.

"The devil took over, I let it. I welcomed it. The power, the anger, I felt like I'd been reborn into something better and stronger. Someone who couldn't be broken with whips and harsh words, who couldn't care less about the people who—" his voice broke. Darek shot to his feet, stood on trembling legs as he fought for control.

"Oh, my love," Mila murmured, "you've been through hell, haven't you?"

He spun around, momentarily forgetting everything as her words resounded in his head. She reached out, taking his hand, and pulled him back onto the bed.

Darek smoothed his hair back, curling his fist around his hair, letting the physical pain distract him from the more frightening world inside. The compassion in her eyes, the silent urge to go on, to get it all out, forced him to face it. He'd gotten this far, he might as well tell her everything. Shifting away from her touch, he took a deep breath and went on. "It haunts me every time I close my eyes. I feel the rain on my skin. The weight of her body in my arms." His eyes flickered to Mila's, taking in her shocked expression before letting his gaze fall to his lap. "No one helped us. She was dying but no one stopped to ask. The doctor next door refused to even look at her. They laughed, they fucking laughed, they watched her die and they laughed."

Tears welled in Mila's eyes.

"I dug her grave in the backyard." Darek's voice grew distant as the memories pulled him under. For a moment he was there, watching the rain fill the hole and slipping in the mud. The pain was as clear as it had been then, but he didn't try to stop it. It never worked. He couldn't hide from the memories any more than he could change the past. The only thing he could do was turn the pain into anger. It was what he'd always done. It kept him alive as he went through the worst days of his life.

"I never tried to fight the power, I welcomed it. I used it for revenge and I'll never stop using it. They deserve to die. They all do!"

"Hey." Mila's hands on his cheeks slowly brought him back to the room. "Relax," she soothed. Not until he saw his clawed hands, did he understand he transformed without even knowing it. Darek stared down at the deep red talons

135

and wished them away. He once wanted to be a beast, to slaughter every single person who ridiculed him over the years. And he was. The revenge was fiery hot, and it was the best thing he'd ever done. He left the small town in ruins, and every single worm that crawled along the streets of the hellhole he'd grown up in, had deserved *exactly* what they got.

But now, under Mila's soft touch, he wanted to be normal. He wanted to touch her without tearing her skin open. He wanted to hold her, without sinking his claws deep into her flesh. He wanted to be gentle. For her.

"It's burning me alive, Mila," he rasped. "The fire, I can't control it. I'm filled with so much anger and vengeance, it's the only thing I think of. I no longer know where I end and the devil begins."

She stroked his face, his hair, and horns, with each caress calming the inner turmoil until his body stopped trembling and he could breathe cool air into his overheated lungs.

"Don't stop," he whispered. "Just give me this moment to breathe."

For a brief moment, she stared at him, then she threw her arms around him.

"I'll never stop," she murmured. "Everything will be okay."

For a moment, Darek dared to believe her. A brief moment of calm was enough for him to relax in her embrace as she stroked the pain away in a never-ending caress.

When she finally pulled away, Darek knew with certainty. He was meant to find her.

"I can't let you go."

She raised an eyebrow. "I've heard that before."

"Mila—"

She silenced him with a finger to his lips. "I'm not going anywhere."

Darek opened his mouth to protest but closed it again as her words slowly registered. "You—you're not?"

Mila smiled. "I hated you with a passion," she admitted. "Then I saw the man behind the devil." She placed a hand over his heart. "I saw you."

A soft breath slipped past Darek's lips. "Can I touch you now?"

Mila's sudden laugh made him scoff. "Please?" He added in a dry tone.

"No."

"No?"

"I said I'll stay. It doesn't mean I'm ready to sleep with the devil."

"What can I do to change your mind?"

"You can start by removing those claws." Her eyes traveled from his hands, up to his body, and across his face. She reached out, brushing a finger along a horn. "And as sexy as you look in these..." She shifted closer, curling her hand around the bone, running it along its smooth surface until Darek thought he'd lose his mind.

"Stop!" he snarled. "Stop taunting me."

Mila sat back, giving him a sharp look. "You have to work on that."

"What did you expect?"

Mila rolled her eyes. "I didn't know they were connected to your dick."

"Hmph." Darek snatched a pillow, placing it in his lap with a huff. "They're not," he muttered. "You are," his voice dipped into a husky growl, "Every time you touch me I ache for you."

Mila let out a breath, cleared her throat, and looked down at her hands as heat spread across her cheeks.

"What?" Darek arched a brow. "Play with fire and you'll get burned."

DAREK

CHAPTER 24

Why was she holding back? She wanted him like he wanted her. She had no way of hiding, and he wasn't blind. But he made her a promise and he'd stick to it. She had to be the one to make the first move. He wanted to hear her beg. He would wait, even if her mere proximity drove him crazy. Everything about her was drawing him in. She was pure temptation. Every time he looked at her he'd have to stop himself from touching her, and by the looks of her, she was fighting the same battle.

"I need to see Kate and Riley." She shot the bedroom door a look as if contemplating if she could make a run for it. Darek smirked. She was smart, she knew he'd never let her leave alone after what happened.

"The dogs are placed in temporary homes, but there's paperwork, and a million things we have to do."

"Hmph."

Mila's gaze drifted back to Darek. "What's up with that *hmph*?"

"About them..." Darek looked down at his hands, still clutching the pillow. "They might've seen... me. In my full glory."

The confusion that flashed across Mila's face was short-lived. Her eyes grew wide and the curse she intended came out as nothing but a wince.

"What were you thinking?"

"Your blood on that piece of paper... I lost it."

Mila nodded. She didn't even look surprised. Was that a good or a bad sign?

"How did they..." Her voice trailed off.

"I didn't stay to comfort them." Darek snorted. "Hell if I care, they could—"

Mila's glare cut him off. "You have to work on your people skills."

Darek huffed. "I don't like people."

"You like *me*."

"You're... different."

Mila rolled her eyes, then sighed, brushing a hand over his. "I get it. You've had a horrible experience with people. But not everyone is like that. There are good people too, people who care."

Darek scowled. He didn't even *want* to believe her. Why should he care?

"Let me prove you wrong. Starting with my friends."

"I don't give a f—"

Mila silenced him with a finger to his lips. "Come with me," she said. "We'll do this the right way."

"They'll run at the sight of me."

"Then I'll go alone. Your choice." She got to her feet, searched through the closet for anything to wear. Coming up with black slacks and a black and white checkered sweater, she pulled it on and headed for the door.

"Coming?"

Darek exited the bedroom in time to see her shrug on her red coat, and then zipped up a pair of knee-high heels. She straightened, eyeing his black leather trousers, and cleared her throat. Avoiding looking at him, she gestured toward his bare chest.

"You're not meeting my friends like that."

Darek huffed but went back into the room. The next time he emerged, he wore the just as black shirt, buttoned only halfway up. It wouldn't stay on long anyway.

"And those wings stay inside," Mila warned, reading his mind. "No more shirtless in public."

Darek chuckled, promising something he couldn't keep. "I'll do my best."

Mila drove, and Darek didn't mind. He wouldn't have had the patience to stick to the road rules anyway, and the last thing he wanted was her nagging. Her eyes flicked between the road and Darek, and he willed his body to relax. But the tension refused to leave his shoulders as he sat stiffly next to her and tried to pretend her friends would accept him, even though it was obvious they wouldn't. He'd stopped caring. There had been a time when all he wanted was to have friends. Now, all he wanted was to break the necks of everyone who even tried to come near him, and he was more than happy with the transition. Friends were for kids, for pussies. He was neither. He was the devil, for fucks's sake. He didn't need to fit in, why should he? When he was made to stand out?

A soft gasp from Mila snapped him back to the car, and as he followed her gaze, he caught a shadow slipping around the corner of the opposite building. Darek's eyes narrowed. Judging by Mila's sudden tension, she was scared. Was she right to be afraid? Were there more of them out there?

— * —

Mila gripped Darek's hand tight to keep him from backing away as they waited outside of her friend's apartment door. They lived on the first floor, so the climb up the stairs was nothing, still, Darek's pulse hammered in his temples as if he'd taken the full seven floors to the top. His hand clutched in Mila's trembled with the tension of pretending he wasn't ready to burst even before stepping into the anticipated torture chamber. Darek didn't do people. He didn't do visits with friends. He never had, and he was certain he never would.

Staring at the brown door, he jumped back as it swung open. Waiting for the reaction, he tensed further, wanting nothing more badly than to leave, but forced himself to stay. Mila squeezed his hand, but her comfort was of no use as Kate let out a shriek and flung the door shut just as fast. The next time it opened, it revealed a pale Riley. His Adam's apple bobbed as he tried to swallow down the fear.

"Mila?" he asked, shooting Darek pointed looks. "What's—"

"It's okay!" Mila was quick to say. "He's with me, he's..." She threw Darek a look, suddenly lost for words.

Darek scowled at her. What had she been about to say? *He's a good guy? He's not dangerous? He won't bite?* He was, and he would, and Mila knew it just as well as her friends did, so why did she even try?

"I need to talk to you, *alone*," Riley hissed.

"I know what you saw. I know what he is."

Riley gaped.

"It's okay."

Mila talked to him like she'd talk to a scared dog, and Darek was sure Riley knew. Somehow it made him enjoy the exchange a little more than he should.

"Darek won't hurt you or Kate. Can we come in now?"

Darek smirked. Wouldn't he? How could she be so sure? The only one he'd never hurt—was her. Those people she called friends, he wasn't as sure.

Riley visibly shook himself out of his head. Blinking at Mila, he finally dared to shoot Darek a new look.

"He saved my life," Mila added. "Please, give him a chance, for me?"

Riley muttered under his breath, then held up a hand before disappearing into the apartment.

"They're scared," Mila said.

"They should be," Darek growled, glaring at the door. "They're all the same."

Mila opened her mouth to protest but closed it again

141

as Riley appeared in the doorway. His face was stiff and his voice clipped as he addressed Darek. "Don't make me regret this."

He pushed the door open, stepped aside as Mila entered, dragging Darek by the hand.

Sitting on their oversized couch, Darek watched as Mila scratched Kate's Jack Russell dog, who she'd named Jack, while desperately wishing himself away. He knew it would be awkward, but this was worse than even he could have predicted. The silence was palatable, the air so thick he could've cut it with a knife.

Mila studied her friends, visibly cringing as they stared openly at Darek. He refused to acknowledge them, to even look at them and kept his eyes on Mila. She was the reason he did this, she was the reason he took this torture, he might as well enjoy the view while he suffered. Despite his best effort to remain calm, heat radiated off him. He burned under the pressure, and for a moment he wasn't sure if it was because of *them*, or because of the way he imagined Mila without clothes….

Darek's muscles quivered under his shirt, his skin crawling with sweat. The sound of that goddamn dog growling deep in his throat was too loud in the pressing silence. Darek shot him a glance. He was perched in Mila's lap, eyes locked on Darek. The fur on his back stood on end, and his tail twitched stiffly. Mila scratched his neck, soothing his fear while her other hand landed on Darek's thigh. He tensed further, the soft intake of breath echoing through the silence.

"Oh, for God's sake!" Mila's sudden shout made everyone jump. "He's the devil, there, I said it. Can we behave like normal human beings now?"

Kate let out a sharp laugh, teetering on the verge of hysterics.

"Ha, devil, of course!" She shot to her feet, making Jack rush up too. He jumped to the floor and started to bark.

"See!" Kate flew her hand toward the dog. "Even the dog doesn't want him here!"

"Kate!" Mila snapped.

"NO!" Kate shrieked. "You can't do this, you can't bring the fucking devil into my home and expect me to be cool with it!"

"Kate—"

"I saw it, wings, horns, a fucking tail!" Kate snatched the pepper spray off the table, aiming at Darek. "He's a monster, I want him outta here!"

Something in Darek snapped. "You—" He shot to his feet. Claws tore through his fingers as he reached for Kate.

Her shriek echoed in the room, and before Darek knew what happened, a sudden burning pain in his eyes made him stagger back, crying out as he clawed at his face in an attempt to escape the burning heat.

Panic coursed through his system. He couldn't see, and the sudden loss of control tipped him over the edge. He screamed as his wings burst through the shirt in a gust of hot air that sent items flying into the walls. The dog barked hysterically, and Kate shrieked just as bad.

When flames appeared in Darek's hands, Mila flew up, throwing herself at him before he had a chance to act on his impulses.

He felt her hands, her body, and managed to reign the flames in. He stood, shaking with rage as her hands gripped him tight. Darek focused on them, letting them hold him together when all he wanted was to fall apart. To destroy the horrible human who attacked him, to tear her head off for even daring to—

"Listen to me!" Mila demanded. "Darek!" Mila cupped his face, forcing him to be still, to relax. "It's okay, everything will be okay."

143

DAREK

CHAPTER 25

Darek burned. His eyes were on fire and his throat seemed to be closing up. Clinging to Mila's soothing voice, he tried not to panic, to hold onto the last string of control and not torch the place in pure rage.

"You gotta rinse the eyes." Mila's hands were on his cheeks, holding his face to study it. "Come." Her hand closed around his, tugging at him, pulling him into motion. Darek let her lead him, blinded by the heat that made him want to rip his eyes out to escape the sensation. He'd never been affected by fire. Was this how it felt like to burn? If he didn't know better, he would've sworn his skin was ablaze.

The relief of cold water was short-lived, and as the burning flared up again, Darek thought he'd lose his mind. He wanted to kill someone, to unleash his power, and watch everything crumble around him. He wanted them to pay for what they'd done.

"I'm so sorry," Mila whispered.

Something cold and wet pressed against his face. "I can't believe she did that."

Darek let out a shuddering breath, leaning into the touch and the relief. Whatever she did to him felt good. At the moment, all he could focus on was to breathe, to keep from lashing out and destroying everything around him. The bitch deserved it. How he ached to murder her and the yapping beast into silence.

"Is it better?"

Darek managed a short nod.

"Wait here, sit." Mila pushed him down to the floor, pressed something into his hand, and told him to hold it against his face. Darek was too shaken to do anything else but to obey.

Squinting through swollen eyes, he saw Mila leave, then he bowed his face into the damp towel, listening to her voice from the other room.

"What the hell was that?" Mila shouted. "Have you lost your mind?"

"Me?" Kate yelled back. "*He* was going to attack me!"

"You insulted him, you *hurt* him!"

"He's the fucking DEVIL!"

"He's half human!" Mila snapped. "He's a good person."

"Hah! He's not a person, Mila, he's a monster. How could you bring that—*THING* here?"

"Girls! That's enough!"

The shouting match abruptly stopped, then Kate's harsh voice. "You're taking his side?"

"No," Riley said. "But he's with Mila. That ought to mean something."

"It means she has lost her mind!"

The yelling was back.

"You're fucking him? The devil? That's what this is about? Is he that good in bed that you've—"

The sound of a sharp slap of a palm against skin reached all the way to the bathroom, and Darek couldn't help but smirk.

"You bitch!" Kate shrieked. "You—"

"STOP!" Riley's voice boomed, again spreading a silence through the apartment. "You've both lost your minds."

"I wanted to give him a chance." Mila's voice was cold. "I wanted him to see there are good people in this world. People who won't hurt him."

Darek sagged against the wall, folding his wings as a shield around him. She'd been wrong, and he'd known it. There were no good people, not in *his* world. Her attempt to prove him wrong instead proved him right. Added to his hatred, and his belief.

Hearing her footsteps approach, Darek lowered the towel, forcing his devil features to withdraw. Squinting up at her through bloodshot eyes, he read the disappointment on her face. Her anger.

"I told you," he rasped.

She dropped to her knees in front of him, pulling him into a hug. "I'm sorry."

Darek allowed himself to relax in her arms, a brief moment of calm. Then he pulled away. He had enough humiliation in one day.

"I'll wait outside." Without awaiting her reply, he shot to his feet, threw the torn shirt to the floor, and left the room. Crossing the floor in the sitting area, Kate and Riley's eyes were on him, following his every move. Darek threw her a look, flashing red eyes in a threatening glare. Kate staggered back with a gasp, bumping into Mila who chased after Darek.

"Mila."

Riley's voice made him pause by the door. Mila caught up, stopping next to him, one hand on his arm.

"Stay, we'll sort this out."

Darek scoffed, threw them a cold look over his shoulder before yanking the door open. His eyes landed on Kate and narrowed. "I'll show you what a devil I can be when you least expect it."

"That's not helping." Mila's hand on his back forced him into motion. "Don't threaten my friends."

"She—"

"No," Mila said. "If you look at her like that again," she

lowered her voice so only Darek heard her, "you'll never touch this body."

"Hmph."

"No hmph," Mila snapped. "I mean it. As much as I hate her right now, she's my friend."

"Fine," Darek muttered. "I won't kill your friend."

"Good boy." Mila shoved him through the door, slammed it shut before leaning back against it. She looked up at Darek, letting a whining sound slip past her lips. "What am I supposed to do with you?"

Darek looked away as a strange sense of guilt filled him. Even though he had done nothing wrong, he couldn't help but wish for a better outcome. She'd been so eager for him and her friends to get along. It would never happen. Sinking onto the top step, he leaned his head back against the brick wall and allowed the cooler air to soothe his skin.

Mila held out a hand, "Let's go home."

— * —

For a moment, Darek started to doubt everything. Why was he even here? Looking around Mila's tidy living room, he felt like an intruder. It wasn't his home. Everything in this room was hers. The light blue walls and the teal curtains which once soothed him now closed in on him. The black and white striped rug under his feet and the black couch he sat on weren't his to use. It was all hers, and what was he to her? Was he nothing but a stray dog to her, something she thought she could save with a little care and affection? Something damaged she'd taken pity on? An experiment? Was he even welcome here?

Darek looked down at his lap with a sigh. Fresh from a shower, the burning sensation was long gone, and the swelling too. But even though his body was back to its perfect shape, his inner world was far from fine. He hated to admit it, but he'd hoped, too. Taken Mila's words as some sort of truth, he'd dared to believe her friends would treat him like one of them.

Sitting there now, in one of her brother's old T-shirts

147

and boxers which were too tight for him, he had to face the truth. It would never happen. He accepted it long ago, suffered through childhood and teenage years as a victim. He refused to be like that again. He refused to go back there. But once the mental slideshow began, he had no way of escaping the memories.

Darek didn't hear a word of what the teacher said. Clutching the chair, he tried to breathe through the pain and ignore the warm blood trickling down his body. He learned to wear black, to hide the red underneath. It seeped into his trousers, and Darek knew it was a matter of time before it'd drip onto the floor, exposing him to the teacher and the class.

"Rewera! Attention!" The teacher's harsh voice forced him to look up. "You've had enough warnings. Do you want to be suspended?"

Darek gulped, shrinking under the man's cold stare and stern face. He wanted nothing more, but the torture he had to live through in school was nothing to what was waiting at home.

"No, sir."

The teacher wrinkled his nose, eyeing Darek's soaked shirt with disgust. Darek's eyes met his, silently pleading with him for the help no one was willing to offer. Everyone knew of the hell he lived in. They knew why he sometimes didn't show up in class. They knew why he couldn't sit down for weeks and why he refused to take off his shirt in public. They knew why he cried in the school toilets and why he walked too slow when he came out. They knew it all, they just chose to ignore it. And so did the teacher who turned on his heels and left without a word.

The silent snickers and the pointy looks of dozens of eyes made him tremble in his seat. They'd seen the scars he tried to hide, ripped off his clothes in the locker room, and beat him until the lashes from the morning bled.

All Darek ever wanted was to fit in, to have someone to call a friend, to be seen as something more than the child of Satan. He learned the hard way—it would never happen.

People were cruel.

Dreams of a different life were the only things that kept him alive. Useless dreams of courage to stick up for himself, of running away. That's all it was—fantasies. Where would he run when the whole town hated him? He wasn't brave enough to survive on his own. He was nothing. A nobody. And as he clung to consciousness on an old wooden chair, surrounded by people who despised him, he was sure he'd die like one, too.

Mila sat down next to him, placing a hand on his arm. "What happened there?"

Darek blinked her into focus, stuck somewhere between past and present.

"You're not so tough, are you?" she mused. "Deep inside you're just as insecure as the rest of us."

Darek scoffed, refusing to admit to her being right.

"There's more, isn't there? Why do you hate people so much?" Her hand ran along his arm, up to his shoulder, before snaking across his back to pull him closer to her.

"Tell me?"

He tensed from the touch, his breath hitching. Forcing himself to be still, he sat, clinging to the present while his mind tugged him back to the past.

"Hey, Scarface!" The group of teens laughed as Darek couldn't hide the shame. Every time the nickname was thrown at him, he wanted to sink through a hole and never emerge. All the marks on his body had been hidden under clothes. Now he couldn't hide. He couldn't go anywhere without being stared at, whispered about, pointed at. The three lines slashed across his face still stung, stretching and itching every time he moved. Darek wanted to cry, but he learned long ago tears only made it worse. The little hope he had of ever getting out of this town and starting over somewhere where no one knew who he was had died with one slash of his father's clawed hand. His dreams, torn apart along with his flesh as his old man left him biting back the pain and clutching his bleeding face in horror.

Mila's voice brought him back again, and when his eyes shot to her, seeing her study his face, he turned his head away.

Her soft fingers landed on his arm. "Darek," she prompted. "I need to know you, I need to understand you. Don't shut me out."

He let out a quick breath, shaking his head. He couldn't tell her. Where would he even begin? It was too much.

"Hey," she murmured. "It's okay, I'm on your side."

Darek swallowed down the sudden emotion in his throat. She knew exactly what she was doing, he had to hand it to her, she was smart.

"Mila—" He wanted to protest, but she'd broken his resolve, crushed the walls he'd built around his heart, and against his better judgment, Darek felt himself opening up to her.

"Before the devil, I uh—I was weak. A coward. I didn't have the strength to do anything—" Darek's voice broke and it took too long until he managed to gather enough courage to go on. "At the time all I wanted was to have friends and be a normal kid. Instead, I was the punchbag, the pariah, the fucking scapegoat. School was hell, home was worse, anywhere I went—it never ended."

Her arms were back around him, hugging him tight, and this time he didn't fight it.

"Oh, my love," she whispered. "I'm so sorry. It all makes sense now."

DAREK

CHAPTER 26

Darek cursed himself. Why had he said those things? How could he be so dumb? It was personal, and most of all, it was the past. And it should've stayed there, untouched and forgotten. She brought it all back. He should hate her for it, but he only hated himself. He'd been weak. He'd been useless, just like his father said he was.

"Hey," Mila murmured. "I'm sorry about—"

"I don't want to talk about it." He couldn't think of her friends now. He couldn't be weak. He refused to be a pathetic man who cried over his past. It was done. It was over.

"Darek."

"Just leave it."

"You don't have to be ashamed. Kids get bullied all the time, it's—"

"Just stop!" he snapped. "Okay? Fucking stop!"

151

Mila flinched, then pursed her lips and nodded.

"I'm sorry. I-I don't want to think about *that* now," he added in a softer tone, trying to smooth over his mistake.

She studied him, then a small smile crept onto her lips. "What do you want to think of then?"

"This." His hand reached out, tucking a strand of dark hair behind her ear, then letting it linger on her cheek. "I want to think of you."

Mila stared at him, momentarily caught off guard by his bold move, then the smile returned. She caught his hand, placing it over her heart.

"Touch me now," she whispered. "I'm yours."

A soft gasp slipped from his lips, and as Mila looked up, catching the stunned surprise on his face, she couldn't help but grin.

Darek hadn't expected her to give in so fast, but he didn't need to be told twice. Throwing all caution to the wind, he grabbed her, pulling her onto his lap, and held her in place with a firm hand on her back while the other raked through her hair.

His body responded in an instant, and as she tugged at his shirt, he released her long enough to pull it off along with hers. His hands landed on her skin, burning her with the heat and making her tremble for more. He'd waited for too long, held back until he couldn't. The urgency in his touches, the hunger for her body blew his mind. He couldn't care less about going slow, about worries and insecurities. He couldn't even think at all. He needed her, needed to feel all of her, to claim her as his.

"Darek?" she gasped.

"I can't stop now," he hissed. How could he walk away when his whole body ached for her? When he was already throbbing from the pressure of her sexy ass rubbing against him.

"I don't want you to," she breathed. "I want you."

A deep growl against her neck was the only reply she got, but it was more than enough. He couldn't focus on words, all he could focus on was her. His body vibrated with heat, burning for her as she pressed herself against his front. She slid a hand down his body, and Darek tensed in anticipation of the touch. His hand closed into a fist in her hair, guiding her mouth to his and muting his groans against her lips. When her hand slid under the hem of the boxers, he stopped her, removing her hand.

His name rolled off her lips, a throaty moan that made him wish for her to say it again. Then, he grabbed her, hoisted her up with his hands under her ass as he stood. Mila clung to him, wrapping legs around his waist as he carried her to the bedroom.

He lowered her onto the bed, unzipped her trousers, and pulled them down her legs along with her underwear. Staring down at her naked body as she propped herself up on her elbows to watch him, he peeled the boxers off.

Then he was on top of her. Mila reached for him, but he grabbed her hands, pinning them above her head as he leaned in to growl against her lips.

"Are you sure?"

She could only nod, then she stilled, locking her gaze on his as he sunk into her. Darek's low groan mixed with her cry as he stretched her to her limit.

"Fuck, Mila," he rasped. "You're so tight."

He held still, allowing her to adjust to his size while his gaze cast a red glow on her milky skin.

"Darek." Her hips bucked against him, drawing one more groan from his lips. Mila tugged at her hands. He tightened the grip, pinning her to the mattress as he fought for the control that slipped further away with each wiggle of her hips.

"I promised you I'd be gentle," he rasped. He was holding on to the last straw of control, body quivering from held back desire. He wanted everything but gentle. He wanted—

"Don't hold back," she breathed. "I won't break."

A grin spread across his lips as she bucked her hips against him, proving her point.

Darek allowed himself to let go, clinging to her wrists tight enough to leave bruises as the pleasure exploded in his body and his breaths turned into gasps for air. She moved with him, using her body to drive him crazy as she urged him to go faster, pushing him deeper with each thrust until Darek cried out loud and Mila's moans turned into screams. Her head rolled back and her body arched into his with a force that made the fire explode within him. Darek let go of her hands, digging his claws into the sheets as his body shook with the last of energy pulsating through him. Mila's arms wrapped around him, nails digging into his back as she pulled him close enough to feel every ripple and shudder as his body collapsed over hers.

It wasn't until he felt his wings slack, falling over them like a shield, that he realized he transformed into his devil-form. Groaning, he dropped his head forward, horns pointed to either side of Mila's face as he let out a shuddering breath.

She raised a hand, running trembling fingers along a horn. "I'd lie if I said this isn't sexy," she whispered.

Darek shuddered under her touch, but remained still, letting her hand explore. He'd gotten used to the things a normal human had never seen. The horns were just there, an extension of his bone structure, as normal as fingers and toes. They were smooth, warm, and even though he didn't particularly feel her touch on the bone itself, knowing what she did was enough to make him burn under her caress. She stroked the goddamn horn as if it was his dick until he trembled under her touch and she pulled away.

"Are you trying for another round?" his voice came out as nothing but a hoarse rasp, but he couldn't care less. What she did to him, no one else had. He was crazy for this woman and he couldn't deny it. He lifted his head, looking down at her flustered cheeks.

A grin spread across her lips. "Is it working?"

Darek's low chuckle made her falter. "Go on," he urged. "Try me."

His lips curled into a smile. She was...cute. Her white skin pink from heat, and her dark eyes twinkling as she gazed back up at him. Darek's lips parted in awe. She was the most beautiful thing he'd ever seen. And she was his. Overwhelmed by desire, he hadn't even taken the time to kiss her, to touch her, to explore every inch of her body.

"What are you thinking?" she whispered.

Darek wanted to tell her everything on his mind, he wanted to shower her with his adoration. But he didn't have the words. He couldn't even understand the feelings inside of him, let alone explain them to her.

"I can't find the words," he admitted. "What you're doing to me—"

Mila's face softened, and the hand which had played with the horn came to rest on his cheek.

"Let me love you," she murmured. "Let me up."

The moment of confusion froze Darek into stunned stillness. Mila took the opportunity to slide out from under him, sitting next to him as he rolled over to his back.

"Why don't you let me touch you?" She trailed a finger along his jaw as she spoke. "You pin my hands so I can't reach you, what are you afraid of?"

Darek gulped. She figured it out. Shifting away to sit, he shielded his body with a wing, suddenly feeling naked under her gaze.

"Don't," Mila stroked the leathery material of the wing before removing her hand. "Tuck them away."

Darek huffed, not sure whether to feel annoyed or turned on. She was brave, he had to hand it to her. Her unflinching ways pulled him in, right from the start, and how she kept demanding things from him was something he never allowed from anyone else.

Her hand trailed up his thigh, slid under the cover of the wing, and paused. She raised an eyebrow. "You want more?"

"I always want you."

Mila snatched her hand back, gestured toward the wings. "Remove them."

Darek did as she said, but not without a frustrated growl. Mila pushed him back until he was leaning back against the headboard, and watched him for a long time, letting her eyes roam over his body until Darek trembled under her gaze.

When she finally touched him, he had to grip the sheets to avoid flinching or grabbing her hands. Her soft touch drove him wild, but also made him feel vulnerable. He'd walked the streets shirtless, but never had he felt as naked as he did now. The way she looked at him, her eyes so full of compassion and lust, blew his mind. Darek didn't know what to do with the feeling. She didn't just see his skin, she saw his soul, and he was sure she wouldn't like what she saw. He wanted to give himself to her, fully. But to let go of the control... he wasn't sure he could do it. It was all he had.

She ran gentle fingers along the thickest line sliced across his chest. The jagged scar which his eyes always drifted to when he saw his reflection. It was the last one, the worst one. It had nearly cut him in two, torn open his flesh, and created a permanent reminder of the day he'd wished to forget.

"Stop!" He grabbed Mila's hand, removing it from his body. "I can't do this." His hand trembled as it held hers, and the grip he intended to keep her away loosened as his hand fell away. He couldn't stop her, but he couldn't stand the feeling of disgust that crept up on him, either. He was not worth touching with such tenderness. He was not even worth looking at like that. He was damaged goods, carved up like an old cutting board.

Disgusting. Ugly. Freak.

The words from his past echoed in his head. He'd heard them repeated to him everywhere he went. They were ingrained in his soul.

"I wouldn't even touch that if someone paid me to."

Darek looked away. He couldn't stand the pity in her eyes. He didn't need that, it would only make it worse.

"Did you fall under a lawnmower?"

Their laughter echoed in his head, making his throat tighten with held-back emotion.

"Maybe he likes it? Wanna try?" The unmistakable sound of a whip whistled in the air. Darek barely had time to see a riding-whip in one of the boy's hands before they attacked him. Kicks and punches to his stomach made him double over as his breath was knocked right out of his lungs. He couldn't breathe, all he could do was clutch his stomach and gasp for the air that refused to enter. A stinging pain

across his back made him lose his balance and before he knew it, he was on the floor. Terror cut through the pain.

Don't fall.

Don't lie down.

Get up.

Get up, get up! Darek tried, but his body didn't obey. And as the crowd cheered on the boy beating him, the taste of blood filled his mouth and the pressure of tears stung his eyes.

"What's going on here?" A stern female voice cut through the air, and everything stilled.

The boy's voice. "Miss, he was trying to attack us, we had to defend ourselves."

"Attack?"

A girl's voice cut in, "It's true. He's that freak from the—"

"I know who he is. You're late for class, get out of here."

The crowd scattered, leaving Darek trembling on the floor.

"You too, get up."

Darek swallowed down the bile in his throat and tried not to vomit or cry as he struggled to his feet. His back burned from the open wounds, and he couldn't stand straight.

Darek looked at the blood smeared across the floor, to his shirt which was just as red as it lay tossed aside. Glancing up at the teacher's tall frame, he dared to whisper, "I didn't do anything, please... help me?"

The teacher stared at him for so long a small spark of hope ignited in Darek's heart. She scratched her neck, adjusted a scarf, and finally brushed the hand through her gray chin-long bob.

"Clean that mess up. You have ten minutes."

With those words, she turned on her heels, and before she left, she threw over her shoulder, "Put some clothes on before someone sees you!"

"Darek?"

Mila's voice slowly brought him back to the present. He blinked her into focus, seeing her worried eyes as she searched his face for any clues of what he'd been thinking.

Her hand caught his chin as he tried to look away.

"You're beautiful," she whispered. "You're perfect the way you are."

Darek scoffed but couldn't bring himself to argue.

When she kissed him, the pain of the memory dispersed like a cloud, giving room for different feelings. Her soft lips, like a balm to an open wound stilled the fear, eased the pain, rekindling the flame until he burned for her all over again. Darek breathed in her jasmine scent and braced himself for what he was about to do.

"Do it," he gasped onto her lips. "Make me forget."

She pulled away long enough to look at him. Then her hands were back, caressing his face, his neck, down his arms, and back up his chest until Darek didn't know if he was trembling from fear or lust.

Mila paused for a moment, her hands flat on his chest, and her lips inches from his. "If you want me to stop, I will," she said. "You just have to say the word. You're in control."

Darek huffed, half amused, half terrified. She knew him too well and it scared him. She'd figured him out, knew exactly which buttons to push and she pushed them well.

She knew he'd never be able to turn down her touch, not when he was already aching for her. Leaning his head back, Darek prepared for the onslaught of emotion. Bring it on. He could handle it, he'd handled everything else thrown at him. What were a few soft touches of a woman he loved—The word he hadn't intended to think, stunned him. He didn't *love*. It was ridiculous. It was lust, it was sex, it was—

Mila's lips trailing kisses down his jawline drew a moan from his lips. Tilting his head back, he gave her full access. He couldn't do anything else. It felt too good. He'd never been touched that way, never been treated with delicacy, and once he got the taste of it, he never wanted her to stop.

Mila went deliberately slow, teasing her lips and hands down his body until Darek thought he'd lose his mind. He wanted to grab her, to satisfy the burning desire within him. But as his hands reached for her, she slapped them away.

"Patience, my love."

She trailed a fingernail down his stomach, following the veins further down, and deliberately avoided his erection until he couldn't take it.

"Mila—"

She kissed the way up his thigh, closing a hand around him before replacing it with her mouth.

Darek cried out from the sudden feeling. Throwing his head back, he gripped the sheets as he breathed through the overwhelming waves of pleasure rolling over him. She took her time, teasing and working her magic until claws grew from his hands from the effort of holding back. Her perfect rhythm and pressure pushed him right off the edge, and as he tried not to scream, he didn't regret letting her get close to him for a second.

Darek's head spun as he gazed at her through heavy eyelids. To say he was exhausted was an understatement. "Fucking hell," he groaned. "What are you doing to me?"

She crawled up his body, straddling his hips. "That was just foreplay," she licked her lips, hovering them above his.

"You expect me to go again?"

"I do."

"Give me a break," he groaned.

Mila raised an eyebrow. "The big bad devil saying no to sex?"

"Hmph." Darek shifted, flipping her off him. Pinning her to her back, he growled into her ear, "I never said no."

DAREK

CHAPTER 27

"What do you see in me?" Darek asked the question while staring up at the ceiling. The mattress moved as Mila shifted beside him, the rustle of sheets giving her away before her arm slung across his stomach.

"What kind of question is that?" Her fingers traced the ups and down of his abs, and Darek was torn between removing her hand or enjoying the touch. The mere contact left goosebumps on his skin, and as his muscles rippled under her fingers, she chuckled, but let her hand rest. Darek gulped, knowing if she'd do that a few more seconds, he'd be ready for a round four. It didn't matter he was exhausted, his body had no limit when it came to her.

"Answer it," he reminded her.

Mila rolled over to her back, remaining silent for a moment before speaking. "You're more than wings and horns," she said. "I see a man who's been through hell but came out stronger. I see... you."

Darek rolled his head to look at her. "You think I can be more than the devil?"

Her eyes met his. "You already are. I believe in you. You can be anything you want."

Darek had to look away. "I'm not a good person." It was the truth. Hell, he was not even a person. And he sure as hell never cared about being good. Darek scoffed at the absurdity. She'd done things to him, set him on a course which he'd never have taken if he hadn't crashed into her that night.

"Why are you with me?"

He asked the question that burned within him. The doubt ate away at him every time he looked at her. She'd hated him, and somehow that made more sense. It was what people did. But here they were, cuddling in her bed with nothing but a thin blanket covering their naked bodies. Darek never believed in fairytales, but this sure felt like one.

"Why these sudden—"

"Please, just answer it," he cut her off. He needed an answer, and he needed it now before he lost the courage to hear it. Did she pity him? Was that it? Did she see him as one of her rescue dogs? Was he nothing but something broken she'd taken upon herself to put together?

Her extended silence added to his fears. Why had she even taken him in? She invited him into her apartment. She went from hating him, from wanting him to die—to sharing her home with him.

"You see *me*," she finally said, cutting off his train of thought. "You make me feel like I matter, like I'm... beautiful."

Darek couldn't stop the soft breath that slipped past his lips. "You're gorgeous," he whispered. "You're the most precious thing I've—" he cut himself off, clearing his throat. "Go on."

He caught a glimpse of Mila's smile in the corner of his eye.

"I have three brothers, one older and two younger. Peter

161

moved out, got married, had kids. I was left with the other two. It was always the same. *Mila, look out for your brothers. Mila, take care of your brothers, make sure they're safe…* who'd make sure I was safe?" She let out an annoyed huff. "They played boy games, never allowing the girl to join in. Even now, I'm the outsider in their family. We don't get along. I'm the one who never fit in, the one who was treated like their nagging mom instead of the sister."

Darek listened, lost for words. He never had a sibling, never had a family at all. His father sure as hell didn't count, and his mom… he refused to think of her, he couldn't—not without bringing pain back.

"I'm sorry," he whispered. It was all he could say.

"No," she sighed. "*I'm* sorry, I'm selfish. Here I'm complaining about my family when you—"

"I'm fine." Darek regretted the harsh tone the moment the words left his mouth. "Don't worry about me."

Mila fell silent. Her hand reached under the blanket to find his. Darek let her hold it, feeling some odd comfort from the gesture.

"I'm not telling you to get sympathy." Mila went on, "With you, I feel like I matter. Like I'm something more than the invisible sister who everyone took for granted. I feel safe with you."

"That's why you invited me?" he asked, and she let out a humming sound.

"You are a lot of things, terrifying, arrogant, and extremely annoying at times, but I realized one thing that night in the alley."

"Hmph."

Mila giggled.

"What did you realize? Other than how arrogant and annoying I am."

She hesitated for a moment, then whispered, "That you'd never hurt me. That you'd do anything to keep me safe. I needed that. To feel safe. To feel protected. To feel like I come first."

"You do," Darek squeezed her hand. "I'd do anything for you. I kill anyone who comes near you."

Mila rolled over, nuzzling her face into the crook of his neck. "I know."

For a few moments of alarm, Darek tensed. The whole thing suddenly felt too real. What she said—what he said. What he didn't say. He never stayed to cuddle after sex, he'd taken what he needed and left. He never even let the girl touch him, and there Mila was, snuggling up to him as if it was the most natural thing in the world, and he couldn't deny he liked it.

— * —

Darek woke to the sound of someone talking. Blinking into the dark, he tried to focus his sleepy brain enough to understand what had woken him. As his mind cleared, he heard Mila in the kitchen. Rolling to his side, he threw a glance at the clock. The bright green digits informed him it was only five in the morning. A frown settled on his forehead. Who the fuck called this early? Darek sat, brushed a hand through his hair to smooth it back as he contemplated the two options.

Going back to sleep—or eavesdropping. Knowing it was wrong, he decided for the latter, slipping out of the room without bothering with clothes.

As he stopped outside of the kitchen, close enough to hear her but not being seen, he tried to understand the one-sided conversation.

"Seriously!" Mila snapped. "You called me to—"

She gasped, then, "Oh, no! That's horrible, who'd kill a dog—wait, what? A threat to Kate?"

"No. You're wrong."

"When did this happen?"

She was silent, and Darek took the opportunity to rack his brain for an explanation. Who'd killed a dog? Which dog? And what did that bitch Kate have to do with it?

Mila spoke again, and her words made Darek's head jerk in the direction of her voice.

"Darek didn't do this."

He scoffed silently. At least she had the decency to defend

163

him against Kate.

"He was with me."

"I'm certain, he was right here, the whole night."

"Geez," Mila scoffed, and Darek didn't even want to know what the person on the other end had said. "Of course not. I'd never be with someone who's cruel to animals. What happened to Jack is horrible. But it's not Darek's fault. He'd never do such a thing."

Damn right he wouldn't. It was the bitch who Mila called a friend he wanted to break. Not the innocent creature that was stuck in her mercy.

"Scott?"

The mere sound of the name made Darek's hands curl into fists. Why was she talking about him? Why did that bastard's name even have any place in her heart?

"Be careful," Mila whispered. "No. Darek would never let anything happen to me."

The thought of Scott vanished as soon as it appeared, and the anger dispersed, filling his heart with a much warmer feeling. She trusted him, she trusted him to keep her safe, just as she said. Darek untangled his fists, rubbing a hand over his face, catching a few strands of hair that had fallen from his usual sleek style. Pushing them out of his forehead, he couldn't stop a smile from spreading across his lips as Mila's words lingered in his heart.

"He can protect you guys too, he's on our side."

Darek almost gave himself away by letting out a scoff. He'd gladly watch them burn and not lift a finger to help. Hell, he wouldn't mind being the one lighting the fire.

"Fine!" Mila snapped, making Darek suspect the son of a bitch refused the offer. Not that he cared, but he couldn't help but feel insulted, nonetheless.

"Suit yourself. You'd wish for his power when someone grabs Kate, or you."

Darek had to agree with her on that. They would. It didn't mean he'd ever lift a finger to waste his power on people who didn't give a shit about him.

The click as the phone slammed back into its holder made Darek tense. Preparing an excuse, he heard the sound of the coffee brewer, and relaxed. Turning to head back to the bedroom, Darek contemplated the phone call with an uneasy feeling settling in his gut. Were these the same people who'd taken Mila? The group of scumbags which he slaughtered? Were they still out there? Had they upped the game?

Thinking back to the conversation he heard in the basement, the confusion grew.

"Something's not right man, Boss pays us for snatching some chick?"

Boss. Who was the goddamn boss and how could he kill him? His thoughts were cut short by Mila's sudden scream. She called his name, and by the tone of her voice, she was alarmed.

Forgetting he was already halfway to the kitchen and it would be suspicious to appear within seconds, he spun on his heels and found her staring out the window.

Darek grabbed her shoulders, spinning her to face him. "What's wrong?"

"There's someone outside," Mila breathed. "He looked straight at me."

Darek's eyes darted to the window, but he never let go of Mila. "I'll kill them," he growled. "I'll burn the whole fucking city to the ground if I have to."

He had enough. Someone was playing games with him, and he hated it. The longer it went on, the more out of control he felt. It needed to stop. People needed to die.

"Who did you talk to?"

Mila's eyes narrowed. "How did *you* know?"

Darek chuckled. "I'm not deaf, you woke me up."

She pursed her lips but nodded. "Riley. Someone killed Kate's dog. Left a note, saying *'you're next'*. She's terrified."

Darek couldn't help himself. "Serves her right."

Mila shook his hands off of her, stepping away with a scowl. "How can you say that?"

"It's not that hard," Darek muttered. "That B—" he cut himself off before giving Mila a fake smile. She shook her head but surprised Darek by letting it go.

"Tell me everything," he demanded. He needed to know

what they were up against. Some idiot killing dogs didn't seem dangerous, but Darek had a feeling it was more to it than that. It wasn't about the dog, it had just been a pawn. A diversion. Darek was sure of it. It was about him.

Mila sighed and went to sit at the table, throwing occasional glances out the window as she spoke, retelling the phone call in detail.

When she was done, she fell silent, and Darek took the opportunity to process her words. He couldn't help but enjoy the thought of that horrible woman's fear. He didn't care if she was Mila's friend. She had quickly proven to be just like everyone else. Darek wasn't the type to forgive and forget. He held grudges, he believed in an eye for an eye. Kate was no exception.

The dog though, annoying as it was, had never done anything to him. No animal had. He didn't have anything against them, he'd just never gotten the chance to connect with one, given the fact *they* hated him.

"I didn't do this," he said before Mila could jump to the wrong conclusions. She was fast to do so, and Darek knew how it looked. He had threatened Kate, and he'd meant every word. He'd more than willingly strap her to a wall and twist her neck. The only thing holding him back was Mila. He promised her, and he never broke a promise.

He'd have no reason to strangle a dog and stick a note to it. The animals were harmless. They were innocent creatures, stuck in the grasp of humanity, suffering in their hands just as much as he had. No, Darek would never hurt an animal on purpose, it was the humans he went after. They were the cruel species. The ones who deserved everything he could imagine, and more.

"I know. I know you'd never do that."

"You do?"

She smiled, getting to her feet. She reached out, stroking the scar on his cheek. "You're not as evil as you think you are."

"Hmph."

Darek stepped away from her, unsure whether he should feel flattered, or offended.

Mila's eyes traveled down his body, her cheeks growing pink as her eyes lingered long enough for him to squirm under her gaze.

"Get dressed," she breathed, "we're going out."

— * —

Darek waited outside of Kate's door, gladly obeying Mila's order. He'd rather die than exposing himself to that insect's stare. He didn't even want to be anywhere near her place, but Mila's stubbornness was unavoidable. And no chance in hell, he'd let her go alone when there was someone out to get her.

Pacing the corridor as he waited, he let his mind wander. He'd seen girls just like Kate. Mean girls, bullies, and sluts, he'd been exposed to them all. And he hated them with the same intensity as the shame he had to endure.

The first time he ever let a girl touch him would always stay with him. The frustration, the humiliation... Darek tried not to think of it, to keep his mind from going there, but the scorn in Kate's eyes threw him back in time. Back to the toilet in Stackston High.

Tessa had nestled her way into his heart with sweet smiles and seducing hands. He'd believed her when she claimed to want him.

Darek leaned back against the wall as the memories flooded his mind. He felt Tess's hands on his chest, remembered the nervousness and the excitement. At barely sixteen, he'd never touched a girl, he'd never dared to even think of the possibility. When Tessa cornered him in the boy's restrooms, the first feeling that flitted through Darek was fear. It was usually the boys who beat him. The girls simply ignored him and whispered about him from afar.

When Tessa smiled sweetly and her knowing hands pushed him up against the wall, Darek couldn't even breathe.

"I've been watching you," she purred. "I like you, you're different from the other boys." Her lips pressed against his,

and Darek's mind exploded in thoughts. He didn't know what to do. Fear made him tremble under her hands.

She giggled, "You've never done it?"

Darek managed a small nod and she let out a tsk tsk sound. "Do you want to?"

One more nod. Tessa grinned, pulling his t-shirt above his head. Darek held his breath, following her gaze with his eyes. She watched the scars with a grimace that didn't go unnoticed by him.

"They're disgusting," she said. "But it's okay, you can't help how you look."

Darek wanted to run, to take his shirt back on and escape her eyes. Before he could, Tessa dropped to her knees, unzipped his jeans, and pulled them down along with his underwear. Darek stepped out of the clothes on her command, and stood on weak legs, naked in front of her.

Tessa grinned, tugging her panties down from under her dress before kicking them to the side. "I'm ready," she winked. "Are you?"

Darek gulped, fighting against the panic swirling in his gut.

Tessa dragged a long fingernail down his chest. "Don't you want me?"

"I—I do."

"What are you waiting for?" Tessa's lips landed on his throat, nibbling and biting his skin as her body rubbed against his. Darek felt himself respond to her teasing, growing hard under the friction from her dress against his overheated skin.

"That's better," Tessa purred. She dragged her teeth against his neck, stopping as she reached his ear. "Now touch it," she demanded. "I want to watch you."

Darek's mind reeled. He couldn't do that, not in front of her. Starting to regret the whole thing, he looked around for his clothes, but she'd kicked them across the room, and they lay in a pile next to the door. Darek gulped, torn between desire and fear. One part of him wanted to please her, to give her everything she asked for. He wanted her to like him, to keep liking him. She was the only girl who'd *shown any interest in him, and he'd lie if he wasn't excited. Tessa was beautiful. Her blonde hair and slim body was any boy's dream to touch, and she was right in front of him. Her knickers tossed to the floor along with his clothes.*

Darek's hand trembled as he did as she'd asked. He didn't dare to do anything but to obey her.

Tessa grinned, backing away until her back was up against the other wall and her hand reached for the door. "I'm holding it. It's safe. No one can come in. Go on." She reached her other hand down her body until it disappeared under her dress.

Darek's eyes were fixed on her hand, the thought of what she was touching was enough to make him tremble with excitement. He got braver, a sliver of confidence returning as he thought of being wanted by a girl like Tessa.

When the door burst open and the room flooded with laughing people, Tessa joined in. She picked up the clothes, waving her knickers in the air. "Enjoy. Looser."

The laughter faded as Darek's mind returned to the empty corridor. His hands trembled as he slid down the wall, gripping his hair and digging claws into his skull to distract himself from the memories.

They never let him forget that day.

Even after burning every single one of them to the ground, their faces stayed with him, haunted him every time he closed his eyes.

Under the power and confidence the devil provided him, he was still that boy. He never got the chance to heal, he never allowed himself to feel anything other than anger. Mila changed it, and he hated her for stripping him just as defenseless as Tessa had. This time, he wasn't worried about his body. It was his soul he feared for. The way he cared about her, the way he couldn't imagine his life without her in it, scared him more than anything. If something happened to her, he didn't know what he would do. He couldn't even breathe without her.

DAREK

CHAPTER 28

Darek's head jerked up by the sound of the door opening. Mila hugged Kate goodbye, making her promise to be careful, and Darek wanted to scream in frustration. As Mila's eyes landed on Darek, concern flashed across her face.

"You brought *him*!" Kate's eyes were on Darek too. "I don't care what you say, all the bad things started with him. He's toxic!"

Ignoring her, Mila darted to Darek, untangled his hands from his hair and he let her, but couldn't help but shudder under her touch.

"What's wrong?"

"You," Darek growled before he could think. "You're bringing it all back."

A few moments of confusion made Mila freeze, then she pulled him to his feet, wrapping arms around his body and pulled him close.

"It's okay to feel," she murmured. "It's okay to be human."

"I can't do this." He abruptly pulled away from her, stood glaring down at her before swirling around, hitting a fist against the wall with enough force to make the bricks crumble from impact. Hands up against the wall, he fell forward, trying to keep himself together as Mila's eyes bored holes into his back.

"That's the perfect gentleman," Kate hissed. "Gosh Mila, get rid of that freak."

Darek slowly turned, claws scraping against the wall as he locked red eyes on Kate. The sound made Mila cringe, but the way he eyed Kate was what made her gasp. Darek didn't care who she was or about his promise to Mila. That bitch needed to learn her lesson. Seeing Kate again, keeping that promise was the last thing on his mind. He moved slow, like a cat stalking its prey. His eyes were locked on Kate, who stood trembling under his glare. Darek's muscles quivered with pent-up tension, the power within him just waiting to be unleashed. He'd rip her throat and paint the walls with her blood. He'd shove her fucking heart down her throat for all the nasty things coming out of her mouth.

Mila stepped in the line of his vision, blocking his way. "Snap out of it!" she hissed. "I don't know what happened, but you've gotta calm down." She turned to Kate, pointing a finger at her. "And you!" she snapped. "Stop bullying him, he's been through hell, he doesn't need you to bring at all back."

Her words snapped Darek out of the killing mode and his line of vision returned to normal as the eyes transformed back to gray. Still on guard, he stood stiffly eyeing Kate as she glared back at him.

Mila took his hand, demonstrating her affection in front of her friend. "He's with me, Kate."

Kate scowled at Darek, then withdrew into her apartment, pulling the door with her.

Mila sighed, returning her attention to Darek. Squeezing his hand, she murmured, "What happened here?"

Darek huffed. The last thing he wanted was to talk about it, to dwell on the humiliation, and most of all, tell her about it.

"No secrets," Mila pressed on.

She led him down the stairs toward the waiting red Kia. Not until they were inside the car, did she go on. "Come on, tell me. Something happened there. I can see it."

Darek balled his hands into fists, clenching his jaw as tight as he could without crushing his teeth. He refused to open his mouth, refused to say one word, no matter how skilled she was with her persuasion.

"Darek."

He shook his head, silently praying she'd let it go, to just fucking drive and leave him alone.

Her hand over his made him flinch, his eyes darting to her.

"I can't talk about it, it's so fucking humiliating." He turned his head to avoid her gaze, and Mila hesitated.

"What happened?"

"Hmph." Darek shot her an annoyed glare. "What part of not talking about it didn't you understand?"

Mila chuckled. "You'll feel better, trust me."

Darek eyed her as she drove in silence. A part of him wanted to open up, to tell her everything she wanted to know and let her soothe the pain with her comforting hands. But the part that would never allow himself to be vulnerable refused to let him. Darek remained silent, knowing he disappointed her by shutting her out. Some things you simply didn't talk about, this was one of those things. How could he explain to her how he still felt disgusted with himself for what that slut had done? How could he explain he'd never let anyone touch him again after those hands had tricked him, he'd never let a girl on top, never even let anyone put their hands on his body since that day?

He was the one in control, and he'd never give it up, not again. He'd lived far too many years in fear and shame to go back to being the victim. He'd outgrown that. He'd gotten the power he needed to rise above those filthy humans who believed they were so special. Not even Mila could make him change his mind. He'd do everything for her, but not that.

Parking outside of her apartment, she sat in Darek's silence, studying him as he refused to look at her. When she finally reached out to touch his arm, he flinched.

"It's just me," she whispered. "Don't shut me out. Whatever it is. You never have to go through those things again. It's over."

"It's never over," Darek hissed, again regretting his words as soon as they left his mouth. Despite knowing he should shut the hell up, he went on, "As long as they're people..."

"Not everyone's a—"

Darek snorted. "Right? You said that about Kate too, before she tried to kill me with that tin of fire." He whipped his head around, eyes blazing red. "I can't stand to even look at people." He snarled, "I'll never be one of them."

"Then be above them, take the power back."

A flicker of confusion crossed his face.

"I don't mean by killing people," Mila rushed to explain. "You're more than the devil, you're strong, you're brave, you're smart, do something with your life. Something good. Something you'll be respected for. Be the boss."

Darek chuckled. Torn between liking the idea and feeling insulted by the simplicity of her words. It sounded good, but she had no fucking idea what she was talking about.

"And how do you suggest I do that?" He cocked his head. "If you haven't noticed, I have nothing. Not even a goddamn place to call home."

Mila reached out, and this time he didn't pull away. Taking his hand, she whispered. "You always have a place with me. You have *me*. We'll think of something."

Her words wormed their way into his heart, making it swell with a sudden wave of emotion. He leaned his head back, closing his eyes. Did she mean that? Was it possible she was the one exception? The missing piece he'd been searching for? He needed her to be. Trusting people never turned out well, but he was shocked to realize he trusted her more than he'd ever thought he could.

He just hoped it wasn't a mistake.

DAREK

CHAPTER 29

"We're watching you."

Darek snatched the envelope off Mila's front door and tore it open with a frustrated cry. A set of pictures fell out, and he knew before even looking at them he wouldn't like what he saw.

"What's that?" Mila asked.

"Nothing."

He bent down to pick the pictures up, intending to throw them away before she saw them. She didn't need one more thing to worry about.

"Don't lie to me." She snatched the pictures out of his hand and gasped. Her eyes shot to Darek, who sighed. He watched her stare at the pictures and tried to keep his calm.

The silent torture was driving him crazy. Seeing Mila's pale face was more than he could take. For the first time in his life, he didn't think of himself. He didn't fear the shadows, the invasion of their privacy, and the fucking asshole snapping pictures of their every move—he feared for her. They'd taken her once, they could do it again. Every second he kept what was theirs, he put Mila at risk. He'd find another way to climb the ladder of life, he'd find a fucking job if he had to.

Grabbing Mila by her shoulders, he stared down at her. "I have to take you somewhere safe."

Mila's eyes widened in alarm. "What do you mean?"

"I've had enough. This shit gotta end." he grabbed her arm, pulling her toward the way they'd just arrived from.

"Wait!" she yanked herself free. "We're safe inside. Please. I just wanna be home. With you."

Darek let out a frustrated growl. Why did she have to argue? People had their eyes on the place. He couldn't leave her here, and he couldn't stay cooped up inside with her either. He had to end this. Now.

"Okay." He guided her inside her apartment. "Stay here, don't open for *anyone* if it's not me," he demanded.

When she opened her mouth to protest, he shook her shoulders. "Do as I say," he snarled. "I can't stand the thought of something happening to you, do you understand? Do you *fucking understand*?"

A small smile played on Mila's lips despite the situation being anything but amusing. Darek huffed as he realized his mistake. Her smile was not of amusement, it was because of him, and what he'd let slip. He'd spoken his feelings out loud, but for once he didn't care to feel awkward. She needed to know. She needed to see what he saw, to understand how important she'd become to him. She needed to remain safe. It was the only thing that mattered.

"I'll return it, fuck them!"

Mila's eyes grew wide, then she flung herself in his arms. "I'm proud of you," she murmured. "You're doing the right thing."

Darek allowed himself to melt into her arms one more moment, then he stepped away. He stood, looking down at her, taking her in as if he never wanted to forget the way she looked. Not even for the short time he'd be gone. He reached out, brushing his knuckles over her cheek. "Stay here," his voice dropped into a whisper. "Stay safe."

"I will. I promise."

Darek turned on his heels and stalked back down the stairs. Once outside, he slipped out of his jacket, changed into devil form, and shot toward the evening sky with powerful wing strokes.

Darek landed in the alley he'd first seen them in. The darkened street was empty. The smell of burnt flesh still hung in the air, making Darek shudder as he thought of Mila tied up to the chair. Feeling his pockets, he tried to remind himself he was doing the right thing. Nothing was more important than her. If this was about what he'd stolen, he had to be the one to end it. No more games. This had to end now.

Darek looked around, ignoring a bad feeling forming in his gut. Were they lurking in the shadows, as they always did? They'd watched him for so long, he had a hard time believing they were suddenly gone. The men he'd killed were not the only ones in their game of hide and seek. They were more, and they were there.

Wrinkling his nose at the stench, Darek began to walk down the alley until it opened up to a bigger just as a rough street. He'd seen the sea when flying, knowing he was close to the docks. Rounding a corner, he stepped out onto what looked like an abandoned parking lot, lined by just as shabby buildings and containers. From between the red and blue cargo halls, the waves glittered in the setting sun.

"I know you're there!" Darek shouted. His voice dipped into a growl, "You can come out now."

A chuckle reached him before a figure emerged from between the containers. "Very perceptive."

Darek huffed, narrowing his eyes as the group of people stepped out from their hiding places.

A tall man strolled up to him, stopping close enough for Darek to reach out and touch him if he wanted to. Darek eyed his black suit and shiny shoes with suspicion. His hair was almost as dark as Darek's, but short-cropped and trimmed to perfection. The four men standing behind him looked just as well dressed, and as far from the drug dealers he'd thought he'd be dealing with.

"Who are you? What do you want from me?" He fished out a pack of bills from a pocket, holding them up for the man to see. "Take it, and leave me alone, leave Mila alone!"

The man laughed. "I don't care about your money." He gestured toward the bills with a flick of his hand. "You can keep those."

A black sedan rolled up next to Darek.

"We've got something more precious, I believe?"

Darek's eyes darted from the car to the man, then back to the car. It slid past him as in slow-motion, and when his eyes caught the sight of Mila inside the backseat, he could have sworn his heart stopped beating. His blood ran cold, and for a brief moment, the world stopped spinning. Fear pushed down on him until he thought he'd suffocate from the intensity. Then his mind cleared, and just as he was about to reach the door, the car sped up, creating a distance between them.

"You do as we say," the man spoke in a calm voice. "Or she dies."

Darek clenched his fists, keeping the flames contained as the anger rose.

"You don't know who you're dealing with," he hissed. "Let her go."

The man laughed. "Oh, but we do know, that's why I have *this*." He held out his hand, showing an item clutched in his grip. "If my finger leaves this button, she'll die. So I wouldn't try to be the hero."

Darek froze, his eyes drifting to the car which had parked in a distance. A safe distance for them to be out of reach of the explosion. Darek shuddered. What he'd thought had been a good idea suddenly took a turn for the worse. How had they even gotten to Mila? He'd specifically told her to not open the fucking door, and yet there she was, stuck in a car which they were ready to blow up if he didn't cooperate. Darek wanted to scream. Weighing his options, he came out blank. He could kill the son of a bitch, but not before the detonator would go off. He could reach the car

in seconds, but would it be enough to get Mila out before...
Darek shuddered at the thought. He couldn't take the risk,
not with her. If he'd be even one micro-second too late,
she'd be history.

"What *the fuck* do you want?"

A woman stepped out from behind the group of men,
and the first thing that caught Darek's attention was the
pink streaks in her hair. But instead of a mini skirt and high
heels, she wore black slacks and a white top, looking just
as corporate as the men lined up behind the one addressing
Darek.

Watching her approach, realization slowly settled around
Darek like a cold blanket. He'd been played. The job, the
cash. Had they taken Mila too, to test him? To push him to
this moment? The more Darek thought of it, the more sure
he became. He walked right into a carefully constructed
trap, and now he had no way out.

"You," he snarled at the woman.

"Hello, devil-boy," she greeted him. "How have you
been? Enjoyed the drug business?"

"Fuck you," Darek hissed.

"I'd love to fuck you," she winked at Darek. "Are you
offering?"

Darek's arms shook from the tension of holding back.
His claws pressed into his flesh to avoid throwing fire on
the bitch. Despite his effort, flames leaked from his hands
as horns grew from his skull. Blood dripped from his hands,
but the pain was nothing to the terror tearing at his insides.
Mila in that car. Mila held captive. Again. Mila's life, so
close to ending. He couldn't let it happen. He'd sworn to
protect her. He meant every word.

"No need to get all worked up," the woman snickered.
Holding up a syringe long and fat enough to make Darek
shudder at the sight of it, she continued. "Now there are two
ways to do this."

Darek stepped back as she approached. "Don't even
think about it," he growled.

"Boss?" she gestured with her eyes toward the car. "Is
Max out yet?"

179

"Yes, it's ready," the man said with a satisfied smirk. "But, Carla?"

Darek's eyes darted between them and the car.

"Let her say goodbye first."

The woman, Carla, laughed as the man held up a radio. Clicking a button, a static noise crackled through the air.

"Miss Shikawa?" he asked. "Do you wish to say goodbye to your devil boy?"

Darek's heart clenched at the sound of her sob. When she finally spoke, her voice quivered despite her effort of trying to sound strong. "Darek, don't listen to them."

Darek snatched the radio, holding it in trembling hands. "Mila?"

"They were already inside," she said. "I never opened the door."

"I'll get you out." Darek could barely contain the anger. "You're safe."

"I'm not, you know that."

Darek turned toward the car. She was so close, yet so far. It could not be more than 100 meters away. Could he fly there in time to get her out before that son of a bitch pressed the button? Maybe. He was fast. Probably faster than these cockroaches had predicted. But could he take the chance? They knew who he was. *What* he was. They had come prepared. He couldn't risk underestimating them. Not when Mila's life was on the line.

"Darek?" she whispered.

"NO!" he snapped. "Don't say goodbye. I'll get you out."

Her soft sobs did something to him, filled him with a pain he never felt. A need, he never felt. He wanted to touch her, needed to feel her in his arms. He needed her like he needed air. He needed her to be alive.

Darek's eyes never left the car. He only had one option, and it didn't matter it went against everything he stood for—he had no other choice. He had to surrender.

Holding out his arm to Carla who approached, Darek squeezed his eyes shut, gripping the radio to the verge of a breaking point as the fat needle stabbed through his skin.

The slight tremble to his voice annoyed him to no end,

but he didn't have time to dwell on it. He needed to hear her voice. He needed her, now more than ever. He could no longer care about vulnerability or being weak.

"Mila?"

"I'm here, baby," she sniveled.

"You'll be fine," Darek choked out as his chest squeezed with emotion. "You have to be."

"Don't! Don't do it!"

Darek opened his eyes, watching the blue liquid enter his bloodstream. "It's too late."

Mila's silence tortured Darek to the point of desperation. He needed her voice again. He needed her calm to wrap around him. It was the only thing he had left to cling to.

A cold sensation traveled up his arm, followed by a painful tingling as his stiff muscles were forced to relax. He started to feel tired, weak. He couldn't focus. The radio in his hand grew blurry as his eyelids turned heavy. He fought against the feeling. He needed to stay alert.

When Mila finally spoke, her voice was just a whisper, "I love you."

The words hit Darek like a bolt of electricity, surging through his entire being. A warmth settled in his heart, and everything fell in place. A lifetime of hatred and cruel words, suddenly turned to its end by three small words. The words echoed in his head, and as he tasted them, silently feeling them on his tongue, he knew the feeling was mutual.

Before he could even begin to form a reply, he staggered. Blinking to keep the world in focus, he felt the shift, the devil pushing through his consciousness, roughly shoving him away as he broke to the surface with an inhuman cry. It was his survival instinct triggered as the poison injected coursed through his system. It was adrenalin blasting every cell in his body with reserve power until he exploded in a cascade of wings and fire. The men screamed, scrambling out of Darek's way, running to safety.

Their voices blended to background noise as Darek's heart thundered in his chest.

"Get away!"

"That was enough to sedate a fucking elephant!"

181

"He's not supposed to react like this!"
"Shoot him!"

Darek flew his arms out, spreading a wave of fire their way. Only one thought circled in his head.

Kill them Burn them.

I love you… Her words swept over him like a cool breeze, making him falter, forcing his focus elsewhere even when controlled by the devil.

Mila.

Darek swirled around, throwing himself into the air, swooping down to grab the car by its roof, he ripped the whole top off with little effort, tossing it aside before reaching for Mila. Hauling her out by her arms, he lifted her like a child, up into the air the same moment the car exploded. Mila's screams echoed in his head, urging him to push harder, faster, even though his energy dropped like a stone.

Darek's head spun, microseconds of darkness flickering through his mind. All he wanted was to fly off into the night, but his wings were heavy, slowly growing numb.

"Darek?"

Mila trembled in his arms, her fear leaking into him as well.

"What's happening?"

She'd noticed his descent. The ground nearing, no matter the struggle to stay in the air. He blinked the world back into focus but drifted off again. He dropped to the ground, his legs buckling the moment they touched the hard surface.

Mila's hands were on him, pulling him up again. "We gotta get out of here!" she cried. "Darek!"

Darek held on to her, feeling himself slip closer to the nothingness waiting to devour him. Even speaking was hard, his lips refusing to obey.

"I. Can't. Move," he choked out. "Go. Run!"

"I'm not leaving you."

Darek staggered, but remained on his feet, supported by Mila's arm around his waist and his hands gripping her shoulders. His hands were weak, unable to hold on, and he could no longer feel his legs. Darek blinked Mila into blurry focus, managing to choke out. "I can't move."

"You have to!" A sudden sharp pain on his cheek snapped him back momentarily. He blinked, realizing she'd slapped him. Before he had time to get angry, he slipped away again. He couldn't think, couldn't focus. Hell, he could barely stand on his own. He could not protect her.

"Go." Darek struggled to even speak. His throat was thick, not letting enough air through, not allowing him to form any coherent sentence. He tried again, but no words came. Panic welled up inside. There was so much he wanted to tell her, so much he hadn't dared to say. Now when he needed her to know, he couldn't speak. Pushing her back, he tried to make her understand he wanted her to run. To get away from the monsters breathing down their necks, to LIVE.

— * —

A gunshot rang out. Before Mila could scream, Darek grabbed her, pushing her behind him as he stood on numb legs, blocking her from the approaching team.

"You're stronger than I thought." Carla clapped her hands. "Well, played."

The man chuckled as she went on.

"Cat got your tongue?"

The man grinned, adding, "Feeling a bit woozy perhaps? Little weak in the knees?"

Darek wanted to snatch those guns and feed them down their throats, but he couldn't find the strength or coordination to even shift one foot in front of the other. Mila ducked under Darek's slouching wings, wrapping one arm around his waist to keep him steady as he wobbled on his feet.

"What did you do to him?" she snapped. "What do you want from us?"

Carla cocked an eyebrow. "And *you* are braver than I thought." She gave a short nod, and a gun pointed straight at Mila. "And dumber. Shoot her."

Darek heard the words as in a haze, distorted and slow. He couldn't think or focus, but somehow his body acted on instincts, swirling around to throw Mila to the ground with the force of a wing, seconds before the shot rang out. The movement sent him tumbling to the ground as well, and as he collapsed next to her, he had no way of getting back to his feet. Even staying conscious was a losing battle. Using the last strength he could muster, he wrapped his wings around them both to shield them from the outer world as his mind drifted in and out of consciousness.

The sound of multiple shots forced a scream from Mila's lips. And once she started screaming, she couldn't stop. A burning pain registered in Darek's brain, forcing him back to reality only to be greeted by a series of bullets tearing through his skin. Darek's body shuddered with each shot, low groans the only sound he could pull off as he balanced on the edge of darkness.

Mila shifted closer to him, crawling into his embrace, comforting, and taking comfort all at once. As she wrapped her arms around Darek, and he collapsed into her embrace, her screams turned into sobs. Darek wanted to hold her, to lift his arms and pull her tight to his body, but his muscles refused to move. A second hail of bullets rang out. Darek's body tensed at the sound, a silent growl vibrating in his chest. Mila buried her face into his neck, holding on to him with all she had as his body grew limp in her arms.

Darek couldn't speak, couldn't move, he couldn't even blink. If it was the injection or the fact his body was riddled with bullets, he didn't know. But as he was ripped away from Mila, he felt her hands trying to hold on to him. Heard her sobs. He wanted to scream, to hold on to her. His body was dead weight, his mind struggling against the pain that threatened to push him over the abyss he refused to fall into.

Their voices drifted to him too slow, distorted, and blurred.

"The devil, giving his life for a human," Carla mused. "Never thought I'd see that happen."

Darek wanted to scream, to tell Mila he was alive. The terrible pain throughout his body made him fear he wouldn't be for much longer. His wings were shredded, bleeding— and so did the bullet holes littering his back as he lay, face down on the cold ground. Blood seeped out from under him, coloring the asphalt red.

One of the men came forward. Darek saw through blurry eyes a pair of long legs. He wanted to blink, to focus his gaze, but no matter how he tried, nothing happened, and instead of clearing, his vision grew foggier until the world started to lose its color.

"Keep the cash." The man tossed Darek's jacket at Mila. "Consider it payment for your part of this."

Something bothered him as the darkness circled him, but his mind was too slow to pinpoint what. He heard Mila's voice and tried to cling to it, fighting to stay afloat in a sea of darkness pulling him under.

DAREK

CHAPTER 30

A bright light glaring directly down at him pulled Darek from unconsciousness. He wanted to close his eyes, to blink at the light blinding him, but couldn't. Indistinct voices reached his ears, but as he tried to turn his head toward the source, his muscles didn't obey. A bolt of fear zapped through him. His flight instinct triggered. His body didn't move, even though his brain screamed at it to get up and away. A slight twitch of muscles, the only response.

Darek's chest tightened with fear, his heart leaping into his throat as thoughts rushed through his head. Where was he? Where was Mila? Why did he feel something was so horribly *wrong*...

As he lay immobilized, the numbness started to draw back and he slowly became aware of his body. The hard surface under him digging onto his bones, the cold metal uncomfortable against his skin, and his wings folded in a painful angle under him. The brief confusion of realizing he was still in his devil-form was forgotten as a deep ache started to spread through his back. Darek tried to shift, to get away from the pain and flex his muscles, but couldn't move enough to escape the growing feeling. Tugging at his arms, he realized they were tied down, held firmly in the grasp of something cold and hard against his wrists. Darek's heart rate quickened, his breath turning fast and shallow as his breathing shifted from calm to gasps as something pierced his back, twisting in his spine like knives. He tried to scream, to arch away from the torture, but something held him down by the waist. Even his legs were pinned to the surface, making it impossible for him to get up.

Somewhere around him, a beeping noise intensified until it echoed in his head. The rustle of footsteps came closer, then the beeping stopped. And a face came into focus above Darek.

"He's awake!" The voice shouted. "Increase!"

Darek slipped back into darkness.

When his vision cleared the next time, he was able to move. Darek blinked at the light, turning his head to take in the surroundings, and tried to focus enough to push through the mental fog surrounding him. His brain didn't work. He couldn't think, couldn't hold on long enough to grasp what was happening. Everything around him was white and steel. Windowless walls were covered in tools and machines Darek had never seen before. They looked advanced for their time, something he would have expected from the sci-fi movies.

Letting his gaze travel down his body, he tried not to panic. It was hard, seeing the long needles shoved into his arms and chest, and the cuffs holding his wrists and ankles firmly against a sleek wall. Darek tugged at his outstretched arms, hoping to break free, but the weak effort he could pull off was nothing. The cuffs rattled against the wall but didn't budge. Darek realized, with a pang of fear, not only his arms were weak, but his legs were as well. They barely carried his weight as he stood, and had he not been tied to his waist, pulled tight against the cold surface behind his back, they would have buckled.

His wings were spread flat against the wall, pinned down by nails and chains with no regard to their anatomy. Darek tried flexing them, but all the motion caused was a shooting pain that spread through the wings and down his spine. He winced, clenching his teeth to ride out the feeling. When it faded, it left a dull ache that made him wish to stretch, to escape it by moving his body, but he could barely move an inch.

The fear turned to anger fast. How dare they? They didn't know who they were dealing with. He'd show them, he'd rip the cuffs as if they were made of paper, he'd burn their ridiculous lab to the ground and stretch his wings to rise above it all. He'd get back to Mila, he'd get back home.

Darek tugged at the cuffs, twisting his body in an attempt to apply more power, and the moment he managed a good strong yank of an arm, a sudden pain exploded in his body. He screamed from the shock as his muscles cramped and convulsed until he shook and his body sagged in the restraints. Then just as fast at it had started, it was gone, leaving Darek gasping for air as his body trembled in the aftermath.

"You're not getting out of those."

Darek's head snapped up, seeing the man from the docks, the one they'd called *Boss*, standing in front of him with a smug smile plastered on his lips. He nodded toward Darek, adding. "Nice try though." The man eyed Darek up and down. "Two weeks and you're as good as new. Your healing abilities are astounding."

Darek's eyes flashed red. "What do you want?"

"What do I want?" the man echoed, putting his finger to his chin as he pretended to think. The gesture annoyed Darek more than it should. The man's calm demeanor, his cold ignorance of the suffering he just inflicted made Darek want to scream. Whoever this man was, Darek had never been surer—he was the real monster. As Darek read the name tag on the lab coat covering a jet-black suit, he hated humanity more than ever.

T. Berner.

"Aren't you gonna ask about your girlfriend?"

Darek tensed, hissing through clenched teeth, "If you hurt her—"

Berner laughed. "Why would we hurt her?"

Darek didn't understand. They'd fired at her, they'd tried to kill her...

Berner nodded as he encouraged Darek's thought process. "Miss Shikawa is safe. She played her part excellently."

Darek's eyes narrowed at the man's words.

"You must admire her acting talent, don't you agree?"

Darek could only stare. What was he insinuating? Mila was in on it? He refused to think so. She couldn't have betrayed him...

"You're lying. She wouldn't." Darek said it with certainty, but couldn't ignore the little seed of doubt growing within him. Could she?

"Oh, but she would, she did. Without her, you wouldn't be here."

Darek tried to swallow down nausea threatening to choke him. He refused to accept it. She was everything. The reason he'd survived. The image he'd held on to when he'd felt like slipping away. He'd balanced on the edge of life and death, too broken to live but too stubborn to die. Images of her had pulled him back to the surface when he'd been so close to drowning in the pain. She'd been his reason to fight. She still was. The thought of being back in her arms kept him alive, kept him from going under.

"No," his voice was strangled, rough from emotions.

"Miss Shikawa would be dead if we *wanted* her dead. What does that tell you?" Berner cocked his head. "No need to fight the truth."

Producing a set of photos from his coat pocket, Berner held them up for Darek to see. "See for yourself." He grinned at Darek's sharp intake of breath.

Seeing Mila step out of her friend's car outside of her home, dressed in Darek's leather jacket broke something in Darek. When he should have been happy about seeing her alive and well, all he felt was a deep pain in his heart. What he refused to believe, was true. They'd spared her. They'd let her go as if she'd never been in danger…

Darek tore his gaze away. He couldn't look at her without breaking. She made him feel so good he'd forgotten everything he learned. He'd fallen for her hard, been blinded by her charm and soothed by her calm. He trusted her.

She'd gone from hating him to—loving him. Darek's heart squeezed at the thought, his throat tightening with the sudden emotion. She'd said she loved him—but she lied.

No one loved him. It was a fact. No one *ever* loved him and he was certain no one ever could. Especially not someone as perfect as Mila.

"Aww," Berner cooed, pressing a hand to his chest. "Poor devil's been played. Does it hurt?"

Darek's claws scraped against the wall with a sickening screech that made even Berner cringe.

"Miss Shikawa did a splendid job. What surprises me is how easily fooled you are. Does it come with the species? You're strong, but clearly lacking in intelligence." Berner gestured towards Darek's exposed body with a disgusted grimace. "You really expect a woman like Shikawa to love *that*? You look like a cut-up bat."

Darek lunged forward, pulling at the cuffs with a cry of rage instantly turned into a cry of pain as the same intense feeling ripped through his body.

When it was over, his legs gave out, and as he hung from his arms, slumped against the wall gasping for breaths while his muscles cramped painfully, he fought against the pressure building up behind his eyes.

Berner chuckled. "In case you wonder, you're rigged with 2.000 volts at 12 amps. That's more than enough to kill a human being, but since you're not, we can't take our chances. You move, you hurt. Easy as that."

Darek stood on weak legs, glaring at the man with only one thought running through his head.

Mila…

His precious flower. His goddess. His Mila. Betrayed him? Sold him out to the monsters who strapped him to a wall to torture him? He couldn't wrap his mind around it. He trusted her, dared to believe there could be one human in this world who didn't look at him like he was trash. One person who wasn't repulsed by his scars and scared of his darkness. He dared to believe she loved him *despite* it all. He believed her words, he'd given his life for her. He *loved* her...

Darek squeezed his eyes shut to trap the pain inside. Trusting her had been his biggest mistake. And as much as it pained him to admit it, Berner was right. How could he have been so dumb to believe a woman like Mila could be attracted to him? He was damaged goods. Scratched and burned, destroyed by the humans she loved and protected.

Darek wanted to cry as he had to face the truth. He let down his guard, and she pulled the rug from straight under his feet. Knocked him down when he dared to start to climb out of the dark hole he spent his life in. Darek hung his head, holding on to the last string of pride as the dreams of power and respect turned flat under the thick layer of betrayal and humiliation.

Strapped to a wall. Stripped of clothes, and in the mercy of humanity once again, Darek didn't know how much more he could take.

Berner was right, he may have the power to destroy the world, but he was impulsive and dumb. He didn't have the patience and the intelligence needed to outsmart them.

The human part of him was a wuss, it had always been. No matter how he dreamed of power and the strength to stand up for himself, for taking control and showing them all he was more than the scared boy they could step on, he'd never amount to that.

The devil part of him had the strength and the power, but it acted on random, lashed out in rage and vengeance, burned cities in blind hate, and killed humans in the blink of an eye, a twitch of a hand, a flick of his tail. He had all the power he needed, he just didn't know how to use it.

"Hang tight there, buddy." Berner's pat on his shoulder snapped Darek out of his head and back to reality. The man spun on his heels, barked out orders to his staff on his way toward the entrance.

"Isolate him. No human contact, no food, no water."

"Will do, Boss."

Darek's eyes snapped up, staring at their retreating forms with a growing dread building up inside of him. Yanking at the chains, a fresh wave of electricity coursed through him. Darek clenched his teeth, refusing to scream and let it rip through his body until he collapsed.

Hanging from his arms, he focused his gaze on the closed door where the group of men had disappeared, letting his eyelid drift close in defeat. Without Mila to go back to, he had nothing left. No reason to fight. No reason to go on.

DAREK

CHAPTER 31

The sound of footsteps made Darek lift his head. Gazing through heavy eyelids, the first thing he saw was a long knife glistening in Berner's hand as he strolled up to the wall.

"Two weeks of isolation and starvation complete. Endurance and energy levels approximately seventy percent higher than the average human." Berner read from a file, nodding toward Darek, then smiled as if he announced top grades for his favorite student. "You passed with flying colors."

Darek scowled at the man.

"Hungry, perhaps? Thirsty? Felt a bit lonely there?"

When Darek refused to reply, Berner shrugged, playing with the knife. He stroked the blade, grinning as he noticed Darek's eyes drift to the metal glistening in the sharp light.

"On to the next stage, shall we?"

Having a bad feeling about the man's intentions with that weapon, Darek braced himself for the pain he had no way of escaping. He was defenseless. Even if he could've moved, he wasn't sure he would have enough strength to do it. He was dehydrated, his throat dry as sandpaper, and the hollow ache in his stomach had long ago disappeared, leaving him with a fatigue trapping him somewhere between consciousness and sleep. He didn't even have the energy to be scared. The only thing that hadn't left him was the thirst. He'd kill for a glass of water.

"We've already seen your healing abilities in action." Berner held up the knife, tapping it in the air as he spoke. "But—" He pointed it toward Darek, who gulped. Wishing he could disappear through the wall, Darek clenched his jaw, glancing at the monitors as they shifted with activity. His heart rate spiking along with the pulse. The response to fear which he had no control over.

"We didn't get the chance to document it." Berner grinned like a kid on Christmas Eve. "Isn't this exciting?"

Darek squeezed his eyes shut, trying to keep his breathing steady. It was going to hurt, no doubt about it. But he refused to scream. He refused to give the sick bastard the satisfaction. When the cold tip of the knife pressed against his stomach, Darek held his breath, clenching his teeth to keep silent as the full length of the blade pushed into his flesh.

"I'm impressed," Berner said. "I almost expected you to cry. But that's fine. Your vitals speak for you." He gestured toward the screens. "How does it feel?"

Darek couldn't speak. He didn't dare to even open his mouth. If he did, he'd never be able to keep it shut. He wanted to cry, just like Berner suggested. He wanted to scream and throw up as his head swam and bile rose in his throat. He didn't do anything. His reactions were the only things he could control, the only strength he had left to cling to, and he refused to give that up, no matter how bad it hurt.

Berner's chuckle made Darek wish for his very slow death. He twisted the knife with a shove before sliding it out, and the sudden shockwave of pain caught Darek by surprise. Biting back a cry, he fought to stay conscious, to ride out the pain and nausea as blood trickled down his legs.

Berner stepped back, wiping the knife on a towel as he studied the blood pooling around Darek's feet. "Don't worry. We won't let you die."

Darek didn't know if his comment was a comfort or a curse. They kept him alive, but just barely. The torture was worse than death.

"You don't know how long we've wanted you." Berner grinned, slapping Darek's shoulder as if he was an old friend, and not someone he'd just stabbed with a five-inch knife and left to bleed. "I can already see the headlines," he went on. "*Berner & Junior* proves the devil's existence." He placed the knife on a nearby steel table before clapping his hands. "What are you? His son? Satan fucked a human chick?" He laughed at his own joke, looking pleased with himself as Darek balanced on the edge of consciousness. Sweat coated his skin, the rush of blood roaring in his head as his pulse worked on overdrive.

Before Darek could even think of a comeback, a female voice cut him to it.

"He's not *the* actual devil's spawn, he's Donovan's son. The Rewera bloodline goes back generations. His old man was the same. A hybrid. Born out of a dark curse. A man selling his soul to the devil."

Darek's eyes snapped up at the mention of the name. His anger spiking by the mere thought of the twisted grin and sickening laugh. The woman with the pink stripes stood before him, camera in hand and a satisfied smile on her lips.

"Aren't you the little expert," Berner chuckled. "Good job, C."

Carla grinned, nodding toward Darek. "I've dedicated my life to this. I know everything there is to know. Even writing a book about it."

"I have a feeling we will do wonders here."

"You wouldn't stand a chance without me."

Berner chuckled, too proud to admit she was right.

"I'll document this." She backed away, looking through the camera. "Stunning." She clicked a few shots before changing the angle. "All the blood makes for a cool effect, don't you think?"

"Indeed," Berner agreed.

Carla shifted closer, taking closeups of his devil features, moving from horns to claws and down his body until she finished with a series of shots of the wings. When she was done, Darek burned with humiliation and the need to shove that camera up her ass.

"Weren't we going to test his temperature tolerance?" she asked as if they were discussing the next baking project and not the next step of his torture.

Berner wrapped an arm around her shoulder, guiding her away. "Easy, there's time for that too. Let him heal first."

Darek watched them disappear, dropping the act as he was again left alone. The wound hurt like a motherfucker, and made him want to double over or apply pressure to it. His whole body was screaming at him to do something, to stop the steady flow of blood coloring his skin red.

He couldn't do that. All he could do was wish for unconsciousness to save him, but he wasn't even granted that relief. Every time he felt himself slip closer to welcoming darkness, the machines beeped, and something jolted him back to alertness.

— * —

Judging by the healing wound, time passed even though Darek felt like he was stuck in a never-ending hell-loop. The echo of pain still lingered every time he shifted. His abdominal muscles clenching in remembrance of the knife shoved deep in his gut.

Berner whistled as he strolled into the room. "Healing time, eighty percent faster than a human body. Pain response: approximately the same as the human body."

Berner's robotic stating of facts made Darek wish to shove that knife up his ass to show him how well *he* responded to the pain. That sick bastard.

"Are you ready to cool down?"

Berner gestured toward the staff, who were always on the

lookout for his orders, and they sprung into action. Pressing buttons and pulling levers, they produced three glass walls that rose around Darek, connecting to the back wall and the ceiling, creating an airtight cube around him.

Darek eyed them suspiciously, trying to brace for what was coming.

"Body temperature: 108 Fahrenheit," Berner stated, not quite hiding his shock. What had the son of a bitch expected? He wasn't human. He was fire. Of course he was hotter than any average scumbag who would've crumbled to pieces anywhere near his temperature.

Cold air seeped into the cube, making Darek huff. That's their next move? They'd be disappointed. He didn't freeze. Relaxing in the cold air, Darek closed his eyes and let out a breath that hung in the air like a cloud of thick smoke. When he opened his eyes again, they were red.

The sudden drop in temperature stunned him. This wasn't the normal winter cold which he expected, and by the looks of the men gathered outside the cube, they were just as stunned. They exchanged looks, checked the monitors, and while Darek could see their mouths open and close, he couldn't focus on what they were saying. The cold air closed in on him, seeping into his nose and mouth until every breath was a struggle he couldn't win. Gasping for air while his muscles shivered and ached, he tried to stay focused. After an eternity of quivering, Darek's body started to grow numb. His fingers grew stiff, cracking in the joints as he tried to move them, and his damp skin was covered in a thin sheen of ice that burned worse than any fire.

When his breathing was nothing more than a faint wheeze, and his eyes were frozen in a red stare, they shut the experiment down.

"Astounding!" Berner clapped his hands. "We'd be long dead. Give him one hour to recover." Berner dismissed the staff who scurried away. He shot Darek a look, then turned on his heels and disappeared too.

Darek's mind was slow, he couldn't catch one thought and hold on to it. Everything seemed to merge until he didn't know what was real and what was not. When the temperature climbed, his bones ached painfully, pins and needles spreading through his fingers and toes up his arms and legs until his skin crawled.

Thoughts of Mila flashed through his mind despite his best effort to banish her from his heart. She never cared, still—he cared for her. The guilt of knowing she'd feel everything he felt, killed him. She deserved it, she deserved everything he went through, and more. She deserved to burn in hell for what she'd done. But what she deserved and what Darek's heart accepted were two totally different things. It refused to let her go even when his brain cursed him for the weakness.

Darek barely had time to breathe a normal breath before Berner came back, flanked by his staff who looked more than eager to jump onto the next experiment. They gathered around the glass cage he was stuck in, notepads in their hands and excited eyes locked on Darek.

"Go on," Berner ordered. "Don't just stand there."

"Sorry, Boss."

They sprung into action, and instead of the cold, the cube filled with warm air. This time Darek didn't underestimate their cruelty. They wouldn't stop at bearable. They'd crank the levels up, they'd roast him alive.

Breathing through the fear, Darek tried to remain calm. What was a little heat? He was the devil for fucks sake, he was created from hell. He was made of heat. He was fire, he couldn't burn.

Encouraged by the thought, he relaxed. Their expressions went beyond surprised, and when the heat started to annoy Darek, they exchanged astounded looks.

"You can't burn me, you bastards!" Darek shouted. "I'm the devil."

Berner hesitated, then gestured toward the man attending the monitor. "Increase!"

"It'll blow the system, sir!"

"Do it."

Darek started to sweat, his skin glistening in the warmth and his heart rate skyrocketed as the heat increased the pressure on his chest.

The air seemed to shimmer and distort until the men outside the cube morphed into faceless lumps. Images filled his head until they felt so real he saw them take shape in front of his eyes. Darek squeezed his eyes shut. He didn't want to see her. He didn't want to be reminded of her, but she was everywhere. Her images were ingrained into his eyelids, forcing him to see her every time he closed his eyes. Darek screamed into the thick air, snapping his eyes open to escape her memory. But she was there too. Soaring in the air in front of him like a mirage in the shimmering heat, her milky skin flustered and damp.

"*Mila.*"

Darek tried to reach for her, only to be reminded of the cuffs. She smiled, stepping close enough to lay her hands on his sweaty body. Darek shuddered under her touch, feeling the cooling effect of her hands as his insides burned along with his skin.

"*I'll find you. You're not alone.*"

Her voice resounded in his head.

Darek's head fell back as her hand slid over his body, touching him, tasting him, teasing him.

An alarm went off as the levels increased further, and Darek screamed into the heat.

When the system shut off and the temperature dropped, Darek's chest heaved as he tried to suck in air that seemed too thick to breathe. His head spun, heart rate still speeding as his blood pressure dropped.

"*I love you.*"

Mila's voice echoed in his head before the room started to spin and his stomach cramped with a sudden rush of nausea. Darek fell forward as much as the restraints allowed, coughing and vomiting blood before the room spun into darkness.

His eyes shot open to the spray of cold water directed to his face. He gasped for air, spurting water, and tried to move his head to avoid the high-pressure spray.

"Thought you'd appreciate a shower," Carla said. "Be still, don't be such a wimp."

"Fuck you," Darek hissed through clenched teeth. When he wanted to do the opposite, he did as she demanded. It was the only thing he could do. One wrong move and he'd be fried. If he activated the electricity, he didn't know if even the devil's power could save him.

Darek closed his eyes and tried to endure the sharp spray as it moved down his body. He never imagined water to hurt, but as it hit his skin it felt like it would tear it right off him. The pressure, the sharp angle it hit him cut like hot blades. As it reached his most sensitive areas, he clenched fists and jaw to avoid screaming or blacking out a second time.

When it was over, warm hands replaced the water. Darek's eyes shot open to the feel of the sudden soft touch.

Carla's pink-striped hair was gathered in a knot on top of her head, and she looked up at him from under a set of long lashes and blue eyes.

"You poor thing," she said without the slightest hint of sympathy in her voice. "Can't have you all sweaty and dirty for this." She ran a hand down his chest, over his stomach, and further down.

"I enjoyed the show." She stepped closer, leaning in to drag her lips down his neck. "You're real eye candy."

Darek rolled his head to the side, and she grabbed his chin with her free hand. "Be still."

"Don't touch me," Darek growled. "Don't you fucking touch me."

"Try to stop me." Carla snickered as Darek trembled with the need to shove her off. He had barely accepted Mila's hands on him. This bitch had no idea how many boundaries she pushed, how much he was dying to get away from this, how many ways he imagined killing her to cope with her soft treatment. He'd take a fucking knife in his gut over this. All he wanted was to rip her hands off his body and burn her to a crisp for even trying to force herself on him, but he couldn't even move enough to get away from her caresses. He could just stand there, willing his body not to react to her knowing hands and squeezing his eyes shut as it did. He imagined Mila in her place, thinking it would make everything better. Instead, he was reminded of the real reason he was stuck on this goddamn wall, and his heart squeezed with the pain. He had trusted her, and she'd turned out to be just as rotten as the rest of humanity. He should hate her, but the thought of her still turned him on.

DAREK

CHAPTER 32

Darek lost count of how long he'd been strapped to that wall, but it didn't matter. The only thing on his mind now was survival, and what he was ready to do for it.

Somewhere between the pain and the fear, he'd stopped struggling. Stopped resisting and started planning. He tried strength, but it failed him. He couldn't even turn enough in the restraints to kill a fly before the electricity set in. Once it started, he didn't stand a chance. It was strong enough to knock out a dinosaur.

He tried anger, but it consumed him. The more he raged, the more pain he was subjected to. He'd given up, withdrawn from his body and his mind for as long as he could. That, too, hadn't worked.

And as he slumped in the cuffs, his legs too tired to hold his weight after the last shock of electrocution, he was back to giving up. It was the only thing he had left to do.

Berner stood before him, but Darek didn't even bother to look up. He had nothing to say to the man. Nothing he did could surprise him anymore. He'd been through it all. When he'd thought things couldn't get worse, that humanity couldn't be crueler, that man proved him wrong. Over and over, until Darek stopped caring.

"Time flies, huh?" Berner flipped through his notes. "Three months." He studied Darek, eyeing him up and down, and nodded to himself. "You really aren't human." He made a sweeping gesture toward Darek's body. "You look like you've been there no more than three hours. All muscled up and tanned as if nothing happened. Can't blame Carla for enjoying herself, now can we? Who'd say no to sex with the devil?"

Darek slowly lifted his head, glaring at the man through slits of red eyes.

"Oh!" Berner clapped his hands. "You didn't think I knew? I know everything." The smug grin on his lips made Darek's hands itch to wipe the grin off of his face. One swipe of his claws was all it would take. One second, and he'd be mopping his blood off the floors.

Berner placed the notepad on the table and reached for a syringe. "Oh don't worry," he soothed. "I just need a blood sample."

Darek looked the other way as the needle was shoved into his vein. When he was done, Berner patted his shoulder, making Darek's blood boil from the patronizing gesture.

He had enough. If he had to look at the man one more day, he'd go insane. He tried everything. But there was one thing he hadn't done. It was the only thing he hadn't dared to even think of, but watching the man stroll away whistling a happy tune, Darek had no other option. If it would kill him, so be it. He had nothing left to lose. Relying on the devil's strength for too long kept him alive. It made him heal from each excruciating experiment and plunged him right into a new one. It kept him alive, but being stuck to this wall was not a life.

Would he be able to reign his devil-side back in after leaving it in the foreground for too long? Did he even know how? And even if he did, would he be able to hold it back long enough to allow his human side to suffer the consequences? The jagged line on the monitor skyrocketed by the mere thought of giving up the power and the control. He'd lie if he said it didn't make him shudder, that it didn't terrify him more than the torture ever could. He was nothing without the extra power.

Darek took a deep breath, preparing himself for what he knew could kill him. He had no other option. He'd never get out of this place if he didn't try. Standing on wobbling legs, he braced himself for the pain and willed the devil to step back. When nothing happened, Darek tried harder, mentally forcing wings and horns to shrink away with the excess strength it carried with it.

The moment it was gone, Darek lunged forward before he had a chance to chicken out. The pull on the restraints sent a shockwave of electricity through him. The devil reacted in an instant, ready to spring back, to survive. Darek held it back, hanging on to consciousness long enough to fry every last cell in his body.

When the sound of footsteps came running, he hung limply in the cuffs, muscles spasming in the aftermath of the shocks.

"What the fuck is he doing?" The alarm in the man's voice was like music to Darek's ears. If he had no control of anything but his life, he'd use it as leverage.

"It's a trick!" another man said. "Let him be."

"He's trying to kill himself!"

Using the last fraction of strength, Darek tugged at an arm, letting loose one more set of the torture.

"Stop him!" Berner hissed. "We need him alive."

With the last weak tug, Darek felt a heavy pressure in his chest, a suffocating tightness cutting off his air supply, making his heart race as a searing pain spread through his chest out his arms. The machines started to scream.

"He's going into cardiac arrest. Get him to the medicals!"

Hands were on him, tugging at his arms and legs.

"Now."

Something urged him to focus. A voice in his head.

"Now! You're free."

Darek slid to the floor the moment he was free. Instead of running, instead of fighting, he did nothing. He was nothing.

Everything was white, a long corridor with no walls and no end. Darek looked around. Seeing nothing. Feeling nothing. He couldn't breathe, but he didn't need to. He floated through the vast space, free of pain, free of fear. It spoke to him, comforting and calming, he didn't want to leave. This place was heaven if compared to that wall of torture. It was beautiful. Time stood still, but he didn't need time. He needed nothing. He was free.

A surge shot through his chest. An electric pulse rushing through his body, pulling him out of the white void of existence.

"NOW!" the voice inside him roared.

Darek let go. A rush of power swept through him, catapulting him through the corridor until he saw red, and his spine expanded into wings which shot him straight up from the table and into the air. The sharp snaps as the restraints ripped from where he'd been tied down made the doctors fly back. Items flew through the air from the power of Darek's extended wings. Fire flared from his hands, torching the men within seconds. An alarm went off, and sprinklers activated, raining down at them as they crumbled to the ground.

When the rush of adrenaline drained, Darek started to feel the effects of the past months. Dropping to the floor as his wings no longer had the power to keep him hovering, he stood, staring at the dead bodies and tried to grasp the shift of reality. He was no longer tied to that wall. He was no longer in the control of the sick bastard who forced him to suffer for months. He was free.

Scanning the surroundings, he contemplated his next move while smirking at the death around him. At that moment, only one thing mattered. He wasn't going back on the wall—he'd die before that happened. He could run, but he'd never be free. These people knew too much, they'd never stop, they'd hunt him down and he'd be right back in their grasp. He needed to take them out, each and every one of them. He needed to take the control back.

"You think you're smart, huh?" Berner appeared in the doorway, studying the roasted men at their feet. "Suicide attempt was brilliant. But you're never getting out of here." He raised a hand, shoving a gun clutched in one hand, while the other gestured toward Darek. "See for yourself."

His gaze followed Berner's, stopping at a syringe still clinging to his skin, stuck deep in a vein and half-emptied into his system.

"What did you do?"

Berner chuckled. "Not me. You've gotta blame the doctor. Didn't want you to wake up like you did."

Darek huffed, ripping the syringe out, and tried to ignore the numbness spreading through his arm.

"You'll sleep like a baby within seconds." Berner's finger twitched, and Darek lunged forward, shoving the needle into his neck the same second the shot rang out. It caught him in the shoulder, making him stagger back. The numbness spread faster through his body until he couldn't feel his legs. Darek collapsed to his knees, satisfied to see Berner on the floor as well. His eyes were open in a motionless stare as he lay on his back. He was breathing, but he wouldn't be for long.

A weak feeling of victory filled Darek. Even though he was on the floor, with zero clothes or dignity. He was alive, and they were not. The thought comforted him as he drifted off into darkness.

He came around to the sound of panicked voices and scurrying feet. Keeping still, he assessed the situation without drawing attention to himself. He could move, he could breathe. It was a good sign. The tranquilizer had worn off. The sprinklers were turned off, too, and as he shifted just enough to see where Berner's body had been laying, he realized the man was no longer there.

Alarm shot through Darek. If he was up, he had no time to waste. Scrambling to his feet, he sent the three young men tumbling to the floor with one swipe of a wing. Darek huffed, ignoring their cowering forms. They were worms, he could crush them in his sleep.

It was Berner he was worried about. That man was pure strength. More than he could expect from a human.

Darek looked down at his body. Loose ropes curled around his ankles, and he couldn't help but chuckle. His eyes drifted to the group of cowards as he cut a claw through a fat rope tied around his wrist as well. He hadn't even felt the bonds.

Berner lay on the table where Darek was not too long ago. Darek didn't need to check his pulse to know he was dead. He scoffed. So much for that strength, but what did he expect? Whatever was in that syringe was meant for Darek. If it knocked him out cold, it would easily kill a human.

Darek couldn't help but smirk as the satisfaction rolled over him. He only wished he'd had the chance to watch him die, to see him suffer and beg like the pathetic insect he was.

He'd been in that man's mercy for over three months. Berner destroyed him over and over, ripped him to pieces, and watched him rebuild every time, only to be torn down again. He watched him suffer and bleed, he enjoyed stripping him of everything he had.

Darek's eyes glowed red. How he burned to do the same.

Robbed of the chance to get his revenge on the man himself, he swore he'd get it in other ways. He refused to let it go, to leave as if nothing happened. He couldn't turn his back to this. He'd show them. He'd once risen from the ashes of the hell that had been his life. He'd do it again, and this time he'd stay up.

No more humiliation. No more shame. No more weakness.

With a new sense of determination, Darek began removing Berner's clothes. They were still damp, but dry enough to take on.

The suit molded to his body like it had been made for him, and Darek couldn't help but enjoy the reflection in the shiny cabinets on the wall. This place had seen evil, but it had not seen him. He'd show them what true power looked like. If that wasn't the ultimate revenge, he didn't know what was.

Setting his eyes on the young men still cowering on the floor where he'd left them, he hissed, "Get up, make yourselves useful!"

DAREK

CHAPTER 33

Darek's body screamed in protest as he forced it to remain on its feet. Even the devil could get tired. Given the fact he hadn't been allowed to lie down, even sit down, for months, he didn't think it was too farfetched to be exhausted. He could barely stand, his legs threatened to buckle with every passing second, but he'd rather die than show weakness in front of the worms and their boss. The older man dropped in not long after being called for. Papers in hand, just like ordered. If something was wrong with his precious company, he came running.

"Someone's here, the lab's office. He wants to see the documents, uh, contract. Please hurry."

Darek was sure he expected the IRS, not the devil, and couldn't help but smirk at the thought. Surprise. You old motherfucker. Did you know your son is already dead and gone? Just like most of your torturous staff.

"I'm so sorry, Mr. Berner, I was forced to call you, I—"

Darek tore his eyes from the papers he was studying, and whipped his head around at the sound of the voice. His red glare shut the young man up.

"What did I tell you?" Darek snapped.

"To be silent. Sir." He backed away into the wall, squeezing in between his two workmates who looked equally terrified. "And to... be still."

Darek scowled at their trembling forms. He'd kill them. They'd seen too much. But at the moment he needed them, and they'd proven to be more useful than he'd dared to hope. They called in the boss of the boss. The fucking owner, and in the back of his head, Darek knew he should probably feel nervous. He'd never been anywhere near people with such rank, but yet, all he felt was a simmering rage and a need to take everything from the old man who stuttered and stammered under his glare.

Looking the man straight in the eye, Darek enjoyed the fear on his face. He was terrified, and he should be. He was the closest to revenge as Darek could get. When the fucking son was already dead, go after the father. Darek was sure the old man knew exactly what had been going on in that lab, given the fact it was *his* lab. He knew, he just turned his back to it and let his son play God and enjoy his sick experiments.

Leaning forward against the desk, Darek glared down at the man, looming over his short, somewhat chubby frame. His stance screamed of danger, but it was nothing more than a pathetic attempt not to collapse, by holding himself up by the strength of his arms. The piece of shit that ran this place didn't need to know.

"Sign it," Darek hissed. When the man still hesitated, he raised his voice, shouting into his face. "NOW!"

The man's hand trembled so bad he dropped the pen, and as he shifted away from Darek's red glare to fetch it, he stuttered. "W-what do you want with it?"

"None of your goddamn business," Darek snapped. "Now sigh the fucking paper!"

"It's over t-ten years of research, i-it's—"

"Research about *ME*!" Darek snarled. "About the devil!" He lowered his voice, remembering calm was as efficient as shouting, and he needed to save all the energy he could. "After what you and that maggot have done to me, it's only fair I get to keep the results."

"You're the d-devil."

"In the flesh." Darek's eyes flashed red, and as he placed a clawed hand on the table, the man broke into sobs.

Darek reeled back, crying out loud, "For fucks sake!" He would have preferred dealing with the younger Berner. At least that son of a bitch wasn't a coward. Darek had to hand it to him. He was brave. Ridiculously so. This man who fell to pieces at the mere sight of him was no match. It was as easy as taking candy from a kid. He could scare him into doing anything he wanted.

"That's right. Show him what you've got," the voice whispered in his head, as dark and tempting as always. *"Take the power back."*

Swirling around at the sound of footsteps approaching, Darek saw the opportunity.

"What's going on in—" The woman abruptly cut herself off, her words breaking into a cry as her eyes landed on the destruction of the room—and the dead bodies on the floor. Two small boys stopped beside her, eyes wide in horror.

"About fucking time," Darek hissed, and before the woman knew what happened, Darek grabbed her neck and with a flick of a hand snapped it. Tossing the lifeless body to the ground, he snatched the screaming kids by each arm and held them dangling in the air.

Eyes locked on the weeping man behind the desk, he snarled, "Sign the goddamn papers, or they die."

"GRANDPA!" The boys shrieked. "MOM!"

A brief flicker of regret shot through Darek as their despair seeped through his anger. His own pain echoed back to him, his cries for a mom who never opened her eyes again.

"Focus," the voice urged. *"Destroy them."*

"You've got thirty seconds."

"T-the lab is just a branch, it's the—a part of the company… I can't just—"

Darek tightened the hold of one of the boy's arms, knowing he'd leave bruises, shaking him until he wailed in fear. "Give me the fucking lab, that's all I want. It's my life documented. It's my right."

"Y-you don't understand—"

"I DON'T CARE!" Darek forgot to keep his cool. The more the man resisted, the more his anger rose. How hard could it be? Pen to paper. Get the fucking drama over with.

"Your son is dead. These two will be next." He tightened his grip around the kid's arms until their screams echoed through the room.

Sobbing, the bald man picked up the pen and signed not only one but five documents.

"I-it's yours." He reached out a hand. "G-give me the children."

"Is it legal? If you trick me—" He left the threat unspoken, knowing the kids were enough proof of what he was capable of.

"It's yours, everything. Give me the boys."

"That's it?"

"You could get it notarized, b-but yes. Y-you just need to sign it."

Darek narrowed his eyes, then lowered the kids to the floor, but held on to them both with one hand. They struggled, kicked and scratched, and cried. Darek didn't even feel it as he scanned the documents.

He hesitated, pen on paper. "The fuck are you doing?" His eyes snapped up, darting to the man. "Berner & Junior?"

"I can't give you the lab alone, it's a—it's a process to sell it independently—"

"What are you saying?" Darek whipped his head around, shouting at the struggling kids. "BE STILL! And shut the fuck up!"

"Please—" the man begged. "Take it all. Do what you want with it, just don't hurt the children."

Darek scoffed. That pathetic excuse of a man who looked like he couldn't count his own toes ran one of the biggest businesses in the city. It was as ridiculous as knowing he'd give it all up for the sake of two squirming brats.

Darek signed the contract with a sliver of dread in his gut. He didn't want the whole fucking company, he just wanted the lab. He wanted the control, the insurance that the devil research stayed in his hands. He'd gotten more than he'd bargained for, and he had no idea of what to do with it all.

Darek snatched the papers, folding them and tucking them away into a pocket, then in one fluid motion sent the kids flying into the wall and grabbed the man with the same hand. He pulled him from the chair, dragging him over the desk and pushed him against the wall, and watched as his face turned blue. When he hung limp in his grip, Darek let go of him with a shove.

The kids cowered on the floor next to their mother's body. Sobbing and whining. Darek looked around, his eyes landing on the young men lined up against the opposite wall, pressed so tight against the wallpaper they merged into it. He scoffed at their cowardliness. Even the fucking kids had more guts. They hadn't run, they hadn't left, even when they'd had the chance. Darek shifted closer to them, studying them.

One of the boys turned his gaze up, locking it on Darek's. For some reason, he couldn't look away. The pain in the little boy's eyes broke something in him. Sent him back in time.

"Rest now sweetheart." His mom stroked his face. "You will feel better soon."

Darek looked up at her face and tried to hold back his tears. "It hurts so much, Mommy," he whimpered. "My back."

"Oh my boy," she murmured. "I wish I could take you to the doctor. You know they don't like us."

"Why is Daddy hurting me? Why doesn't he like me? Why is he so mean to me?"

"There's something evil living in him, baby. It's not really your Daddy. You have to remember that."

"You're lying, it is Daddy. He can choose, but he chooses

213

to hate me—"

Darek blinked the room back into focus, shaken by the memory.

He can choose...

The words lingered in his head, refusing to let go. *Choose.*

Darek tore his gaze off the boy. Angered by the sudden emotion, he turned his head so he wouldn't have to look at them. He'd choose all right. He'd choose to rise above the weakness and the pain. He'd choose *right* this time. No remorse, no guilt. He'd choose the devil, he'd choose revenge.

Holding out his hand, he studied the flame dancing in his palm, and just as he was about to release it on the kids, his mom's face flashed through his head.

"You will face darkness, but don't ever let that darkness take you."

Darek screamed, snuffed the flame, and stepped toward the kids. "Get out," he hissed. "Run, before I change my mind."

The boys looked at each other, then at their mom.

"GET OUT!" Darek's sudden scream made them shoot to their feet, and as they ran, Darek fell to his knees.

He ran out of energy, even breathing was a burden he no longer could carry.

Dragging himself up with the help of the table, he forced his worn body to take him to the chair. Collapsing into it, he leaned his head back and allowed his eyes to close.

The sound of shuffling feet forced him to reopen them. "Where do you think you're going?" he hissed at the three young men who stood frozen under his tired gaze.

"You work for me now, clean this mess up."

DAREK

CHAPTER 34

Later that night, Darek slumped against the bar a few blocks away, feeling the gaze of curious customers at his back. He had nowhere to go, and the only thing he craved at this moment was a bed to rest his aching body. Her bed. *Her.*

But he couldn't go back there, he'd kill her if he ever saw her again, and as much as she deserved it—he couldn't think of her dead.

Being out, feeling the crisp air in his lungs and the light rain on his face, Darek had never appreciated freedom as much as he did then. But the relief was dimmed by the dark thoughts circling his head. He'd never been so set on murder as he was now. It took him everything he got not to slash every throat within reach, not to burn down everything in his wake. His whole body vibrated with the need to do *something. Anything.* To feel the strength he'd been deprived for too long, to be the devil he was meant to be. Most of all, he wanted to burn *her*. He wanted to rip her heart and feed it down her throat. He wanted her out of his head, out of his heart. He wanted her gone. He wanted her… Darek cursed out loud. He couldn't lie to himself. He wanted *her*. Even when he hated her, he wanted her.

"But she never wanted you."

The voice was back, making Darek scowl into the glass of gin clutched in his grip. It was right. She wanted him gone from the start, now he was. Guess she was happy now?

Darek emptied the glass, wishing he could get drunk enough to not have to feel, to not have to think, but it was the downside of being the devil. The alcohol affected him, but not nearly as strong as he wished to. Signaling for more, he pushed the thought of Mila from his head and glanced around.

The bar room was dimly lit. White curtains were framing the windows and chandeliers hung from the ceiling. The more Darek took in the surrounding, the more out of place he felt. This wasn't the typical dive he tried to get drunk at. If the sleek, spotless design and the furniture didn't show off the class, the people occupying the place surely did. This was not a place for jeans and sweaty t-shirts. Every single human in the bar or at the tables looked like they came straight from the office.

Darek squirmed in his stolen suit, trying to shut out the imposter syndrome as it closed in on him. He looked like the perfect businessman. Dressed up and professional, when in reality he'd never worn a suit until this day, and he had no idea of how to run a business.

The fact he dreamed of a position just like this was one thing. He never thought he'd get this far. Now here he was, the legal owner of *Berner & Junior*, the fucking leading pharmaceutical company in the city and he didn't even want it. He acted on impulse, as if driven by an inner force telling him what to do when he'd been too tired to think for himself. He already regretted it.

That old man had lost his mind. Giving away his life's legacy, for what? Those squirming brats? Darek didn't understand, but people did stupid things out of fear, and the old man had been ready to shit his pants at the sight of his devil side. Darek couldn't help but smirk at the thought.

Run, run and hide, cockroaches.

A tap on his shoulder jerked him out of his head.

"Sir."

A young woman, possibly not older than seventeen, stood behind him. She wore a black skirt showing off long, slender legs, and a matching black and white striped button-down shirt.

"What?"

"There's someone who wants to see you, alone. She's waiting by the restrooms."

Darek huffed. Alone? Him? Restrooms? Not fucking likely. If he could even stand up, he'd be happy. Casual sex was as far from his priorities as it could be.

"Tell her to go fuck herself."

The girl snickered. "She says it's important. I think you better see her, or you might regret it."

Darek didn't understand. It couldn't be... Mila's face came to his mind and he tensed. He couldn't see her, not now, not like this. He'd rip her heart out...

"Sir—"

Darek let out a cry of frustration as he slid down the stool to land on aching feet. He winced, but forced his body to move, following the slender blonde to the back of the room and through an archway.

He stopped, eyeing the empty space outside the restrooms. "Where's the—"

"Give me your wallet, or I scream," the blonde demanded. "Now!" She held out her hand, snapping her fingers at Darek who stared.

"Seriously?" He cocked a brow in disbelief. Who did she think she was? Scoffing, he added. "Even if I wanted to, I don't have—" he cut himself off, searching his pocket to find a slim wallet stuffed into it. He'd almost forgotten, he'd taken the clothes off Berner. The sadist who ran the fucking multi-million company. Of course he had a goddamn wallet.

"I'll scream that you're trying to rape me, I swear I do.

217

Doubt that's good for your business."

Darek's low chuckle caught her off balance. For a brief moment, she paled, throwing a glance over her shoulder almost as if she'd expected to have been caught. Darek couldn't help but admire her skills. The girl was smart, he'd give her that. She'd even tricked him. She was perfect.

"Hmm," he thought out loud, picking out a business card from his pocket. It still said *Berner & Junior*. He needed to change the name. If he had to see it one more time...

Darek handed the card over to the girl who took it, looked at it with clear surprise written on her face. "As in the medicine company?"

Darek nodded. "I believe so."

Her eyes narrowed. "Believe?"

Ignoring her, Darek blurted, "Work for me."

She burst into laughter. "Are you insane? Why do you want me?"

"You're exactly what I need."

She was clever, manipulative, and seemed to know enough to get her around the important people. With a person like her on the inside, he'd get a steady stream of information.

"As what? I'm not educated for—"

"Who the fuck cares?" Darek snapped. "You'll start tomorrow."

She scratched her head, then a smile broke out across her face. "All right. What do you want me to do?"

Darek didn't know. He didn't even know what he was dealing with. All he'd seen was the lab, and he never wanted to go back there. He couldn't look at those walls and the equipment, not yet. Maybe never.

"Sit with me," he muttered, pushing past the girl and back to the bar. He collapsed at the nearest table, momentarily leaning his head in his hands. When he looked up, she sat opposite of him, a mix of confusion and expectancy on her face. She flashed a smile, pushing her glasses up the bridge of her nose.

"Do you know your way around this company?" Darek asked.

She frowned, then nodded slowly. "I've slept with a few men in there," she grinned. "Even been at the top floor."

Darek scowled but didn't bother commenting.

"You'll blend in," he stated. "I want you to be my eyes and ears. Report everything back to me."

She laughed, nervously now. "At *B&J,* why? Who are you? You're not a terrorist, are you?"

"Hmph." Darek looked offended. "Do I look like a fucking terrorist?" He straightened, trying to look his position. "I'm the new owner."

She sucked in a surprised breath and let out a whistle. "What happened to the Berners?"

"They died," Darek growled. "Now stop asking dumb questions and do as I say."

She scratched her head. "I'd lie if I said I'm not intrigued. I'm in!"

"This will be all over the city tomorrow." He stated the obvious. The rumors would spread like wildfire. They always did. But whatever he'd done in the past was child's play. This was the real deal. He'd not just torched a random rathole, he'd lured out the big rat and shaken the entire hierarchy of the corporate world.

This was riskier. The stakes were higher. Did he even want to get involved with something this huge? Something so life-altering?

"No shit!"

The girl snapped him back to the room, back to her. She grinned. "You've gotta tell me everything." She studied Darek for a long time, then adding with a wry smile, "Boss."

— * —

Darek woke up to the strange smell of food and no memory of where he was. Sitting up, he stared at the beige walls and white couch in disbelief. It wasn't until a female voice reached his ears that last night slammed back into him.

He was no longer tied to that wall, he was no longer stripped of clothes and pride. He was free. Darek sagged in his seat, letting himself fall back against the soft cushion as he relaxed.

"I believe I didn't get your name." The blond girl from the bar came into focus. Darek arched a brow, studying her until she squirmed under his gaze.

"Rewera." He gave her his surname. It was enough for her, it was what he'd use from now.

"That's an odd name," she said. "I like it. I'm Catherine, but everyone calls me Cat."

Darek huffed. How fitting.

"You seriously don't have a place to sleep, or this was just a failed attempt to get into my pants?" Cat asked, gesturing to Darek's makeshift bed on her couch. "A bit odd for the fucking owner of *Berner & Junior* to be homeless."

Darek clenched his fists. "Stop saying that name," he snapped. *Berner, Berner, Berner...* if he heard it one more time he'd kill someone.

"It's Rewera now, Rewera Corp." He lifted his gaze, trying to keep the red from his eyes.

Cat grinned. "I like you."

"Hmph."

DAREK

CHAPTER 35

One week later, Darek stood outside the building, scowling at the giant sign above the entrance. *Berner & Junior*. Fuck that man and his father. He deserved to burn in hell for what he'd done. If he could kill him twice, Darek would enjoy every second of torturing that man until he begged for death.

Tuning out the traffic from the busy street the three flights of wide stairs below, he tilted his head up, trying to see the top of the tower. The sleek walls of steel and glass rose into the sky, disappearing among the low clouds swirling across the sky. Darek gulped, channeling all the fake confidence he could muster, calling in the devil to empower him. Surrounded by five-star restaurants, hotels, and skyscrapers towering over him, he never felt smaller.

Logos of all the important brands and companies glared down at him, reminding him of how much of an imposter he was.

"Coming?" Cat gestured for the massive double doors. "We're running late."

Darek closed his eyes, saying goodbye to his previous life. Once he stepped into this building, it would never be the same. Having no idea of what he was getting himself into, he snapped his eyes open and stalked into the main entrance with Cat by his side.

Stealing glances as he walked, he was ready to run back out to the street. Everything was too shiny, too expensive, too high quality. He didn't belong here, he was a fraud. Even the people's clothes looked like they cost more money than Darek had seen in his life. He might be the owner, but that was just a piece of paper stating a fact he killed for.

Stepping into a shiny elevator that rose toward the sky with a few touches of sleek buttons, his heart rose along with it until it was stuck in his throat.

When Darek stepped out on the top floor, he was sweating under his stolen suit and his stomach was in a knot. Even the devil felt out of place here. He hesitated. Images of people spitting at his feet flashed through his head. Words from his past slid into his mind, making him tremble under curious eyes.

Freak. You should not exist. Scarface. Loser. Go back to hell where you belong...

Darek touched the scar on his cheek, knowing all too well people whispered about it, but tried to ignore it. Clenching his fists, he dug the growing claws into his skin to avoid showing them to the people who stared holes into his back as he walked through a shiny corridor.

"How did you become the fucking owner?" Cat hissed as they walked. "And why?" She grabbed Darek's arm, pulling him to a halt.

"Let go of me," he snarled, yanking himself free. "Don't fucking touch me."

"Geez." She did as he said, looking slightly taken aback by his sudden reaction.

Darek huffed, scrubbing a hand over his face and through his hair.

"You're sweating, you're fucking steaming. Going to go in like that?" Cat whipped out a napkin, handing it to Darek. Scowling, he took it, wiping sweat off of his face before shoving the tissue into a pocket.

"What are you even doing here?" Cat went on. "Seriously? It couldn't be clearer, you have no freaking idea what you're doing!"

Darek swallowed down the lump in his throat. She was right. More than right. He had no clue, but he wasn't going to let it stop him. He could do this, he was the devil for fucks sake. He could do anything. If everything else failed, he could at least burn the damned building to the ground. That would show them.

Encouraged by the thought, he shot Cat a death glare, then set his eyes on the tall double doors that hid the CEO's office behind the shiny white paint. Grimacing at the color, Darek made a mental note to re-design the place. Everything was too bright. Too fucking white.

"We have an appointment," Cat announced their presence to what looked like a secretary, or a guard dog, sitting at a lone desk on the way to the big guy's office.

The woman behind the desk adjusted her glasses, squinting at the couple. "Name please?"

Darek opened his mouth to snap at her when Cat beat him to it. "Oh, of course, Miss. This is Mr. Rewera, the new owner of the company, I'm his assistant."

The old lady's eyes widened. "New owner? Nonsense! Mr. Berner would never—"

"The son of a bitch is dead!" Darek hissed, leaving her staring after him in stunned silence.

Cat's heels clicked against the floor as she ran after him. "What the hell was that!" She breathed. "You can't talk like that!"

"Hmph."

Enough of the bullshit. Flinging the double doors open, he stepped into the office—and froze.

"You look good in my suit."

Darek's jaw dropped. *He* was dead. The son of a bitch was supposed to be dead. But there he was, sitting in a fancy chair behind an even fancier desk, smiling a mocking smile that made Darek's blood boil.

The last months flashed before his eyes. The pain, the shame, the *hell* he'd been through, and he couldn't hold back. Exploding into devil form, he flew out his hand but caught the flame before it could fly off. Burning him was too easy. Too fast.

"Lock the door." Throwing one look over his shoulder, he expected to see Cat. She lay on the floor, clearly passed out. Darek huffed. She wasn't as brave as she let on. One look at his true form floored her, just as it did any human. Anyone but Mila…

Flinging his tail in the direction of the door, he flicked it shut with the force.

"Get out of that chair," he snarled, moving deliberately slow as he closed in on the man who'd tortured him for three months. Darek didn't forgive and forget, he'd return the favor, with interest. Berner would wish he'd died. He'd beg for death and Darek wouldn't grant him. He'd make him suffer the worst way, he'd watch him bleed and cry.

"Get up." Darek reached out a hand, ready to *help* the son of a bitch to his feet.

"I wouldn't do that if I were you."

"Shut up!" Darek snapped, but let his hand drop. "How are you alive?"

Berner chuckled, then shrugged. "It was a sedative, not a death injection."

"You'll wish it was." Darek leaned forward, hands on the desk. His voice dipped into a growl. "You'll beg for mercy like the pathetic worm you are."

Berner rolled the chair back to get out of the glare of Darek's red eyes. "That's how you talk to your employees?"

His words caught Darek off guard. Did Berner know the reason for his visit? Was he the fucking CEO they'd come to see? Reality hit, slamming down at him like a bucket of ice water. Of course. He should have realized. No one with a lesser position could get away with a secret lab, with

224

torturing people under the protection of the shiny logo. A smirk crept onto Darek's lips. It was perfect.

Imagining the things he could achieve with this firm as a safety net was enough to dim the anger. The possibilities were endless. If he played his cards right, he could rule the world, just like the voice in his head had once told him. He could have humanity in his mercy. He'd control their medicine, their vaccination, their lives.

"If I leave this chair, an alarm will go off. You'll be dead within seconds." Berner warned. "Don't you think I knew you'd come? That you'd try to take over. I'd like to see you try."

"I will."

"Just because you scared poor ol' dad into signing the papers doesn't mean you're an expert. You may be the owner, but you're still a nobody," Berner laughed. "You know nothing. You'll run the company to the ground. You need me, you need my expertise, my experience."

"What I need is to see you bleed."

"Holding a little grudge, are we?"

Darek lunged forward, reached over the desk, and grabbed Berner by the throat. With eyes blazing red he glared at the man, "I'll get you."

Berner held up a hand, waiting for Darek to release him before speaking.

"One more thing." He reached into a drawer, pulled out a file, and handed it to Darek. "If I were to... let's say, disappear, *she'll* be paying the price. My men have orders to take care of her the moment I don't pick up this phone."

Darek ripped open the folder, spilling a series of photos onto the desk. For a short moment, the anger dimmed, replaced by a rush of emotion as he saw her for the first time since that night. Even in the pictures, she looked stunning. She wore the red coat again, and her skin was paler than he remembered, but her hair was just as silky, framing her flawless face. Darek picked up a photo, and as he studied her, the reality seeped back like poison in his veins until he saw red.

He threw the picture away and jerked back with a huff.

"I don't care." It was a lie, but he needed it to be true. After what she'd done, he *couldn't* care. "Kill her if you want."

Berner chuckled, picking up a picture showing Mila on her front stairs, looking up at the dark sky. Her coat was opened, revealing a white sweater underneath.

"Do you want me to kill the baby, too?"

Darek's eyes darted to Berner. Had he heard that correctly? What baby? Mila didn't have—Darek's eyes drifted back to the picture, settling on her hand, cupping her belly. No. He refused to believe it. It was a trick. It was nothing but a pure coincidence. Her posture didn't mean—

"Let me guess." Berner pretended to think, stating the thoughts running through Darek's head. "Did she fuck some other dude? Is it yours? Why didn't she say anything?"

Darek gulped.

"She didn't say anything because you are dead to her," Berner went on. "Don't worry, she did grieve. Too long if you ask me, I mean what are you worth?"

Darek's body quivered with the held-back need to rip the man's throat. He burned to destroy him, to make him suffer, but he had to be smart. Tearing his gaze from the photo, he spun to face away from Berner. It was the only option he had left. If he looked at him one more second he wouldn't be able to contain his rage.

"Oh, I almost forgot," Berner called out. "Miss Shikawa never worked for us, she was just a pawn."

Darek swirled around so fast his wings sent items flying off the shelves from the sudden wind. "You're lying."

"It was Carla's idea to lie to you, I just went along with it. She wanted you to herself, for obvious reasons." Berner chuckled. "The poor woman always picks the wrong Daddy materials."

Darek shuddered as the memory of that woman's hands on his body crept into his head. He didn't know what had been worse, her, or the torture.

"You've spent three months hating poor Shikawa when in reality she never did anything wrong," Berner laughed. "How comical." He shifted, leaning forward, hands on the desk. "I'll make you a deal. Sign the company back to me, and I'll give you enough money for you and Miss Shikawa to live happily ever after. I'll get you anything you need, as long as I never see you in this city again."

DAREK

CHAPTER 36

Darek paced Mila's street the rest of the day, contemplating whether to knock on her door or leave and never look back. Was Berner telling the truth, or did he lie to cover up his previous lie? Was it all just a game to trick Darek to give up the ownership of the company? Was Mila the carrot he knew Darek couldn't resist? Did he offer him the happily-ever-after fairytale in hopes of getting rid of Darek? Or was Mila innocent, as that son of a bitch had claimed?

She hadn't tried to find him, she hadn't tried to help. Whether she was innocent or not, she'd left him to rot on that wall. Forgotten about him and moved on with her life. The pictures were proof.

The more Darek thought about it, the more the uncertainty killed him. He had to know. The hate toward her burned like a steady flame deep in his core, and the only way to satisfy it was to feed it. He lived on hate, powered by vengeance he never seemed to get enough of. The list kept on growing longer. He never wanted Mila to be on that list, but as he stared at her dark windows, her name stood out the most. He hated to admit it, but nothing hurt as bad as knowing she, of all people, had lied to him. He expected nothing but pain and misery from every other human, but he'd never expected it from her.

"Don't be a fool," the voice in his head hissed. *"She's a worthless whore. Kill her."*

"Don't call her that!" Darek snapped into the air.

The low chuckle somewhere inside him made his skin crawl with the need to silence it, to rip the owner of that voice to pieces.

"She deserves to burn. You know that."

When the sun dipped beyond the rooftops, casting a blanket of darkness over the city, Darek considered burning it all to the ground and never looked back. It was the easy option, it was the fastest way to get out of the mental torture he'd been thrown into. But it wouldn't end there, and he hated to admit it. He could burn her house, her body, wipe her from the face of the earth, but he could never burn his memory of her. She was a part of him, tucked away in the deepest corners of his heart where not even the devil could reach. She'd been from the start, and Darek knew she'd always be, no matter where he, or she went. She'd be there, eating him alive from the inside. Taunting him, reminding him, stealing his breath with every thought of her lips against his...

A movement across the street caught his attention, snapping him from his head and back to the moment. Her red coat made his heart skip a beat. He'd come to find her, now he wasn't sure he could face her.

She stopped on the front stairs, visibly worried as she gazed into the dark. Darek inched forward. She looked so small, so fragile. He just wanted to...

"Who's there?" Mila's voice slammed into him like a punch to the gut. Darek stopped dead, suddenly finding it hard to breathe. She'd seen him... or *someone*, judging by her question. She was afraid.

Darek wanted to move, but he didn't know in which

direction. Should he run from her or to her? As if encouraged by his reaction, she shouted, "Leave me alone you bastards!"

Darek's heart thundered in his chest, pumping blood faster and hotter until the air vibrated around him, filling with smoke-like steam as he burned under his stiff posture.

Mila threw one last look across the street, then yanked the door open, and Darek couldn't hold back. A strong flap of his wings took him through the air, closing the distance in less than seconds. He slammed the door shut in her face before she could enter, sending her staggering back from the sudden gust of wind.

He wanted to grab her, to shake the truth out of her, but the moment her eyes traveled up his body, settling on his face, he froze under her stunned gaze.

Darek caught her when she collapsed, scooping her up in his arms, and kicked the door open. Torn between the need to hold her, and the urge to drop her from a rooftop made him pick up his pace. Stalking into her apartment, he dumped her onto her bed with a huff. Sucking in a few deep breaths, he tried to calm down, to reign in the fire seeping through the cracks of his fists. He'd never get the answers if he roasted her along with her bed. Darek backed away and stood, staring down at her as his head spun. He couldn't focus around her. He couldn't hate her, but he should. Or should he?

He had no choice but to catch her as she fainted, but staring down at her now, he wasn't as sure. Why should he care? Why would he even bother? His skin tingled from where she'd been just moments ago, pressed against his chest, making him shudder from the mixed feelings it woke him in.

Mila stirred, letting her hand stroke the sheets as a confused look came over her face. Then her eyes snapped open and she scrambled to sit, whipping her head around to stare at him. Their eyes met, and something in Darek stilled.

Her eyes traveled over him, once again her face shifted into confusion as her eyes lingered on his ripped suit jacket. She gulped, tearing her eyes away, and sat motionless and silent long enough for Darek to squirm in the pressing silence.

Eventually, she looked back, blinking up at him as if doubting her eyes.

"Darek?" her voice was just a trembling breath, his name rolling off her lips like a soft caress. He shuddered, his soft breath echoing in the silent room.

"You're really here?" Mila sprung to her feet, reaching for him and Darek wanted nothing more badly than to allow her arms to hold him, to soothe the turmoil and still the fire. He stepped away before she could touch him, crossing his arms over his chest, and tried not to let her stunned expression get to him. She had no right touching him. She had no right to even look at him like that.

His voice was just a growl. "Sorry to disappoint you, darling."

She blinked, inching closer to him. "What?"

"You hoped to never see me again, didn't you?"

Mila stared.

Darek backed away, hissing, "Don't play games with me."

"I'm not, I'm—"

"Lies!" Darek grabbed her arm, spinning her around to throw her up against the wall. "Tell me the truth." His hands shook as they squeezed around her wrists, and not even her whimpers made him loosen the grip.

"You're hurting me."

"She deserves to bleed," the voice urged. *"Don't you want to be more than her slave?"*

He did, and he would be. He'd had enough of holding back, enough of everything. But before he could do anything, he needed to know.

"Why?" he snarled. "Why, Mila?"

"WHY WHAT?" Her sudden shout hit like a slap to his face. Squirming in his grasp, she angled her face up, challenging him with her eyes. "What are you accusing me of?"

Darek looked away, not wanting to risk falling for her hypnotizing gaze, to fall into her calming trap. "You know damned well what I mean."

When she didn't respond, and a puzzled look came over her face, Darek couldn't wait. He had to know or he'd lose his mind.

"You worked with them." He made it sound like an accusation, rather than the question he intended. "You got me caught." He looked back, and Mila flinched from the intensity of his red gaze. "The truth!" He pushed against her wrists, drawing a cry from her lips. For once, she looked genuinely scared. There were no snappy comments or demands, just wide eyes and pale skin as she stared up at him.

"The truth," he repeated, dipping his voice into a menacing snarl as he went on, "Tell me the fucking truth or I swear I'll rip your throat." He let go of her with a slash of a hand, nearly making the threat reality as his claws graced her skin.

Mila staggered back, falling back on the bed in her hurry to get away. "I didn't do anything," she cried out as Darek inched closer, leaning down to trap her between his arms. She scooted back, out of reach. "Why would you even think that?"

Darek huffed, and pushed off the bed and away from her.

"I'd never sell you out, I tried to find you." Mila scooted to sit on the edge of the bed. "I thought you were dead," she whispered. "Then I felt you, I felt everything." Tears welled up in her eyes. "I felt—" her voice broke. She looked up, holding his gaze as she closed the gap between them. As she reached out to touch him, Darek flinched, barely containing his impulse to slap her hand away and instead balled his hands into fists.

"I felt your pain. What did they do to you?"

The air vibrated with tension, his body quivering as he stood glaring down at her and tried not to let his anger consume him. He had to focus, to think. But it was nearly impossible when he balanced on the edge of wanting to kill her or fuck her. Darek let out a breath through clenched teeth and tried to hold himself together long enough for her to speak.

Her voice was hesitant. "Why would you think…" her

voice trailed off, and a hurt expression came over her face. "How can you think I'd do that to you? Didn't you hear me that day?" She took a hesitant step closer, and this time Darek forced himself to stay put as her hand landed on his arm. "I'd never betray you, I love you."

Darek spun on his heels, facing the window. He couldn't think of that. Not now. Being here, in her presence, was enough to tear his walls down. He made a mistake. He should have stayed away, should've focused on what mattered, and left her alone. He couldn't risk falling for her lies one more time. He couldn't—

Mila's hand landed on his back, making him flinch. Each muscle in his body tensed, ready to act, but he forced himself to be still, to be silent, to not break under her touch.

She hesitated, hand still on him. Darek held his breath, trying to still his speeding heart and force his muscles to relax. He'd forgotten how good it felt. How much he needed her, how she managed to make everything feel better with a simple touch. Her arm snaked around his waist, and before Darek could get away, her body pressed against his back as she hugged him from behind.

"Everything will be okay," she murmured. "They can't hurt you anymore."

They stood in silence for a long time, and when Darek finally forced himself to step away, tears clouded his vision.

"Oh my love," Mila reached up, cupping his face in her hands. "I'd never do this to you, you have to believe that."

Darek wanted to believe her, to trust her, but he didn't dare. He couldn't risk it.

"Hey," Mila stroked his cheek. "Look at me."

He did and immediately regretted it. How could he look at her angel face and not drown in her dark eyes full of tears? How could he have any doubt when she touched him so gently, when she looked at him with so much compassion.

"I'm sorry you had to go through that."

Darek squeezed his eyes shut, clenching his jaw in a desperate attempt to keep the pain off his face. Mila smiled through her tears, keeping her soft hands on his skin until Darek broke under her loving touch.

DAREK

CHAPTER 37

Darek was horrified. He couldn't remember the last time he cried, and here he was with pressure behind his eyes he couldn't force back or fight with anger. Her gentle touch and soft words brought it all to the surface. He survived the last three months by distancing himself from it, by separating himself from the devil and letting that part of him take all the pain. He'd lost himself, and he'd done it willingly. It kept him alive and sane, there was no other option.

Being with Mila, he couldn't hide. She brought back the things he'd hoped to never have to face. He wanted to fight it, to push it away, to stay focused, to stay alive. He tried and failed, just like he always did around her. She brought the walls down and cracked him open like a fortune cookie. She looked at him with so much love it was impossible to hate her.

"I don't know what they told you," she whispered. "What

lies they told, you've gotta believe me." She reached out, placing a hand over his heart. "I tried to find you."

Darek believed her, and he didn't know what was worse. Had he hoped she'd confess to betraying him? Had he hoped for his fears to be confirmed? Had he waited for the chance to prove himself, right? No one loved him, no one was supposed to. But there she was, showering him with affection and sympathy until he broke in her embrace.

Accepting the truth was harder than believing the lie. In one way, it had been easier to accept she'd been part of it, that she'd gone behind his back and gotten him captured. That she'd stood by and watched him being tortured and nearly killed. It was the only thing he'd known, why would she be different?

Looking at her now, he was reminded who she was. Mila was the only one who'd seen him, *really* seen him, and she still did.

She wiped his tears with gentle fingers, smiling up at him with her dark eyes so full of compassion it made him choke on the emotions he tried to stuff back down his throat. He couldn't hold himself together, but he refused to let go. He'd been strong for too long. Not just the three months of hell, he'd been strong his whole life. He'd always bit back the emotions and locked away his heart. He'd thrown away the key, never expecting her to find it and bring it all back.

Darek crumbled in her arms, allowing her to lead him to the bed and sink down onto it as she stood between his legs, gathering him in a tight embrace.

"You're safe now," she soothed. "Let it out."

Darek stopped trying, stopped fighting. He was too tired to do anything else.

When he thought the emotions would consume him and the pain was too much to bear, she held him tighter, lending her strength when he couldn't find his own. At that moment, she was his life. His everything, and as long as he was in her arms, everything he'd done, everything that had been done to him, faded until it was too far out of reach to hurt him.

When she pulled away, he wasn't ready to let her go.

Mila sat next to him, laying a hand on his arm. "How are

you here?"

Darek searched for the right words. How could he explain to her what he barely understood himself? The months tied to that wall felt like a fog. One part of him was convinced it was nothing but a nightmare and he'd finally woken up, the other part of him who knew the truth refused to face it. It was too much, too real. The first week of freedom was the same. He remembered every detail, but his actions didn't feel like his own, and he knew why. The devil had pushed him, throwing him on the path he'd never would've had the courage to choose for himself.

"What happened?" her soft voice reminded him of her question.

Darek shook his head. He couldn't bring himself to talk about it. He couldn't face the pain one more time. He couldn't even look at her as the memories again filled him with a deep agony he was sure would never fade.

He'd carry those months with him like he did with all the rest. One more emotional scar that would never fade, one more proof humanity was as rotten as he'd always known them to be.

"I can't talk about it," he said at last.

"You'll feel better," she coaxed.

It took all his willpower not to explode from the sudden burst of anger flaring up within him. *Feel better*. It was bullshit. He'd never feel better. He didn't even want to. He didn't want to *feel* at all. Darek dug his claws into the mattress to keep from using them on her. He was the devil for fucks sake, he didn't *feel*! But he did, and it made him even angrier.

"Hey," her voice was hesitant, and so was the hand on his arm. "I'm sorry."

Darek let out a shuddering breath, trying to reign back the devil when all he wanted was to let it rage. But he couldn't, not around her. If he'd snap and hurt her, he didn't know what he'd do.

"I'm losing control," he confessed. "It's getting stronger. I let it. I had to." He glanced at her, seeing her lips part in a silent gasp. Then she nodded, sliding her hand down his arm to take his hand.

"Fight it."

"I can't." Darek looked down at their hands, his voice dipping into a growl. "I don't want to."

"That's the devil speaking."

The tremble to her voice didn't go unnoticed by Darek. He huffed. She was scared. She should be. She should hate him. If she knew what he'd done, she would. A part of him was tempted to tell her every detail to push her away. The other part of him wanted to cling to her, to the hope of redemption and the love she was willing to offer even though she knew he was nothing but a monster.

"That's what I am, Mila."

"You're more than that," she whispered. "You're also human. Choose."

The words hit him like a sledgehammer, knocking the air out of his lungs. *Choose.*

"There's something evil living in him, baby. It's not really your Daddy. You have to remember that."

"You're lying, it is Daddy. He can choose, but he chooses to hate me—"

Images flashed through his mind, throwing him from scene to scene so fast it made him lightheaded from the sudden assault.

Berner's sick grin.

Carla's seductive hands.

Blood, so much blood...

Darek pressed a hand to his head, digging claws into his skull as if trying to tear the memories from his head. He refused to go back there. Not now. Not like this.

"It's okay," Mila breathed. "Relax." She untangled his hand from his hair, ignoring his bloodstained claws, and wrapped her hands around his.

Darek's mind spun, he didn't even feel the stinging pain his claws left behind. When the slideshow of mental torture finally subsided, only one thing was stuck in his head. Guilt. He killed without regret, burned down cities

237

without remorse. He left bodies in his wake, torn families apart, and destroyed lives, and he enjoyed every second of it. Yet, the two pairs of tear-filled eyes as those little boys had looked up at him that day, refused to leave him alone. Darek squeezed his eyes shut, trying in vain to banish the feeling.

"What are you thinking?"

"Nothing," he choked out. He could never tell her. She would never understand when he couldn't even understand it himself. Why them, why now? He never cared, never felt the weight of his actions crush him, and he'd done things far worse.

"Darek," Mila's voice was soft, comforting. So were her hands, still wrapped around his. "Don't torture yourself, it's over."

"No," he said before he could think. "I did things, Mila… things I… regret."

She frowned. "Then make it right."

"I can't." Darek hung his head, too tired to fight the feeling. He could pretend all he wanted, hide from the truth. But he knew why those eyes haunted him, why he felt bad for the first time in his life. He saw himself in them. The despair, the pain, the fear. He saw his own eyes looking up at the man looming over him, silently begging to make everything all right, even when he knew it was too late.

"Talk to me," Mila coaxed. "I can help you."

"No."

"Darek."

"I SAID NO! Don't fucking force me!"

Mila flinched, but the hand never left his.

"I won't force you," she murmured. "It's okay. I'm not the enemy. I just want to help you."

Darek gave a short nod. Would he ever be able to accept that? Would he ever be able to fully trust her?

A deep silence fell between them, and Darek was glad she'd given up. He'd do anything for her, but not that. He couldn't stand the thought of her looking at him differently. As much as he hated to admit it, he needed her. He wasn't ready to lose her. Not again.

238

"Whose clothes did you steal?"

Her sudden voice made Darek jump. His eyes darted to her, blinking her into focus as her words drifted into his overheated brain too slow.

"Hmph." Darek scowled at her as the son of a bitch Berner's face flashed before his eyes. He'd wanted the man dead. Instead, he'd stepped right into his shoes, taken over his life, in more ways than one. How ironic. Yanking his hand from Mila's grasp, he shrugged out of the suit jacket and tossed it along with the shirt aside.

"Sorry." Mila gave him a sheepish smile. "I'm sure you looked dashing in that suit before you tore it to shreds."

Darek couldn't help but groan. The disadvantage of having fucking wings which he had no control over.

"I'm not used to seeing you so dressed up."

"Better get used to it," Darek muttered. "Do you know how to run a business?"

Mila's brows shot up. "Why are you asking?" Her eyes narrowed in suspicion as she eyed the clothes with a new interest. "What aren't you telling me?"

Darek let out a short laugh. "I just happen to have this multi-million dollar corporation on my hands and I—don't know what to do with it."

Mila gaped. "Are you serious?" She frowned. "How the hell did that happen?" The hidden accusation in her voice sparked Darek's anger.

Before he could stop himself, he snapped, "I got them to sign me the fucking lab they used to torture me." He scowled at the memory. "It's my life, *mine*, every result, every file—" he cut himself off and stood. "No one else should have access to that, to what they did!" He snarled. "I took it, and the son of a bitch signed the whole fucking company instead."

Darek paced the floor, digging claws into his palms, overwhelmed by the rush of reality washing over him. "I never asked for it! Never wanted it, do I look like a fucking businessman?"

Mila's hand on his shoulders calmed him immediately, and he felt the horns pull back before they had the time to

239

emerge.

"You do." She smiled. "You look stunning. Like a boss."

"Hmph."

"I do know how to run a business. At least the basics, we can do this. Don't panic."

Darek collapsed onto the bed, letting his head fall into his hands. "You know how to run a goddamn dog shelter, this is—"

"What?"

"Heard of fucking *Berner & Junior*?" He spat the name out. Judging by Mila's gasp, she had. Darek looked up, locking his now red eyes on her. "Do you know how to run *that*?"

She gaped, no words leaving her mouth.

"Because I'm dying to throw that bastard of a CEO out the window."

"Darek!" Mila snapped. "I'm not letting you throw anyone out the window." She shook her head in exasperation. "But I will help you." She scratched her neck. "Is this even legal, how can someone just sign—"

"It is."

"*Berner & Junior* is private limited? Because if it's not—" she cut herself off, smiling at Darek's perplexed expression. "You really do know nothing?" She seemed to think, then spoke again. "*Berner & Junior* is huge, I find it hard to believe they'd have full right to just sell it. What about shareholders? What about—"

Darek cut her off, "They run a fucking torture chamber, they're shady as fuck, they'd never let outsiders in on that. Neither will I."

"It's not that easy, there's a chain of people…" Mila trailed off, sighing at Darek's frustration. "We'll figure it out. Maybe you're right. I guess it's not impossible."

Darek huffed. She was just saying it to calm him down. But he *was* right. After what he'd done, they'd never dare to cross him. Not a fucking chance. Darek shook his head to clear it of disturbing images, to get those eyes to leave him alone.

It was legal. Why was that cockroach Berner so eager

240

to bribe him into signing the company back to him, if it was not? It was legal, Darek was sure of it, and he had no intention of giving it back. Not that he wanted the goddamn firm or cared what happened to it. He just wanted it long enough to destroy the sick bastard and take the rest of humanity down with him. This was an opportunity too big to let slip. It was everything he needed and more. With a little bit of planning and a whole lot of secrecy, he could take over the world without leaving the building. He needed people he could trust. People who would do as he told them with no questions asked. He needed someone with no morals and no heart. Darek smirked at the thought. He'd do what no one before him had done. Modern times called for modern measures, and he had the right tools to accomplish great destruction, right under his nose.

"First thing we're doing is changing the goddamn name."

MILA

CHAPTER 38

Mila heard him in the other room and considered getting up to check on him. She'd tried to persuade him to sleep, and he said he would. Three hours later she woke up to an empty bed. He never even stepped into the bedroom.

Gazing at the clock, she memorized the time and closed her eyes. He needed time to process everything, she wasn't going to push him. Only yesterday she'd been convinced she'd never see him again. She'd been ready to accept the fact, but never the feeling. Lying in her bed now, suffocating desperation swept over her like a blanket, sending her back to the lonely nights trying to reach out to him through her thoughts.

"I'll find you. You're not alone," she whispered into the dark. *It had become a ritual, based on the tiny hope he could feel her, too. If he could feel how much she missed him, would it offer him some comfort?*

Mila buried her face into the cold leather jacket, inhaled his lingering scent, and prayed for it to be over. The connection they had, started to feel like a curse. The cycle never ended, and even though she knew she only felt a fraction of what he went through, Mila couldn't help but wish for a way out. She wasn't strong enough to handle the pain. There were times she wished he'd just die.

Curling up on her side, she imagined him there with her. Closing her eyes, she could almost feel the warmth radiating off him. Mila stroked the cold sheets where he should have laid, and tried not to cry. She didn't want him dead. She wanted him with her. She wanted him so bad it hurt.

When she opened her eyes again, the room was bright. Mila's eyes darted to the clock and widened. She was supposed to meet Kate two hours ago. Scrambling out of bed, she threw on her robe, shuffled to the kitchen, and grabbed the phone.

Riley answered on the second ring. "I overslept," she breathed. "Can you tell Kate I have to reschedule?"

"Sure, you okay?"

"Yeah, just didn't sleep well," she lied. "See you tomorrow?" Mila felt bad about missing out when they were so close to reopening. Since the fire, they'd received generous donations for the rebuilding of the shelter. That, and the help of the insurance, Lucky Paws was about to open up within days.

It had been her only anchor, the only thing she'd focused on to keep her sane. Mila opened the fridge, snatched the orange juice from the shelf, and drank straight from the bottle as her thoughts drifted to the shelter.

Inside, everything looked the same but yet so different. The smell of fresh wood hung in the air, a scent Mila always loved. She sniffed the air like a dog, making Kate laugh.

Running her finger along the fresh walls, she took everything in, in awe. Everything was upgraded. The kennels, the yards, the endless supply of blankets and dog accessories in shiny cabinets.

A full smile spread across Mila's lips. The first she'd smiled in months, she realized with a pang of guilt. She was happy while Darek was being tortured somewhere.

Mila's smile faded, and she sunk into a chair.

243

"What's wrong?" Kate was quick to ask, having gotten used to her sudden shifts of mood.

Mila gave her a faint smile. "I'm fine, just—" she let out a deep sigh. "I feel like I'm leaving him behind. Christmas is just around the corner and everything's changing." Mila looked up at Kate, whispering the last words. "He's still out there somewhere."

Kate sat too. "You've tried everything. The police tried, you have to let him go."

Mila shook her head. "How can I? I feel him."

"You weren't connected before meeting him. Go back to that. Cut the tie."

"I don't know how." Mila let her gaze fall on the cages lined up against a wall. "I don't want to."

"You've suffered enough because of that man," Kate's voice grew impatient. "If he truly cares for you, he'd want you to be happy. He'd understand. Throw away that old jacket, use the money for the shelter. Take your life back." Kate reached out across the table, placing her hand on Mila's. "He's not coming back."

It was no secret Kate was happy about Darek's absence. Even though she tried to look sympathetic, she was relieved. Mila couldn't blame her, but her friend's hatred toward Darek bothered her, especially now when he was back.

She was torn in two. She couldn't imagine leaving Darek alone when she'd just gotten him back, but bringing him to the shelter... she didn't dare take the risk. His last encounter with Kate had gone horribly wrong, and now, if possible, he was even more tense.

Mila found him in the living room, staring through a window. She stopped in the doorway, watching his broad shoulders with a deep sorrow filling her heart. The scars on his back always made her sad. To think of the things he had gone through, to imagine how his life must have been, almost brought tears to her eyes. That the three months away had been hard on him was obvious, but as she watched his tense posture, she realized she knew nothing. She'd suffered along with him. But the ghost pain she'd endured had been just that. A ghost. The moment it was gone, she was fine. She was safe. But he hadn't been. He'd never had the relief of curling up in a soft bed or eating ice cream out of the box in self-pity. He'd never had anyone to even hug him and tell him everything would be alright.

"Hey," she greeted. "You didn't sleep at all?"

When he didn't offer anything, and instead of facing her, kept on staring through the window while a noticeable aura of steam rose from him, Mila, knew something was wrong.

She crossed the room, laying a hand on his back. The moment she touched him, he jumped, letting out a sharp hiss. Mila staggered back, suddenly uncertain of how to act.

"Darek?" she whispered. Her hand reached out, and before she could touch him again, he swirled around, out of reach. His eyes roamed over her, from head to toe and up again, briefly pausing at her middle. Mila held her breath. The way he looked at her made her feel like he knew. But he couldn't. Only Kate and Riley knew, she hadn't told anyone else.

"Open it." He made a swift flick of a hand toward her robe. Mila's heart skipped a beat before jumping into her throat. He knew. She didn't know how, but the way he looked at her was all the proof she needed.

"Darek..." she began.

His voice was just a hiss, "Do it."

Mila briefly wondered why he was just standing there. Why wasn't he touching her, why wasn't he pinning her to a wall and breathing down her neck?

Keeping her eyes on his face, she opened the knot and let the robe slip open enough to reveal her belly. Darek paled visibly, his lips parting in an inaudible gasp.

"I wanted to tell you," her voice betrayed her by trembling. "I just didn't know how, I'm—" the words died in her throat as he shifted, taking one step closer to her before stopping again. She tried to read his face. What was he thinking? Was he excited? Was he as horrified by the thought of this thing growing inside of her, as she'd been? Would he run and never return? Mila couldn't blame him. She would've done the same thing if she could have. She'd

245

been so close.

"The child you carry is evil. He will grow into a monster. He will hurt people, he will hurt you. He will be the death of you."

Mila pressed her hands to her ears. Was she going crazy? Was she scared, yes. Did she have doubts about keeping the baby, yes. But the voice was as clear as day. She didn't imagine it. It was there in her head, filling her with a strong need to act upon the impulses. And as she stood outside of the abortion center, with her hand on the doorknob and a lump in her throat, shifting her weight and trying to gather up the courage, she knew she had to do it.

"You're doing the right thing." The voice was soft, comforting, speaking to her as a loving mother.

"Stop," Mila cried. "Please stop."

"Don't be frightened."

Mila raked her hands through her hair. It was not real, the voice was not real.

"You know what you have to do."

"No."

"You feel it. The darkness."

Mila drew in a trembling breath, her fingers curling around the knob. She did feel it. The constant feeling of doom never left her heart. It was growing in her belly. It would eat her alive, it would be the end of her life as she knew it. She didn't want it. She didn't want this baby...

"It's not too late," the voice whispered.

Mila squeezed her eyes shut and breathed in a few deep breaths. She loved puppies, she loved life—but she wanted to kill her baby? The thought made her feel sick to her stomach.

Mila blinked the room back in focus. Watching Darek as he stared back at her, the same feeling of doom came creeping over her. It wasn't just her. He wasn't ready to be a father, just as she wasn't ready to be a mom. But there was no stopping it now. Mila swallowed down the fear rising in her throat. He had the choice she'd never allowed herself

246

to make. He could turn his back to it, to her. He could run.

His eyes sought hers, and Mila flinched from the intensity of his sudden red gaze.

"Is it mine?"

His question took her by surprise. She'd never considered the thought he could have any doubts. She'd just assumed—

"Tell me," he snarled. "The truth."

Mila only managed a small nod, stunned by his sudden fierceness. How could he even doubt it? Who would she have been with, and when? Did he think she'd been with other men while he'd been tortured in some secret lab? Did he think she could even stand the thought of anyone else's hands on her body?

"Holy shit! It's his?" Kate's shriek made her grimace. Mila didn't bother to even nod. Of course it was his. Kate knew it as well as she did. Swallowing down the uneasy feeling, she pulled her shirt down to cover herself up.

"Why didn't you tell me?"

Mila looked down at herself, letting the hand linger on her belly before dropping it into her lap. Deep down she knew why, she just wasn't ready to admit it. It hurt too much to accept the truth.

Since he'd disappeared, a part of her had been cut out along with him. A part which was now replaced by the baby residing in her body. She should be happy for the part of him he'd left behind for her to love. But the thing was, she wasn't. She didn't feel happy. She didn't love the THING inside of her. She wanted it gone.

"Mila?"

She looked up, blinked away tears, and finally whispered, "I wanted him to be the first to know."

"It's always been you," she whispered. "Even when I hated you, I wanted you."

A shadow of a grin flashed over his face.

"There has been no one else, during..." he trailed off, and Mila's heart ached as she saw the pain written all over his face. She shook her head, stepping closer to him.

"No one. I love you." She reached out a hand, taking his in hers. He tensed but remained still. "I meant it, I still do."

"I know it's a shock," she went on. "I'm not particularly happy about it either. I didn't want it, not without you." She brought his hand to her chest, squeezing it between both of hers. "Say something," her voice was just a whisper. He was too calm, too still. It wasn't like him. Mila held her breath, waiting for him to explode.

He slowly backed away, pulling his hand from her grasp until he was free. He paused, eyeing her in silence as her heartbeat echoed in her head.

"Darek?"

His eyes traveled from her face to her belly and then up again. When he brushed past her and steered straight for the front door, Mila didn't try to stop him.

The door slammed shut, leaving her emptier than ever. She couldn't blame him, she really couldn't. But she also couldn't deny she hoped for a different reaction. She'd hoped he'd stay. She'd needed him to. She needed him.

Mila looked at the closed door, silently praying for it to open again. For him to come back. When she'd stared at it for what felt like hours, she sunk to the floor, letting the tears roll down her cheeks.

DAREK

CHAPTER 39

Darek paced the floor of Cat's tiny studio and tried to listen to her frantic rambling and failed attempts to make him leave. He didn't even know what he was doing there. He'd fled in shocked panic. He needed air, needed to breathe. But the further away from Mila he was, the harder it was to do so.

"Be still!" Cat finally shrieked. "Sit, please, you're freaking me out!"

Darek stopped with a huff. "I'm trying to focus." He continued to pace. The more time passed, the more unsettled he felt. He'd left her. His mind was a whirlwind of thoughts which he didn't know how to process. He'd left her. Was he planning to return?

Darek didn't know. Could he? He didn't know that either. Did he want to? He paused. Yes. He wanted her like he had from the first time he'd seen her. It hadn't changed.

Everything else had. She had. He had. It was too late, no chance of getting back to how it had been. No more carefree days locked away from the rest of the world.

"Will it even be human?" he asked Cat. "Will it be like me?"

Cat let out a sound, a laugh, and cry mixed into one. "Are you seriously asking me that!" She rushed out of the way as Darek continued the pacing. "This isn't happening," she chanted. "This is a dream. What I saw in that office was a dream. Right? You're—" she gestured toward Darek. "You have a normal body, a human body."

Darek stopped, hesitated, then removed his jacket and started to unbutton his shirt.

"What the hell are you doing!"

"The fuck does it look like?" Darek shifted into devil-form before Cat could ask again.

She screamed, scrambling back until she hit the wall. "Shit!" she cried out. "What are you?"

"Do I look like a father to you?" he shouted. "Does— THIS—look like dad-material? Do you see these scars?"

Cat's mouth opened and closed several times with no words. "I pretty much only see wings," she finally gasped. "Am I going crazy?"

Wings… "Oh fucking lovely!" Darek's shout made Cat jump. "A flying baby! I can't go back."

"Are you some kind of an angel?"

Darek's eyes snapped to her, a cold laugh erupting from his throat. "I'm the devil, you idiot."

Cat slid down the wall, burying her head between her knees. "I'm going to die," she wailed.

Darek huffed. "If I wanted to kill you, you'd be dead long ago, now focus!"

Cat shot to her feet at the sound of his tail cutting the air like a whip. "Focus?" she breathed. "Oh, I'm focused all right. I'm in the same room as the fucking devil!" She pointed to Darek's blood-red wings. "Why did you show me?"

"What?"

"Why did you show me your—" she gestured toward his

250

body, not finding the words.

"To shut you up, to get the goddamn charade out of the way," Darek snapped. "This is who I am. Accept it or die."

"Good options," Cat breathed. "I guess I'd prefer the first one."

Darek turned away with a huff.

"I'm going to be a father," he stated the obvious.

"Oh great!" Cat collapsed onto her couch. "That's what the world needs, a mini-devil. As if we're not fucked up enough as we are."

Darek clutched his head, trying to breathe through the panic welling inside of him. Was she right? What about Mila? She was human, could she survive a non-human birth?

Darek suddenly felt nauseous. What had he done to her? "Why are you here?"

Cat's words snapped Darek back to reality. He had no answer. He didn't even remember.

"The business—" he tried to focus, to steer his mind toward something he had control over.

"Oh, no, no. I'm not working for you anymore if that's what you're—"

Darek flung his arms out, making the couch skid across the floor from the heat wave bursting from him. "You are."

Clinging to the couch, Cat nodded frantically. "Okay, okay, okay, I am. What do you want me to do?"

Darek stared at her as he thought. All he could think of was Mila and that baby. All he could feel was the burning need to be back in her arms.

"Recruit," he said the first word coming to his mind. "I need more people."

"For what?"

"I'm replacing the lead, those assholes are loyal to that worm Berner. Find others. And find out how to change the logo. He will die along with his name."

"I'll look into it. I think I know exactly where to start."

Darek nodded, letting his thoughts drift back to Mila, to the life growing inside her. *His baby.* Darek couldn't wrap his mind around it. Mixed emotions made him lightheaded. His heart was a pendulum, going from the darkest of feelings to love, then back again. He didn't know where it would stop, where he wanted it to stop.

Between the panic and fear, something so much bigger and warmer grew within him and he couldn't put it into words. It spread within him like cancer, overpowered the need to run away and the fear of turning out just like his own father.

"Why are you still here?" Cat asked, raising a brow. "Do you want it?"

"Want what?"

"The baby. The girl, the freaking happily ever after you're running away from."

"Hmph." He studied Cat. How did she know? "I'm not signing it over to that worm," he snapped.

Cat held up her hands in defense. "Geez, I'm not saying you should." She frowned, then seemed to understand. "He asked you to?"

"He threatened Mila."

A thoughtful look came over Cat's face. "I can't believe I'm saying this, but I'm on your side. I never liked that man, he's a creep."

Darek arched a brow. "And I'm not?"

Cat let out a nervous laugh, eyeing his still exposed devil features. "You're okay, for being—" she gestured toward him.

Darek couldn't help but chuckle.

"Why aren't you killing me?" Cat blurted.

"I didn't know you wanted me to." His eyes flashed red and Cat flinched, gulping visibly.

"I didn't mean—" She climbed out of the couch, keeping her eyes on Darek as she moved to stand behind the tipped-over table. "Just that—" she gestured with a hand toward his devil form. "You could. Easily."

Fear radiated off her as he inched closer. "Don't tempt me."

Cat slid out from her position, crossing the room to keep a safe distance to Darek, who scowled at her pitiful attempt.

"Okay!" Cat breathed, "Look! Go to her, why are you

here playing cat and mouse with me? She's clearly all you think of."

"Hmph."

MILA

CHAPTER 40

Kate's horrified gasp made Mila's head snap up from her position on the floor. The pitbull she'd been brushing, rushed up too, growling in the direction of the door. Mila followed the dog's and Kate's gaze, eyes landing on Darek as he stood, arms crossed and casually leaning against the doorframe.

"You're alive?" The venom dripped from Kate's voice.

Mila blinked at Darek, not able to grasp what was happening. He'd left, he'd run, yet there he was, eyes blazing as they stared past Kate and straight at Mila.

Kate grabbed the dog's leash, pulling him away from Mila while she hissed, "Why didn't you tell me?"

"I found out last night, I didn't—" her voice died as Darek pushed off the wall and stepped closer.

"Explains where your mind has been all day," Kate muttered. "I'll take Spade. Here." She hurried through the back door with the growling dog, and Mila turned her face up.

"I didn't think you'd come back."

A shadow of guilt flashed over Darek's face. Silently, he held out a hand. The moment Mila took it, heat rushed along her arm, and exploded in her body. She bit back a gasp, but couldn't stop the shiver. Darek's smirk made her squirm. He'd noticed. Feeling her cheeks burn, she let him pull her to her feet. Once standing, she'd expected him to let go and jump away like he had the previous times. As if he was repulsed by touching her. But instead, he stood motionless, holding on to her hand as if it was his only lifeline.

"Have you seen him?" His voice hinted of the fear he hid inside.

Mila didn't need to ask. Following his gaze to her belly gave her all the information she needed. She shook her head. "I didn't want to, didn't—dare."

Mila swallowed down the lump in her throat and forced herself to speak. "I swear if it's like you, I'll kill you myself."

Darek let out a sudden laugh, then his face fell and a pained expression came over his sharp features. "Mila, I'm—sorry."

Her eyes bulged. An apology? From him? That was the first.

Her eyes narrowed. "For what, exactly?"

He squirmed, suddenly looking like he wanted to be anywhere but there. "Everything—but mostly—" He grimaced, flicking his eyes toward her belly.

Mila gaped, lost for words. She'd seen a lot but never had she expected *that*. She didn't even know what to say.

Darek shifted his weight, smoothed out invisible wrinkles of his shirt as he waited for her to speak. Mila watched him suffer, and somehow enjoyed it, letting him sweat.

"Where were you?" she asked at last.

Darek just shook his head. "Does it matter? I'm here now."

"You have to do better than that."

He looked away, but not before she saw his jaw tense, and his eyes flicker red. A pang of regret shot through her. Was she wrong to push him? He'd said it himself. He was losing control. He was not the same Darek as she'd known. He was rough, on the verge of cruel. Was that something she wanted to poke? Did she want him to snap and break her neck?

Mila eyed his stiff posture and tried not to pull her hand free as he held it in an iron grip.

"Listen…" she began.

His head snapped back to her, his gaze so intense it made her flinch.

"I was with a workmate. Cat. I needed to—" he cut himself off, and Mila wondered if it was the look she hadn't been able to keep off her face, or simply his own fear of talking about his feelings that stopped him.

He scoffed. "No need to be jealous, darling. You're the only human I can even stand to look at."

Mila made a face, not sure if she should be relieved, or offended.

"Mila. I'm trying."

She tilted her face up, watching his expressions shift, and when he spoke again, his voice was just a whisper, "I don't know who I am anymore."

Tears sprung to Mila's eyes, and when she tried to speak, her throat closed off.

Darek grabbed her shoulders, stepping closer.

"I'm not going anywhere," he growled. "I'm with you, and the boy."

A soft gasp slipped past Mila's lips. He was so close she could kiss him. His scent filled the space around them until it lit every cell of her body on fire.

"How do you know it's a boy?" she asked the first thing coming to mind.

"There's always been boys in my bloodline." His eyes lit up, shining bright red as they gazed into hers. The way his jaw tightened told her he wasn't as amused as he let on. He was scared, too.

"Let's break the chain," she murmured. "Let's have a girl."

Darek let out a controlled breath, warm and tempting against her lips. His hands slid down her arms holding them tight as he leaned in. Hovering his lips above hers, she felt his hands quiver, the steam rising off his body, increasing temperature around them.

Mila tugged at her arms. She wanted to wrap them around

his neck, she wanted to touch him. But he didn't let her. He didn't even kiss her. Instead, he just stood, torturing himself and her with the proximity.

"What are you waiting for?" she breathed. "Kiss me, you idiot!"

Darek crushed his lips against hers, blowing her mind with an intensity and leaving her breathless and aching for more. When she finally tugged her hands free, she didn't hesitate. Wrapping them around his neck, she pressed herself closer, moving in for more.

"Ehm."

The sound made them jump apart, and Mila's gaze snapped to Kate who started back at them with pure horror on her face.

"Whoa!" Riley entered from the other door, oblivious to the scene. "Is it hot in here?"

Mila's cheeks turned red, and Kate burst into a fit of nervous laughter.

"What's so fun—" Riley's eyes landed on Darek, and widened? "I'd be damned. I thought you were—" he cut himself off, eyeing Mila's flushed complexion and Darek's ruffled clothes.

"Did I interrupt something?"

"That guy—thing," Kate waved a hand at Darek. "Is steaming, I mean literally."

Darek's whole body tensed. He shot her a glare, stiffening further until Mila thought he'd snap from the tension. When the steam turned into a deep scent of smoked wood, and his muscles quivered with the effort to not act on whatever murderous impulse he had, a bolt of fear zapped through Mila.

"Kate," she warned. One more word from her and she wasn't sure Darek would be able to stop himself. Not this time. Mila forced her voice to sound calm even though she wanted to cry or scream.

"Maybe you should try to keep the insults to yourself." She took Darek's hand, hoping the gesture would soothe him. "He's not a *thing*." Looking up at him, she added. "He's the father of my child. And I love him."

257

The room fell silent as all three stared at her in stunned silence. Mila took the opportunity to whisper to Darek, "That's who you are."

He only managed a stiff nod, but his hand tightened around hers and Mila knew. He'd never let her go. Just as he'd promised from the start. Just as he'd sworn every time she wanted him as far away as possible. How had she gone from hating his guts to needing him like she needed air? It didn't make sense, but Mila didn't try to figure it out. She was content with what she felt and knowing somewhere deep inside him, he felt the same.

"I'm fine with you, man," Riley broke the silence. "I heard what you did for Mila. Not many would do what you did."

Darek looked at him, a guarded look on his face. Mila poked his side, "See, some people are good, you just need to give them a little time."

Darek's huff made her chuckle. It was clear he had a hard time believing that, and after what he'd been through, she couldn't blame him.

Riley grinned. "Truer words couldn't be said." His eyes landed on Kate, urging her to join in. Mila's eyes traveled to her as well, demanding her to speak up. Kate squirmed under their eyes, letting hers dart to Darek, then back to Mila.

"I want to be okay with him but—" she gestured toward him, hissing. "He's the devil, The fucking devil, how can I be friends with *that*? I'm scared, okay?"

"Kate," Mila begged. "He's also human, look at him." Mila looked as she said it, seeing nothing *but* the human in him. Seeing through the tough exterior and the permanent scowls. Seeing his bruised soul and feeling the pain he tried to hide deep inside. He wasn't evil, he wasn't hellbent on killing them all, he was just suffering from a life of abuse and mistreatment.

"He's been through hell, eh, not literally, he just needs someone to care, a friend."

Darek turned with a huff, shaking off Mila's hand, and stormed off before she could stop him. She winced, she'd embarrassed him, possibly even touched a few sore spots he didn't want to be touched.

She looked between the empty place he'd disappeared from and back to Kate. "Give him a chance. He gave his life for me. He was tortured for three months, you know it, you saw it through me. Those months nearly killed me. It's been his life since he was born. Where do you think those scars are from?" Mila lowered his voice. "He hates people because he sees nothing but pain and suffering when he looks at them. He's not evil, he's just in pain. Don't be the one to add more."

Kate sighed. "It's really that bad?"

Mila nodded, blinking away her tears.

She left Kate to think of it, and went to find Darek.

He stood outside, melting the snow around his feet. His head snapped up as he saw her, and the scowl deepened. "I don't *need* anyone," he hissed. "Especially not *her*."

"Oh my love," Mila brushed her hand over his arm. "I just wanted her to understand. It's important to me you two get along. I love you both."

"It will never happen."

"Dar—"

"NO! I swear I'll kill her if I have to see her again."

Mila sighed, looking down at the ground. Darek cursed under his breath, then he sighed, and added in a strained voice, "Sorry."

Mila looked up, studying his face as he seemed to battle his own demons. She reached out, touching his chin, and forced him to look at her.

"You really are trying, aren't you?"

He gave a short nod, then squeezed his eyes shut and let out a long breath. "I was with Cat for about a half an hour. She convinced me to go back, but I—" he cut himself off, snapping his eyes open and resting them on Mila, seeking the courage to go on. "I don't want to hurt you. When I'm like this, I... could."

"No." She took his hand. "You won't. You're doing good."

"I spent all night fighting the fucking devil, I'm

exhausted, I can't do it."

"You didn't hurt Kate."

Darek's scowl said at all. He wanted to. He'd been dying to. Mila cringed but didn't say anything.

"I won't let him win, I won't let him take you," Mila said.

Darek muttered something under his breath, but let it go. Mila smiled, patting his shoulder. "Good boy." Standing on her toes, she kissed his lips, drawing a deep growl from his throat. When she was ready to turn and head back into the warmth, he grabbed her, pinning her to the wall as he caged her in.

"Not so fast, darling."

Mila looked up, startled from the sudden shift in his mood. Heat spread around her as he stepped closer, touching his body to hers with a notable gentleness that took all his willpower to maintain.

"I can't wait nine months," he growled into her neck. "Being around you and not touching you is torture."

Mila didn't bother to correct him, and she had no intention of waiting the remaining six months. She needed him just as bad. If they hadn't been on a busy street, she would have begged him to take her, right then and there.

"Then don't," she breathed. "Take me home."

Darek stepped away, his eyes narrowing in confusion. Mila stepped into his arms, wrapping hers around his neck. "Make use of those wings."

DAREK

CHAPTER 41

Darek lifted the sweater over her head, watching as her dark hair fell over her shoulders, dancing over her white skin with a delicacy making him tremble. Crouching before her, he unzipped her jeans and peeled them down her legs. She stepped out of them, standing before him in black lace underwear and a nervous look on her face.

"You're beautiful," he growled. "Just looking at you..."

He held her hips, studying her belly with an intensity that made her tremble under his hands.

The flat tummy he remembered, showed a clear bulge. He couldn't stop staring at it. Wrapping his mind around it was hard. His son—or daughter, was growing in there. *His*. Should he be proud or nauseous? He promised her he'd stay, and he meant every word, but he wasn't ready to be a dad. How was he supposed to take care of a kid when he could barely take care of himself? He had no idea what to do with a kid. But he would never leave her because of it. She was too precious, too special. Had it been anyone else, he'd be long gone. But Mila was different. Mila was his reason for breathing. His obsession with her hadn't faded, and it never would. She did things to him, things he'd never felt. Things that terrified him, but also thrilled him.

She was his, now more than ever. His claim on her grew inside her belly. She'd always be his. Nothing could take that away now.

Darek's hands trembled as they slid from her hips to her stomach. Her skin was smooth and warm. So full of life. The curve of the life force growing inside her mesmerized him. Knowing was one thing, but seeing...

"Darek—" she began, her voice uncertain.

"No." He knew what she was thinking, but she was wrong. He didn't find it repulsive, fat, or ugly. He was in awe.

Rising to his full height, he touched a finger to her lips. "Don't say it." He trailed his knuckles over her cheek, down her jaw before letting a thumb trail the contours of her lips. They parted with a soft moan.

Darek ran his hands down her sides and then up again, hooking them under her arms and lifting her like a child. Mila's surprised yelp melted into his mouth as he laid her down onto the bed and kissed her. Holding himself up on his arms, he hovered over her, scared to touch her, yet dying to.

"I'm pregnant, not poisonous. What's wrong with you?"

"I don't want to hurt you"

"You won't."

"The baby—"

"Sex can't hurt the baby," she said. "Now shut up and—"

Darek didn't let her finish. His mouth was back on hers, his hands following. He couldn't get enough of her. Touching her, tasting her, every inch of her body left him burning for more. It had been too long, but he still remembered every curve, the way she squirmed when he kissed her neck, the way her body arched as he trailed the tip of his claws down her sides. Darek had never cared about being gentle, about giving pleasure instead of pain, but with Mila, he couldn't think of anything else. Even now, when he was more devil than man. Even when he'd been consumed with anger and pain, he'd held on to her, stubbornly refusing to give in and lose himself completely. He'd been close, but her presence brought him back. Brought him to this moment, when he was back in her arms and all he wanted was to love her. Even if he didn't know how.

He wanted her to beg, to scream, but for the opposite reasons than what he usually craved.

Darek helped her remove the last distraction of underwear and stood, fully clothed, staring down at her naked form. She was the most precious thing he's ever seen. She was like the moon and the stars, all wrapped into the shape of her mouthwatering body.

"Why am I the only one naked?" she whispered.

Truth was, he didn't know. Had he grown so used to the torture he wanted to torture himself, as well? Every cell in his body was ablaze. He was burning up under the tight suit he insisted on keeping on. The need to feel her skin against his was so strong it hurt. Yet, something stopped him.

He climbed onto the bed, straddling her hips, and leaned down until his lips hovered over hers. Her arms snaked around his neck, pulling him down. A traitorous groan escaped his throat at the mere contact, his muscles tightening until they quivered with held back desire.

When her hands tugged at his shirt, he grabbed them, pinning them to the mattress. Before she could ask, he returned his lips to hers, stealing her breath and making her beg for more.

Mila tugged her hands free, but before she could reach him, Darek slipped to his knees on the floor. One hand on each of her thighs, he yanked her closer to him, gazing up at her through red eyes.

He dragged his claws across her thighs, watching her back arch and her hips buckle.

"Darek," she moaned.

"What was that, darling?"

"I need you," she whispered.

A smirk crept onto Darek's lips. He'd give her what she needed, and more. Lowering his lips to her leg, he trailed his mouth over her porcelain skin, enjoying her moans as he found the spot between her legs.

Mila grabbed the sheets, clutching them until her knuckles whitened and her body shook. When she cried out loud, Darek nearly gave in. If he had to wait one more second, he'd burst.

Her pleasure rolled over her in waves, her body shuddering in the aftermath, and as she slumped against the sheets, panting for air, Darek shot to his feet and left the room before she had time to ask.

Staring out the kitchen window, he adjusted his pants in a useless attempt to ease the discomfort. He bit back a groan, clenching his fists at his sides to keep his hands from going there.

"What's wrong?" Her voice made him tense, breath hitching in his throat. Through the reflection of the glass, he saw her enter the room. She was still naked. Darek clenched his jaw, feeling his teeth crash together until the tension made his head hurt. Why did she have to be so irresistible? Why did she have to be so—her hand landed on his back.

Fuck. Darek squeezed his eyes shut, trying to block her out. He couldn't do this. Not now. He didn't want to remember.

"Is it because of the baby?" she asked.

Her question caught him by surprise, and before he could stop himself, he spun around to face her. "No," he snapped. "It's not the baby, it's—me."

Mila frowned, reaching out for him, and he backed away shaking his head. She'd never understand. He didn't even want her to. He was too fucked up to even understand it himself. "I can't do this."

Mila caught his arm as he tried to run, holding on to it as he snarled. "Don't touch me!"

"Darek!" Mila raised her voice, yanking him to a halt. "Look at me!"

He scowled but did as she said.

"It's just me, you're safe."

264

Darek let out a sharp breath. Trying to hide his true feelings with a scowl led him nowhere. She saw straight through him, and he hated it. Just the thought of her hands on his body sent him straight back to that wall. He couldn't be that powerless, that vulnerable, he couldn't even stand the thought of being naked around her.

"I don't know what they did to you." Her hand traveled down to his hand, lacing her fingers in his. "But it's over. Let me love you."

Darek's resistance didn't stop her from leading him back to the bedroom. "Don't you want me?" she asked, dragging a hand down his chest. "Don't you want—" she trailed the hand down, stroking him through the pants, "This?"

A traitorous groan escaped his throat. How could he say no when his whole body demanded the opposite?

He caught her hand, removing it from his body, and stood, clutching her wrist and staring down at it while his mind raced along with his heartbeat.

"You're scared." She stated the fact but made it sound like a question.

Darek turned from her with a huff. "That's ridiculous."

"Is it?"

He didn't bother to reply. What did she think? He was some little girl? He wasn't fucking scared. He just didn't want to relive the horrors etched in his mind. The further he drifted from the devil's mentality, the more he felt it, and he hated it enough to consider giving it all up. It would be so easy to let the devil take over his mind, to let it rule him with its ruthless cold. He didn't have to think or feel. He didn't have to suffer.

"That's right," the voice in his head coaxed. *"Let it go."*

Mila's voice snapped him back to the room. "What happened there?"

He shook his head. He didn't have to do this. He didn't even have to be here with her. What was she? A mere human. A worm, just like the rest. And there she was, trying to get under his skin, into his heart…

"She will only give you pain. She will make you weak."

"Darek! Talk to me!"

"Powerless."

"Nothing you want to hear about," he snapped.

"Pathetic."

"Don't shut me out."

"Kill her!"

Her hand on his shoulder made him swirl around, ready to scratch and bite.

The hurt expression on her face and genuine fear in her eyes broke something in him. Darek froze, feeling the anger disperse like smoke in the wind. The devil was wrong. She cared. She was his strength. He was better *with* her.

He wanted so badly to shut her out, to shut *it* out. To turn off everything inside that hurt, and let the anger swallow him up, but he couldn't. Not this time.

He needed her like he needed air. Shutting her out was nothing but a slow death. He needed her, needed the calm relief she offered, now more than ever. Needed the love. He refused to let the devil stand in the way.

"Mila," his voice was raw, but he forced himself to go on, "Touch me. Make it okay again."

Tears spilled from her eyes, but she smiled despite them.

"Don't you want to talk about it first?"

"No," Darek growled. "There's nothing to talk about. I know you felt it."

A puzzled look came over her face. He studied her in tense silence, waiting for the realization to hit. She'd said it herself, she'd felt the pain, the torture. Wouldn't she have felt the other things, too? Hands on his body, disgusting hands where they shouldn't be. His body, betraying him by accepting what his heart refused to. The humiliation...

Her face fell, mouth dropping open as she stared up at him through wide eyes. "No," she whispered.

For a long time, Mila just stared at him. Darek stared back, his heart throbbing against his ribcage, his pulse echoing in his head.

"I don't need your pity," he growled at last. "Just go."

"Oh my love," she stepped closer instead, hesitating only a few seconds then wrapping her arms around him. "I'm so sorry you had to go through that." She pulled him closer, burying her face into his neck as she stroked his back. "The bitch had no right to touch you."

Darek stood rigid, fists clenched to his sides as he tried to wrap his mind around her reaction. He'd expected her to be angry, disgusted even. He thought she'd look at him differently, hoped she wouldn't want to touch him after knowing the truth. Was it cheating if he hadn't willingly participated?

Mila's soft body pressed against his, proved everything he'd thought, wrong. And as he dared to relax enough to untangle his fists and rest his hands on her bare back, a calm surged through him. Darek let out a slow breath, tightening his arms around her in return.

MILA

CHAPTER 12

"You don't have to do this," Mila gazed into his gray eyes while trying to keep tears from spilling from hers.

"No." He looked up at her from his position on the bed. "I do."

"Darek," she whispered. "I didn't know, I didn't mean to—"

He let out a sound, a mix between a scoff and a laugh, cutting her off. "If you don't touch me soon, I'll combust."

Her eyes involuntarily drifted down to his lap. "I can see that." A smile crept to her lips. "You haven't changed that much."

"Hmph."

"Are you sure?" She brushed a hand over his shoulder, letting her fingers rest on the button of the shirt.

"I'm the devil, not some fucking—"

Mila quieted him with a finger to his lips. "Stop! You're not *the* actual devil." She demanded. "Just because you're *a* devil, doesn't mean you don't have a right to feel."

The scowl on his face made her roll her eyes. "You're also human. And trust me, we feel a lot of things. It's normal. It's okay to be stressed out. To feel hurt, exposed.

Most people would suffer from severe PTSD after going through something like that."

Darek scoffed. "I'm not *most people.*"

She hushed him again. "You say that, but your body language says something different."

"Oh, for God's sake Mila, *just fucking do it*!"

"Relax." She shook her head in exasperation. "Alright." Keeping her eyes on his face, she began unbuttoning his shirt. It gaped open, and as she pushed it off his shoulders, he tensed for a brief moment, then shifted, pulling his arms free from the fabric, and tossed the shirt aside with a huff.

"That's the devil I know." Mila grinned, placing her palms on his chest to push him back. He didn't protest but tensed further. Leaning back, propped up on his arms, he studied her hands as they worked on his belt.

Mila listened to shuddering breaths, studied his stomach muscles flex, and tried to decide whether it was from unease or arousal. Judging by the tightness of those trousers, she hoped for the latter.

Darek's eyes never left her as she peeled the fabric down his legs, exposing his naked body in all its glory. Before she could touch him, he slipped off the bed, snatched her up, and flipped her over, pinning her to the mattress. Straddling her, he held her down with the weight of his body to her hips, staring down at her with an urgency in his eyes that made Mila shiver. She blinked up at him, stunned by the sudden shift.

Supporting himself on his arms, he lowered himself over her, keeping a gap between them she was dying to close.

"I need this," he growled against her lips. "The control."

Mila managed a weak nod, and it was the only sign he needed. He grabbed her hands the moment she tried to touch him, holding them firmly with one hand above her head, as his other hand reached between them, guiding himself into her with one powerful stroke. Mila tugged at her arms, wanting nothing more than to feel him under her hands, in her arms. He held her in an iron grip, and as she listened to his shuddering breaths, the heat from his body wrapped her up like a blanket. Mila's body moved on its

269

own, reaching for him, craving the heat, the touch of his skin against hers. As if he'd read her mind, he straightened, letting go of her hands and gripped her hips, raising her to match his movements. The need to touch him was forgotten as the feeling exploded within her. Instead of reaching for him, she grasped the sheets, curling her fingers into the soft fabric as her body arched against his.

"Darek," she breathed.

He paused, holding still as he gazed down at her, chest heaving and muscles flexing in a show of ripples and shudders. Just looking at him was enough to push her to her limit. With his glistening skin, ablaze from the inside, he was the most stunning thing she'd ever seen. Fog-like steam rose from his skin, filling the room with the scent of freshly snuffed candles and burned wood.

Mila arched her hips, urging him to go on. Faster. Harder. A grin spread across his lips as he obeyed, granting her wish.

"Don't hold back," she breathed. He hesitated for a beat, then let go. His jaw slacked as the tension left. His mouth falling open in a silent groan as he allowed himself to really feel, to relax enough to lose himself in the pleasure.

Mila flinched as the horns grew from his skull, and his eyes flashed red. Wings sprouted from his back, filling the room with their width and his grip of her hips tightened along with his body.

The burst of power shook Mila's body, drawing a gasp from her lips. Her eyes flickered to the wings, to his tail as it twitched from side to side from his movements, then back to staring at his face, breaking the eye contact only when hers fluttered close with the wave of warmth washing through her. Darek cried out, collapsing forward. Holding himself up on strong arms, he tipped his head forward, leaning his forehead against her chest, caging her in with his horns on each side of her head.

Mila let out a shuddering breath, lifting a hand to stroke the horn while her pulse throbbed in her temples. "Holy shit," she breathed. "They always come out, when..."

Darek rolled over. Collapsing on his back, he draped a wing over Mila in the process. She rolled to her side so she could watch him, feeling oddly protected under the leathery shape of his ruby wing.

"I can do it without, but it's not as good," he muttered.

Mila grinned, leaning in to place a kiss on his jaw. "It's okay."

Darek rolled his head to watch her. "How can you be so okay with this?" he asked. "How can you not be—repulsed? Scared?"

Mila reached out, caressing his face. "Because I love you," she murmured. "Are you alright?"

Darek only managed a weak nod, but it was enough for Mila to smile. "Next time you'll let me touch you."

Darek huffed, scowling at her.

"Come on," Mila protested. "I can't do this '*look but don't touch*' any longer, you're too tempting."

Darek chuckled, then his face turned serious. "What are you doing to me?"

"What do you mean?"

"You're—brightening up my dark. I thought I was lost. I was ready to rip out your heart for fucks sake! You make me want to be good." He scoffed as if he couldn't believe he was saying it, "For you."

Mila's heart swelled and tears sprung to her eyes. "Isn't that a good thing?"

Darek considered it. "No."

She snorted. "Says the devil." She stroked his arm. "You're more than that, Darek. You can be good, you can do good. You just have to choose a side and stick to it."

"I choose you."

A wide smile lit up Mila's face. "I love you."

Darek opened his mouth, then closed it. Several tries later, he gave up, turning his head with a huff.

"You don't have to say it," Mila soothed. "I know you love me too."

His head jerked back to stare at her.

"Don't look so surprised," she chuckled. "When the devil wants to convert to the good side, that's pretty much a dead giveaway." A sad look came over her face as she went on, "Plus, you sacrificed everything, for me."

Darek looked up at the ceiling, a tortured look settling on his face.

"Hey," Mila pushed herself up to a sitting position, draping his wing over her lap and caressing its smooth surface as she studied him. "It will be okay, nothing bad will happen. We'll stick together, I won't let anything come between us again."

Darek hesitated, then reached out a hand. Mila took it, brought it to her lips and kissed it. She lowered it in her lap, playing with a claw and testing its sharpness with her finger. When the tip pierced her skin, she yelped, snatching her hand away.

"Holy crap, they're sharp!" she breathed. An embarrassed look came over her face. She patted his hand. "Sorry, I'm dumb. Shouldn't have done that."

"I'm not a vampire." He gestured with his eyes toward her bleeding fingertip. "Give me that."

Mila hesitated, reaching out her hand to him. He sucked the blood off her finger, then placed his thumb against the cut, keeping the blood from dropping.

"Sure you're not a vampire?"

"You'd rather have it all over the sheets?"

Mila grimaced.

"It'll stop," Darek muttered.

"I'm not worried." Her voice rose with alarm as she studied him, "It won't make me a devil or something?"

His sudden laugh made her jump.

"It doesn't work like that."

"How does it work, can you make a—" her voice died in her throat. When her eyes met his, she knew the same thought had crossed his mind.

"Mila, I'll take you to that fucking ultrasound kicking and screaming if you don't—"

Mila swallowed down the sudden lump in her throat. "I'll go tomorrow."

DAREK

CHAPTER 43

Mila parked outside the shelter with an amazed grin still plastered on her face. "You have no idea how relieved I am," she exclaimed. "It's a baby, a normal *human* baby."

Darek chuckled, feeling slightly better himself. The fact he hadn't impregnated her with the devil's spawn was good news, so why did he feel so shaken?

He had an important meeting right around the corner, but all he could think of was the black and white image taken from Mila's belly. The lack of tiny horns and wings wasn't enough to excite Darek as much as it had Mila. The small shape of a human that was their baby threw him completely off balance and he couldn't seem to regain it.

The range of emotion had him in a vacuum. This was really happening. They were having a baby. A boy. Darek wasn't surprised, even though he'd hoped for a girl. He didn't want a mini version of himself to remind him of things he wanted to forget. He wanted a girl, a baby girl like Mila. She didn't seem to care about the gender, she was just relieved it was no devil. Darek scoffed at the thought. Did it even matter? Devil or not, it was a boy. A fucking boy. Maybe if he'd take his looks from Mila, he'd be—

"Darek?" Mila poked his arm, snapping him back to the car. "What are you thinking?"

"It's a boy," he muttered. He'd known it. But having it confirmed crushed the last hope of ever breaking the chain.

"A *human* boy," Mila said. "Relax, my love, he won't grow up like you did. We will give him a good life. Don't worry."

Darek nodded. When she said it, it made sense. Just because the boy was a boy didn't mean he was doomed to grow up in the hell Darek had. This baby had Mila. He had Darek—he frowned at the thought. Was that a good or a bad thing? Could he do this? Would he be a bad influence? Would he push the boy to the dark side just by being in his life?

"I'm the—"

"Devil," she filled in, "I know what you're thinking. Look at you, you're not as evil as you think. The baby has nothing to worry about."

Darek huffed, offended by her comment, but didn't know why. Hadn't he decided to choose the good side? To choose her. Those words should be a compliment, yet, he couldn't shake the annoyance bubbling up within him.

"I'm only good when I'm around you."

"You're on the right path, you'll get there." She leaned in to steal a kiss. "Plus, I'll be there. We're in this together. I won't let you slip."

Darek flashed her a quick smile. She was so confident he could do this. It made him feel like maybe he could. For *her* he could, for her—he wanted to.

Darek kissed her goodbye until the windows steamed up and he'd forgotten he needed to go. When she pushed away from him, he growled deep in his throat.

"Hold that thought," she winked, brushing a teasing hand along his thigh. Darek shuddered, watching the hand travel up. He grabbed it before it reached his crotch, breathing deeply to calm his pulse. He couldn't do this, not yet, not like this. Her touches, even though driving him wild, also threw him straight back to that wall of horror. He had to keep his head clear. He had to focus.

"Don't taunt me," he growled. "These pants are too tight already."

She giggled. "See you tonight." Mila slipped out of the car, tossing the keys to Darek. "Be careful."

— * —

Half an hour later, Darek pulled up outside of a small house in the suburbs. He eyed the once white walls and a broken fenced-in patio with a growing feeling of dread. Even though the area was shabby and old, he didn't belong here. He didn't belong anywhere where there were people.

He got out of the car, smoothed down invisible wrinkles in his new suit, and strode up the stone path to knock on the door before he had a chance to chicken out. He was not a people person. People annoyed him. People were something he'd learned to stay away from—or kill. Playing nice was something he was not used to, and he had no idea how to do it.

The door flung open, almost smacking him in the nose. Darek jumped back, digging claws into his fists to keep from acting out on his impulses.

Standing face to face with a man, possibly in his mid-forties, all Darek felt was a deep desire to slit his throat. Reigning in the devil, he forced a polite smile.

"Richard Evans?"

The man nodded. "You must be the infamous Mr. Rewera. Miss Catherine told me you'd be dropping by." The man chuckled, adding, "Everyone talks about you, and trust me, it's not good."

Darek huffed. The sudden swap of ownership had left the whole company reeling in the news. The news that damn Berner was spreading. Darek was sure the bastard did everything in his power to make Darek look like the bad guy, the enemy.

"Come in." Richard made a wide gesture, slapping Darek on the back as he passed. "I'm impressed. I have to say, I believed you'd be older. How did a young man like you get a hold of a company like Berner & Junior?"

Darek stopped in the middle of the room, unsure of what to do next. "I'd rather not get into details," he muttered. He studied the man. He was tall and well-built, almost as tall as Darek, and his dark blond hair was messily strewn around his long face. A twisted grin played on his thin lips. He was dressed in faded jeans and a black t-shirt with a skull printed on, looking as far from the businessman Darek expected, but looks were deceiving.

"Coffee?"

Darek shook his head. He wanted to get this over with and leave, not stay for pleasantries. He wanted to be with Mila.

"Take a seat." Richard gestured at an old wooden table and a few chairs. Darek hesitated, then did as the man said, trying to look professional, even though he was already sweating. Richard took a seat opposite of him, and Darek tried to resist the urge to snap his neck. Being around people and not killing them was not his strong side. His fingers itched with held back power, the fire burning hotter within him, just waiting for an outlet. Darek kept his hands in his lap, tightly balled into fists to keep the flames contained, and prayed the man wouldn't notice the strange heat filling the room.

"What happened to your face?" Rickard asked.

Darek's eyes snapped up to glare at him, and it took all his willpower to keep them from going red.

"Sorry," Richard chuckled. "I bet you hear that a lot. Just curious though."

"I bet you are," Darek's voice lowered into a growl. "No one lives to hear the answer."

Richard gulped visibly, momentarily paling as he stared back at Darek who held his gaze without as much as blinking.

Richard averted his eyes, then cleared his throat before

going on as if nothing had happened. "I hear the old man Berner is dead?"

Darek's eyes narrowed, silently warning the man not to push it. There was no limit to his questions. Darek didn't know what was worse, that idiot asking about his scars, or mentioning the name he couldn't stand hearing.

Richard cocked a brow as if waiting for an explanation.

Hiding the fire-storm underneath, Darek managed to speak with a calm that even surprised himself. "I heard he broke his neck. Should've been more careful."

A sly smile played on Richard's lips. "Is that so?"

"You've been in jail?" Darek abruptly changed the subject, making Richard laugh out loud.

"You're not beating around the bush, are you?"

Darek couldn't hide the scowl. He couldn't do small talk. He had to get out of there before he snapped and killed the man. The only reason he hadn't already torched the place was because he needed him alive. Cat had done her research, and she'd done it well. According to her, Richard was the perfect candidate. Now, just to convince Richard himself. "Do you want revenge? Power?"

Richard's grin spread. "I'm listening."

"You're exactly what I need."

"An ex-con?"

"Did you not hear me?" Darek scoffed. "You're already corrupted."

"So?"

Darek's blood boiled, steam making the suit cling to his body. For a moment he questioned everything. What was he trying to achieve? Was this arrogant son of bitch someone he wanted to deal with on a daily basis? Could he? Without losing it and cutting his head off?

Richard cleared his throat, giving Darek a pointed look.

Darek turned away, facing the old wallpaper and the stack of newspapers lined up on the table. Judging by the man's home, he wasn't doing as well as he let on. He was poor. He was jobless, just as Cat had said. He *was* perfect.

"You'd work for me, no questions asked. No moral lessons, no crying to the law."

Richard chuckled. "What exactly are you trying to accomplish?"

"I don't know." It was a lie. He did know, but spilling his plans to a stranger was not only risky, it was dumb. Richard didn't need to know. He'd have to kill him if he knew the plan taking form in Darek's brain. "I'm new to this, once I get the hang of it..." he left the sentence unfinished, the unspoken promises of something big hanging in the air. "Are you in?"

Richard held up his hand, a gesture to calm down. "What exactly are you asking me to do?"

Darek's mind went blank. He hadn't thought that far. He knew nothing of the business lingo, even Mila had caught him off guard. He needed to learn, to fucking study. Darek huffed at the thought.

"I'm replacing the top, handpicking people who suit Rewera Corp."

"Rewera Corp, huh?"

"The name changes today, including that awful sign. Fucking Berner is history," Darek's voice dropped into a growl. "In more ways than one."

"Count me in." Richard slapped his hands together. "Anyone who can bring down that man is my kind of person."

"He turned you in?"

"He destroyed my family, my life. I've spent ten years behind bars because of that son of a bitch."

"Do you have the competence to take his seat?"

Richard's blue eyes bulged. "As the CEO? Are you serious?" Then he nodded, laughing out loud. "Of course I have, I grew up in a suit. I was the head of ZionGen before the bastard got me."

"What did you do?"

"Rather not go into details." Richard grinned at Darek's scowl. The man was smart, Darek had to hand him that. Smart, *and* shady. He considered it. Anyone was better than that bastard Berner. If he could have taken his place himself, he would have. But even though he hated to admit it, he'd never manage it. He knew nothing, Berner was right. He'd destroy the company before he'd even get the chance to learn. He needed someone like Richard to hold the reins until he could take over. He needed someone to teach him.

"That office is mine," Darek stated. "But you can have the position, the salary, the power, on one condition."

Richard raised an amused eyebrow. "Which is?"

"You'll teach me everything you know. You follow my vision, and you do it without questions. No matter what you see."

"Can't see why that would be a problem."

Darek chuckled. "Oh I can, and *you* will."

"What if I don't agree?"

"Either you're with me, or you're dead."

Richard guffawed. "Deal."

A smirk played on Darek's lips. "Welcome to Rewera Corp."

MILA

CHAPTER 44

Bright rays of sun shone through the teal curtains the next morning. But it wasn't what woke Mila. He had. Before she opened her eyes, she felt his heat as he lay next to her. It radiated off him, making her smile into the room. She'd been lucky. After everything that happened, there had been a time when she was convinced she'd never see him again. That the baby would have to grow up without a father.

But he found a way back to her. He survived, and even though he never spoke of it, she knew better. He did it for her.

After too much time to think about it, Mila had pieced the puzzle together. They told her that night, but not until later had she understood and accepted the full truth. She'd been a pawn in their games since day one. The moment she'd fallen for Darek had been the start of his downfall.

The terrorizing, the stalking, the shadows outside her windows, her kidnapping, it had all been a part of their study, their plan to lure Darek right into a trap with no escape route. Falling for her had been his biggest mistake. They used it against him, used his feelings for her to force him right into their grasp.

Mila shifted, propping herself up on one elbow to watch him as he slept. In sleep, he looked peaceful. Without the permanent scowl on his face, he looked so much softer. If she hadn't known better she could never have guessed what was hiding inside that perfect body. The only thing that gave him away was the faint scent of candle smoke coming from him, and the fog-like smoke rising from his skin.

Mila reached out, brushing a hand over his chest. He was as warm as he looked, burning on the inside, even in sleep.

"My love," she whispered.

Darek stirred, his eyes snapping open so fast it made her flinch at the sight of the deep red glow. The moment he saw her, he relaxed, his eyes changing back to normal gray.

"Are you watching me sleep?"

Mila smiled sheepishly. "Couldn't help myself."

"Hmph." Darek sat, catching her by the neck and guiding her lips to his. When he was done kissing her, Mila wanted nothing more than to stay in bed and continue what he started.

He grinned. "Keep that thought. I have to arrange a few things first."

"First? Like... right now?"

He nodded, jumped out of bed, and got dressed in a rush. "I'm late."

Mila sat, staring at him. "For what?"

"Patience, darling."

"Have I told you how gorgeous you look in that suit?"

A low chuckle rumbled in his chest. Winking at her, he turned and left.

— * —

Mila spent the day at the shelter, catching up on missed time with the dogs and taking walks in the nearby park.

The black pitbull tugged at the lead, eager to explore the fresh layer of snow. Mila laughed at her as she threw herself on the ground and rolled. The carefree life as a dog, like a child, full of innocence and joy, often made her joke about wanting to be a dog in her next life. There was a small amount of truth in it.

"Wait for me!"

Kate's voice forced her back to the present, and she smiled as her friend came running toward them. Sheila's ears peaked, her tail wagging as she launched herself forward in excitement.

"She thinks you've been gone for weeks," Mila chuckled. "Not just hours."

Kate dropped to her knees in the snow, while the dog tried to reach her mouth with sloppy kisses.

"Where's Riley?" Mila looked around.

"It was weird, he said he needed to go help a friend, wouldn't tell who."

"Maybe he wants to surprise you."

Kate laughed. "He's not that clever, unfortunately." She giggled. "If he says he helps a friend, he helps a friend. He can't keep secrets."

"Point taken."

They walked in silence, and Mila's thoughts wandered to Darek.

"It was never his fault, you know that."

Kate's eyes darted to her, and it didn't take long for her to follow Mila's train of thought.

She sighed, catching snow off a hanging tree branch as they walked. She formed it into a ball and threw it for the dog to chase before admitting, "The incident reports show traces of gasoline. It was arson."

Just as Mila opened her mouth to ask, it dawned on her. The fire.

"Why didn't you tell me?"

"You had enough on your plate."

"Darek doesn't need gasoline to—"

Kate held up a hand, cutting her off. "I'm not blaming him." She rolled her eyes, grimacing. "I'm saying I know it wasn't him."

Mila stopped, eyeing her friend suspiciously. "Are you serious?"

Kate grimaced again, but nodded. "Doesn't mean I trust him."

Mila opened her mouth to protest, but Kate cut her to it. "I'm not blind. I can see you love him. And he did kill for you. Probably even intended to die for you. I guess I can't ask for more than that from my best friend's boyfriend."

A small smile tugged at Mila's lips. "Thank you," she whispered.

"It's getting dark, let's go."

Back at Lucky Paws, the dog's fur was covered in snowflakes which she shook off on the floor in the reception. Kate took her leash, gesturing with her free hand through the window.

"There's your devil."

Mila's eyes darted to the window, and there he was. On a safe distance from Kate, no doubt. He stood in the midst of the snowfall, wearing nothing but a three-piece suit.

"Doesn't he feel cold?" Kate asked.

Mila shook her head, never taking her eyes off Darek. "He's warm," she murmured.

Kate groaned, muttering under her breath. "Enjoy. Don't do anything I wouldn't do."

"Hi, Mila!" Riley stepped through the door, tipping his hood back and sending a cascade of snow through the air.

"You're worse than the dog," Mila complained. "The floor will get wet." She frowned, adding, "Where were you anyway?"

"Just had to run a few errands. Someone is waiting for you outside. Dress warm."

Mila stared after Riley as he crossed the room and disappeared through the same door Kate had. Dress warm? For what?

More confused than ever, Mila threw on a red hat matching her coat and stalked toward the winter street outside.

"Dress warm?" she asked as a greeting. "What are you up to? Did you just come in with Riley?"

Darek raised an eyebrow but remained silent as he wrapped Mila in a tight hug. When he stepped away, he studied her for a long time before asking. "Do you trust me?"

"Of course."

"Then do as I say. No questions asked."

"What are you—"

He shut her up with a kiss. "I said, *no* questions, darling."

Mila clamped her out shut, and Darek chuckled.

"Follow me."

He led her around the corner, out of sight of the trafficked street and passing pedestrians before unbuttoning his suit jacket.

"Hold on to this." He handed it to Mila, shredding the shirt as well and all Mila could do was stare. Standing in the heavy snow, wearing nothing but a tie and pants, he grinned at her stunned face.

"Come here."

He held out his arms, inviting her. Mila didn't hesitate, letting him wrap her into a tight embrace. Face pressed against his chest, she felt the surge of power ripple through him as his wings emerged from his back.

"We're flying, should have guessed."

She groaned, holding on tighter in anticipation of the weightless feeling she hadn't yet gotten used to.

Before she could think further, a strong gust of warm air washed over her, then she was airborne. Mila squeezed her eyes shut, never daring to look as they glided through the night sky like birds.

The light thud as he landed let her know it was safe to open her eyes. Darek held on to her, spinning her around so her back was pressed against his front, then folding his wings around her to shield her from the biting wind.

"Where are we?" Mila gasped. The view was breathtaking. Far below, a canvas of city lights spread out as far as she could see. Big fat flakes of snow swirled around her face, weightlessly dancing in the wind as they fell toward the streets.

"On the top of the Rewera tower."

Mila gaped. "It's amazing, I didn't realize it's so tall."

A low chuckle reverberated in Darek's chest. He stepped away, taking away the heat.

"Turn around."

Mila gulped, suddenly feeling the altitude. Without his support, she felt like she'd slip and fall off the moment she moved. This was no tourist attraction, there were no security net or high railing to keep her safe. They were on a flat roof, and she was certain the fresh layer of snow had made it slippery.

"I won't let you fall."

Mila managed a weak nod. That's what the wings were for. He still had them out. She clutched the shirt he told her to hold on to as if it was a lifeline, eyeing his bare chest and wings, and couldn't help but gulp as the mere sight of him stirred something deep in her belly. *That* was her security-blanket and her source of heat. She smiled at the thought, no matter how terrified she was, she was just as certain he meant every word.

Mila slowly turned and gaped. Spread out on the roof was a blanket big enough for four, and thick enough for blocking the biting cold. A row of lanterns surround the area, the flames flickering even though they were safe behind glass. Mila's eyes traveled over each and every one of them until skipping to the middle of the blanket. To the basket, to the smell of food.

Darek's arms were back around her waist, guiding her toward the safety and comfort of the fluffy black blanket.

"Sit," he demanded, and Mila gladly obeyed, placing the clothes next to her for safe-keeping. She adjusted her scarf, trying to block the snow from slipping into her coat, then ran a hand over the blanket.

"You did all of this?" she asked, staring in awe at the setting.

"With a little help from Riley."

"He was up here?"

"Fuck no, he shit his pants by the mere mention of it."

Mila laughed out loud. She wouldn't have expected anything but. Riley had a fear of heights, and this was pretty much as high as they could come in this city. If she didn't count The Needle.

"Then what did he…" her voice trailed off as he began opening the basket, revealing the wonderful smell she'd caught a whiff of a moment ago.

"Pepperoni pizza!"

"Someone told me it's your favorite, plus, this location calls for finger food."

Mila could only stare as he popped the cork of a bottle and poured it into two glasses. "It's alcohol-free, for the little one."

Mila wiped her eyes, stunned at her reaction. She never cried. She wasn't the type. Blaming the wind, she took the glass he offered her and sipped the drink.

"This is amazing," she whispered. "I didn't pin you as the romantic type."

Darek raised an eyebrow. "I have my moments, darling."

"Let's eat." Mila scooted closer, taking heat from his body as she munched on the pizza and overlooked the city below. If this wasn't a little piece of heaven, she didn't know what was.

"I can totally hear *'Top of the World'* by The Carpenters play in my head now," she spoke with her mouth full, grinning at Darek's puzzled face.

"The fuck's that?"

"This." Mila made a sweeping gesture around. "I love you."

Darek flashed her a smile. "Hold that thought."

They ate in silence, and when Mila was stuffed enough to not get one more bite down, Darek shoved the basket to the side.

"I should probably do this properly… human-ish, but—" he gestured toward her. "I'm not taking any chances. It's slippery as fuck up here."

"I'm not leaving this blanket." Mila threw a look out across the night sky, then back to Darek. "What's going on? I don't mind your devil-looks," she added with a wink. "It's hot."

Darek chuckled, then his face grew serious.

"Mila," he took her hand, and they both looked down at his dark red claws as they curled around her delicate hand. "I don't know how to do this, I wanted to leave you with a card and…" he reached into his pocket, producing a small velvet box and held it for Mila to see, "...this. And, uh, give you time to think about it, without me breathing down your neck."

Mila stared at the box sitting in his palm, while her pulse skyrocketed. Was that what she thought it was? Her eyes darted to his face, and the moment she saw his expression, she knew she was right. He sat paralyzed, eyes locked on her, and she could've sworn he wasn't even breathing.

Pulling her hand free from his, she hesitated for a beat, then reached out to lift the box from his hand. She opened it, staring down at a diamond ring.

"Darek?" she breathed his name, looking back to him.

He swallowed hard, rasping, "Marry me."

She smiled at the lack of a question mark. He made it sound like a demand, but she saw beyond the words, saw the emotion in his eyes, the doubt, the fear. The vulnerability.

"Say something," he hissed.

"You were going to leave me a card?"

He looked away, cursing under his breath, and Mila almost felt bad for letting him sweat a bit.

"You thought I'd say no?"

"I wanted to give you the option," he spoke without looking at her. "I'm not the typical husband material."

"Oh, my love." Mila picked up the ring, sliding it onto her finger before scooting closer. "I couldn't ask for a better husband." She cupped his chin, forcing him to look at her. His eyes were deep red, but the color didn't fool her. The way he refused to meet her gaze spoke of the uncertainty. He was nervous, waiting for her reply with dread he couldn't mask behind devil-eyes.

"Didn't you already call me your wife the first time we met?"

"I did."

"Where did that confidence go?"

Darek let out a sharp laugh. "I wanted to fuck you then, now I want to give you my life."

Mila smiled through sudden tears. "You can do both." She held up her hand, wiggling it so the ring caught the moonlight. It sparkled on her finger, bringing new tears to her eyes. "I'll marry you."

"Oh, thank God," Darek breathed. "You scared the shit out of me."

Mila laughed, throwing herself into his arms.

He held her to him as if he'd never let her go, as if he needed to feel her to really dare to believe that she was his. And at that moment she truly understood. What he'd just done was one of the hardest things he'd ever done. Putting himself out there. Opening himself up to rejection, to the possibility of getting a *no*. He'd taken the chance on one human, and she was sure if she'd broken that trust, he would have broken him along with it.

When she pulled away to look at him, she saw her thoughts reflecting in his eyes, and in the wet trail on his cheeks. It wasn't the show melting on his skin, no matter how he tried to make it look like it.

"I love you," she whispered. "I'll love you forever."

DAREK

CHAPTER 15

Five months later

"I don't want to—"

"Shush!" Mila slapped Darek's arm. "No more complaining. I don't care if you've never celebrated your birthday, from now on—you will."

Darek groaned, slumping onto the couch in defeat. Mila watched him, hesitation flashing across her face. Darek huffed. Now she was having second thoughts? After torturing him with the party-talk weeks before *the* day. He wanted nothing more than to run and hide like the little boy he suddenly felt like he was. The way she forced this on him made him want to scream or throw some sort of anger tantrum. But he couldn't do any of those things. He cared too much about her to ruin it for her. She tried so hard, she was always there. Every slip, every mistake. Every bad thought he had, she'd been there to soothe it down with her soft words and gentle touches. She'd never given up. He refused to be the one to let her down, even though he was slowly dying inside by the mere thought of celebrating the day that meant nothing but pain and darkness for him.

Sixth of June. It meant nothing to normal people. It was just a date, a sun-soaked summer day with birdsong and flowers and green grass. For Darek, it represented everything he despised—and thrived from. The date was what set him apart from the rest of the humans. It was what caused his misery, but also the source of his revenge. Without the powers he acquired that day, he'd still be the nobody who suffered under the lash of the man he'd thrown into the fire and watched burn.

Mila studied him as he sat, legs crossed and a deep scowl on his face as they waited for the guests. Did she know what was on his mind? Did she worry? Darek tried harder. Tried to relax, to untangle his fists and smooth out the wrinkle between his eyes. He tried to look happy.

Darek's eyes fell on the golden ring on Mila's finger, and he automatically touched his own. Spinning it on his finger to keep himself busy, he allowed his mind to wander.

He wasn't sure what surprised him the most, that she'd actually agreed to marry him, or the fact he even asked her. Sliding the ring onto her finger and promising to stand by her forever was one of the strangest things Darek had done. Before Mila, he'd scoffed at the idea of binding himself to a human. He'd seen no point in doing something so ridiculously dumb. After meeting her, everything changed. The same reason that once made him scoff became his main focus. He wanted her, needed her, and he refused to stop until he made her his. The golden band on his finger was not just a sign of his success, it was proof she was really his. Their names were etched into the ring. It was his claim on her.

"The fuck is she anyway?" Darek paced the church floor, impatiently waiting for Mila to appear. Looking out across the empty hall, he raked a hand through his hair, smoothing

it down, and wiped his palm free of sweat at the same time.

"Never thought I'd see you nervous," Riley grinned.

Darek stopped with a huff, eyeing the man. Riley looked good in a suit. So different from the jeans and t-shirt he was used to seeing him in. His hair was slicked back, mimicking Darek's style.

"This place—" Darek cut himself off and sighed. He never felt more out of place as he did. He never set his foot in a goddamn church in his life, and he'd been sure he never would. But Mila insisted, and he'd never been able to say no to her.

"I want to burn this place down," Darek muttered, drawing a nervous chuckle from Riley.

"Huh," he breathed. "I don't think it's appropriate to talk like that in the house of—" he cut himself off before he could say the word God.

Darek raised an eyebrow. "So, me being here, is?"

Riley gulped. "Point taken."

They fell silent as both of them stared down the aisle.

"Why the empty rows?" Riley asked.

Darek wasn't sure what he was supposed to say. 'Because I hate people?' 'Because I had no one to invite?' Instead of answering, he remained silent, thinking about Mila's words as they'd planned the day.

"Just let Kate and Riley come."

"What about your family? Don't you—"

"No, they don't really approve of... let's just say it would be a disaster."

Darek never asked why, but he was sure it had to do with him. And he was just as sure she was right. About them not approving, and about the disaster.

Music started playing. The church door flung open, making Darek's heart skip a beat. But instead of Mila, Cat stood in the door, accompanied by Richard.

"You think you can get married without us?" The music died down as Cat stalked down the aisle, wearing a silky light green dress and matching flowers in her hair. "Congrats, you devil."

Darek grimaced at the name, wondering briefly how long

291

it would take Richard to find out the truth, and if he'd look so happy around him when he did.

"Good job, son," he grinned, "Mila is one fine lady."

Darek tried to ignore the strange feeling spreading in his chest. It wasn't like him to be emotional. But something about the man's words made his heart clench.

Before Darek could dwell on it, the music started again, and Mila appeared in the door. Darek's eyes locked on her, and time stopped. She was the most beautiful thing he'd ever seen. She wore a white dress that enhanced her body, softly following her curves, and not quite hiding the baby bump. Her dark hair was pinned up on top of her head, and a few curls hung loose, framing her heart-shaped face. Darek couldn't take his eyes off her, not even when she came to a halt in front of him. Kate walked to stand next to Mila, and when the music stopped playing, the young priest stepped forward. He spoke, but Darek didn't hear the words.

Not until Mila took his hands did he snap out of the trance.

"Darek is the best thing that ever happened to me. There's nothing he wouldn't do to keep me safe. I couldn't ask for a better man," Mila smiled through her tears, and Darek choked back the emotion rising in his throat. She mouthed the words 'I love you,' before leaving the word to Darek.

Darek had rehearsed it, prepared a few lines of affection which he would be able to speak out loud in front of the tiny crowd, but as he stood there, he remembered nothing.

Mila grasped his hands tighter, urging him on with a small nod.

Darek gulped, stumbling over the words. "I wanted to make her mine the first time I saw her." It was the truth. He'd even called her his wife. Darek smirked at the memory. "Mila changed my world. She's the angel in my life, the light to my dark, I'd die for her, I— " Darek finished the sentence in his head—I love her.

"And you make one stunning couple," the priest smiled a warm smile. "I hereby declare you husband and wife." He turned to Darek. "You may kiss your bride."

"About time." Darek grabbed Mila, pulling her body

292

flat against his, and kissed her until the priest blushed and looked away.

Five months had changed a lot, and Darek could never have imagined he'd be where he was now. Mila couldn't be happier, she'd said it too many times for him to miss that part, and he couldn't deny he felt the same, even though he never dared to admit it out loud.

She'd married the devil. Darek still had a hard time understanding she was so okay with *that* fact. She joked about it, throwing the word around as if it was the most natural thing in the world. It wasn't, and if someone overheard her talk about her hubby-the-devil, they took it as a joke. Darek knew better, and he admired her for everything she'd done. For every time she'd seen past his mood swings and dark thoughts. For every time she'd brought him back to the right path. But Darek hadn't been the devil for a long time. He kept his word. He was as much of a normal man as he could be. He'd done it for her, and he'd keep doing it.

Mila sank down next to Darek on the couch, rubbing her belly and bringing him back to the room. "I can't believe I have to do this one more month. My back is killing me today," she groaned. "It doesn't go away."

"Call it off," Darek took the opportunity to find an excuse to not have the birthday party. "You're not feeling well, don't strain yourself."

Mila snorted. "Nice try. The party is happening." She brushed a few dog hairs off of his black trousers, then patted his thigh. "The best way to get over the past is to create new memories, overwrite the bad ones." She took his hand, brushing her thumb over his skin. "Nothing bad will happen today."

Darek let out a deep sigh. "I just have to restrain from killing a bunch of idiots on the worst day of my life, lovely."

Mila grimaced, and Darek sighed. He hadn't meant to say it out loud. But it was true. He didn't know how he was going to survive this while staying sane and pretending all was fine. It was not. He could never forget. Almost four years had passed since that awful night, but it felt like yesterday. The moment he closed his eyes he saw his mother's dead eyes stare up at him, heard his father's sick laugh as his belt dug into his chest. Darek clenched his teeth, breathing in deep from his nose as he tried to settle his nerves and soothe the pain. He could do this. He was not there. Time had changed everything, but it hadn't healed the mental wounds, it never would.

"Darek—" Mila began.

"No," he rushed to say. "It was a joke."

She didn't look convinced. "Is it too soon?"

Darek gulped. This was his chance. He could stop it. He didn't want a bunch of people breathing down his neck. He wanted Mila, and Mila alone. He wanted her arms around him, her soft body wrapped in his, he wanted her to make him forget.

"No, it's fine," he lied. What else could he do? She worked too hard to make it perfect, to make it special, he didn't have the heart to ruin it. He'd survive. He always did.

The knock on the door announced the first guests. Mila struggled to her feet, but Darek jumped up, pushing her down.

"Sit," he demanded. "I'll get it."

Growling to himself, he went to open the door. Let the fucking hell begin.

"Happy birthday, man!" Riley looked like his old self in jeans and a shirt. His dark blond hair was messy as if he'd been out in a strong wind, and a friendly smile played on his lips. He pulled Darek into a one-arm hug, patting his back and Darek tried not to tense up, not to shove him away in horror. The man had been nothing but friendly toward him during the last months, and as much as Darek hated to admit it, he didn't dislike him as much as he had from the start. Restraining from killing Riley had become remarkably easy, he even found himself chuckling at his stupid jokes.

Riley stepped away, and there was Kate. Darek's whole body tensed at the mere sight of her. Her hair was braided, hanging down either side of her neck like two rat's tails. Cold eyes stared at him, despite their warm brown shade. They stood staring at each other for too long before Darek turned away with a huff.

294

"Hey, guys!" Mila tried to break the tension. "I'd get up but—" she gestured to her round belly. "My back is killing me."

Kate shot Darek a look before plopping down next to Mila. "Damn." She eyed Mila with concern in her eyes. "You look pale."

"I'm as okay as I can be with this bad boy kicking up a storm in there."

Kate giggled. "Should have thought about that before sleeping with the devil."

Mila rolled her eyes. "It's a normal baby," she muttered. "Stop calling him a devil."

Darek couldn't help but smirk. He'd sworn not to harm the bitch, but it didn't mean he couldn't take pleasure in her defeat.

Kate looked offended. "I called his *father* a devil," she shot Darek a look. "And we all know I'm not wrong there."

"True," Mila said. "But he's *my* devil, and I wouldn't want him in any other way."

Darek's heart swelled with emotion. This was why he tried so hard. These were the moments he knew he was doing the right thing. He just wanted her to be happy. His pain didn't matter. He could even tolerate her horrible friend if it meant putting a smile on her face.

The bell rang again, and as Darek pulled the door open, Cat's bright smile was the first thing he saw.

"Hey there!" She stepped inside, followed by Richard. "This is for you, bad boy." She tossed her blond hair over her shoulder with a flick of her head, handing Darek an envelope. "I didn't wrap it, figured you'd be too impatient for such nonsense."

Darek couldn't help but chuckle. She was right. Tearing it open, he took out a white piece of paper with the name *Berner* written in the middle. The name had a fat red cross over it, and a smiley was drawn under. Darek lifted his gaze to Cat, then let his eyes drift to Richard before going back to Cat.

"The fuck's this?"

Cat started to laugh, and Richard joined in. He slapped

Darek on the arm before pulling him into a man-hug.

"What do you think it means?" he asked. Cat wiggled her eyebrows toward Richard. When Darek still didn't get it, Cat exclaimed. "He's gone! The son of a bitch is gone!"

All eyes in the room fell on her.

"Sorry, too loud!" Cat waved at Mila and her friends with a grin.

"He resigned?"

"Of course!" Cat said, "He had no other choice, he just held on as long as he possibly could. Suddenly so strict about the *law*."

"I'll start first thing tomorrow," Richard informed with a grin. "Berner is history. Kicked to the curb like the trash he is."

"When did this happen?"

"Yesterday, I waited to tell you. Birthday surprise and all."

Darek grinned, feeling an old spark flare up inside. That cockroach may be crawling in his own misery, feeding off scraps and licking his wounds in the streets, but Darek wouldn't settle with that. No matter how good he had become, he was still the devil. And he'd be damned if he let that insect get away with his limbs intact. Ruining him wasn't enough. If the man had been dumb enough to invest all his savings and possessions into the company, that was his problem. Darek smirked. What wouldn't he give to see the look on that man's face when he'd been forced to face the fact he lost everything he owned. All the luxury he'd taken for granted, down the drain.

"You'll move into the penthouse?" Cat asked with a grin. "I've never been up there, but I've heard it's fit for a king. Just one elevator ride away from the office."

Darek frowned. "I haven't had time to think about that, Mila is—"

"I know," Cat cooed. "Baby boy is top priority."

"How far gone is she?" Richard asked.

"Baby's due in one month," Darek threw a look at Mila as he spoke, seeing her throw a glance at the clock hanging on the wall.

296

5:15.

The catering should be there any second. Darek groaned, again regretting the whole fucking thing. Birthday party. It was ridiculous. He never celebrated one in his life, and why would he? It had been just any ordinary day when he was growing up. The lashes hadn't stopped just because it was his special day, the pain had been just as bad, the blood just as red, and the cuts just as deep...

"Got a name?" Richard asked, abruptly snapping Darek back to the moment.

"Wh—what?"

"For the boy? A name?"

"No, not yet."

Darek threw a glance at the card still in his hand, huffed at the name staring up at him, before tearing it into pieces.

He'd done what he'd never thought he could do. He not only pushed the devil so deep down he never climbed back up, he had not just created a family, but also a legacy. The company which had been nothing but a complication he didn't want, turned into so much more. He had the power and the control he fantasized about while bleeding on that hard chair back in school years ago. He settled into his new role as a businessman. He found his place, and he felt like he was handmade for the position. The dream was no longer just a dream.

"What did he do to you?" Cat asked.

Darek's head snapped up, eyes growing wide as the question registered in his brain. Before he could even open his mouth to form any sort of a reply, Richard beat her to it.

"Shame on you! Are you seriously asking him on his birthday?"

Cat's cheeks flushed red. She made a face. "Sorry, I just see the hate burning in your eyes every time you mention him."

Darek clenched his fists. Oh, there was hate enough for a lifetime. He just held it back, waiting for the right moment to let it all out.

"He screwed me over too," Richard said. "I couldn't be happier to know he finally got a taste of his own medicine."

Darek's eyes narrowed as a thought struck him. He'd been surprised by that man's strength... was it possible—

"DAREK!"

Mila's shout cut off any thought he'd had. The alarm in her voice snapped him into action.

He found her in the kitchen, clutching her belly and leaning forward against the stove.

Darek stared at her, momentarily frozen in place.

"What's—" His eyes drifted to a puddle of water around her feet, and widened in alarm.

"I said nothing would happen today," she winced. "I think I might've been wrong. He's coming."

Darek staggered back, bumping his back into the doorpost, muttering the word *no*, over and over. He refused to hear it. It was wrong. The wrong month. The wrong fucking day.

"Darek!" Mila exclaimed. "Snap out of it! The baby is coming!"

"It's too early." Darek dragged a hand through his hair. "This can't be happening." He grabbed Mila's shoulders. "You *can't* give birth to him today!"

"It's not up to me you idiot!" Mila screamed, grabbing his shirt to hold herself up. "Hospital, now," she hissed through clenched teeth.

Darek gaped, suddenly too stunned to move. His head was spinning, thoughts and feelings mixing into a whirlwind freezing him into paralyzed shock. It was supposed to be a normal baby, he was supposed to have a normal birthdate. But he chose this day? Of all the fucking days in the year.

"What's—shit!" Kate's shriek pierced the silence. "Oh, my God!" She spun on her heels, shouting for Riley. He came running, with Cat and Richard following close behind.

"Holy fuck!" Cat exclaimed, slapping Darek's back. "You're about to be a dad!"

Mila stared at them. "Don't just stand there!"

A new wave of pain had her crying out loud, her grip of Darek's shirt tightening until the fabric ripped.

"I'll call the ambulance." Kate pushed her way past them and grabbed the phone.

"No time," Mila wailed. "Oh, God." Her legs buckled, and before she hit the floor she was in Darek's arms, clutched to his chest.

"I got you," he breathed. "Hold on."

Everyone scrambled out of the way as he steered straight for the front door. It took all his willpower not to let his wings out and fly straight through the roof.

"He'll drive her?" Richard asked, sounding confused.

"Something like that," Cat grinned.

Darek left them behind. The moment he was out of sight, the wings burst from his back, launching him into the air.

DAREK

CHAPTER 46

Darek's heart raced, his pulse echoing in his head as sweat broke out across his skin. Light-headed and overheated, he tried to breathe through the suffocating pressure on his chest and stay calm. Mila looked so small in the hospital bed, so pale. Her hair lay spread around her head like a dark halo, her hand gripping his so tight it would've broken a regular person's bones.

A quick glance at his wristwatch paled his skin to the same level as Mila's.

5:50.

Darek squeezed her hand right back, praying for him to be wrong.

"Mommy? When was I born?"
"Why do you ask, baby?"
"The other kids say I'm evil because I was born on a bad

day and a bad time. Is it true?"

"Of course not honey, you're not evil. You're mama's little boy."

Darek blinked away tears, not believing her. "But I'm a triple six."

Darek blinked away the memory, throwing one more glance at the watch, and cursed out loud. A few odd looks from the nurses increased the scowl on his face. The baby wasn't supposed to be born now. He was one month too early. He wasn't supposed to be a fucking triple six copy of him. But here they were, minutes from the disaster Darek dreaded but talked himself out of.

Just because he was a freak didn't mean his son would be. He'd been a normal baby on the screenings. He *was* a normal baby now, too. He had to be.

Mila's sudden cry made Darek jump, snapping him back to the moment.

Her eyes were on him. "You did this," she hissed. "I hate you!"

Taken aback by her sudden outburst, Darek could only stare, and when her head rolled back and a new cry tore from her throat, he nearly passed out. Her pain was killing him. He hated himself, too. He *had* done this to her. He'd put her through hell, and for what?

His free hand shot out, grabbing a nurse by the arm. "Do something," he snapped. "The fuck are you just standing there for?"

"Sir." The woman tugged at her arm, trying to remain professional even though it was clear his grip hurt her. "Your wife is doing fine, let her take the time she needs."

Darek let go of her with a scoff. "Does that look fine to you?" he snarled. "She's in pain."

"It's normal."

Darek averted his gaze seconds before his eyes flashed red. He refused to make a scene by scaring the nurses off. He refused to be the one to make it all worse. But if they didn't do something right now he was sure he'd snap and kill them all. Mila's cries and whimpers tore through his

301

heart like knives. It screamed at him to act, to destroy everything in his way, to help her. But he couldn't take this away any more than he could stand to see her in pain. The only thing keeping him together was Mila's sweaty hand wrapped in his. When he was the one who was supposed to stay strong for her, he was the one falling apart. Darek let out a shuddering breath, focusing all his willpower to remain calm. The nurses were right. It was natural. It was normal. And it would be over soon.

"Darek?" Mila breathed his name in a gasp, but it was enough to snap his attention back to her.

"I'm here." He hated how his voice trembled, but couldn't keep it steady no matter how he tried. "I'm right here, darling."

"Sorry about the party. I didn't think—" She squeezed her eyes shut, and Dared watched in horror as her face twisted in pain and tears leaked through her eyes. "I'm scared," she whimpered.

Darek's heart clenched.

"I won't let anything happen to you." He brushed damp strands of hair from her face, fighting the swell of emotions threatening to choke him.

"Almost done, sweetie," the nurse coaxed. "One more big push."

Mila's eyes darted to Darek's, her fingers tightening around his hand as her body tensed.

When her scream faded, a high-pitched cry reached Darek's ears, and when his head snapped to the direction of the sound, his eyes fell on a tiny creature, cradled in the nurse's hands.

A gasp slipped past Darek's lips. One glance at his wristwatch confirmed what he'd already known.

Six P.M. sharp.

His growl was cut short by Mila's shaky voice.

"Is he okay? Is he—normal?"

Darek knew what she was asking.

The nurse smiled a warm smile, wrapping the baby in a light blue blanket before handing him to Mila's waiting arms.

"He's a perfect healthy baby boy. Congratulations."

The nurse's voices faded to a background hum. Mila started to cry, and the flood of relief that washed through Darek nearly floored him. No horns? No tail? No wings?

Time stopped as he stared at Mila and the baby. The way she looked at it broke something in him. Feeling the pressure build-up behind his eyes, he quickly looked away. He refused to cry.

Mila looked up from the baby, resting her eyes on Darek. "Wanna hold him?"

Darek's eyes darted back to her, growing wide. He blinked in shock, unable to move. When Mila reached out her arms, holding the baby over her chest, he had to fight the urge to run out of the room.

"I can't—"

"Darek," Mila murmured. "Hold your son."

Darek shifted closer in his chair. Close enough to gaze down at the tiny baby in her arms.

He held Mila's gaze, letting her tired smile encourage him. Darek looked down at the tiny face in awe. Two big brown eyes looked up at him. Darek could only stare. The baby had Mila's eyes. The color, the dark brown that almost looked black, the depth that drew him in like a moth to a flame. But his face, his little nose and lips were Darek's. Staring down at the copy of himself, Darek forgot to breathe. He thought he'd feel bad, that he'd be repulsed by the idea of a mini version of himself, and he'd been prepared. But he'd never been prepared for the warmth that filled him, for the love he felt for the tiny human in Mila's arms. The little baby mouth opened, letting out a gurgling sound, his arms reaching out as if he wanted to touch Darek.

"He looks like you," Mila murmured. "Isn't he beautiful?"

Darek only managed a weak nod. The baby was nothing of what he expected. His big eyes shone with an innocence making Darek feel scared to even be near him.

"Take him," Mila whispered.

"I—" He looked away, trying to win time, to find an excuse. He couldn't tell her, but he was terrified. The boy was so small, so fragile. So precious.

"You won't hurt him."

Darek's eyes darted to her. Had she read his mind? Embarrassed of being caught, he reached out. It was just a baby. How hard could it be? Despite his best effort to act tough, his hands trembled as he took the bundle from his mom.

Darek shifted the baby to one arm, cradling him to his bare chest while he let his free hand touch the tiny pink cheek. Those big brown eyes stared up at him, his little mouth opening and closing as if he was trying to speak. Instead of words, little *aah* sounds slipped from his mouth.

"I can't believe he's ours," Darek whispered. His eyes met Mila's. "Promise me he'll never be like me."

"Oh, my love," Mila whispered. "He won't. Look at him."

Darek nodded, trying to accept she was right. She had to be.

— * —

Darek spent the night pacing the floor while Mila slept. No way in hell was he leaving her and the baby alone with a bunch of idiots. Though Mila reassured him there was nothing to worry about, it didn't stop his mind from spiraling.

The longer he was left with his thoughts, the more he started to fear things weren't what they seemed. Everything was too calm, too perfect. Darek never believed in fairytales, and as much as it pained him to admit it, he was sure this wasn't one either.

He never asked about his own life. He never cared, until now. And when he was dying to get the answers to the fears eating away at him, he had no one to ask. There was only one person who knew the truth, and she was dead.

Leaning back against the wall, he slid down until he hit the floor. Clasping his hands together, he drew his knees up, rested his elbows on them, and let his head fall forward.

"What are you waiting for?"

"Your birthday surprise, what else?"

The words echoed in his head until he had more questions than answers and the whirlwind inside made him want to scream out loud. Before looking into his son's innocent eyes, Darek never even considered the possibility of himself being born without devil powers. Had they grown on him? Had he been a normal human baby at birth? Or had he been different already from his first breath?

He couldn't remember ever being treated like a normal human child. He never had friends. He couldn't remember ever being around other children growing up. Was that because he was different from them? Because he'd hurt them if they came close? Or had the fear of his father kept everyone at a safe distance, refusing to interact with him already before he had been big enough to feel the pain of being left out?

Darek didn't have the answers. But one thing he knew—he'd never allow it to happen to his son... he'd make sure his life would be nothing like the hell he grew up in.

Picking himself up from the floor, he sunk into the chair, resting his gaze on Mila, and tried to relax. Her peaceful form as she slept settled the turmoil inside, calmed it to a low simmer, allowing him to breathe deep enough to fill his overheated lungs with soothing air.

He wanted to be good for her, and he had. She'd been his reason to fight the darkness. She still was. She would always be. It hadn't changed, it multiplied. In the blink of an eye, his whole life changed.

He was no longer the impulsive teenager he tried to outrun, no longer the angry devil who destroyed everything in his path. Everything around him changed, hell, even *he* had, whether he wanted it or not. He was no longer the same person. He was a man—a dad.

— * —

"He needs a name," Mila whispered, careful not to wake the sleeping baby once he'd finally fallen asleep.

Darek stood next to her, his eyes locked on the tiny form sleeping peacefully in his pram next to the couch.

They'd been home two weeks, settled into somewhat normal routines. As normal as it could be, juggling work and a newborn baby who he had no idea what to do with.

Mila's brilliant remark, '*Think of him as a puppy,*' meant nothing to him, but she seemed to be doing great as if she'd never done anything else.

"Can you at least sit down," she hissed.

Darek sat with a scowl, throwing a look at his wristwatch.

"I have a meeting—"

"With Richard or Cat? I'm sure they can wait."

Darek forced a smile. It couldn't wait. He hated to lie to her, but he had no choice. The last thing he wanted was for her to worry, to think he slipped back to being *evil*. The last he wanted was to disappoint her, but this had to be done. And if he enjoyed it, too… well he couldn't help that. But it was nothing she needed to know.

"I have to do this today, it's important."

It was the most important thing he would ever do. Two days had passed in slow motion, and every noise, every little shadow had him on edge. He hadn't slept more than five minutes at the time. The threat to Mila followed him every waking second until he was sure he'd snap from the stress. He couldn't wait any longer. Berner was down, but it meant nothing when his words echoed in his head.

"If I were to… let's say, disappear, she'll be paying the price."

It wasn't going to happen. Not on his watch. He'd burn down the world to keep her safe. Locating the bastards had taken longer than he'd wanted, but from the second Cat called with the information he needed, he'd been dying to get to the office and then straight to wherever the cockroaches were holed up. He just hadn't gotten the opportunity to slip away.

Mila's groan cut him off. "I liked you better when all you wanted was to bone me."

Darek chuckled. "Oh, I still want to do that."

"I just gave birth to—"

"I'm aware. That's why I don't."

"Point taken." Mila gestured toward the baby, "Does he

look like David, to you?"

Darek scoffed, feeling more offended than he should by the name suggestion. "You're not naming my son after some fucking king."

Mila grimaced. "Actually... I want to name him after you," she said, shooting Darek a look to see his reaction.

Darek's eyes widened in surprise, and for a moment he looked confused. "Devil?" he said with a sneer. "How about Lucifer, Satan, Beelzebub?"

Mila stifled a chuckle, rolling her eyes. "What about Devin?"

Darek frowned. "It sounds an awful lot like *devil*."

"Am I weird for liking that?"

Darek huffed, making Mila cringe.

"Let me explain." She held up a hand, preventing Darek from talking, and took a deep breath as to brace herself before bursting into a flurry of words and gestures. "I want him to know his roots. We're not going to hide what you are, the baby will know. I want him to know, to feel the strength of what he came from, to feel protected under the wings of a dad who'd go to hell to keep him safe. Because you would, like you did for me." She paused to breathe, allowing Darek to take everything in. He sat, staring at her in stunned silence. The thoughts she had of him were overwhelming. She spoke of him as if he was an angel, instead of his more sinister nature. But she was right, they could never hide it from the boy. He'd eventually notice. It was better he knew from the start.

"Say something," she coaxed.

Darek swallowed, opened his mouth to speak, but closed it again as he didn't find the words. Mila took his silence as doubt, and went on, talking while Darek turned his head to look at the boy.

"I want him to feel how special he is, and to never forget it no matter what people say. To carry it with him like a shield. To empower him, to make him proud."

Darek took his eyes off the baby to look at Mila. "He's not a devil," he muttered. "Didn't we establish that fact?"

"But *you* are."

"So?"

Mila sighed. "You're special, I want him to remember who he is, where he came from. I want him to know he's special, too."

"By naming him after the devil?"

Mila smiled at his confusion and clarified, "After *you*. His father."

Darek huffed but didn't protest. After her speech, he had no clue what to say.

Mila shifted, straddling Darek's lap and smiled at his stunned expression. "Don't get your hopes up," she warned. Placing her palms on his cheeks, she leaned in to softly kiss his lips. "I love you. The baby couldn't have a better dad. I want him to know that."

"Oh, for fuck's sake," Darek muttered. "Devin it is, then."

Mila stifled a squeal, throwing her arms around Darek's neck. "It's perfect for him."

When she pulled away, Darek's eyes glowed a deep red, and he had no way to hide it. Mila's soft gasp deepened the color, making him ache to feel more of her. It had been too long. The weight of her body over his wiped all thoughts of baby names from his head, filling it with less innocent ideas. Before he could stop himself, he'd grabbed her hair, holding her face in place, inches from his.

"Darek," Mila warned. "It's too soon, I can't—" The way her voice trembled gave her away. She was tempted. A smile crept onto Darek's lips as she wetted hers in anticipation of the kiss. Darek pulled her closer, catching her mouth with his. She was first to pull away, grinning at Darek's expression.

"Want more of that?" she asked. "Then stay."

Darek was tempted, and for a brief moment, he considered giving in. Then he remembered why he was going, and his mood shifted.

"I have to go." Without warning, he lifted Mila off him and stalked toward the door before he had a chance to lose his determination. If she kissed him like that again, he wasn't sure he'd be able to go.

Mila caught him in the door, grabbing his arm. Before he could speak, she shushed him with a finger to his lips. She stood on her toes, whispering in his ear, "Come back soon." She trailed a fingernail down his chest, teasing, tempting.

"You don't have to rush it," his voice couldn't hide the desire for her to do just that.

"I'm off-limits." She jabbed him in the chest saying, "But you're not."

It took a moment for him to get it, and when he did, he gulped. Mila ran her hand down his body, brushing it over the tightness of his pants. "It's time you let me touch you."

"Mila." He grabbed the doorframe, scratching the wood as claws grew from his fingers. His voice was nothing but a growl.

"What are you doing?"

Darek was torn between removing her hand and enjoying it.

She grinned up at him. "Giving you a reason to hurry home." She watched his lips twitch in a silent growl, feeling his body shudder underneath the suit as she stroked him through the thin layer of clothing.

"*You* are the reason, I don't need sex to—" he cut himself off, biting back a groan. Fuck, she sure knew how to make him lose his mind. Did she do it on purpose? She sure seemed to be in the mood now.

Was the *I've-just-squeezed-a-baby-out-of-there*-talk just a charade to push him to the point where he'd have no choice but to let her touch him? If she starved him of the real thing, he had to give in? Darek had to admit it was working. He was close to surrender, to let her do whatever she wanted with him. Fuck the disturbing images that flashed through his mind, fuck the pink-striped bitch who'd disappeared into thin air before he'd gotten his hands on her, fuck it all. He was better than then. They'd broken him, but he refused to stay broken, and who was better at fixing him than Mila?

"But you want it."

His voice dipped into a husky growl. "I always want you."

Mila stepped away, winking at him. "That's what I

thought, now go. I need to take a nap while the little one is still sleeping."

Darek adjusted his pants with a scowl settling on his face. *Now* go? He no longer wanted to. All he could think of was how good her hands felt, how he craved more. Darek let out a shuddering breath, silently cursing himself for falling into her trap. Mila raised an eyebrow at his attempt to hide his desire for her, gesturing toward the aching bulge in his pants.

"Good luck with that."

"If I didn't know better, I'd say *you're* the fucking devil." Darek turned with a huff, leaving her with an amused grin on her lips.

She called out after him. "Don't forget Devin's checkup today, I expect you to be
there."
Darek nodded, silently cursing the distractions. "I'll meet you there."

MILA

CHAPTER 47

Little Devin was two weeks, and Mila was stunned to see time fly by so fast. Hadn't it been only yesterday he'd been born? Pushing the pram into the doctor's office, she dreaded the crying she was sure would come.

A young woman smiled at her as she settled into a chair, one hand on the pram to keep it softly rocking.

"Two-week checkup," she said, as if the doctor didn't already know why she was there. Doing a double-take, she furrowed her forehead. "Haven't we met before, Doctor... You look familiar."

The woman held out her hand, "Lucy, and I'm just the nurse, Dr. Brown will be with you shortly.

Lucy? The name didn't ring a bell, but her face did. Her friendly smile, the curly blond hair, and the little mole on her cheek. She'd seen her before, but she couldn't pinpoint where.

"I'm sorry, I don't think so," the nurse scratched her neck as she thought. "I look like any average nurse, I'm sure," she added with a grin. "Must be mistaking me with someone else."

Mila chuckled. She was probably right.

"How's baby boy doing?"

"He's fine, he sure knows how to keep a girl awake."

The nurse laughed. "They do, don't they?"

Mila grimaced.

"We're waiting for a daddy or it's just us?"

"He should be here," Mila threw a glance at the clock perched on the wall above the doctor's desk. Where was he anyway? He'd promised to be there.

The door flung open, and there he was. Dressed in a three-piece suit and slick hair, he looked like the perfect businessman. The mere sight of him spread warmth through Mila, a fire she could never put out when she was around him.

"Speak of the devil," she grinned. Her eyes lingered on him, taking the moment to appreciate his looks. She'd never get enough.

"Am I late?" Darek raised an eyebrow in the direction of the nurse before stepping into the room. The door slid shut behind him, and instead of sitting, he came to stand behind Mila. Hands on her shoulders, he burned her skin from the simple touch, making Mila ache to turn around and wrap herself into his strong arms.

"I take it you're the daddy," Lucy's voice held a slight tremble. Mila no longer wondered why. It was a common reaction to Darek, and in some way, she enjoyed it more than she should. The way he managed to intimidate people just by entering a room was not only convenient in his line of profession, but it was also sexy.

"Is Devin okay?" he asked, skipping the formalities just like she knew he would.

The nurse flashed him an apologetic smile. "It seems like Doctor Brown is late, I should, eh—" she gestured toward the door. "I'll be right back."

She darted to the door, opened it, and slipped out, leaving Mila staring after her.

Shifting in her seat, she angeled her face up. "You scared her off," she giggled. "Big bad Devil."

Darek huffed. "I did nothing."

Mila grinned, slipping a hand inside his suit jacket. "You

312

don't need to." She ran the hand up his stomach to his chest. He didn't need to show off red eyes or horns, he radiated danger and power without even trying. And what scared others to their core, added to Mila's sense of safety. As long as she was with him, nothing could harm her. No one would even dare to try.

Darek caught her arm, guiding her hand back to herself with a deep growl rumbling in his chest. "What the fuck are you doing?"

Mila grinned, taking his hand. "I missed you."

"I'm here now."

Before Mila could reply, the door opened, and a man appeared. His white doctor's coat stretched over a stomach that looked like it had seen too much fatty food, and his eyes twinkled with warmth as he looked at the baby sleeping in his pram.

"I'm sorry I'm late." He held out a hand to Mila, then to Darek. The moment he grasped Darek's, his eyes widened, and he held on a moment too long before stepping aside.

"You're burning up," he stated. "I'd suggest you go home and rest—"

Darek's scoff cut him off, and Mila tried to stifle her laughter. The poor doctor had no idea.

"He's fine," she said at last. "We're not sick, just—" there was no logical excuse for Darek's heated skin, and she'd given up trying to explain it long ago.

The doctor hesitated, then nodded. "Alright, let's see the baby."

The short examination left Devin crying and Mila fighting the need to cover her ears. The doctor chuckled as he gave the baby back to Mila.

"He has strong lungs, I'll give him that."

Sitting at the desk, he began filling in Devin's information.

"He's fine though? Nothing... odd about him?" Mila had to shout to be heard.

"Odd?" The doctor looked up from the files. "He's perfectly fine. Healthy as a horse."

"No need to kill me yet," Darek spoke in Mila's ear, making her jump from his sudden proximity. He chuckled.

"Give him to me."

Doing as he wished, she scooted the baby over to his waiting arms. It didn't take long until the crying subsided.

"He likes me."

"He sure does." The doctor looked surprised, but Mila knew better. It wasn't the first time Darek's heat had soothed the baby within seconds. Cradled to his chest, the warmth from Darek's skin had him wrapped in an invisible blanket of comfort and safety. The sight never ceased to leave Mila in complete awe. Darek was good with the baby, something she never thought possible before witnessing it. She'd seen him gentle, but the way he touched her was nothing compared to the tenderness he showed his son.

The doctor said his goodbyes and left them alone in the room.

"What were you expecting?" Darek asked. "Sudden wing growth?" Placing a now sleeping Devin back in his pram, he turned to Mila. "He's not like me," he said it with an urgency that blew away the last of her doubts. He wasn't. He wasn't *allowed* to be. He wouldn't be.

"I know."

"Let's get the hell out of here." Darek didn't wait for her to reply. Mila let him go first, enjoying the sight of him wheeling the light blue pram as if it was the most natural thing in the world.

"Hey." The nurse, Lucy, stopped her on her way to catch up with Darek. "You were right."

A smile spread across Mila's lips. "I knew it. I rarely forget a face." Her smile faded. The face she remembered, but that was it. "Care to enlighten me?"

Lucy gestured toward Darek with a tilt of her head. "You *did* marry him, huh?"

Her words catapulted Mila back in time. Back to the hospital he took her to after crashing her car. Images flashed through her head like a fast-forwarded movie.

"That is Darek Rewera, you must've heard of him?"
"You're married to that guy?"
"He's not my husband, he's a freaking stalker. Help me

314

out of here before he finds me!"

"You're the nurse from Westwood?"

Lucy nodded. "That's me. Moved to Seattle a few months back." Her eyes drifted to Darek, her face taking on a thoughtful expression. "What did you do to him?"

"What do you mean?"

"He's... different."

Something in Mila clicked. The pieces falling on places. "You see auras, right?"

Another nod.

Mila hesitated, then went for it. "How bad is it? His?"

"No." Lucy eyed Darek as she spoke. "It's good, better. Calm."

Mila couldn't stop a gasp. Had she done that to him? After everything bad he'd suffered through, she'd been convinced he'd been damaged permanently. Was it possible he was healing, that she was helping him stay clear of the darkness within?

"Thank you," she whispered. "I needed to hear that."

Lucy placed a hand on her shoulder. "I won't lie. I still sense danger from him. Darkness. It's there, he's just keeping in check. Be careful."

"I will be. Maybe I'll see you for the next check-up."

— * —

Lucy's words echoed in Mila's head as they drove home. Darek sat in silence, his face hard and arms tense as he gripped the wheel.

"You heard her," Mila stated the obvious. "Hey." She reached out, placing a hand on his thigh. "It's okay."

"Hmph."

"Come on," Mila coaxed. "Out with it, what's bothering you?"

"She practically told you to wait for me to snap." He shot Mila a look, holding her gaze for a brief moment before returning his eyes to the road. "The fuck am I supposed to do with that information?"

315

"Nothing. Forget it. I know you won't. You're not like that anymore."

"Aren't I?"

"No!"

"I'm still the devil."

"You're so much more than that. You're doing great. I'm proud of you."

Darek sighed, driving the rest of the distance in silence. Not until he pulled the car over outside of their apartment complex did he speak.

"I'd never hurt you. Either of you."

Mila snapped off her seatbelt, shifting in her seat enough to grab his shoulders. "I'm *not* worried. I know you won't."

Darek nodded, then sighed.

"There's something else, isn't it? Why did her words bother you so much? Why are you so worked up?"

It took a moment, then he shook his head. "Forget it. I overreacted. I'm fine. I made you a promise and I'll fucking keep it."

Mila grinned. "Let's not go home." Before he could protest, she added, "A change of environment will do us good."

"I have to do something, it can't wait."

Mila sighed. "Not again, come on, two hours max, relax. The office will be there tomorrow too."

Darek gave a short nod, flashing her a smile. "Where to?"

Mila considered it. "Ever seen the city from the other side?" The lost look on his face sealed the deal. "I know where to go. You'll love it! Get out, I'll drive."

"Hmph."

— * —

Despite his protests, Mila parked the car, dragging Darek and the baby along to her intended destination. Pier 55. She pointed to the ferries labeled *water taxi* and Darek huffed.

"Don't be such a bore," she complained. "Come on! It's twelve minutes. You'll love the city view from over there."

She led him over to the queue, paid for their tickets, and

316

waited to board the ferry.

The seaside smell and the fresh salty air forced a small smile to his lips. Taking his hand, she led him up a flight of stairs to the top terrace where the view was brighter and the wind cooler.

"Told you, you'd like it."

Darek chuckled. "It's relaxing." He slung an arm around Mila's shoulders, pulling her closer to his body. "Soothing. Just like you."

She stepped into his embrace, hugging him tight. "Water has that effect. I guess especially on you." She nuzzled her face closer, inhaling his fiery scent, and smiled against his suit.

"Aren't you the miss-know-it-all?"

Mila giggled. "You're welcome."

Darek held her tighter, his hand in her hair warm and firm as he pressed her to him. The unspoken gesture confirming the words he never spoke out loud.

"I love you too," she murmured.

He kissed the top of her head, before tilting her head back to claim her mouth with his. He kissed her until she blushed under the staring eyes of strangers and steam rose from his skin.

"Hold that thought." She pushed away from him, grinning at his tortured expression. "Don't wanna get arrested for public indecency now, do you?"

Darek smirked. "Maybe I do."

Jabbing him in the chest, Mila turned away, facing the sea. "Behave," she hissed. "Have you forgotten about Devin? And the rest of the boat. There are *people* here."

"I'm on my best behavior, darling." His arms snaked around her waist, his body pressing against hers, hard and hot. Mila shuddered despite the heat surrounding her. His breath smoky and warm in her ear, his voice nothing but a growl. "I'll tell you what I want to do with you."

Mila's knees were weak as she stumbled off the ferry, and he knew it. The smug bastard. Scowling at his attempt to act unaffected, she pushed Devin's pram a little harder, increasing the distance between her and Darek. She could not look at him and not wish to rip his clothes off. Not after his devilishly graphic narrative in her ear.

A hand on her shoulder pulled her to a halt. "Where's the fire?"

Mila swirled around, hands flat against his chest, she hissed, "*You* are the freaking fire."

He chuckled, then his voice dipped into a husky growl. "I can have you in our bed faster than you can scream."

Mila pushed away from him with a shove. "Don't even *think* about flying. It will scare Devin."

Darek raised an eyebrow, then grinned, looking around. "What to do around here?"

Mila let out a shaky breath, waiting for her pulse to settle.

"Nothing," she said at last. "Just enjoy this moment together as a family."

Darek's face softened, eyeing her with a new set of eyes. Reaching out, he tucked her hair behind her ears, letting his fingers linger on her cheeks, he murmured, "I'd love that."

DAREK

CHAPTER 48

Later the same night, Darek left the car outside of an abandoned factory and continued by air. The dark sky concealed him, making him invisible to the car creeping along dark alleys. Tracking the bastards had taken more time than he hoped for, and as he hovered above the car as it finally pulled up, and two men slipped out, his patience was running low.

Mila was waiting at home. She started to worry, and Darek wanted nothing more than to be there, to finish what he'd started on that goddamn boat ride.

"Why did her words bother you so much?" Mila's words resounded in his head.

"Forget it. I overreacted. I'm fine. I made you a promise and I'll fucking keep it."

Darek hated to lie to her. But he had to do this; he did it for her. Not that she'd ever know. He'd sworn to her to be good, to do good—she didn't know about the darkness that drove him to a hidden warehouse in the pitch-black night. She didn't know about the threat to her safety, and how he was about to turn the table by some good old-fashioned devil-work.

Thanks to Cat's spying skills, he knew who Berner relied on to do his dirty work. Darek smirked into the night. If he only knew how dirty it was about to become.

A door shutting echoed across the empty back street. Darek lowered himself onto the ground, touching the asphalt with a low thud and a swoosh as his wings folded.

His eyes flashed red, illuminating the old metal door before swinging a foot toward it. The sound as the door ripped from its hinges and flew inward echoed through the night.

Two guns pointed toward Darek the moment he stepped into the dimly lit space.

"One more step and you're dead!" A pale man with short-cropped blond hair stepped forward. He wore a jeans jacket with a set of spikes sticking out from his shoulders, and his brows were pulled tight in a deep glare.

Another man stepped forward, his dark complexion a stark contrast to the first man. "Who the fuck are you?" he waved a gun in Darek's face. "The hell you doing here, man?"

Darek's eyes darted to the third person. He stood hidden behind the two, silently watching. Hiding behind his guard dogs. How pathetic.

"No more games," Darek hissed. "I'm done playing nice."

Before either of the idiots had time to react, Darek lunged forward, snatching the weapons from their grips, and fired a series of shots toward their stunned forms.

Stepping over their collapsed bodies, he ignored their cries and screams, leaving them to bleed as he zoomed in on the man staggering away as he neared.

"Not so brave now, are you?" He flashed his eyes, chuckling as the man stumbled and fell in his hurry to get away.

320

Darek crouched over him. "Did you think I'd let you get away with it?"

"W-who are you?" the man stuttered. "What do you want?" He tried to crawl away. Darek caught him by his thigh, burying claws into his flesh, and yanked him back with a sharp tug that had the man howling in pain.

His hands searched the floor, trying to find something to hold on to, to pull himself away from Darek while his body twisted and turned in a blind panic.

"You have your filthy little eyes on my wife," Darek spoke with a deadly calm, his cold voice showing no sign of the fire raging inside. "You've been spying on her, taken pictures of her, you have orders to HURT her."

Wings burst from his back, and in one fluid motion, he grabbed the man by his collar, launching him into the air in less than seconds. He slammed the man against the wall, leaving his feet dangling far above the concrete floor. Holding him in place with one hand, he produced a flame in the other.

"Am I right?" he snarled. "Speak!"

The man grabbed Darek's arm, trying to loosen his grip, and clinging to it at the same time. "Let me down," he yelled. "I just followed orders."

Darek played with the flame, the beat of his wings making it flutter, reaching for the squirming worm in his grasp.

Despite knowing exactly whose orders he followed, Darek needed him to say it. "Who's your boss?"

"Mr. B-Berner, please let me down." His eyes drifted to the floor far under them.

"As you wish." Darek let go, watching the man drop like a stone. The scream as he hit the hard surface muted the audible pop as his bones snapped.

Hovering in the air above him, Darek scowled at his pitiful form. They were all worms, a pest that needed to be wiped from the earth.

Darek flew his arms out, releasing a burst of fire from the motion. One powerful flap of his wings fanned the flames, and as they flared up all around him. Darek lifted toward the ceiling, breaking through the material effortlessly as he flew into the night.

One down, one to go.

Darek's car pulled up to the street outside the Rewera tower. The bold red letters illuminated the ground like freshly drained blood in the puddles left by the previous rain.

Stepping out, he tilted his head up. The building rested in darkness, except one floor. Dimly lit windows on the top floor made his blood boil. The son of a bitch was still there. In *his* office. In *his* building. Darek dug his claws into his palms, focusing on the pain to keep him anchored. Staring up at the lit-up windows, all he wanted was to fly up there and rip the man to pieces like the trespasser he was. He had no right to be there. He had no right to cling to what was no longer his.

The bastard had no idea what was waiting. He not only took months from Darek's life, he destroyed him in the process. He still couldn't let down his guard around Mila. He couldn't stand the thought of giving up the control, of surrendering himself to her, and there was only one person to blame.

All the anger he suppressed the previous months flared up. He promised Mila to be good. He'd chosen, and he'd chosen *her*. He still did. But this was something he couldn't turn his back to.

His fingers itched with contained power as he unbuttoned his shirt. He couldn't wait to bury his claws into that cockroach's flesh.

Unleashing the devil after too long of restraining it felt good. Once the power flooded his system, there was no turning back. He needed this. The revenge, the satisfaction. The small sliver of guilt that made it into his heart was not strong enough to keep him on the ground. A few powerful wing strokes lifted him into the air, leaving the ground far below as he closed in on the light shining through the top windows.

As his eyes landed on the man, blurred by the night sky reflecting in the glass, the last ounce of Darek's patience vanished. He waited almost half a year for this. He had enough. Even thoughts of Mila couldn't hold him back.

The glass shattered the moment he allowed his full power to surface, exploding into the office in a cascade of broken glass. The sound so sharp it pierced the night air, traveling over the streets. Shards rained down in fragments sharp enough to cut, hitting the floor with clinks that echoed in the following stillness.

Darek landed in the middle of it, standing with his wings raised above his head, and his eyes blazing red as he stared down at the man ducking behind the desk for cover.

"Get. Up."

Berner slowly straightened and stood, looking around as if trying to find the fastest escape route.

"Forget it," Darek growled. "You're not getting out of here, alive." He inched closer to the desk, tiny pieces of glass crunching under his shoes. The only obstacle standing in between him and the man he fantasized about ripping to pieces every night before falling asleep.

"Be smart," Berner's voice was surprisingly calm. "I hear you're a dad now, wanna risk your son's life, along with your wife's?"

Darek huffed. The motherfucker didn't know his little pawns were wiped out. For the first time, Darek had the trump card, and he was going to play it well. Being patient did pay off.

"Better worry more about *your* sons," Darek hissed. "Ever thought about what will happen to them—" he stepped closer, wiping the desk clean off items with one flick of his tail before placing his palms against it, leaning forward to hiss, "When you die."

Berner gulped visibly, his skin paling and the veins in his neck shining blue as they bulged with fear.

"You can kill me." Berner's eyes locked on Darek. "But you'll never be free. You'll never sleep one night in peace, you'll never fuck your wife without thinking of me."

Darek's claws dug into the wood, tearing through it with a screeching noise that made Berner cringe away from the sound.

"Hit a sore spot, huh?" he taunted. "You pretend to be

so tough. You don't even dare to let your wife touch you. You're pathetic."

Before Darek could think about the consequences, the desk flew into the opposite wall, which cracked as the building shuddered from the impact. His hand had Berner's throat in a death grip faster than he could blink. "How dare you."

Berner grinned despite the lack of air, and the gesture fueled Darek's anger to the point where he wanted to snap his goddamn neck and throw him straight through the window. Berner's hand closed around his wrist, his grip tight as he tried to yank himself free. He was strong, too strong. And when he pushed himself off the wall, making Darek stagger back from the unexpected movement, he knew something was wrong. The grip around Berner's throat faltered, and the man took the opportunity to rip himself free. Darek's hand shot out to grab him, but he ducked, again stunning Darek with his speed.

"I know things." Berner's eyes bore into Darek's, a challenge he refused to accept. He refused to spare this son of a bitch, not again. Fuck being good. He couldn't have it all, no matter how he desired it. This was who he was, this was who he was *meant* to be. Everything else he tried had been a failed attempt to go against his nature. He was the devil—time to act like it.

"Nice try."

One swift movement, a flick of a clawed hand had Berner howling in pain, and Darek's skin splattered with warm blood. Berner clutched his chest, trying to stop the blood from spilling from deep gashes.

"You think you can *BEAT ME*?" Darek snarled. "You think you're *FAST*?" One flap of his wings sent Berner flying back, crashing into the wall with an audible thud. Before he could scramble to his feet, Darek lifted him by the collar of his suit jacket. "Think you're *STRONG*?" Dragging him over to the broken panorama window, he pushed him back enough to dip him into the air, his grip the only thing keeping him from tumbling to certain death. "Think you're *BRAVE*?"

324

"Please," Berner gasped.

"Please?" Darek hissed. "Fucking *PLEASE*?"

"Don't do this."

"And why the fuck not?" Darek pushed him further out, letting go for a fraction of a second, but caught him before he fell. Berner's scream formed a smirk on Darek's lips.

"I'm sorry!"

"I don't want your apologies."

"What do you want?"

Darek let go, then again caught him before he fell out of reach, yanking him up and hurled him through the room as if he weighed nothing.

Looming over Berner as he tried to crawl away, only one thought spun in Darek's head.

"I want to watch you bleed."

His hand shot out, burying claws into Berner's chest as effortless as digging them into clay. Enjoying Berner's screams, Darek curled his fingers, lifting him by the grip. Warm blood pooled around his fingers, running over his hand and down his arm, coloring his skin red, and as he listened to Berner's shallow breaths and cries of pain, he'd never felt better.

"Now who's crying? How does it *feel*? " Darek pushed against him, drawing another cry from his mouth. "How does it fucking *FEEL*?"

Berner didn't speak, but the sound coming from him was all Darek needed to hear.

Darek released his grip, watching as he sank back to the floor.

"Now speak, or I'll rip your fucking heart out."

Berner let out a strangled noise, pressing a trembling hand to his chest.

"Talk." Darek crouched over him. "Why are you not dead? You are stronger than a normal human. Why?"

Berner managed to produce a mocking grin, rasping, "What do you think?"

"Don't. Play. Games. With. Me."

The icy calm in Darek's voice made Berner recoil. Darek studied him, making him tremble under his flaming gaze, then faster than Berner could react, he had his hand in a firm grip, cracking one of his fingers as if it was a twig. When Berner still didn't speak, he went on to the next. When he was about to snap the fourth, Berner broke.

"We took your blood," he gasped. "It was an experiment."

Darek's head snapped up, staring at the man in disbelief. "You tried to turn yourself into a devil?" His sudden laugh made Berner flinch. "You're fucking insane!"

He let go of the hand, but not before giving it a good hard squeeze causing Berner's bones to grind. Darek shot to his feet, raking a bloodied hand through his hair as he thought. The fuck was this idiot doing? How was it even possible?

As he stood there, a sudden wave of fear washed through him, sending chills running up and down his spine. Darek couldn't stop the gasp as little as he could stop his rapid heartbeat.

Mila.

It was her. It wasn't the first time he felt her through the unexplainable link they shared. He felt her pleasure, her pain, he felt it all when he hadn't been able to be near her. And he felt her now.

Darek's eyes darted to Berner as he lay, barely conscious against the wall, bleeding all over the floor.

Mila.

Her face flashed before his eyes, filling him with a pang of guilt he tried to push away. He hadn't done anything wrong. The son of a bitch deserved every ounce of pain. It wasn't wrong, it was revenge.

"You're more than the devil, Darek." Mila's words echoed in his head.

Cursing under his breath, Darek grabbed Berner by the arm, kicking the doors open, and stalked toward the elevator. He promised her. He kept that promise. He wanted to, needed to. Now, he wasn't so sure.

But he knew one thing with certainty. *She* needed him... He had to go home, he had no time for this bullshit. But he couldn't walk away from what he'd started. No matter what Mila believed, he didn't have it in him. He didn't forgive and forget. He wasn't the angel she thought he was, and he'd never be.

He wasn't done with Berner. He wasn't going to let him get away that easy. Killing him was too kind. He wanted to watch him suffer, he wanted him to wish he'd die, but not let him.

"You can be good, you can do good."

He couldn't. Not now. He tried and failed. All he wanted was the complete opposite, and he wasn't going to let a few soft words stop him.

They reached the bottom floor, deeply hidden underground and with access only granted to Darek. Yes, he'd set it all up, just waiting for the day he'd get his hands on the maggot who'd tortured him for months. A twisted grin spread over Darek's lips as he dragged Berner along the dark corridor. Pushing a door open, he threw the body inside, as abruptly as he could for good measure. Berner's low whimpers made him scoff.

"Good for you, you stole my blood," he snapped. "Heal up, I'm not done with you."

"Wait." Berner's weak voice made Darek pause.

"What?"

"I'm not like you, I'll bleed out—"

Darek cut him off with a cold laugh. "You did just fine when you survived that injection, you son of a bitch!" It had knocked Darek out for hours. Should have killed a human easily, stopped his heart in seconds. It hadn't, and now Darek knew why.

"Choose a side and stick to it."

Slamming the door, he checked the handle to make sure it was locked, then spun on his heels and ran the way back up the corridor. Mila needed him. He felt her, her despair.

Ready to kill the elevator for going too slow, Darek counted his breaths to keep from flying straight through the roof. He already caused enough of a problem by destroying the office and spilling Berner's blood all over the floor. He didn't need to cause more of a scene than he already had by ripping a hole in the fucking roof as well.

Sprinting back to the office, Darek changed back to devil-form as he ran, launching himself straight from the broken window and into the air.

"I choose you."

The moment he stepped through the door at home, he knew something was wrong. He didn't need the connection to feel it. Call it a sixth sense, an intuition. Whatever it was, it was enough to make Darek's blood run cold.

MILA

CHAPTER 49

Mila blinked into the dark. Something had woken her. A sound. It took too long for her sleepy brain to connect the uneasy feeling twisting her belly into a knot, to the sound of a crying baby. She sat bolt upright. He wasn't crying for attention, he was crying with… fear.

Mila sprung to her feet. The baby bed next to hers was empty. Following the sound of the crying, her eyes fell on a tall figure pacing the living room floor. The only light was what the street lights provided outside of the windows, and the shadows covering the person's face sent a chill down her spine.

"Darek?" her voice was hesitant. What was he doing? Why didn't he try to soothe the baby? He didn't even look at him. Mila inched closer. "Dar—" her voice died in her throat. It wasn't Darek. Was she so sleepy she hadn't noticed it at first glance? He was too skinny, and he reeked of booze instead of Darek's intoxicating scent.

"Give me my baby," she snapped, flicking on the lamps. The room bathed in light, and for a few seconds, she didn't see anything. Blinking at the blinding brightness, she squinted at the man who looked back at her with a sneer on his face.

"Princess Shikawa."

"Scott, you sick bastard!" She strode closer, reaching out her arms to grasp Devin from his arms. "Give me my baby! How did you even get in here?"

Scott took a quick step to the side, revealing a knife pressed up against the baby's throat. A bolt of fear zapped through Mila, making her cold all over and skyrocketing her heart rate.

Scott laughed at her expression, a noise she barely heard above the pounding of her heart.

"Yeah, I wouldn't try anything if I were you," he sneered. "Now step back."

Mila fought back tears but did as Scott instructed.

"He's just a baby!" Her voice went shrill. "Don't hurt him."

"You took my child from me!" Scott's sudden shout made Mila flinch, and Devin started to cry louder. "You took my child, now I'll take yours!"

Mila fought to find her voice, trying to keep it from trembling. "You abused her! I did what I had to do! You're sick, Scott, don't you understand, you need help!"

"*I'm* sick?" His laughter echoed in the room. "You're sleeping with the fucking devil!"

His words caught Mila off guard. How did *he* know?

"That's more than enough to declare you unfit to be a mother." Scott jabbed a finger in the air. "I've got you, this time I've got you."

"What do you want from me?" Mila wiped her eyes, furious at herself for crying. She wasn't the crying type, and this wasn't the first fight with Scott. Why was it so different? Why did it scare her out of her mind to see the knife held against little Devin's throat? Why did it fill her with a deeply rooted need to plunge the same knife into Scott's heart for even attempting to threat her baby?

"What you took."

"You're never getting Chrissie back. She's in a good home, with people who adore her."

"I don't care about the brat!" Scott shouted. "I want the

money, the property which *you* are the fucking guardian of. YOU! You weren't even family. It should've been mine. I can't wait until she's eighteen. I need it NOW!"

Mila's blood ran cold. All the things she hadn't understood before, suddenly made perfect sense. The fact that Scott was a psychopath was nothing new, but this took everything to a whole new level.

"You want to use your daughter's legacy to buy drugs?"

Scott let out a hysterical laugh. "You'd never understand. You're a little miss perfect." Scott backed away. "You'll see. I'll get it all back. The child is not safe here, and neither are you."

"Since when do you care about my safety?" Mila's eyes darted to the clock above the couch. It was way past midnight. Where was Darek?

"I don't give a fuck about you or your demon child. But the cops will. *Social service* will. You'll see."

"You're wrong," Mila hissed. "You won't get away with this. Darek will find you, and you don't want to know what happens when he does."

A shadow of fear flitted across Scott's face, then he let out a sharp laugh.

A thud as the front door shut, reached her ears. Mila's eyes shot to the door. She held her breath, praying it was Darek and not some of Scott's friends.

A faint scent of candle smoke allowed her to relax slightly. Mila wanted to scream, to alert him of the danger, but she held her tongue in fear of what Scott could do to Devin.

The moment Darek stepped into the room, and his eyes fell on Scott, she knew she didn't need to worry. He'd never allow anything to happen.

Scott let out a nervous chuckle. "Speak of the devil, huh?"

"Give me the baby, Scott," Mila begged, her eyes darting to Darek, and widened in alarm. He stood frozen to the spot, his bare chest stained with what she could only assume was blood. His hand was just as red, and so was half of his arm. The color drained from Mila's face, and for a moment she

331

thought she'd faint. The range of scenarios that rushed through her head made her dizzy, and as she stared at him in paralyzed shock, his gaze drifted from her, to Devin.

His eyes blazed red as he took in the scene, and the air seemed to grow thick around him. "Get your hands off *MY* son," he snarled.

Scott scrambled away. "I'm not afraid of you!" He shouted as he backed. When his back slammed into the wall, he jumped forward as if he'd been struck. His eyes darting between Mila and Darek, he realized his mistake. Mila glared at him, taking deep satisfaction in his defeat. Her stalling him had paid off. He was trapped, and Darek was here. Her eyes shot back to him. Was it too soon to be relieved? Was he injured? Was that *his* blood? Or someone else's? For a confused moment, Mila didn't know what was worse. Darek's full focus was on Scott, and somehow it made Mila relax slightly.

Devin would be okay. He had to be. Mila's eyes settled on the knife, wishing it away with all she had. Even Darek realized danger, inching closer to Scott so slow she could barely see him move at all. His body was as tight as a wire, ready to spring into action. The sight of him sent a chill down Mila's spine. He was deadly, a panther sneaking up on his victim. The absolute focus, the predatory look in his blood-red eyes. Everything about him screamed danger. Scott had signed his death note. Mila couldn't see Darek sparing him this time, and she was shocked to realize, she didn't care.

Scott had taken everything from her. He'd sabotaged her life since she'd rescued his daughter from him. She'd thought he'd been after some sort of revenge, but not until now did the truth dawn on her. It wasn't revenge. What he wanted was a way to keep up his criminal activities. He'd killed for it. Her dog Maddie was gone, and he'd taken Bosco, too. He'd burned down the shelter with no consideration of the dogs inside, he'd even threatened Kate and brutally murdered her Jack just to terrorize Mila. He'd destroyed everything she'd loved, and now he was after her baby.

"You're not supposed to be here," Scott shouted at Darek. "You should be locked up in that torture chamber!"

Mila's eyes darted to her husband, seeing him tense further. She held her breath as his teeth bared in a feral snarl. She whispered his name, more to herself than to him, silently begging him to stay calm, to not let Scott get to him. It was too late. It had been too late the moment he walked through that door, covered in blood. Mila didn't know what happened, and she wasn't sure she wanted to.

Scott's next words turned into screams as Darek's devil features emerged in a heatwave sending Mila staggering back. Scott fell back, his arms flying out as if to shield himself, sending the baby out of his arms and into the air.

Time seemed to slow down. Mila watched the scene as in slow-motion, hearing her own cries as in a haze. Darek lunged forward, catching the baby with gentle hands while his tail whipped out to twirl around Scott's legs. Scott tumbled to the floor, snapping Mila out of the trance. Her pulse throbbed in her temples while Darek cradled the baby to his chest. His little arms flailed, tiny hands reaching for something to grasp.

"I've got you," Darek's voice was just a growl, but Mila knew better. Within seconds, Devin stopped crying, snug against Darek's warm skin, oblivious to what was happening around him. The room fell silent.

Mila could only stare, her mind blown by the stark contrast of devil and man. He was heaven and hell all wrapped into one. Lethal but also gentle. Seeing him in his full glory, a pure killing machine, holding the tiny baby brought tears to Mila's eyes. She'd known it, but knowing and seeing were two totally different things. She couldn't have found a better man, a better father for her child. His strength would always keep her and Devin safe. She was his weakness, his soft spot, but she figured even the most powerful needed to be vulnerable sometimes.

"I'll take him." Mila brushed a hand over his arm, catching his gaze for a brief moment before shifting the baby to her arms. "We're okay."

DAREK

CHAPTER 50

Darek watched Mila draw back into the bedroom, to safety, cradling Devin in her arms. He wanted nothing more than to be with her, to hold them both and promise them to burn everyone who even dared to look at them in the wrong way.

Scott tried to crawl away, his hands dragging his body over the floor while Darek's tail held him back. A flick of the tail jerked him into the air, and before he collapsed back to the floor, Darek's hand shot out, catching him by the throat.

"I should've ripped you apart the first time I saw you," he growled.

"You and I," Scott's wheezed, clawing at Darek's grip. "We're the same."

Darek flew him into the wall, watching with a smirk playing on his lips as his skinny body slipped to the floor.

"I'm *nothing* like you."

Scott looked up from his position on the floor. "We both want revenge. We both want what's rightfully ours."

"Hmph."

"She's hiding things."

Darek's eyes narrowed. Hating that tiny sliver of doubt Scott's words awoke, he crouched down over Scott, playing with a flame in front of his face.

"Talk," he snarled.

"She took my daughter," Scott blurted. "She got custody of the child and the property. She took everything from me."

The flame died as a strange hollowness filled Darek. Mila had never mentioned having a daughter. She'd never said anything about Devin not being her first... he'd thought... Darek was at a loss for words. Everything he'd believed, was a lie?

Feeling her presence, Darek glared over his shoulder. "Is it true?"

Mila nodded. "Except one thing." She kicked Scott's thigh. "He forgot to mention one important thing."

"What?" Scott shot back. "That you're a psychotic bitch!"

The lie made Darek numb. He couldn't even react to Scott's harsh words. When he normally would've ripped his throat for uttering such words about Mila, he couldn't even lift a hand.

"You never wanted her, you never cared!" Mila snapped.

"Neither did you! She's not even *with* you!" Scott bounced back. "What about the boy huh, you didn't want *him* either, did you?" Seeing the shock in Darek's eyes, he added, "Mila only cares about dogs."

"That's why you targeted the dogs? You bastard?" Mila snapped.

Scott burst into laughter. "You figured it out, first prize goes to Princess Shikawa."

"Stop calling me that!"

Darek shot to his feet and stood, staring down at Scott as he struggled to stay ahead of the whirlwind inside. He should be angry, maybe he was. He just didn't know who to direct his hatred to. Scott or Mila? He didn't want to believe it, but her words confirmed it. She didn't deny the child's existence. She didn't even deny taking her from Scott.

"Darek? Darek!" Mila's voice penetrated his thoughts, snapping him back to the brutal reality. The numbness started to lift, giving way to a flood of emotion. Darek swirled on his heels.

"You lied to me!" He took a step toward Mila, who gulped and backed away. Darek scowled at her. She was afraid. She *should* be.

"Darek, please, calm down." She reached out to place a hand on his chest. He jerked back with a hiss in her direction. "Why didn't you *TELL ME*!"

"About what?" The confusion on her face triggered Darek's anger further. How dare she pretend to be oblivious to what she'd done.

"I did everything for you," Darek's voice dropped onto a menacing growl. "I *died* for you."

Mila came closer.

Darek took a step back. "Do you even care?"

"I don't understand, why are you angry at me?"

The pain in her voice threw Darek off balance. For a brief moment, he wondered the same thing. Then, Scott's words came back, along with the feeling of betrayal, and the anger flared up again.

"You protected him, you didn't want me to hurt him," Darek growled. "Well, it all makes FUCKING SENSE NOW!" His sudden shout made Mila flinch. She opened her mouth to speak, but closed it again and kept on staring at Darek in bewilderment.

Feeling Scott's movement behind him, he flicked his tail, and without even looking, sent Scott tumbling headfirst into the wall.

"You still love him. Who is he, your first? Did you fuck him behind my back? Is Devin even mine?"

Darek's eyes bore into Mila's, demanding answers, ready to kill anything that moved as the pressure inside made his muscles quiver with the power waiting to be unleashed.

After a silence that nearly destroyed the last ounce of

resistance, her eyes widened and she finally spoke.

"You mean Scott? Why would—" she buried her face in her hands, mumbling a set of '*Oh, Gods*' that made Darek shake with pent-up anger. He'd caught her, and now she had no place to run. Darek dreaded hearing the truth, but he had nowhere to run, either. He crossed his hands over his chest, tightening his fists into balls to avoid lashing out.

Mila locked her eyes on his, giving a perplexed shake of her head.

"Darek, Scott is my brother."

"What?"

Had he heard her right? It didn't make sense. The child... Was this worse than even he had dared to imagine?

"You have a child with your brother?"

Mila stared at him in disbelief. "Why would you think— oh, my love." She stepped forward, grabbing his upper arms to keep him from stepping away. "You've got it all wrong. I only have one child, and he's sleeping in there." She gestured toward the bedroom with a tilt of her head.

"Relax," she soothed.

Darek stared at her.

"What happened to you?" Mila took the opportunity to ask. "Why are you so worked up?"

Darek blinked, his eyes landing on her hands still holding his arms.

Before he had the time to reply, Scott started to cough. Darek swirled around, ripping Mila's hands off him, and nearly knocked her down with a wing.

Looming over Scott, Darek forced himself to be still when all he wanted was to rip his head off.

"Tell me one thing."

He spoke with a dead calm, giving nothing away. Scott gulped visibly but didn't dare to move.

"Who do you work for?"

Darek already knew, but he needed to hear it, to confirm his fears. Scott knew about the lab, about the torture. He couldn't know those things if he hadn't been in contact with that fucking Berner or his slutty sidekick.

Mila's gasp reminded him of her presence. Ignoring the

brief feeling of guilt that zapped through him, he focused all his attention on the cockroach on the floor. He needed to be crushed, like the insect he was. He'd deal with Mila later. It was already too late to pretend he hadn't slipped back to being the devil they both knew he was.

"I don't know what—"

Darek crouched down and hissed in Scott's face, "Who?"

He dragged a claw across Scott's throat, slow and promising until the man trembled under him.

When the claw slit the skin open, drawing a thin line of blood, Scott stuttered, "I don't know... I don't know her name, don't kill me."

"Hmph."

"No, please, I was just—"

"WHAT?" Darek's sudden roar made both Scott and Mila jump. Darek shot to his feet, dragging Scott's trembling body with him to his full height, slamming him up against the wall with a force enough to crack it and knock the breath out of Scott.

"Just *what*?" Darek hissed. "You think this is a game? You think this is fun?"

Scott stammered a series of incoherent words before starting to cough. "Mila?" he rasped.

"No," her voice was surprisingly cold. "I'm done, Scott."

"You're my sister."

Mila scoffed. "Oh, really? *Now* I am your sister? What about when you tried to cut Devin's throat, when you burned down my shelter? When you took Maddie and Bosco? You sick bastard! Where is he anyway? What did you do to him?"

Darek couldn't hold back a grin. Backup from Mila was the last he expected, but oh, did it feel good.

Mila's hand landed on his arm. "Hold on," she warned, then directed her attention to Scott.

"Answer the questions, or I swear I'll let him kill you."

Scott's eyes bulged as Darek added pressure to his throat. "With pleasure."

"Where is Bosco?"

"Northgate. Brady Parson."

Darek's hands burned with contained fire, steam swirling around Scott's face as he pressed harder against his neck to keep the flames under control.

"Who is the woman?" Mila asked the question he dreaded hearing. "Tell him the truth."

"I don't know her name. She has pink in her hair."

"What did you do?"

"Nothing! I just —told her where to find you. Gave her the key to the apartment. Might have bugged it."

"Key?" Mila asked.

"Found your spare. Making duplicates was easy." Scott grinned as if proud of his accomplishment.

"You sick fuck!" Mila's voice was harsh. "You sold us out for drugs? You knew what those people would do to him?"

"I didn't know—"

The look on Darek's face made him rethink, stuttering a raspy. "M-maybe I knew."

"That woman—" Darek couldn't keep his voice steady no matter how he tried. For a few seconds, he was back there on the wall. For a few moments of horror, he was forced to relive the shame, the pain.

"It's—"

"I know," Mila whispered. Her hand on Darek's arms tightened. "I saw her that night."

"Mila?" Darek squeezed his eyes shut, focusing on her touch to keep him together. He was so close to breaking, to ripping the bastard's head off. He couldn't even care if Mila saw him, but he should care. He promised her. He promised...

Devin started to cry, and in a flash, Mila's hand fell away as she stepped back. Darek heard her footsteps as she ran to the bedroom.

Images of Scott's hand with a knife to little Devin's throat flashed through Darek's mind, and it was all it took. The fraction of control he clung to vanished.

Darek pushed himself off Scott's body with a scream that shook the walls, and in the same fluid motion twisting his body, slitting Scott's throat with a slash of his claws. Scott dropped to the floor, and not until his blood created a pool around his body did Darek calm down enough to realize what he'd done.

Somewhere in the back of his head, he knew he should feel ashamed, feel bad. But he couldn't find those feelings. All he felt was deep satisfaction.

Devin's cries and Mila's soft humming drifted to him, filling him with a calm that ripped the last energy from him. When he shifted to his human form, the impact of his actions crept up on him.

Darek stopped in the doorway, watching Mila as she sat on the bed, rocking the baby in her arms. Her gaze drifted to him, her humming faltering as her eyes widened at the sight of the fresh blood-stains all over his skin, and the red dripping from his fingers.

She swallowed, then with her eyes locked on Darek, she continued to softly sing. Darek held her gaze, letting the soothing melody calm him, as well as the baby. He didn't doubt for a second; she knew what happened the moment she left him alone. Yet, she just continued to hum the tune as she stared at him.

Darek inched closer, sinking onto the bed next to her but couldn't bring himself to look at her. What was worse, that he lost his temper with *her*, or slit her brother's throat?

Blaming her for the withheld information wouldn't lead anywhere, and even though he wanted to be angry at her, he couldn't. It was all on him. He lost his temper, he let her down. The promise to her suddenly meant nothing.

Devin had stopped crying. And after a long silence, Mila's low voice reached his ears.

"Where were you?"

Something in Darek's stomach tightened. Despite her soft tone, the accusation was as clear as if she'd been shouting.

"I had to take care of something."

She didn't need to know the details, she didn't need to know she'd been that bastard Berner's safety net. She was no more, and neither was he.

"If you'd been here this would never have happened. Devin could have died."

340

Darek gulped. She was right.

"Mila—"

She shook her head, and Darek fell silent. Thinking of the dead body in their living room, and his unexpected connection to Mila, he couldn't keep from asking, "Why didn't you tell me?"

Mila refused to look at him and spoke staring into the dark window. "It never occurred to me you might think he's something else," she muttered. "Everything he said..."

"Is true." Darek filled in. "Don't lie to me."

A shadow of shame settled on Mila's face. She hung her head. "I wasn't ready to be a mom, but I couldn't see that little girl being abused. I did what I had to do, what no one else dared to do. Scott got furious, but not because he lost the child, but because he lost the property she inherited."

"Where was her mom?"

"She died, she was—my best friend. She'd made me the legal guardian of her property, and the girl. She thought I'd raise her, keep her and her legacy safe until she turned eighteen. I wasn't ready for that responsibility. I was just seventeen and I was going through a really bad time. I arranged with my oldest brother, he has a family, a kid the same age as Chrissie. He took her. I let my friend down, and I hate myself for that, but I had to do what was best for the child."

"It's still signed to you? That's what he was after? Cash?"

"Scott is a drug addict and a psychopath. He's done everything to destroy me and my life. If it's for the money, if it's out of revenge, I don't know."

"I do," Darek's voice dropped into a growl. "I know exactly what he wanted."

"How—"

"He wanted to break you, to show everyone you're the unstable one."

Mila sat in silence, staring down at the sleeping baby in her arms. Darek followed her gaze.

"You didn't want Devin either, did you?"

Mila's silence was all he needed. Scott was right. She only cared about the dogs.

341

"Do you want me to pick him up for you?"

"What are you talking about?"

Darek huffed. "The goddamn dog. Your most prized possession."

"Shut up."

"Hmph."

"I'll pick him myself." She fell silent, sighing deeply before adding, "About Devin... You were gone, I was going through hell along with you, I was terrified. There was a voice in my head. I mean literally."

"A voice?"

"I know it sounds crazy, but I swear I—"

He cut her off, "It's not crazy." He knew all too well what it was like, he just never thought she'd hear it too. How was it even possible?

"What does it say?"

Mila's eyes drifted to the sleeping baby. "That he's evil. That I had to kill him."

Darek couldn't keep the shock from slipping from his lips. "The fuck?"

She cringed. "It was just once, I never heard her again."

"Her?"

She nodded.

"It's a woman?"

Another nod.

"And she's gone?"

One more nod. "What does it mean?"

"I feel like I *should* know. That it's connected to me, but I don't."

A pressing silence crept over them, giving Darek the time to ponder her words. Someone or *something* warned Mila about the baby? Made her believe he was evil before he'd even been born? The thought was enough to make Darek's blood boil. Devin wasn't evil. He was no devil.

"I should've been there," he growled. "But I would never have thought I needed to protect him from *you*."

"You didn't even know I was pregnant!"

"That's not the point!" Darek snapped. "You wanted to *kill* him."

"I didn't—"

"You just said—"

"I LOVE HIM! I can't see my life without him!"

Darek stared at the boy, breathing through parted lips to calm his temper. She was right. Things changed. He never imagined himself in this situation either, but yet here he was. A dad. A husband. A businessman. A devil... Darek cursed under his breath. If he just stayed at home...

"Mila—"

"Don't."

"I—"

"What!" she hissed, finally turning to face him. "You're going to apologize?" She scoffed. "To say you didn't *mean* to attack me? That you didn't *mean* to kill Scott? That you didn't *mean* to come home covered in blood? Who *else* did you kill?"

Darek no longer knew who he was, what he was supposed to say or focus on. When he'd only been the devil, it had been easy. He'd known nothing else, now he was pulled in different directions, and he didn't know which way was the right way.

Silently he took Mila's hand. She flinched, trying to pull away but he held on. "I don't expect you to forgive me. I failed you."

"You're damn right about that."

Her words hit Darek like a knife to his heart. He hung his head, the weight of his actions crushing him. The blood on his skin started to itch, to disgust him.

"I had to do it. What he did to me—"

"He?"

"The son of a bitch who—" Darek cut himself off. He didn't want to say it, to even think of it. He'd been ready to let it go. He expected to come home to Mila's loving arms, he expected pleasure, instead of pain. He'd done everything wrong. Yet, he only felt bad about disappointing her, not about what he'd done.

Glancing up at Mila, he was struck by her cold gaze.

She looked at him in silence, then her eyes drifted back to Devin.

"Promise me one thing."

Darek managed a weak nod.

"Never let anything bad happen to our son."

Darek swallowed down the lump in his throat. "I promise."

DAREK

CHAPTER 51

Three years later

Darek kept the promise. He protected the baby with his life. Mila too. With Berner safely stored in the sub-levels of Rewera Corp, and Scott out of the picture, things were calm. Mila never asked what happened to Scott's body, and it suited Darek just fine. She didn't need to know. He'd taken care of it, just like she'd demanded. Two months after his *disappearance*, the police declared him dead. The time Mila spent away from Darek, with her parents and brothers, felt like years long.

"I need space. I can't be around you now."

"If you go—" he swallowed hard, forcing himself to admit what he didn't want to face. *"I'll lose myself."* The

345

devil was too present, whispering to him of the pleasures of darkness and sin. The temptation burned hotter than ever inside, tearing at him every time he dared to let his guard down.

The tension between him and Mila added fuel to his fire. The cracks of their foundation, giving the devil more wiggle room to lure him to the wrong side.

"You only got yourself to blame." Mila backed away as Darek reached for her. "You chose the devil over me. Over our family. You did horrible things, and for what? Revenge? You're better than that. You were doing good. You were good."

"I didn't choose—"

"Don't lie to me."

Darek fisted his hair until the pain made him wince. She was right. He'd briefly chosen the darkness over the light. He'd chosen revenge. Murder. Torture. He'd craved the warmth of human blood on his skin and the satisfaction of hearing their cries.

"You don't know what it's like."

For a moment, her features softened. She sighed. "You're right. I don't."

Darek stepped closer, encouraged by her words. Throwing her packed suitcase a glare, he swallowed down the desperation swirling in his gut. "Don't go." He reached out, brushing his knuckles over her cheek. "I need you."

Her dark eyes found his, and for a moment she hesitated.

"No," she whispered at last. "You need to work on yourself. Take this time to figure out what you want."

The pained expression he couldn't hide made her smile. Taking his hand, she brought it to her chest, cradling it over her heart.

"I love you. But I need to know I'm still your first priority."

Darek's chest tightened with emotion, and as he spoke, the words came out as nothing but a rasp. "You are. I choose you. I choose Devin. Always."

"I'll come back. I just need a little time with my parents after everything that happened. Okay?"

They lived the perfect family life on the outside, but Darek knew better. He tried. He tried so hard it crushed him, but he refused to let her down again. He promised her, and he'd rather die than break that promise.

He'd chosen her, shoved the devil away into the darkest corner of his soul, and refused to let it surface. The struggle left him exhausted. There were nights he didn't dare to go home at all. He could never fool Mila, he learned the hard way. He had a darkness in him he couldn't brighten, and when it got too pressing, he learned to avoid her instead of seeking her soothing calm. It wasn't that he didn't want to. He did. He craved it, and deep down he knew it was his only salvation. But he couldn't put it on her. He couldn't come running to her every time he was overwhelmed by dark thoughts. Mila deserved better than that. She deserved a man who could take care of himself. She deserved a rock. He wanted to be that, he wanted to be her everything. But he was no rock, he was a volcano, and he didn't want to be anywhere near Mila when blowing its top.

The beeping of an incoming call brought Darek back to the office. He pressed a button, allowing Cat's voice to drift into the room.

"Good morning, Boss," she chirped. "One more all-nighter, huh?"

"What do you want?" Darek never cared for her chitchat, even though she never failed to try.

Cat groaned. "Someone woke up in a bad mood."

"I didn't sleep, Cat. Get to the point."

"Richard called in this morning, he's not feeling well. You gotta take his meetings."

A bolt of alarm zapped through Darek. He wasn't ready. He'd make a fool of himself. He feared this day. Richard had pushed him, but he'd refused. Three years were not enough, even though Richard had claimed he was more than ready to face the big men.

"I can't, I—" Darek cut himself off, thinking of an excuse. "I'm busy." It was no lie.

"Then reschedule. You don't want to miss this

opportunity. If we land this deal—"

"Got it," Darek snapped. He didn't need to hear how important it was. He wasn't dumb, he knew what was at stake. Richard taught him well, but he never thought he'd be the one walking into that boardroom. Darek gulped. He could do this. He had to.

"Okay." He spun the chair, facing the panorama windows outlooking the city, reminding himself he had nothing to fear. He knew business. It was his family he was failing in.

"Cat, I need to see her."

There was a long silence, then she finally spoke. "I'll see if I can get a hold of her."

He'd spent most of his time in the office instead of in Mila's arms. But now he needed her, needed to see her smile and feel her soothing hands on his skin.

— * —

Darek paced the floor in anticipation, and when the soft knock on the doors reached his ears, he hesitated.

He couldn't hide the slight tremble of his voice as he called out, "Come in."

The black double doors parted, and there she was, dressed in a red coat so similar to the one he'd first seen her in. Her black hair was gathered in a high ponytail, and a white scarf loosely slung around her neck. Darek forgot how to breathe. Every time he saw her he was in awe of her beauty, and the effect her mere presence had on him. The fire within him stilled, his tense shoulders relaxing, but his heartbeat skyrocketing.

"Daddy!" Devin pushed his way past Mila's legs and ran straight toward Darek.

Darek scooped him up, holding him over his head with his hands hooked under his armpits, and spun him in the air until he screamed in delight.

"I'm flying, Daddy!" he giggled.

"That's right, Firefly."

The smile on Devin's face vanished, and a frown ceased on his little forehead. "Why don't you come home? Mommy

348

was crying last night."

Darek lowered the boy, holding him on one arm as his gaze traveled to Mila. She looked embarrassed.

"I had to work, little one," he said at last. Putting Devin down to the floor, he watched him run off to climb his office chair and winced.

"Be careful, don't—" Darek cursed under his breath, stalking over to the boy to remove him from the desk. If he messed up the carefully organized piles, he'd be in big trouble. Shifting the stacks to a shelf where Devin couldn't reach, he looked around for something to distract the boy. Finding nothing but a black marker and a few old papers, he gave it to Devin who was more than excited for the gift.

When Devin was busy drawing squiggly lines on the papers, Darek turned to Mila.

"I should've been there."

Mila snorted, leaning back against the wall. "I waited for you."

Guilt wormed its way into Darek's heart. He let her down, again. On nothing less than their wedding anniversary. He should have been there. Yet, he spent the night in his office.

"I was—" What was he supposed to say? I was a wreck? I was worried I'd snap? I didn't want to worry you. All of the options would have been better than what he said, "I was busy."

"Why am I here?"

The hostile tone broke Darek's heart. He swallowed down the pride, he had to tell her, or he feared he'd lose her. "I need you," he managed to whisper. "I'm—sorry."

Mila's expression softened. Closing the gap between them, she lay her hands on his upper arms, gazing up at his face, and for a moment everything felt all right again.

"What's going on with you?"

Darek didn't know. All he knew was that it was hard. Every day was a struggle he couldn't win. What had once been easy was getting impossible. The force burning within him was stronger. It kept on growing stronger, demanding more space, more power.

As Devin grew older, the darkness within Darek grew

thicker. How could he explain this to Mila, when he didn't even understand it himself? How could he tell her he had moments when all he wanted was to watch the world burn? He promised her to be good. After the slip with Scott, he tried harder, and he'd done well. But just because he hadn't snapped and killed someone didn't mean he didn't want to. He was dying to, aching for the satisfaction. He just denied himself the outlet for the dark desires swirling within him, redirecting the energy to the business.

"Tell me the truth, Darek. Why are you living in this office?"

"I—"

"No!" she barked. "Don't lie to me."

"Because I'm protecting you!"

His words cough Mila off guard. Her mouth opened, then closed. On the second try, she managed to ask, "From what?"

Darek scoffed, facing away from her as he regretted the outburst.

Her hand landed on his back, making him shudder under her touch. Darek spoke facing the windows. "From me."

Mila's hands on his arms spun him to face her. "What the hell is that supposed to mean?"

"It's growing stronger, Mila. I didn't want you to worry."

The moment of confusion quickly turned into realization. Her features fell. She shook her head, refusing to accept it. "No." She stepped closer, circling her arms around Darek. "Don't you dare try to wiggle out of this. Fight it!"

Darek swallowed down the emotion. He was a different person when he was with her. One part of him wanted to let everything else go and never leave her side. But it wasn't possible. Even if he gave up the company, she still had the shelter. She still had a life that didn't involve him. He couldn't force her to give up her dream, just to stay cooped up in her apartment to babysit him.

"I'm trying."

"Try harder," Mila demanded. "If not for me, then for Devin."

"I'll do anything for you." It was the truth. He'd die

for her. He'd sacrifice anything to keep her safe. Even if it meant his own happiness.

"Come home, take a few days off. We'll do something, just the three of us."

Darek couldn't do anything else than nod.

"I'm proud of you." Mila stepped away, smiling up at him. "You've got so far, you do wonders with the company."

"Do I sense a *but* in there?"

"Don't forget you have a family, too."

Her words caught Darek like a kick to the gut. He hadn't forgotten. She was all he could think of. She was his reason for breathing.

"Everything I do, it's for you," he whispered. "To keep you safe."

She smiled, gesturing toward the tall ceiling. "When are we moving into the penthouse?"

"Soon."

She snorted. "I've heard that the last three years, you haven't even taken me to see it."

"I'm—" Darek looked down. He avoided it. He didn't need the reminder of the lie. Mila thought Berner was long dead. He had to close that chapter before he could move on. He had to finish what he'd started. He refused to live in that man's home and see him everywhere he looked, he'd barely been up there himself. Briefly, when the curiosity got too much. Cat had been right. It was pure luxury. It was what Mila and Devin deserved. He just didn't know how to take the step.

"I haven't had time, it's—it needs to be renovated. I can't…"

Mila understood. "It will remind you of that man. It's okay, our little place is good, I don't mind it."

"No, I'm sorry. I'll have a team fix it up ASAP, I can't wait to share it with you."

She blinked away tears. "I love you."

Darek couldn't bring himself to say it back. The only person he'd ever said it to had died. The little words burned within him, and he knew one day he'd have to speak them out loud. But he wasn't ready. Instead of speaking, he grabbed Mila, wrapping her in his arms as tight as he could without crushing her.

Mila was first to pull away. Standing on her toes, she reached up to pull him down for a kiss. Once he had her lips on his, he never wanted to let her go. When she pulled away again, he caught her, pressing her flat to his body and catching her mouth with his. He kissed her until they were both gasping for air and his slacks were painfully tight. Darek was tempted to leave everything and take her right there, it wouldn't have been the first time. Fuck the meetings, fuck everything. He needed to feel her skin, to bury himself in her and forget about the world.

The angry beeping of an incoming call snapped him back to reality. Cursing out loud, he left Mila, snatched the receiver from the cradle, and listened to Cat's voice. Throwing a look at his watch, he paled. He'd lost track of time.

Cutting the call, he swirled around to face Mila. "I have to go."

"Right now?"

Darek adjusted his pants with a huff. He was late for the goddamn meeting, and all he could think of was how Mila's naked body felt under him.

Muttering a string of curses under his breath, Darek began gathering the documents.

"Daddy, look!"

Darek jumped at the sound of Devin's voice. He'd almost forgotten he was still there. Twisting his neck to see where the boy pointed, his eyes grew wide at the sight of a big black crisscross of lines drawn on the bottom corner where the panorama windows met the floor.

"That's, uh—nice," Darek raked a hand through his hair, smoothing it back. "I'll treasure it, little one." He flashed a smile and Devin beamed as if he'd drawn a masterpiece.

"Now go with Mommy." Shooing the boy back to Mila, he gestured toward the doors and let out a ragged breath.

"You seem nervous," Mila stated the obvious, and Darek let out a sharp laugh.

"I never did this," he muttered. "Richard is not here, I

can't afford to screw this up."

Mila's calming hand on his chest allowed him to suck in a deep breath, calming his nerves.

"You'll do fine," she murmured. "I'll be waiting at home," she added with a wink.

Darek stepped away with a huff. *That* wasn't helping. Storming out of the office, all he could think of was her and all the things he'd do to her once he had her alone...

MILA

CHAPTER 52

"I'll be waiting at home…"

She'd been waiting all right. She waited two nights. When he finally came home, she hadn't even bothered to look at him, let alone give him the chance to offer her any excuses.

"Go on, I'm sure you have work to do. I'll be with our son."

Mila closed the book, smiled down at Devin's sleeping form, and leaned in to kiss his cheek. "Goodnight, baby," she whispered.

Time passed fast. It still felt like yesterday when she held him in her arms for the first time. Now he was over three, and quite the little man. The child she never wanted was suddenly her whole world.

Mila gently peeled the blanket off Devin and cringed at the sight of the bruises on his upper arm. The perfect mark of a hand gripping him too tight. She didn't know when it had happened, but as much as it pained her to accept it, she knew how.

Scott had been right. Devin wasn't safe. Mila didn't want to admit it, but it was time to face the truth. The perfect family was over. It had been for a long time. Darek had changed. It had happened slowly, crept up on them like slow-growing cancer. She hadn't caught it before it was too late. The bruises on Devin's arm were enough for Mila to know she had to do something. She'd taken Chrissie away from Scott for the same reasons, she had to take Devin to safety, too. No matter how it hurt, she had no choice. He came first. She could not risk his well-being because she was in love with the devil.

It didn't matter that the mere thought of leaving Darek broke her heart. Devin had to come first.

Darek hadn't come home that night he'd promised, and she wasn't surprised. But she was disappointed, even though she should have gotten used to it by now. If she didn't know better, she'd have thought he was avoiding her. As she left the bedroom, their last meeting in the office replayed in her head.

"It's growing stronger. I didn't want you to worry."

He was trying. But it wasn't enough. Not anymore.

"I'll do anything for you."

It sounded good. And she was so tempted to believe it. To let his words fill her with that same security it had from the start. Then he'd done anything to be *with* her, now, he was doing everything he could to stay away.

She closed the bedroom door, turned, and nearly tripped over Bosco. He'd been waiting outside the door, silent but never leaving her side.

"Hey," Mila cooed. "Who's jealous of the human baby?"

The dog waved his tail, nudging his face into Mila's belly. She smiled down at his silver fur, stroking it with loving hands as she recalled the day she brought him back from the asshole who kept him hidden on Scott's demands.

Mila shuddered as she crossed the lawn to a suburban house. The neighborhood looked just as rough as its inhabitants. People dressed in shabby clothes drifted along the streets, and groups of teenagers she'd run from if she met them on a dark night, stared at her as she hurried up to an old brown door.

The moment it opened, she blurted, "I'm here for my dog."

A bald man with a large beer-belly stared at her, dumbfounded and mute.

"The gray Pitbull," Mila clarified. "My brother Scott left him with you. I want him back."

The man grimaced, spit out a mouthful of loose tobacco, and disappeared into the house. When he came back, he had Bosco on a tight leash.

"This your mutt?"

Mila dropped to her knees and the dog jumped straight into her outstretched arms the moment he let go of the rope holding him away from her.

His happiness answered the question. And as he wiggled his body in joy and licked Mila's face until her skin was wet and she had to push him away, the man slammed the door.

Mila got to her feet, removed the old leash, and ran back the way she'd come. Bosco flew into the back of her car the moment she opened it.

"Let's go home."

She'd been lucky. The sleepless nights she'd been so sure she'd never seen him again had been plenty. But he was safe. He was home. Lifting her gaze from the dog to the man on her couch, her mood shifted.

Darek was home too, but he wasn't really there. Mila found him with his nose in a bunch of files. He didn't look up, not until she snatched the papers out of his hands and threw them to the floor.

"What the fuck?"

"You have no right to say that!" Mila hissed. "Look at you!"

Darek shot to his feet, drawing a deep growl from Bosco who'd followed Mila.

Shooting the dog a look that could kill, he gathered the folders and placed them on the table before facing Mila. "What? Isn't this what you wanted? That I do something with my life?"

Mila snorted. "Don't put this on me. I never wanted to

lose you to that goddamn office."

"I'm right here," he snapped.

"Only two days too late!"

"Hmph."

Mila grabbed his shoulders, searching his eyes for that old warmth which he'd reserved only for her. The eyes that stared back at her were cold, piercing. She had to look away. "You're not *you* anymore. You're so far away I can't reach you."

Darek's silence only added to her despair. She dreaded having to say it.

"You're hurting Devin."

His scowl made her want to slap him. How could he stand there looking pissed? Couldn't he at least pretend to be remorseful? To explain.

"No child should have bruises like that, what did you do?"

Darek jerked her hands off of him with a huff. "I'd never hurt him." He swirled around to leave, but Mila caught his arm.

"Don't walk away from me."

"Or what?" he growled.

"Darek, please." The desperation in her voice reached to him. His tense stance softened as he turned to brush his knuckles over her cheek.

"I don't want to fight," he whispered. "I'm—lost." His eyes sought hers, and for a moment she saw the Darek she used to know. "I don't know how to fight it, sometimes I don't even want to."

Mila threw her arms around him, breathing in his smokey scent while fighting back the tears. She pulled away enough to look at him. It was so easy to give in, to let him sweep her into the fantasy bubble and pretend nothing changed. But it had. And no matter how much her heart ached for him, how much her nature craved to rescue him, to not give up, she had to think of Devin. She had to choose him.

"Oh, my love." She cupped his cheek, watching him with a growing feeling of guilt in the pit of her belly. He deserved better. Someone who'd fight for him. He wasn't evil. She believed without a doubt he'd never hurt Devin on purpose. She trusted the man with her life, but the devil was a different matter.

Mila stroked his face, brushing gentle fingers over his scars. "I love you." She let her hand fall, forcing the next words out of her mouth. "But I can't do this anymore. I have to put Devin first."

Darek's face shifted from confusion to pain, and settled on anger. His eyes lit up, casting a red glow on his cheeks as those eyes bore into Mila's.

"No," his voice was calm, too calm. "I won't let you go."

"You have to."

When he didn't speak, Mila took the opportunity to go on, "You don't need us, you're never home. And when you are, all we do is fight. It's over, it's been over for a long time, you know that too."

Darek's hand shot out faster than she could dodge. With a yank, he had her trapped against his body. "It's not true," he growled in her neck. Backing her up against the couch, he pushed her down onto it, pinning her hands over her head as he held her in place with his body. "You are *not* going anywhere."

Mila's eyes narrowed. "Get off me or I swear I'll hurt you."

Darek scoffed. "I'd like to see you tr—" A knee to his balls made him cry out loud. She thought he'd let go of her, but instead, he gripped her harder, collapsing on top of her body.

"Fucking—" He cut whatever he'd been about to say in half, retreating to a strained groan.

"Are you okay?" Mila couldn't help but ask. How could she feel bad? Once, she'd been attracted to his dominant streak, now it just aggravated her. She was not a little girl anymore. She was a mom. So much had changed.

Darek lifted himself on strong arms, hovering above her with a predatory look on his face. Mila gulped. Okay, so she may not be immune to it. He might have changed, but he was still sexy as the sin he was.

"Am *I* okay?" he growled. "What do you think?"

Mila squirmed under his glare. "Darek..."

"Don't go, Mila." His gaze softened, old pain leaking through. He hung his head, whispering the last words, "I need you."

Mila swallowed down the emotion. "Can you fight it?"

Darek lifted his gaze. The red faded, returning his eyes to the normal gray.

"I can," he said with such certainty, that for a moment she believed him. She wanted to believe him, wanted him to be right.

"Make love to me, like we used to do."

Something lit up in his cold eyes, a smirk settling on his lips. "You shouldn't have crushed my balls if you want sex."

Mila couldn't help but snort. "You're the devil, you heal. I'm sure they're fine by now."

"Hmph."

Mila lifted the same knee, this time rubbing it against him, drawing a low groan from his lips.

"Let my hands go, and I can do that better."

"I'm not letting any part of you go."

His lips cut off her retort, and in the few seconds of confusion, Mila was torn between sticking to her plan or giving in to her needs. Her body and heart won over her brain. She loved him like she had from the start, she needed him like she had before even realizing it. He was still everything she desired, and he was right here. Mila couldn't push him away, not when she finally had his full attention.

She didn't want to go. She didn't want him to let her go.

Darek released her arms to strip off their clothes, and before she had time to think, he was back in her arms, one hand pinning hers above her head, and the other lifting her hips to his. Mila stifled a cry as he thrust into her. The last thing she wanted was for Devin to wake up.

Darek moved with an urgency, a hunger for her that couldn't be satisfied. It had been too long. Their bodies knew it. Mila slung a leg over his waist, urging him closer, deeper. Her mind swam, the dormant passion awakening by the flood of pleasure and the sounds Darek couldn't hold back.

"Be silent!" she hissed. "Devin—is—

"Mommy!"

Their bodies froze as the wail reached their ears.

"Oh, for fucks—" Darek groaned.

"I have to go to him."

"I'll do it." Darek pulled away, throwing on his pants. Mila couldn't help but smile at his discomfort, and the low hisses as he adjusted the pants as well as he could. Devin wouldn't notice, but that bulge was all Mila could think of as she watched him disappear into the bedroom.

Mila wrapped a blanket around herself and tiptoed up to the door.

"Mommy is busy right now, Firefly." Darek stroked Devin's head. "I'm sorry, son, I've been busy too. I missed you."

Devin shifted, hesitating, then threw his arms around Darek's neck. "I missed you, Daddy."

Tears welled up in Mila's eyes. She'd been wrong. He did care, he just needed to be reminded of what truly mattered. He needed his family. He needed her.

Darek tucked Devin back in. "Sleep now, little one."

Mila could tell he'd fallen asleep, but Darek lingered at his side. His fingers brushing through his hair with a notable gentleness that made tears roll down her cheeks. Darek whispered to him, words Mila couldn't hear. But she didn't need to. His actions spoke louder than the words he didn't dare to say out loud.

DAREK

CHAPTER 53

At the end of the following day, Darek sat in the car outside of their little apartment, torn between going in, and going straight back to the office. The raging fire within him made him long for Mila's soft voice and calming touch. But that same power left him feeling like a bomb ready to blast, and he didn't want to be anywhere near her or Devin if that happened. Even thinking of walking into their home in his state of mind was selfish. But he wanted to breathe again, to fall into her arms and allow himself the comfort. He needed it now more than ever. He needed her to set him straight, to save him from the dark.

"It's time for you to die," Darek's voice was cold and emotionless. Keeping the cockroach Berner alive for three years lost its charm. His suffering no longer did something to Darek. He needed it to be over. He needed to be a better

361

man.

"Please, let me go, I won't tell anyone."

"Hmph." Darek stared down at the man hunched into a corner on the cement floor. A flame danced in his palm. Darek studied it, allowing his lips to twitch into a smirk.

"I believe this is gonna hurt."

"No, please."

The screams as the flame engulfed him was like music to Darek's ears. When the scream died down, Darek turned and left, knowing the body would be nothing but ashes within minutes. It was over. Now he had to go home.

Darek felt numb as he stepped into the foyer. The pleasure he'd expected when killing Berner faded the moment he left the body to burn in the room. The closure he needed left nothing but a deep ache in him. An ache he couldn't dull with either family or work, a thirst that couldn't be satisfied with living the lie he clung to. When staying good took more out of him than it gave, Darek didn't know how long he could hold on. Sometimes he didn't know what he was fighting for.

He could never be enough for Mila, but it never kept him from trying. He couldn't lose her, couldn't imagine his life without her. How would he even breathe without her? She was the calm in his storm, the soothing balm to his fire. Yet, he felt it in every fiber of his body—she was so close to slipping away. So close to that decision which he'd talked her out of.

"Daddy!"

Devin's voice snapped him from his thought, and he forced a smile as the little boy came running to greet him.

"Hey, Firefly." Darek scooped the boy up, holding him effortlessly on one arm as his thoughts wandered.

"Devin has bruises on his arms."

Darek had seen them, and he knew as well as Mila did what caused them, and it broke his heart. He'd never do that. Willingly.

"What did you do?"

Darek's heart clenched at the memory. That she'd even

accuse him was enough for him to want to scream. Didn't she know he'd never hurt her? Or the boy? Didn't she know how many nights he'd suffered alone at the office just to keep them safe from him? Didn't she understand he sacrificed everything for her, that he let himself fall further into the darkness just to keep her in the light?

"I love you. But I have to put Devin first."

The sudden sting of anger toward the boy stunned Darek. He wanted to shake it, to forget it and pretend it hadn't happened, but he couldn't. The feeling clung to him as tight as Devin's little arms. Filling his heart with darkness and his head with sin.

Before he could rationalize it, before he could prepare himself, the images slithered into his head, filling him with a deep desire to execute the impulses.

It was wrong, it made him sick to his stomach, but it was there. The strong and sudden urge to tear his claws into Devin's little body. The shock coursed through Darek like a cold stream, momentarily freezing him to the floor.

He wished his son away.

Wished he'd never been born.

Wished for his blood on his hands.

Darek put Devin down, swallowing down the disgust crawling up his throat. He adored the boy. He'd done everything to keep him safe. To protect him from the horrors of the world. He couldn't count the sleepless nights imagining Devin in the same nightmare as he'd grown up in.

"Daddy," Devin complained. He reached his arms up, wanting back up, and the little scowl that settled on his face as Darek refused only fueled the irritation instead of making him chuckle as it always had. The little boy mastered the Rewera scowl already at three. Darek had been proud of his temper. Now, all he felt was annoyance.

"I have to put Devin first."

Darek cursed under his breath. When had it come to a choice? When did it become okay to dump him and take his son? How had the little devil-child wormed his way in between them? Destroying what they had? Destroying him.

"Daddy!"

"Not now, Firefly."

"But Daddy!"

Darek clenched his fists, burying claws into his flesh until the blood dropped onto the floor.

"Go to Mommy," Darek managed. "Run. Get away from me."

Devin's eyes widened, his lower lip quivering as if he was about to cry. "But—"

Darek squeezed his eyes shut, choking out, "Daddy is not feeling well."

He heard the sound of little feet, then the silence wrapped around him like a dark cloak. When a hand landed on his arm, he jumped, snapping his eyes open, and just barely managed to keep from exploding.

"Devin said you don't feel well, what—" Mila grabbed one of his hands, holding it up. "You're bleeding. What happened?"

Darek snatched the hand away. "I am the bad thing, Mila."

She stared at him, not understanding.

"That's not true. What are—"

"I promised you."

"Promised me what?" Mila's hands landed on his upper arms. "Calm down, everything will be okay."

Darek shook his head. It wouldn't. It couldn't.

"I promised not to let anything bad happen to him. *I* am the bad thing."

"My love—"

"NO! Don't!"

"Darek!" Mila raised her voice. "Listen to me!"

"He's not safe with me. You said it yourself."

"I didn't mean—"

"Stop!" Darek snapped. Raking his hands through his hair, he gripped it, focusing on the pressure of the claws against his skull to keep from lashing out. He'd never felt so out of control, and the power swirling inside him both terrified and thrilled him.

"Don't hold back. You know what you want to do."

364

"No," Darek hissed. "Shut up. Go away!"

"Darek?" Mila stared at him with a look of caution on her face. "Who are you talking to?"

"I have to go." Darek spun on his heels. It had been a mistake coming home. His mood was dark. He'd thought she could make him feel better. He'd been selfish.

"You just came!" Mila's hand on his arm made him stop, but he didn't turn. He didn't dare.

"You can't do this." The accusation in Mila's voice broke something in him. His blood boiled, his body burned, every cell of his being aching with the contained power.

"You can't run away every time there's an argument."

Darek clenched his jaw, grinding his teeth so tight his head hurt while trying to remind himself this was Mila. If something happened to her, he'd never forgive himself.

"She's controlling you. You're dancing on her strings," the voice in his head taunted. *"Do you want to be a pussy-whipped sap for the rest of your life?"*

Darek ached to prove his inner beast wrong. He was no pussy. He was not like the goddamn humans he despised. He was stronger than them.

"What are you waiting for? Shut her up once and for all. Take. The. Power. Back."

"Are you even listening to me?" Mila snapped.

Darek reached for the door, setting the flames free the moment he opened his fist. He closed it, slamming it into the door with pure frustration. Leaning forward on trembling arms, he fought to breathe, to suck in enough air to soothe his burning lungs and clear his head of intrusive thoughts.

"Mila?" His voice was just a rasp, a silent plea for her to save him from himself.

"What?" Her sharp voice cut through him like blades, pushing him further into the fire. He wanted to beg, to scream at her to hold him. To keep him from falling, but before he could even begin to form the words, she went on.

"I can't do this, Darek!" Her hand on his shoulder felt everything but soothing. "You're right, *you* promised me, you promised me you'd fight it, so *fight*!"

His voice was just a whisper, "I can't."

"I can't hear you."

His voice rose into a growl, "I said I can't."

Mila's hand fell away. "Can't, or won't?"

The fraction of control he'd clung to pulled out from him like a rug under his feet. The rush of power, blasting from his core. He swirled around, turning on her as he exploded in a flurry of wings and heat that sent her flying back from the blast. Darek reigned the powers in, but it was too late. Mila hit the wall back first, the force knocking the air right out of her lungs. She slid to the floor and lay there unmoving and small.

The shock overpowered the darkness, the realization of what he'd done almost bringing him to his knees. Darek couldn't breathe. He stood, paralyzed while his heartbeat hammered in his chest.

Mila. He whispered inwardly. *I'm sorry. I didn't mean to hurt you. I'd never hurt you.*

Mila coughed as she tried to breathe, the effort dampening her skin and leaving her with flustered cheeks. A stark contrast to her ghostly pale skin and wide eyes as she looked up at him from the floor. The moment her gaze locked on his, the last hope he'd clung to shattered like glass under a stone.

"You're not safe with me," he whispered.

When he hoped for her to deny it, to stick to her conviction that he still had the chance of redemption, she just shook her head. The small gesture, speaking volumes, saying what her words could not. *He was right.* Darek clenched his jaw to avoid screaming. He didn't *want* to be right. He wanted to be wrong. He'd give anything to be wrong, to be proven wrong. But instead, she gathered her legs and leaned back against the wall he just threw her into.

Darek could only stare. She looked so small, so fragile. A few seconds of lost control was all it had taken. A fraction of untamed anger, a slip of the devil, and she paid the price. He could have crushed her skull against the wall, he could have snapped her neck—he could have killed her.

"Say something," he whispered. "Mila?"

She looked up, meeting his eyes. "What do you want me

to say?" her voice was flat. "That you're wrong?"

Darek struggled with the whirlwind of thoughts and feelings. He wanted nothing more badly, but they both knew the truth. He'd changed, and he couldn't go back to what he'd once been.

Devin had bruises on his arms. And even though Darek tried to deny the truth, they were his. He tried. He'd given them all he had, and it had been enough—until it wasn't. Until the devil had grown stronger, slowly taking more power than what he should have. It had happened slowly over the years. They both closed their eyes to the evidence until it had been impossible to ignore. Until he stood staring down at her bruised body, knowing he did that to her.

He hurt her. The only woman he ever loved. The one he'd sworn to protect with his life. The one he'd sacrificed everything for. The light in his life, the love he needed like he needed air. He'd been selfish to come home, but he couldn't be selfish now.

"No," he finally said. "Don't say that."

Mila struggled to her feet, taking a few hesitant steps toward Darek. "Fight it," her voice trembled. "Devin needs his dad." She inched closer, placing a hand on his chest. "I *was* wrong. I need you. I need the Darek I fell in love with. The Darek who chose to do good, who chose me. Come back to me."

Darek squeezed his eyes shut. Her touch still had the power to soothe him. It was the only thing he had left, what kept him from slipping over the edge. When he was with her, it was easy to believe in the change she craved. It was the time away from her that destroyed the chance he had left of a happily ever after with her.

"I can't." It wasn't that he didn't want to. He couldn't. He meant it. The influence was too strong. He'd been a nobody for as long as he could remember. He refused to go back. Once he'd gotten the taste of power and authority, he craved more. It was a thirst he couldn't slake by staying away. He didn't even want to. He wanted it all. The power, the family, the job. He never thought he'd have to sacrifice one to have the other.

Darek placed his hand over hers, momentarily letting himself get lost in the feel of her soft skin against his. He'd held on to her through it all. Refused to let her go even when she'd despised him. He'd gotten exactly what he wanted, and more.

Now he had to lose it.

"I love you," Mila whispered. "Devin adores you." Her hands reached his cheeks. "You're stronger than this, you *can* fight it, you *can* win."

Darek let out a shuddering breath. With her so close, everything seemed possible. He couldn't fall for that again. He tried too many times and failed. He held on to her out of selfish reasons. He hurt her. He would do it again. He'd wanted to hurt Devin, and those images scared him more than anything.

He shifted, wrapping his fingers around her wrists. The way she tensed hurt like a knife to his guts. She was scared. She had every right to be.

She removed her hands, and Darek backed away. "It's too late"

She stepped forward, and a flame shot out from his hand. She yelped, staggering back. "Darek, my love—"

He shook his head, clenching his jaw tight enough to send stabs of pain to his skull. He refused to cry. Where was the goddamn devil when he needed him? "I can't do this."

"Then don't." Silent tears rolled down her cheeks. "I know what I said, but I changed my mind. I'm sorry. I don't want to lose you."

Darek shook his head. "Tell Devin I—" he couldn't say it. The three little words burned within him, but instead, he said nothing.

"Darek, please," Mila whispered. "I should never have said those things. Stay. You're choosing wrong."

"I'm choosing *right*," he hissed through clenched teeth. Her safety was the top priority. He chose *that*. He chose to break his own heart by doing the thing he'd never thought he would.

Darek gave her a long look, "Don't come after me." With those words, he turned and walked the short distance toward the door. The few steps felt like miles long, the further away from her, the harder it was to breathe.

As the door closed behind him, he knew he'd never hold her again. It was over. Everything was over.

Darek's wings burst from his spine, launching him into the air with a scream that shook the building he left behind. If doing the right thing hurt this bad, he'd never do it again. He wouldn't have a reason to. The devil could do whatever he pleased as long as Mila was far away from it. Darek was done playing nice.

Mila was safe. Devin was taken care of. He'd grow up and have a good life. He'd be better off without Darek in it. Everyone would. He was no dad, no husband, he'd never been. He'd managed to fool everyone, even himself, but as his true colors shone through, it was time to run.

Images of Mila flying through the room replayed in his head over and over until he thought he'd burst from the emotion. Her delicate body crashing into the wall assaulted his vision no matter how far he flew.

Leaving her was the only option. If it'd be the last good deed he'd ever do, at least he'd know he could never hurt her again.

He'd taken her for granted. Chosen work over her, and now she was gone. The realization slowly sunk in. She was really gone. He could never go back. If he did, he wouldn't be strong enough to walk away a second time.

A sob tore from his throat, his wings growing heavy. Letting himself sink to the ground, he fell to his knees the moment he touched the street. A row of houses lined up on either side of him. He didn't know where he was, and he didn't care.

Mila wasn't there to scold him. Her calming touch wasn't there to stop him—Darek tilted his head back and screamed into the night. Throwing his arms out, a blast of fire exploded from him, spreading outward in pulsating ripples. Within seconds it spread across the streets, catching the wood until the suburb was ablaze. Screams and fire alarms rose into the night sky, and as the chaos raged around him, Darek fell forward as sobs shook his body.

A hand landed on his shoulder. "Sir, you need to evacuate."

Darek's head snapped up, two blazing red eyes set on the person who'd dared to come near him. The man staggered back at the sight. One flap of his wings lifted him to his feet, and in the same fluid motion, he landed a punch sending the man flying across the street and into the flames.

"Leave me alone!"

MILA

CHAPTER 54

Mila watched the news on the small screen in the reception of Lucky Paws, fighting back the tears. She refused to cry.

"I hate to say it," Kate wrapped an arm around Mila's shoulders. "But you're better off without him. That man is evil. He always was."

Mila shook her head. In denial? She wasn't sure anymore. She'd been so convinced Darek wasn't the bad guy. That he was more than the devil. That she could save him from himself, all it would take was a little love and affection. It had been enough, he'd been good, he'd been hers.

Mila sniveled, wiping her eyes. "He just walked away. From me, from his family."

"It sucks," Riley sighed. "I liked him, I did."

"He is the devil," Kate countered. "I'm not surprised."

Was Kate right? Had she simply been blind the whole time? Had he never loved her the way she'd loved him? Was he even capable of such emotion?

Darek's last words to her echoed in her mind.

Don't come after me.

That's it? Three years, and that's all he could tell her before disappearing from her life? Mila knew she should be angry, but all she could muster was disappointment.

"He never said it back," she whispered, regretting it the moment the words left her mouth. Kate looked confused, but as she saw the pain on Mila's face, she understood.

She grimaced, steering Mila away from the TV and the destruction they both knew too well who caused.

"Trust me, hun, if he hasn't said it in over three years, he won't. You deserve someone better."

"But I love him," Mila whispered. "Devin loves him." How was she supposed to explain to a three-year-old his daddy no longer wanted him? The thought of it was enough to make her tears fall at last. He didn't want them. He'd chosen power, work, and everything that wasn't her and Devin.

"He's still small, he'll be okay. Come, let the puppies cheer you up, it works for Devin."

"He's with the pups?" Mila wiped her eyes, following Kate through the door to the backroom. The first thing she saw was the receptionist, Jenny, sitting cross-legged on the floor with Devin on her lap, the four pitbull pups tumbling all around them.

"They like him," she whispered, smiling through her tears. No dog had ever gone near Darek. Their aggression toward him made her worry about letting Devin near them. She kept Bosco at a safe distance, never letting him into the same room as Devin. She'd kept him away, too scared to face the possibility of him hating the boy just as bad as he hated his dad.

Seeing the interaction warmed her heart. Devin's little giggles as the pups played with his feet was the most beautiful thing she'd ever seen.

"Why wouldn't they like him?" Jenny asked.

"Uh—" Mila squirmed, muttering, "They hated his dad, I just assumed—"

Jenny let out a sharp laugh. "That guy's scary as fu—" She clamped a hand over her mouth. "Sorry!"

"It's okay," Mila lied.

— * —

372

Mila spent two weeks expecting Darek to come walking through the door at the end of the day. When the days marked the beginning of the third week, she tried to accept it wouldn't happen.

He really left. The fact he was just fifteen minutes away hurt her more. He was so close, yet so far away. He hadn't called, not even to check up on Devin. If she hadn't seen the news, she'd thought he'd disappeared off the face of the earth.

No. He just disappeared out of her life, and he'd done it with a dedication she never expected.

Leaving Devin at the shelter, she steered her car toward the place she hadn't brought herself to go.

She pulled over at the street below the tower, stepped out of the car, and let her eyes linger on the giant blood-red sign.

Rewera Corp.

A fresh stab of pain shot through her heart. It felt like yesterday. She'd been so proud of him, his hand in hers had been so warm against the frosty air. She'd whispered *I love you*, and he'd looked at her as if he'd felt it, too. He hadn't said it, though. Mila hadn't thought much about it, not until now. She'd said she knew, that he didn't need to say it. That he would when he was ready.

That day never came, and now he was gone, making her wonder if he'd ever loved her at all.

"*Darek*," she whispered the name into the evening air, tilting her face to the sky as she tried to see the top windows. He was up there, so close, yet so out of reach.

What had been the most normal thing in the world, was now foreign and off-limits. She knew her way around the building, hell, she'd spend days there by his side. How many times during the past years had they made love in his office? How many times had she been amazed at how patient little Devin was as they left him to play with Cat?

Mila grabbed the car door to keep herself from crossing the street. It was so easy. Just a few buttons of the elevator and it would take her right up to him. She could be in his arms within minutes.

Mila tore her gaze away. He didn't want that. He didn't want *her*. Slipping back into the car, she knew what she had to do.

She couldn't stay in the apartment. It held too many memories. Even the streets did. He was everywhere she looked. His scent lingered in her sheets, even in the car. That intoxicating smell of candle smoke and burnt wood which she once adored now made her nauseous. How had she ever thought the freaking smell of fire was sexy anyway?

She hit the brake too hard and the car came to a screeching halt outside of the shelter.

"I'm moving to the lake house."

Kate and Riley's eyes grew wide as she burst into the room. The dogs started to bark, and the puppies came tumbling toward her.

"Mommy," Devin hugged her legs. Mila dropped to the floor, hugging him to her while her free hand pet the pups.

"Do you want to go to the lake house, baby?" she asked. "There's a big lawn where you can play with the puppies, you're gonna love it."

A frown came over Devin's face. "Will Daddy be there?"

Mila squeezed her eyes shut to trap the sudden moist. Why did he have to ask *that*? She shook her head. "No, baby, Daddy has to work."

"I miss Daddy."

Mila pulled him into a tight embrace, whispering. "Me too, honey. I miss him too. But it's just you and me now."

She glanced up at Kate. "I have to do this. I'll still come here. But I can't *live* here, in the city. Not anymore."

"The lake house is not too far away," Riley said. "But it won't be the same."

Mila let go of Devin, watching him crawl across the floor to play with the puppies, and smiled through the emotion tearing at her heart.

"I know. But I can't keep seeing all the things that remind me of him. The freaking tower is even visible from here. Knowing he's up there—" her voice broke. "It's time for me to say goodbye."

Kate nodded, wrapping Mila into a hug, and when she spoke, she spoke for everyone. "We'll miss you."

DAREK

CHAPTER 55

Darek watched her far below on the street, pressing a palm up against the window, wishing he could touch her instead of the cold sheet of glass.

The weeks away from her had been torture. Keeping his distance was the hardest thing he's ever done. His willpower fractured every night when he lay alone in the empty penthouse, wishing for her soft body to hold.

He could never let her go. She was a part of him. She was in every fiber of his being. He could pretend all he wanted, he could act as if he didn't need her, while in reality, he craved her like a starving man craved food. He missed her so bad it hurt. He missed Devin's little arms around his neck. He missed tucking him in and whispering to him when he slept. The words he never said to listening ears, the words he never dared to speak out loud.

Darek let his head fall against the window, pressing his

forehead to the glass.

"*Mila.*"

She slipped back into the car, starting with a jerk before disappearing into the traffic. Darek kept his eyes locked on the spot where she'd been, letting the three little words slip past his lips.

"*I love you.*"

The window fogged up from his proximity, leaving a palmprint when he pulled away. Darek stared at it, imagining her hand covering it as he staggered back to collapse into the chair.

A knock on the door snapped him out of the trance. "WHAT?" he barked toward the closed door. It slid open, and Cat peeked in.

"Just me, Boss." She gave him a grin, pushing her glasses up the bridge of her nose. "Where were you lost?" She stepped inside, closing the doors behind. "Thinking about her?"

Darek turned away from her with a huff, facing the windows to make sure she couldn't read the emotion on his face.

Cat's heels clicked against the floor, and the thud as she placed something on the desk didn't go unnoticed by him. Before she turned to leave, she stopped, reached out to place a hand on his shoulder.

"It's not too late to change your mind, you know. Even the devil deserves to be happy."

Darek spun the chair back, eyes blazing red. "I'm doing this to protect her, what part of that don't you understand!"

Cat stood her ground. "You keep saying that. Mila can handle you, you know that."

Darek shook his head. "Not anymore." He looked down at his clenched fist, seeing the fire seep through his skin. When he refocused back on Cat, his voice was just as cold as his face. "Get out."

"Darek," she began.

Flames burst from his fists as he shot up from the chair. "Don't call me that!"

Cat scrambled away, shouting, "Shit! Don't do that!"

"Get out," Darek took a threatening step toward her, raising his voice into a shout, "GET OUT!"

Cat shot him an exasperated look, muttering under her breath as she turned to leave.

Darek glared at her retreating figure. Her long blond hair danced on her back with each step, her ass swaying in the too tight skirt. The door clicked shut, snapping him back to the moment. She was wrong. It was too late. What he had with Mila should never have happened. Those years were nothing but a reminder of what he could never have again.

Darek sat, snatched up the phone, tapping his claws against the receiver as he waited for Cat to reach her desk.

Her breathless voice came onto the line, and he wasted no time.

"I want you to set up a monthly transfer to her account."

"Eh—okay." Cat's confusion was clear in her voice, and Darek pretended he didn't notice.

"How much?"

"I don't care. Enough for her to never have to worry about money. Make it anonymous."

"Okay, Boss." Cat's breathing let him know she was still there. "You're making a mistake." She finally dared to say. "Mila doesn't need your money, she needs *you*."

Darek was tempted to throw the phone across the room but managed to control himself enough to hold on to it.

"Just *do* it."

"Will do."

"Hang on." Darek put the phone down, searched through a folder until he found what he'd been searching for. The picture of two boys slid out onto the desk. They looked like they were around five or six in the picture, and Darek didn't know why he kept it. He'd thrown out everything that reminded him of Berner. Had the whole tower remodeled to his liking, and the office was as good as new. The gray walls and black double doors were as far from Berner's white as he could come. The sleek *less-is-more* design of the skyscraper made him feel like the businessman that he'd been made to be. The dark color scheme and the luxurious modernity fit him to the bone. It spoke of power and authority. It was handpicked by him and reflected his personality down to the knife-sharp furniture, and the blood-red Rewera logo on the wall above the sitting area of the office.

He'd wiped the building clear of its previous owner, and made damn sure that whoever dared to mention the name didn't live to regret it. But he kept the picture of the sons. Darek scoffed at the stupidity.

"Boss?"

Cat's voice snapped him back to the moment.

"Do the same for the Berner boys."

The silence that followed made Darek's blood boil, and before Cat could even begin to question him, he snapped, "Don't ask why, just fucking do it."

"I wasn't going to ask why, I was going to say, 'that's a very honorable thing to do'. I knew you still had it in you."

"Hmph."

Cat chuckled.

They'd lost everything because of him. Normally Darek didn't care. He killed people with a flick of a hand, never knowing who or whom. But those eyes. Those goddamn eyes never stopped haunting him. He'd done his research. The boys lived with an aunt, and they lived in utter poverty. Even though they had a place to call home and scraps of food in their stomachs, Darek didn't call life in such misery a life.

"They can never know where the money comes from."

"Why—"

"You think they'd take money from the man who killed their parents?"

Cat's gasp made Darek snort. "Don't pretend you didn't know."

"I'm not pretending—fuck, Darek! What did you do?"

"Forget I said anything," Darek muttered.

"I need to know, what if someone asks me? What if the cops come snooping?"

"It's long ago, they won't. I'll tell you everything, just stick with me."

Cat's silence made Darek's pulse quicken. He had been careless, so distracted by thoughts of Mila he didn't pay attention to what he said.

"You won't get rid of me that easily, Boss."

"Now do your work." He hung up with a huff. Why Cat had stayed with him, he didn't know, but he'd lie if he said he didn't appreciate her dedication. She knew what he was, and she never tried to change him. She never tried to convert him to the good side—Like Mila. Darek let out a shuddering breath. The moment she crossed his mind, that never-ending pain came creeping back. He could distract himself with work, he could pretend he wasn't hurting. He was. It fucking killed him every day to wake up and remember he could never touch her again.

— * —

Time passed in a blur. Days turned into weeks, and weeks turned into months. Darek kept his promise. He stayed away. But he couldn't forget. He couldn't let go. Not completely.

On Devin's sixth birthday, Darek watched from the shadows of the tree line, wishing with all he had he could hold them, one last time. He'd give everything to feel her in his arms, to feel her soothing hands on his overheated skin, to breathe in her calm.

She was as beautiful as he remembered. Despite the years that had gone by, she didn't look a day older. Devin, on the other hand, had grown a lot, and every time he saw the boy, he was shocked at how much like Darek he looked.

Despite the birthday party Mila had thrown, Devin didn't look happy. He stood staring at the visiting kids, his mouth pressed into a thin line and eyes brimming with tears. Two identical boys pointed at him, whispering and giggling until the tears he tried to hold back rolled down his cheeks. The boys ignored him and played with a dog who did its best to jump and steal the sandwiches from their hands.

"Mom?" Devin's voice was small as he pointed at the dog. "Why doesn't he like me?"

"Sweetheart." Mila kissed Devin's forehead. "Give Rex a little time. He's new here. Play with the twins, I'll bring the cake."

Darek watched her leave, following her every move as she crossed the lawn and disappeared into the house.

Ignoring her advice, Devin inched closer to the dog. Rex's head snapped up, a low growl erupting from his throat. Darek held his breath, wondering if the dog would bite him or accept him.

"Good boy." Devin held out his hand, his fingers trembling as he offered the dog his uneaten sandwich. "You can have it."

Rex's ears peaked, his nose twitching as he inhaled the scent. He took one step closer, and Devin gasped in hopeful glee.

Rex stopped, bared his teeth in a silent threat, then he trotted away and sat, glaring back at Devin from a safe distance. Darek silently cursed. Why didn't the goddamn dog accept Devin? The fact that the four-legged creatures always hated Darek was something he hadn't thought too much about, but when the same happened to his son, he started to feel like there was more to it.

Tears spilled down Devin's cheeks as he let the sandwich fall to the ground.

"He hates you!" one of the twins called out.

"Yeah," the other one agreed. "No one likes you. Not even the dog." They started giggling, causing Rex to bark in excitement. Darek tensed, digging growing claws into a tree trunk as he wished he could bury them into that brat's throat instead.

A stone hit Devin's head. "Go away, freak!"

"Yeah, loser!"

Devin rubbed his head as dark clouds chased away the sun. "Why don't you like me?" he asked in a small voice.

The twins guffawed, and Darek's hand trembled with the effort to hold on to the tree and avoid flicking a ball of fire at the bully. For a brief moment, he was there in Devin's place, subjected to the harsh words and the pain ripped through his heart.

More pebbles flew through the air, peppering Devin's face and chest. He held up his hands as a shield and shrieked, "Stop!"

A sudden thunderclap made him jump, bringing more laughter from the twins.

"What will you do?" one of the boys taunted. "Call your dad?"

"He doesn't have a dad," the other added. "He didn't want him either."

The words struck Darek like a slap to the face. They had no fucking idea. They didn't know what they were talking about.

The kids continued throwing stones at Devin. Their taunting voices blended with Devin's screams as he pressed his hands to his ears, begging them to stop, to leave him alone. They didn't stop. They didn't know they were playing with fire. Darek untangled his claws from the wood, ready to torch the brats. It would teach them a fucking lesson. No one messed with his son.

Devin opened his mouth to scream, and before Darek had a chance to act on the impulses, something shifted within him. A strange pull, as if his insides were pulled in different directions. A wave of dizziness rushed over him, making him stagger as a flash of lightning blasted the backyard. The sudden light was so sharp it blinded him, sending him staggering back from the power spreading from the impact. The light faded as fast as it had begun, and when Darek blinked the backyard into focus, the twins lay motionless on the ground. The grass, scorched and dead underneath their bodies.

Darek gaped, not sure what he'd witnessed. He wanted to take the credit, to believe somehow he had done that, but he knew better. Even though he felt drained, it hadn't been his powers that wiped out those kids and the dog. He used fire, and even though the result looked similar, that light had been nothing like Darek had ever seen.

It was Devin.

There was no doubt, but still, Darek didn't want to accept it. Devin was supposed to be normal. He was supposed to grow up like a normal kid, have a normal life. But the dead kids on Mila's lawn was the only proof Darek needed. He not only gave her a son, he'd given her a devil-child.

"Promise me he won't be like me."

The truth hit him hard. He should have known. Should have realized. What had he expected to produce? Something normal? He was anything but normal, it only made sense his son wasn't, either. Darek stared at Devin as he dropped to his knees next to the dog. His little hand trembled as he reached out to stroke his fur.

"Get up," Devin cried. "Rex?"

Darek turned away. He couldn't see this, couldn't stand the thought of what was obvious.

History was repeating itself...

DAREK

CHAPTER 56

The sound of his footsteps echoed in the empty corridor back at Rewera Corp. When he came to a halt outside the doors, he hesitated. He never felt the need to know, never craved the figures and the facts. But he needed to know what he'd seen. In his heart, he already knew. He *felt* it. The fading left side of his tattoo was just another hint of his power fading along with it. The fucking ink covering his torso wasn't a regular tattoo, it wasn't anything he ever wanted, it had just appeared as he grew. He didn't need to see Devin's chest to know the same thing was now taking form on his skin.

Darek shuddered at the thought of losing the powers. The fire within him wasn't as intense. It was there, but the difference was just as clear as what Devin had done, and he didn't like any of it.

Darek swiped the access card, gulping as the security locks clicked open. The years had done nothing to ease the discomfort clenching his stomach into a tight knot as he entered the lab. He hadn't been able to face it, and instead locked everything up and made it very clear—whoever dared to set foot on this floor of the building—were dead.

The threat worked. The layer of dust on the floor and the spider webs clinging to the equipment spoke for itself. It was abandoned, just as it should be.

The sound of his heartbeat echoed inside his head as he stood in the pressing silence. Throwing the old shackles still hanging on that goddamn wall a glance, he shuddered at the memory. Images flickered through his head.

Berner's sick grin.
Carla's hands.
Pain.
Humiliation.
Defeat.

Darek shook himself out of the past and headed straight for the cabinets in the office section of the lab. Browsing through the files, the amount of information stunned him. Every minute of his time there was documented. Written down in numbers and graphs. But he didn't need it confirmed he was above the average human being in every possible way, he already knew that.

High body temperature.
Abnormal resistance to cold & heat.
The ability to heal with an abnormal speed.

Darek scoffed. What did they expect? He was the devil for fucks sake. What he needed to know was why Devin was too.

Brushing the dust off an old folder, he flipped it open and stood face to face with history. There were his parents' names and all their details. Their birthdates. Their death dates. Darek tensed as his eyes lingered on his father's name.

Donovan Rewera.
Born sixth of June...

Darek stared. How had he lived a whole life and not known his father's birthday? He never celebrated, and not until now had Darek realized why.

Died on the same date thirty-eight years later.

The handwritten notes scribbled in the margin made Darek snort.

'Both parents died on the son's eighteenth birthday. Coincidence?'

They knew nothing. The motherfucker hadn't died together with his wife. It wasn't some fairytale romance. If they knew everything else, how could they fail to know Darek killed the son of a bitch, himself? Burned him to the ground along with the rest of his past.

Darek flipped the page and froze. How these people had dug generations back was a mystery, but he didn't care to dwell on their research methods. What bothered him was the patterns.

Something cold settled within Darek, an unease he couldn't pinpoint, but the past was enough to make him dread the future.

The death of his parents could be no coincidence, and neither could the history repeating itself four generations before Darek.

Darek's eyes were locked on the chart as he fought for air that suddenly was too thick to breathe.

Written all over the page was the number six.

666.

Everywhere.

Birth.
Death.
Birth.

Death.
Birth.
Death.

The color drained from Darek's face. It was no coincidence every fucking son before him met the same fate. Born on the sixth of June like the goddamn devil-child he'd been bullied for. It was also no coincidence every mother had died on the same day eighteen years later. On the exact time. Six o'clock.

The folder fell from his hands as images assaulted his mind. His mother's pale face, her limp body in his arms. The chime of the bells as they'd struck six. When her face morphed into Mila's, Darek screamed, staggering back until he hit something cold. Jumping forward, he gripped his head, digging claws into his skull to keep himself from falling apart.

Was she going to meet the same fate? Were her days counted? Did she have nothing but twelve years left of her life? Darek fell forward, leaning against his palms as his head spun. It was his fault. If he'd never met her, never insisted on keeping her... If he hadn't gotten her knocked up—

A gasp slipped past his lips. It wasn't *his* fault. It had never been the father's fault. It had been the son. It was connected to him. The moment he was born he doomed his mother to die the moment he turned eighteen. If the son hadn't been born, if he didn't exist. There would be no turning eighteen. There would be no reason for the mother to die...

Devin...

Images of the little boy's face flashed before Darek's eyes. The innocent little boy whom he'd loved. Whom he'd sworn to keep safe. He never needed Darek's protection. What he needed was for Darek to finish him before he could kill them all exactly twelve years from now. It already started. He turned six. With the new information, it made perfect sense.

Darek dragged a hand through his hair, curling it into a

fist. It was too much. It was insane. What did he have to do to break the chain? Did he have to kill his son?

Darek imagined Mila, lifeless and rotting in the ground, and the decision was simple. He'd do it. He'd do anything to keep her alive. This had to end.

The world was only big enough for *one* devil, and that was going to be *him*. Not some spoiled little—Darek's train of thought came to an abrupt halt. By instinct, he touched his chest, as if he could feel the fading tattoo underneath the clothes.

Devin wasn't just *a* devil, he was *his* devil. He still felt the drain of energy as the boy had taken it from him, morphed it into something he despised more than anything.

"Mommy, why's Daddy making it thunder?"

"Honey, don't be silly, it's not Daddy. It's God. Daddy is just angry."

"You're lying! He puts the lightning in the sky, I saw him."

The reality slammed into him in full force. He created the boy, he was made up from his genes. His blood and his DNA. A small dose had been enough to mutate that cockroach Berner into something stronger. What did he think a child who was born out of his genes would turn into?

Devin hadn't gotten his power of fire, he'd gotten something so much worse. Something Darek couldn't even stand the thought of. Something he'd never believed he'd have to see again.

Darek cursed under his breath as it lay clear before him. How was it possible he hadn't thought of it sooner?

The devil powers didn't just appear out of thin air. They transferred. He had given—Darek huffed, straightening to his full height, eyes flashing red. He hadn't *given* anything. The boy *stole* it, ripped it from his body and he'd keep doing it until he was old enough—until he took enough to transform.

Darek refused to let that happen. He'd get it back. He wasn't going to be a half-anything. He'd keep the boy alive for as long as it would take to get back what was his. If he had to wait twelve more years, so be it.

Darek slammed the doors shut on his way out. He'd seen enough. He'd seen more than he'd been prepared for, and now he didn't know what to do with it all.

Deep inside he knew he couldn't do anything. No matter which direction he chose, he'd be the one paying the price. Mila's face flashed before his eyes, and Darek picked up his pace. He couldn't think of her now. He couldn't deal with *that* too. It had to be another way. Darek hated to lose, but this was beyond his control. Was what he read in there the truth or nothing but speculations based on a madman's theories? Could he live with the consequences of ignoring it?

The options weighed heavy on his shoulders as he waited for the elevator to take him back to the top floor.

He had to choose, but how could he choose between the two pillars of his life? The two things he couldn't function without?

No matter what he'd choose—he'd choose wrong.

DAREK

EPILOGUE

12 years later

They say time heals all wounds. That the years go by and paint over the old, coating the hurt and the grief with layers until the old can't be touched. That it fades away as if it had never been there at all.

It was bullshit. The years had done nothing to change the cuts etched into his body and soul. The scars were just as present on the inside as the ones covering his skin. He hadn't forgotten, he just pretended to. He lied. To everyone around him. To himself.

Staring out at the heavy rain outside of the panorama windows of the Rewera tower, Darek couldn't pretend not to feel the weight of his actions. He did what he knew he would. Nothing. He ignored it for so long it started to feel

389

like a sinister fairytale. He closed his eyes to the signs, to the patterns, and hoped for it all to be wrong.

But as he emptied another glass of gin and stared out at the stormy sky, he couldn't deny the ominous feeling within. Everything was too still, too calm as if the world held its breath along with him.

Darek survived every birthday over the years, buried himself in work to distract himself from the pain and the longing for her to take it all away. He never stopped needing her, never stopped craving her touch, never stopped imagining her warm body right next to his as he lay alone at night.

Darek let out a shuddering breath. Thinking of her never ended well, and here he was, trying to drown her in gin as her whispers resounded in his mind and his body trembled with the need to feel her again. After all those years, thinking of Mila still made him hard. And the aching in his soul never lessened no matter how much he tried to deny it. He left his heart with her, and he never reclaimed it.

A look at his wristwatch made the blood freeze in his veins.

5:50.

Darek touched the ring, the only thing he had left of her. He'd never taken it off. He couldn't bring himself to do it, he couldn't say goodbye.

"What are you waiting for?"

"Your birthday surprise, what else?"

Darek shook his head to clear it from intrusive memories. He couldn't think of that now. Just because his eighteenth birthday had been a tragedy, didn't mean Devin's would be the same. Everything would be okay.

One more look.

5:55.

Darek's breath hitched. Who was he trying to fool? It wouldn't. Deep down he knew it. But it was too soon, too fast. He wasn't ready.

His eyes darted to the window. Was it too late to find her, to warn her? To tear Devin's heart out and break the fucking curse that had him fighting to catch his breath in a darkened office. Was it too late to fix what he'd done? He'd chosen, and he'd chosen wrong.

Darek shot to his feet. He couldn't lose her. He couldn't even imagine it. He'd lived so long without her, but she was still his world. She was the air in his lungs. How could he breathe without her?

The room suddenly felt too small, the walls closing in on him. Darek's hand trembled as he placed the bottle on the desk and steered for the doors.

His heart hammered in his chest as he waited for the elevator to open up at the bottom floor. Cold sweat breaking out across his skin despite the heat burning within. He needed air, needed space. He needed *her*.

The moment he stepped outside, he stopped to suck in a deep breath of the crisp night air. Tilting his head up, he let the cold rain beat down on him; thousands of needles prickling his face. Praying he was wrong, even though he knew he was right, Darek stood motionless, waiting for the shift. There was no time to run. No time for regrets.

Images of a time long ago flashed before his eyes.

His mother's blank stare as he held her in her arms.

Her body going limp as she drew her last breath.

His tears as he cried to the sky.

The night so long ago reflected back to him in the sheen of water coating the streets, calling to him from the distant rumble of the skies. Everything was the same, yet it was so different. He'd been a scared boy, now he was a man, but it didn't make him feel any stronger than he had back then.

Time didn't heal anything, it carried with it what could never be forgotten.

A sharp thunderclap shook the earth, followed by lightning that briefly lit the dark. The pressure in his chest intensified with the growing storm, and when the second lightning blasted the sky, a blinding pain surged through his body. It grew from the inside, spreading like hot lava through his system until he felt like he was torn and ripped to pieces.

The pain spread through him until his body shook and his eyes rolled back in his head.

Clenching his jaw to avoid screaming, Darek focused

391

on memories of Mila to distract himself from the agony as panic overpowered his senses.

The images faded in the roaring of his own blood rushing through his veins. His heart thumped dangerously fast, and as blinding hot pain gripped his spine, Darek couldn't breathe, he couldn't even move. If he did, he'd lose the control he clung to. Physical pain he could stand. It was what followed he dreaded.

The agony faded minutes after it had begun, and without looking at his watch, he knew it struck six.

The shift within was crystal clear. He sensed the rebirth of the devil, and why wouldn't he? Devin had taken half of Darek, ripped his powers straight from his body. His insides still tingled from the trauma of splitting, blood rushing through his veins as his body fought to rebuild itself to something new.

When everything settled, Darek felt it. The hollowness. The empty vacuum inside, and it was so much worse than any pain he ever endured.

Something in him stopped, stilled, and he knew what it meant. The unexplainable connection they shared made him feel her. He lived through her, shared her moments of happiness when he couldn't find his own. The mere thought of knowing she was alive and well had given him the strength to go on without her.

He didn't feel her anymore.

Choking back a sob, Darek closed his eyes, letting the rain rinse away the tears he had no control over. They fell from his eyes, silent and calm. It was over. The world as he'd known it, stopped existing. His heart stopped beating. He couldn't breathe, and he didn't want to.

He'd carried her with him, safely stored in his heart and soul. She'd been his reason to breathe. Even though he wasn't with her physically, he'd been with her in every other way.

Everything around him slowed down, wrapping him in a vacuum as the thunderstorm raged over his head.

"Boss!" A hand landed on his shoulder. "What the hell are you doing outside in this weather?"

Darek stood motionless, not even when Cat's face appeared in front of him did he react.

Her blond hair clung to her skin in wet strands and her eyes shone with worry as she gazed through rain-splattered glasses up at him.

She tugged at his shoulders. "You can't stay out here, lightning will strike you."

Devin's face flashed before his eyes, and as he opened his mouth to speak, his voice sounded as dead as he felt. "It already has."

Maybe not physically, but he sure as hell felt like it. He was dead inside, drained of power and emotion. Only a gaping black hole filled him. If he didn't know better he thought he died too. He wished he had. Without Mila, there was no light left in his world.

Before Cat could ask, he left her standing there, walking in a haze with no goal or destination.

—— * ——

When the shock lifted, only one feeling remained, and it burned stronger than everything.

Devin was going to feel his pain, tenfold. If it was the last thing he'd do, he'd bring him down. No one took what was Darek's, and the boy had not only taken *his* powers—he'd taken Mila.

Darek's eyes glowed red. Fueled by thoughts of revenge, his life force returned, flooded his system until the wings shot from his back. The blast of power spread outward in pulsating waves of fire, sending everything in its way flying back before going up in flames the heavy rain couldn't extinguish. Darek stopped, standing still in the midst of the chaos. Tilting his head to the sky, he let the well-known hatred burn inside until his muscles quivered and his wings expanded to their full width.

The fact that Devin was his son meant nothing. Not anymore. Mila was gone, and it was Devin's fault. He'd get back, get even. He'd rip the life right out of his body and crush him like the parasite he was. He wasn't going to let him get away with what he'd done. Darek shot toward the sky with powerful wing strokes.

Devin would wish he'd never been born.

Darek & Devin's story continues in
Book two of the Devil Within Trilogy.

COMING SOON

Read the first two chapters here

DEVIN

CHAPTER 1

A strong feeling of guilt coursed through his body when he opened his eyes.

Taking in his surroundings, the panic simmering below the surface intensified. The destruction around him stretched as far as his eyes could see. A heavy scent of burned wood hung in the air, and as he touched the charred ground he lay on, a sliver of fulfillment rushed through him. Horrified, Devin scrambled to his feet, spinning in circles as the thoughts swirled in his mind. The remains of a forest lay in scorched pieces around him, the ground cracked and the air filled with debris made him cough as he tried to breathe through the rising fear. Thoughts slammed into his mind faster than he could think of an answer. Where was he? How did he end up here? And the most important question which made his insides clench with dread. What had he done?

It wasn't the first time he blacked out, and each time

it happened, the media spoke of horrible things which he refused to accept he could have had any part of. But the nagging feeling inside told him differently. It refused to go away, it was almost as if it wanted to take the credit.

There was something wrong with him. He'd accepted that, but he hadn't been able to figure out what. Thoughts that weren't his own whispered in his head. Telling him to do things he couldn't even imagine, urging him to let go, to stop the fight.

Devin's hand trembled as he fished out his cell phone and dialed a number. The last thing he recalled was a heated argument with his coworker at the factory. The call went straight to voicemail, and for a reason Devin couldn't explain, he feared it had nothing to do with his friend's unwillingness to speak to him.

It wasn't the first time they fought, but something told him it had been the last. Shoving the phone back into a jeans pocket, he suddenly noticed the lack of clothes on his upper body and froze. He'd worn a hoodie in the morning, he was sure of it, and he had no memory of taking it off, but there he was, shirtless—with no memory of how, and why.

With his heart hammering against his temples, Devin started to run. He needed to get back to the city. He needed answers.

After what felt like forever, he was forced to stop. Leaning his hands on his thighs, he gasped for breaths while the fear grew in his gut. Everywhere he looked, the land lay in chaos, and the feeling deep inside of him telling him it was his fault, refused to go away.

An eerie silence closed in on him like a suffocating shroud, denying him the air he needed to fill his lungs. Devin straightened, eyes darting in different directions. Everywhere he looked, it was the same. Gray. Black. Dead. Nothing could tell him where he was, and nothing could distract him from his mind. Nowhere to run.

"Not now," he whispered into the air. A voice in his head snickered, making Devin tremble with the effort to shut it out. Once the whispers started, they were hard to chase away. Devin's mood sank as the darkness spread inside of him along with the blinding need to act upon those suggestions. He clenched his fists until his muscles shook and his fingers ached.

Shut up, shut up, shut up.

"You can't fight forever," the voice whispered. *"You're not strong enough."*

Devin clutched his head, curling trembling fingers in his hair as if he could rip the uninvited voice out.

"Let go."

Devin screamed out loud, "Leave me alone!"

The voice laughed inside of Devin's head as he ran. This time he didn't stop. He didn't know where he was going, he just ran, powered by desperation and the need to outrun the mental torture.

The blackened forest slowly transferred into green lush, but Devin barely noticed. Tripping over roots and stones, he got back up and pressed forward. When his lungs ached with the effort and his legs barely carried him, he was forced to slow down. Trying to catch his breath, a sound caught his attention. Devin's head snapped up, eyes narrowing as he tried to locate the low humming noise of what could only be passing traffic.

Between the tree trunks, fast glimpses of silver and red swished by. Devin picked up his pace, and when he broke through the forest and stepped out onto the hard surface, a sudden flash of fear zapped through him.

He looked down the road. Somewhere out there was the truth—was he ready to face it? Turning to gaze into the forest he just came from, he was tempted to go back, to run as far from humanity as he could and never have to face the consequences.

"Where are you heading?"

The sudden voice made Devin jump. He swirled around to notice a car had pulled up behind him. The driver leaned over the passenger seat and shouted through the opened window.

Devin tried to find his voice.

"Seattle ahead," the guy informed. "Wanna hitch a ride?"

"How far—"

"I'd say two hours max."

Devin nodded while his mind tried to make sense of this new information. Two hours from the city. How was it even possible?

"Jump in."

Devin hesitated, but in the end, exhaustion won, and he accepted the offer. Strapping on the seatbelt, the voice in his mind snickered. Devin clenched his teeth, taking a few deep breaths to focus.

"Visiting someone?" the stranger asked, then he exclaimed, making Devin jump from the sudden sound. "Gosh, I haven't even introduced myself. I'm Steve."

Devin forced himself to speak, muttering his name under his breath, "Devin."

"So what are you doing out here in the middle of nowhere? Shirtless even."

Devin frowned, desperately racking his mind for an answer. In the corner of his eye, he saw Steve throw him a glance, and the need to say something made his stress level spike.

"I uh—"

Before he could figure out what to say, Steve held up his index finger as to shut him up, then his hand shot out to turn the volume up on the radio, and Devin immediately knew what it was all about.

Feeling the color drain from his face, he held his breath as he waited for the doom.

"...The latest blast at the Dawson and Co. Factory has left all of Seattle in shock. Hundreds of men and women lost their lives this morning, and as far as the investigators can tell, the cause is still unknown. Was it an accident? Was it yet another attack? I can speak for the whole nation when ..."

Devin zoned out as his vision blackened. The reporter's words echoed in his mind. *Hundreds dead. Blast. Unexplainable...* just like the other times. He'd been there, but he wasn't one of the dead. Instead, he'd woken up in an annihilated forest with no memory of how he'd gotten from A to B.

Nausea rose in his throat. He couldn't explain how, but he'd never been surer. He killed those people.

"You okay?"

Devin focused his gaze on the road and in a useless attempt to silence the voice within.

"Hey! Devin?"

The marks on the dark asphalt swished by too fast, blurring into a whirlwind of yellow and black in front of his eyes. His heart pounded in rhythm with the crackling song now playing on the radio. In the corner of his eye, he saw Steve reach out to fine-tune the channel. But the static noise kept on cutting the song into short fractions of distorted tones.

"That's strange," Steve muttered. "Never had a problem with the stereo before." He threw Devin a quick glance. "Hey!" he called out. "You sure you're okay?"

Fighting the urge to rip the guy's throat, Devin managed a stiff nod and the silence that followed only made it worse. The radio kept making noise, and Devin clenched his jaw as he held on to the last string of self-control.

"I'm sorry," Steve went on. "Did someone you know work there?"

Again, Devin managed a nod.

"Oh, man," Steve said. "It's a tragedy. Family member?"

Devin's head jerked to the side, glaring at the driver through narrow eyes. "Friend."

"Sorry to hear that. I know many who lost a loved one today." Steve's sympathetic voice wrapped like a coat around Devin, sheltering him from the darkness and giving him the opportunity to breathe deep enough to relax.

He drew in a shuddering breath and focused his eyes on his clasped hands. "Do you think—" his voice broke. "Could it have been an accident?"

Steve's silence crept over him, making him restless. Knowing his question was as useless as the little sliver of hope igniting in his heart, he already regretted it. It was no

5

accident.

"No."

The simple word cut like a slap to his face. Devin closed his eyes, trying not to panic.

"But it could have been." Desperate to hear the words he wanted, he asked again. "Right?" his voice was just a weak whisper.

Steve sighed. "That's what you want to hear?" He clicked his tongue and stared ahead at the road, then went on. "I get it, accepting someone would do this on purpose is not easy. I don't know if it was a bomb or…" his voice trailed off. "Whatever happened there, it didn't happen by accident."

Devin's world collapsed around him. Steve didn't say it was his fault, but he might as well have. There was no other explanation. It wasn't the first time strange things happened around him, yet he had no memory of any of it. That alone was enough to terrify him.

It had to end. The voice, the strange pull, and the unquenchable thirst to destroy everything in his wake. Devin didn't understand, but there was no denying it. He was losing his mind, and people were suffering because of it.

As a child, people walked in circles to avoid him. He could recall the whispers and the odd looks, it still hurt to think of the ways the other kids had avoided being paired up with him in school. He'd eaten his lunch alone every break and spent the long hours in class in silence while the other kids had giggled and joked.

No one talked to him, and if they did, it was to tell him what a freak he was. Truth was, Devin never felt normal. If it was because of being treated like a ghost, or if the feeling was based on something more sinister, Devin never knew.

Growing up, the only one who'd ever cared about him and treated him like a normal kid was his mother. She never acted weird around him, never shied away at the sight of him. She'd been all he had. When she died, she left Devin alone and lost in a world that hated him. He couldn't remember much after her death. The pain and the desperation he'd never forget, but if someone was to ask him where he'd gone and how he'd survived after such tragedy, he wouldn't have a clue.

He'd turned eighteen that day, the sixth of June, and as he held her dead body in his arms, he'd not only lost the most important thing in life, he'd also lost his mind. The three years that followed was a black hole. The harder Devin tried to remember, to make sense of the loss, the darkness surrounding it only grew thicker. She'd left him with questions that had no answers, but somewhere deep inside he had a disturbing feeling of already knowing. That the answers were hidden within him, and he just refused to see them.

Sitting in the car with the latest blackout fresh in his mind, he had his answer. He didn't need to know what happened or what he'd done. It wasn't important. What was important was making sure it would never happen again. As long as he was free to walk the streets, the world was in danger. It didn't make sense, and Devin was sure he'd never understand. But at the moment, he didn't care. He had enough of the mental torture and the struggle to fight his own mind. It terrified him to admit it, but he could not hide from the truth. Something was horribly wrong with him.

A hand on his arm snapped him back to reality and he flinched away from the touch, startled by the sudden contact.

Steve chuckled slightly. "Where were you lost?"

Devin shot him a look, not understanding.

"I talked forever until I realized you were somewhere far away."

Devin scowled, annoyed at the abrupt interruption. "Just thinking," he muttered. "How long until we're there?"

"You sound like my boy," Steve said. "He's the most impatient little fella I've ever seen."

"You have a kid?" Devin didn't know why it surprised him. Steve didn't look much older than Devin's twenty-one, but then again, there was no age limit for being a dad.

"Nic isn't mine, he's my nephew. His dad died in an accident when he was two. He's been with me since then.

He's five now."

Devin felt a twinge of sympathy. "I'm sorry," he said. "Must've been difficult."

Steve laughed. "I was ready to sign him up for adoption," he admitted. "I was nineteen and not ready to be a dad. My friends were out partying and I was stuck at home with a baby." Steve grimaced as he seemed to remember the time. "Mom forced me to keep him. Said I would regret it later."

Devin remained quiet, and Steve went on. "She was right of course. My brother chose me for a reason, and I'd never have forgiven myself if I'd let him down. Plus, I love the little homewrecker."

Devin nodded in thoughtful silence, wondering how it would feel to have full responsibility for another human life. Then he remembered the incidents and his mood darkened. He didn't need to have a kid to know the feeling.

"Drop me off at the police station."

DEVIN

CHAPTER 2

Devin said goodbye to Steve and watched him drive off with a feeling of relief filling his body. He'd survived one more human encounter without giving in to the sickening impulses going through his mind.

He didn't know where it came from or what it meant, but he knew it had to end.

Pushing the door to the Seattle police station opened, he hesitated in the doorway before stepping inside and let the door swing shut behind him.

As he crossed the floor to the main reception, the light above flickered. During the few milliseconds of darkness, Devin wanted to turn and run back into the safety of the trafficked street. Where the sound level was high and the buzz of the city light was enough to keep his mind occupied.

The lights flickered on, and Devin blinked against the

sharp light.

"What the hell is wrong with the lamps?" a guy called out. Someone answered, but Devin couldn't make out the words. He was too busy wondering the same thing. But his main focus was not the lamps, it was him. The static electricity that followed him around made him feel even more like a freak. It wasn't the first time lamps exploded in his presence. The flickering lights and charged air around him, he's grown used to, but even though it no longer surprised him, it scared him more than he was willing to admit.

A voice from somewhere in the building called out. "Can someone fix the goddamn lights!"

Devin cleared his throat. "Sir." He went up to the desk, leaning forward to get a glimpse of the man searching the bottom drawers on the opposite shelves. "Excuse me."

His head popped up, and he smiled. "One second." Before he could turn his attention back to the items of his hunt, Devin spoke up, "I have information about the blast."

The young man scrambled to his feet and stood, rooted to the floor as he stared at Devin. Then, without another word, he ran off and soon came back with an older man in a police uniform. He gestured toward Devin, saying something Devin couldn't hear.

"I hear you have important information, Mr.—"

Devin managed a stiff nod, suddenly starting to feel like he might have made a mistake.

"Shikawa." He held out his hand, and the police shook it with an expectant look on his face. "Follow me, Mr. Shikawa."

Devin walked behind the officer through a corridor and into a room, where he gestured at Devin to sit. Obeying, he tried to remember why he was there and keeping himself in the chair when all he wanted was to get up and run.

The officer took a seat opposite of him, placing his hands on the table as he gave him a once-over that made Devin cringe in his borrowed t-shirt and clammy skin. "What can you tell us?"

Devin swallowed down the lump in his throat and tried

10

to find his voice. Looking at anything but the officer, he took a few deep breaths and said, "I think I did it."

The silence that followed buzzed with tension, and when Devin was about to explode, the officer hummed. "Think?" he asked. "What exactly does that mean, Mr. Shikawa?"

"Uh—" Devin hadn't thought any further, and now he didn't know what to say. "I don't remember."

The police officer sighed. "Okay," he began. "Let me ask you a few questions." From his voice, it was clear he'd given up on getting anything useful out of Devin but had to follow up on the strange confession.

"Where were you at the time of the incident?"

"I was there." Devin shuddered at the thought. "I work at the factory. I had an argument with Bri—uh, my coworker. I lost my temper and—"

The officer nodded, urging Devin to go on.

"I woke up two hours from Seattle in a forest. It was destroyed, like the factory. I don't remember how I got there."

"Hmmm."

Devin's head snapped up, an unexplainable irritation filling him. "Hmm?" he echoed. "Aren't you going to arrest me?"

The officer laughed. "Based on what?"

Devin's voice was unnecessary sharp. "I did it, I killed—" his voice broke, and he had to look away. Even thinking about it was too much. He couldn't say it out loud. It would make it too real. Too painful. When he glanced back up at the officer, he whispered. "Please, I don't want to hurt anyone else."

"I don't suppose you have access to explosives?"

Devin shook his head.

"Any other weapons?"

"No," Devin's voice was small.

"Then explain to me how you caused the incident?"

Devin was at a loss for words. Staring back at the officer's face, he suddenly realized he had no idea of what even happened there. He just knew it was bad. Just like all the other places he left in pieces.

11

"I don't know," he said. "Sir." He shifted his weight, crossing his legs, then uncrossing them and tapped his fingers against the table as sweat broke out across his skin. "There's something inside of me, a force. It..." He struggled with the words, feeling himself choke up the more he tried to explain. As if something kept him from talking. "Something evil," he managed to say. "A voice in my head, telling—" his throat tightened with sudden emotion. And instead of telling the police the truth, he fought against his tears.

The older man looked around the room as if he expected to find a solution. Sighing, he pulled out his radio and spoke something which made no sense to Devin.

Then he smiled politely back at Devin and said, "We are talking about massive destruction. I'm sorry, kid, but I believe you may be better off talking to a doctor rather than the police."

Devin couldn't bring himself to reply. Feeling stupid, he hung his head as the shame wrapped around him like a heavy blanket. He's bared his soul in hopes of getting someone to help him. Somewhere deep inside he wasn't surprised by the reaction. He hadn't expected to be taken seriously, but the let-down stung. Humiliation and despair weighing heavy on his heart. If the police wouldn't believe him, who could he turn to? Who could help him? Who would save him from himself?

"Mr. Shikawa?" the officer waved his hand in front of Devin's eyes, and as he blinked the man into focus, he frowned. The uncertain expression on the older man's face told him he'd been somewhere far away. That too wasn't the first time.

"I want to hurt people," Devin whispered. "I can't control it."

The man's eyes flickered to the clock, then to the door before resting on Devin's trembling hands, and said. "Don't worry, son, it will be alright. I've called someone who will help you."

Devin's heart leapt. Was it possible? Had this old fellow listened despite his patronizing comments?

As he waited, the silence filtered into Devin's mind.

Counting the seconds as they ticked by too loud, he started to panic. It was too quiet, too much room for the inner demons to come out and play. As on cue, the whispers began. Devin curled his fingers into tight balls as he focused on the tension instead of the voice telling him to punish the old son of a bitch for mocking him. Devin started to breathe faster, sucking in shallow breaths as he fought against the need to throw the table and the old man through the wall. He could even see the scene play out in his mind. The shocked expression on the little man's face. The fear in his eyes and the screams before the broken furniture pieced his flesh. Devin smiled at the thought of his blood trickling to the floor.

The door clicking close snapped him back to reality and the whispers faded with the last wavering resistance. Devin sagged in the chair as relief flooded him. He'd been lucky this time. The presence of another human being had saved him, but he knew not everyone would be that lucky.

"Hello, young man." A handsome man in his mid-fifties reached out a hand to Devin. "My name is Dr. Shaw. I've been told you have some issues you want to discuss?"

Devin's hand trembled as he greeted the doctor, and as he held it, letting his eyes travel over the man's face, a small sliver of hope zapped through him.

"Come with me."

Devin followed the doctor through the door and out onto the street. There he stood, staring at the passing cars with a deep feeling of dread circling in his stomach and a strange tingling in his hands.

"Take me away from here," he said. "Please."

Dr. Shaw placed a hand over his back and guided him to the waiting car. "Can you tell me what you're afraid of?"

Devin didn't need to think twice. "Myself," he said. "I don't trust myself."

As they got into the car, and Dr. Shaw steered the car into the heavy traffic, he asked in a calm voice, "What do you mean when you say you don't trust yourself?"

Devin had to think. How could he even begin to explain things which he didn't understand? How could he expect this stranger to believe him when the things didn't even make

13

sense in his own mind? How could he talk about the voice, the deep ache to act upon the impulses and the burning urge to do horrible things. How could he expect another human being to listen to his crave for death and destruction when he couldn't even think the thought without feeling sick to his stomach?

"I can't do this," Devin gasped. "It was a mistake."

"You are doing the right thing," the doctor said. "There's nothing to be afraid of." His calm voice managed to soothe Devin's nerves, and for some reason he couldn't explain, he found himself relaxing in the seat as the man went on. "Nothing bad will happen. I promise you. You'll be safe."

"Where are you taking me?"

"We are going to the hospital," Dr. Shaw said. "It's temporary, but a necessary procedure. You will be evaluated, and then if we see it—"

Devin cut him off. "It is," he snapped. "I wanted to throw that officer through a wall and watch him bleed. Is that not enough to lock me up?" He added in a low voice, "It's getting harder to resist. I don't know who I am anymore."

Dr. Shaw kept his cool, and nodded calmly as he turned into the parking area of the mental ward wing. "It is enough."

Devin scowled at the white sign lighting up the evening air. It had to come to this. But what else could he do? His mother's words echoed in his head and the pressure of her words crushed him under the weight of the guilt. He'd let her down. He wasn't strong, he'd never been. Yet her last words to him had made him swear to fight. And he had, even though he didn't know what he was fighting for, or against.

Be strong.

It meant little when he didn't know what he was losing to. But he was losing. And no matter how he tried, he couldn't find that light she'd seen in him. The darkness was too pressing, too heavy to hold off with nothing but a weakening mind.

There was no other way out than to accept defeat. He was broken, and he had no idea what broke him.

Fighting his own mind was a battle he didn't know how to win. When the person to defeat was himself, how did he know if he'd come out on top? When the thoughts blended together until he didn't know which belonged to him and which were the intruders, then how could he know which one was the right one to act upon? Devin didn't know. Torn between the burning desire to watch the world crumble at his feet, and the shame the same thoughts brought with them, he no longer knew what was right or wrong.

There were moments when he'd been so far away in his mind that he'd been sure he'd never find the way back. When Hell had seemed like home and the feelings of belonging had been so strong he'd wanted to unpack and live in the comfort of the darkness for the rest of his existence.

The car door slid open, and Devin turned his gaze up to find the doctor looking down at him. "We're here."

Devin nodded, swallowed down the nervousness, and let himself be led away.

THANK YOU

If you enjoyed this book, please leave a review on
Amazon or Goodreads!

For more information about my books,
follow me on Instagram,
or visit my webpage.

www.dariapaus.com
www.instagram.com/dee_sahiba

Other books by Daria M Paus.

Johnny & I
Me, Myself, & I

ABOUT THE AUTHOR

Daria comes from a family of artists whose creativity has been passed down by generations.

Inspired by her great-great-great-grandfather, the renowned author L.T, she is honored to pass on his legacy. She writes contemporary fiction about the flawed, the broken, and the dark.

With a background of arts and illustration, Daria paints vivid pictures of colorful characters that come alive on the pages.

Daria lives and works on her farm near Stockholm, Sweden, and spends her free time with family and pets.

Printed in Great Britain
by Amazon

68534152R00251